PRAISE FOR KATE MYLES

"Kate Myles takes no prisoners and leaves no skin on the bone. *The Receptionist* is a riveting and disturbing evisceration of twenty-first-century Hollywood greed and ambition. Überagents, self-improvement gurus, desperately ambitious actors—none of these denizens of sun-drenched Los Angeles are safe from Kate Myles's scalpel-sharp pen."

—Christopher Rice, *New York Times* and Amazon Charts bestselling author of the Burning Girl series

"A dark, gripping tale that won't fail to captivate."

—*New York Times* bestselling author Robert Bryndza

"*The Receptionist* is the best kind of guilty pleasure. Unlikeable characters? Check. Twisty plot? Check. This book has a pervasive sense of dread throughout, which made me turn the pages even faster. I couldn't wait to see how it ended."

—Samantha Downing, *USA Today* bestselling author of *My Lovely Wife* and *He Started It*

"*The Receptionist* is compulsively readable and deliciously disturbing, perfect for readers who enjoyed Gillian Flynn's *Sharp Objects*. Myles has written a genuinely unnerving thriller that I couldn't put down."

—Jess Lourey, Amazon Charts bestselling author of *Unspeakable Things* and *Bloodline*

"*The Receptionist* starts as a scathingly funny, deftly observed comedy of Hollywood manners—then twists, changes gears, and gathers the tense, heart-palpitating momentum of a runaway train."

—Jon Evans, Arthur Ellis Award–winning author of

~~Dark~~ Places and *Invisible Armies*

"Kate Myles's *The Receptionist* is a terrific thriller and a mesmerizing character study; I read it faster and with more pleasure than any crime novel I've picked up in months."

—Scott Phillips, bestselling author of *The Ice Harvest*

"*The Receptionist* is a freight train, hurtling toward a sheer drop. Kate Myles's razor-edged debut offers a bitter satire of LA society (or lack of same), told with the pure, pulse-pounding abandon of a 911 call. Myles's villains are delightfully awful, and her dialogue shines bright and cuts deep, but what makes her a tale spinner on par with the greats, like Patricia Highsmith and Tana French, is her recognition that the most thrilling moment of that fatal train ride comes not from the pounding of the engines or the fiery conflagration of landing but from the moment of weightlessness as you fall."

—Nick Seeley, author of *Cambodia Noir*

The Receptionist

The Receptionist

KATE MYLES

Text copyright © 2021 by Kate Myles
All rights reserved.

Epigraph, "Wherever you come near the human race, there's layers and layers of nonsense," is reprinted from *Our Town* by Thornton Wilder. Copyright © 1938 by The Wilder Family LLC. Reprinted by arrangement with The Wilder Family LLC and The Barbara Hogenson Agency, Inc. All rights reserved. To learn more about Thornton Wilder, go to www.ThorntonWilder.com.

No part of this book may be reproduced, or stored in a retrieval system, or transmitted in any form or by any means, electronic, mechanical, photocopying, recording, or otherwise, without express written permission of the publisher.

Published by Thomas & Mercer, Seattle

www.apub.com

Amazon, the Amazon logo, and Thomas & Mercer are trademarks of Amazon.com, Inc., or its affiliates.

ISBN-13: 9781542027458
ISBN-10: 1542027454

Front cover design by James Iacobelli
Back cover design by Ray Lundgren

Printed in the United States of America

In memory of my parents, Monica and Pat, who stocked our home with love and literature.
And for Peter, my heart.

Wherever you come near the human race, there's layers and layers of nonsense.

—Thornton Wilder

PROLOGUE

Nothing was left of the crime scene. The home had been sold, torn down, and was replaced by a stone-walled mansion with a new address designed to foil the last of the curiosity seekers. It was the original house number that drove so much of the morbid tourism. One didn't even need to have listened to the 911 call to recite it from memory.

"ONE NINE FOUR SEVEN TWO!"

The address became a meme. A joke. A public service announcement reminding people to remain calm in emergencies.

Eventually, the terror in the caller's voice persuaded a judge to redact the audio of all but the 911 operator—a ruling meant to balance the interests of the public and the wishes of the victim's family.

But no judge had the power to rid the internet of the photograph.

The picture was gruesome, released not in the public interest but for the financial gain of an anonymous functionary in the police department: black and white, degraded, printed out and scanned back in, with crease marks showing how the paper had been folded, secreted out of the station in a pocket or backpack.

The family tried to make it go away. They sued. They shut down websites. But the image always reappeared, floating to the surface of some grimly titled URL, until it was finally discovered by an eleven-year-old girl.

Unschooled in the visual vocabulary of true crime, the child initially mistook the pool of darkness on the floor for a throw rug and the smudges up the door for dirt. It took days of fixating, studying photo captions, and rereading descriptions of the crime before she understood.

PART ONE
EMILY AND CHLOE

CHAPTER ONE

EMILY

Oh my God, this girl is fucking my husband.

That was my first thought when Chloe showed up outside my office. She was too striking, lingering there in the doorway in her pencil skirt and tank top, with a face that somehow managed to appear both cherubic and angular. She raised her fingers to the doorjamb, hesitating, waiting for me to invite her in. Her bare shoulder caught the light of the hallway fluorescents, giving her the faintest shimmer of a halo. She smiled.

"Thank you so much for meeting with me," she said.

I ignored her and turned to my laptop. I'd already told Doug I didn't want to see any more of his "hungry creative" types. His company was bursting with these day jobbers who'd stayed too long in entry-level positions, hoping to expand some hustle in content creation. "My wife's an agent," he liked to brag before signing me up for another favor meeting, another waste of my time.

Chloe took an exaggerated breath and stepped toward my desk with her hand extended. I gripped the rounded arm of my chair and tried to control my breathing in the face of this nerve, this absolute gall.

Was he actually sending me his side pieces?

"Mr. Markham said you're a great agent," she said.

"Please," I said slowly. "Call him Doug."

She blinked and wiped her palm on her hip, easing herself into the seat across from me.

I wasn't jealous of her beauty. That wasn't it at all. I'd grown accustomed to the gorgeous. They were everywhere in my work, filtering through the waiting rooms of the entertainment industry, their cheekbones and long layers bowed toward scripts and iPhones. They whispered to themselves and emoted silently and were often objects of ridicule until they became wives or became successful.

But outside my world, even a few miles down the 10 freeway at Doug's office, the simple, supple fact of Chloe would have been a confrontation. She'd have stood out as a goddess amid the scattering of hip nerds and tech bros and fierce young women in communications. I couldn't picture a scenario where he wasn't sleeping with her.

She made a show of looking around my office, opening her arms to the space. "I love this building," she said. "Is that a real Calder in the lobby?"

"What do you think?"

"Okay," she said, nodding to herself. She was silent another moment before starting off in a shaky voice. "I guess I'll tell you about me? I've been in LA two years. I'm the receptionist at Beyond the Brand, Doug's company. But that's just my day job. My real work is with this group, Common Parlance. We're performers. Well, we don't call ourselves performers, really. We do pop-ups. But not like a restaurant pop-up. It's immersive. We wear carnival masks."

There was something odd in her manner. Her hands were trembling, along with her voice, and her eyes kept fluttering to her lap. The people I normally dealt with were so slick; I almost didn't recognize the behavior of a nervous person. I pushed my chair from my desk and sat back, taking a better look at Chloe's outfit. Her tank was thin cotton, like something that came in bulk packaging. Her skirt was pilling at the waist. She needed a pedicure.

She trailed off as I looked her over and chewed the inside of her thumb.

"So you do *happenings*," I offered.

"I guess you could call them that."

"What would you call them?"

"We're trying to figure it out. I like 'guerrilla theater,' but nobody else does. Whatever happened to plain old 'performance art,' right?"

Her smile was goofy, friendly.

"How old are you?" I asked.

"Twenty-four."

"I don't believe you."

"I am! I don't like lying about that stuff. I think . . . never mind."

"What were you going to say?"

"It's stupid."

"Go on."

"Oh gosh, it's just that I'm trying to approach everything in life like I approach my art. I want to make sure everything I do is real, you know?"

I focused on her eyes. They were round and clear, with a lack of guile that would have been charming in someone a few years younger. Maybe she *wasn't* having sex with Doug.

"Like, if you're mostly telling the truth," she said, "and that's what we do as artists, right? Tell the truth?"

"I'm not an artist."

"But you work with them."

"Actually, I work with experts: psychiatrists, former FBI agents, people you might see on a talk show."

"Oh," she said and looked confused. She edged to the front of her chair. "Well, I have this belief that if there's something fake in there, people will see it. Even subconsciously, they'll know something is wrong."

No, I decided. She was too sincere. She'd never have been able to pull off this meeting if they were having an affair.

I felt a ball of warmth inside me then, solid and radiating and about the size of a lemon. That was how big the pregnancy books said the baby was now. I was four months along. I hadn't told Doug. I brought my hand to my belly. It was barely perceptible, the tightening, the roundness under my palm. I wasn't going to be able to keep it secret much longer.

But Doug knew. Of course he did. The one time he didn't clear his internet search history, I saw what he'd written. *Wife hiding pregnancy.*

I could tell him now. We could start being honest with each other. Because Doug had sent Chloe to me as a sign, a peace offering, an example of someone he could have slept with but had chosen not to. I moved both hands to my desk and straightened, overcome with an unfamiliar sense of well-being.

"Tell me, then—how can I help you?" I asked.

"I was hoping you'd come see us perform."

I paused and raised my eyebrows. "Can I be honest?"

"Please."

"You've been talking about your group for a while, but I still don't understand what you do."

Chloe sat back. "I'm sorry," she said. "We do site-specific performances, like street theater. It's improvisational. We start out really subtle and play off what's happening around us, like we interact with reality, if that makes any sense."

"Do you have any press?" I asked.

"We do Snap and TikTok. Oh, and YouTube."

"What kind of hits do you get?"

"I can tell you . . ." She pulled her phone out of her pocket and frowned at the screen. "What's your Wi-Fi?"

"Never mind," I said. "I get it. You're alternative. But this is RFG."
I waited for some recognition from her, some acknowledgment she was
out of her depth. "We're a major agency. We don't pluck people out of
obscurity."

The disappointment flushed across her face. She certainly hadn't
thought anything was going to happen here? I was hoping to make the
rejection painless.

I softened my voice. "I work with the elite. People we can market
across different platforms: publishing, retail, that kind of thing. It's hard
to get there. I mean it's impossible."

She narrowed her eyes, ready to take me up on a challenge I hadn't
given her.

"Do you want advice?" I asked.

"I'd love some."

"Your group needs a hook. Something simple that tells people who
you are."

She pursed her lips and swished them to the side. "Would the
masks count as a hook?"

"Maybe. But think in terms of what's out there already, like Blue
Man Group. You've heard of them? They're blue men. They're easy to
understand."

Chloe propped her arm on the back of her chair. It was a pose,
exquisite and still. Doug had told me she'd been a backup dancer for
Fefu Fornes, the latest child actor turned racy pop star. "Yes, but we go
deeper than that," Chloe said. She sounded like she was talking down
to me. "We're beyond entertainment, beyond language, beyond form,
even. Like, there's this undercurrent to every crowd and interaction. We
tap into what's really going on and bring it to the surface."

"Sounds exciting." I flashed her a smile and stood to start the process of getting her out of my office. "You have a great look. Have you
done commercials?" I grabbed a business card from my desk. "Send me

your headshot, and I'll forward it to our commercial agents." My hand was on her shoulder, and she was almost out the door when she stopped.

"Wait," she said. "I forgot to give you a flyer for our next show."

"Don't worry—" I started, but she'd already unzipped her hand-bag, a cheap yellow-leathered overnight bag of a purse, full to the top with faded receipts and free-floating tampons. I saw a flash of hot pink that might have been underwear. She shoved it under the hairbrush and stapler, all tangled up in what looked like two different brands of computer cable.

"I'm sorry. I know I put the flyers in here." She leaned on the arm of my tufted leather sofa and lowered her head, plunging her arm into her purse and churning. "I'm sorry," she said. I wanted to tell her to stop, to email it to me, but her movements picked up speed. "I'm sorry," she repeated. She started trembling again.

"Where is it?" she whispered with an intensity so out of place in my cool, professional world. It was something from the domestic sphere: intimate, desperate, with a hint of violence at the end of it. "I'm sorry," she said again, shaking her head in a tiny, frantic figure eight.

"Chloe." I put my hand on her back. "It's okay."

She stopped and slumped and reached in once more, grasping a handful of something inside. "I must have taken them out for some reason." She tried to perk up with a smile, but it was too late. The entire meeting must have been an exercise in keeping it together.

I remembered this kind of unraveling from the early days of my career, trying out unproven clients. The crazies always made for a good story. But Chloe was so young and pretty. I had an urge to help her.

I thought of taking her purse from her hands and showing her how the yellow was cracking near the bottom seam. *Look,* I wanted to say. *This is why your bag is so crappy. The leather was colored with a surface dye. It's like the manufacturer slapped paint on skin.*

I wanted to take my Bottega Veneta from the back of my chair and let her run her fingers over the soft woven pattern. *Leather needs to breathe,* I wanted to tell her. *See how you can still see the grain? That's called aniline. It's been dyed all the way through.*

These are the things you should be focusing on, I wanted to say. *This is what you should aspire to. Everything else is madness.*

Maybe I should have said it. Maybe she would have taken the advice, embarked on a shallow existence, and left us alone. Maybe she would have dismissed me as a materialistic loon. I refuse to speculate. Turning philosophical is the last refuge of the pathetic.

I believe in judgment. I believe in assigning blame. Everything that came after was Doug's fault.

And I did try to help Chloe that day in my office. I used my gentlest tone as I said, "You'll need to upgrade that purse if you want to be taken seriously."

She looked like I'd smacked her.

I almost said I was sorry, that I didn't mean it to come out that way. I almost told her not to worry about any of this because life was long, and she was young and probably wouldn't even remember this in a couple of years. But I said nothing.

You have to be careful of people.

CHAPTER TWO

CHLOE

Chloe makes a wrong turn out of Doug's wife's office. She's desperate to escape Emily, escape the RFG Entertainment building, but nothing is ever easy. She starts left instead of right. The assistant jumps up from his desk and says, "No, this way."

"I'm sorry," says Chloe. She stumbles as she turns, and her cheeks—she can barely see over them. It's like they're bulging, like her whole body is swelling with shame.

Just twenty minutes earlier, she was fearless, bounding down this same hall with disorienting optimism. She had a meeting at RFG! She had a contact! Contacts. Networking. *It's who you know.* That's what everyone says. But these things that work for other people, they never work for Chloe.

She lunges for the elevator button. She can feel the agents and their underlings on the floor behind her, watching. The elevator is empty, thank God, and for a moment, she's safe. But then, every few seconds, it stops with an agonizing bell chime. The doors open to clone after clone of Doug's wife. They crowd the car in groups of two and three, and it doesn't matter if they're male or female; they're the same, all bundled against the air-conditioning in their sleek gray suits and closed-toed shoes.

Chloe's instinct is to smile, to offer them tiny greetings. But no one reciprocates. Instead, each person gives Chloe a hard once-over, and not with jealousy or lust like she's used to but with an authoritative sweep from her hair to her roman sandals. They assess and ignore, and Chloe stares down at the nail polish chip on her right big toe and wonders, *Why, oh why didn't I get a pedicure?* These are the type of people who notice feet.

She hits the lobby atrium and winces at the sight of the giant Calder mobile. It's imposing now, casting its translucent shadow across the marble floor. On the way in, she was comforted by the artwork, by the thought that it had started just as an idea in someone's head. Chloe swallows. She focuses on the front door as she passes the guard booth. She's almost out of the building when she senses she's in trouble. It's always there, that feeling she's about to be yelled at, but right now it's strong.

"Miss," she hears. "Excuse me."

It's the security lady, calling out to her.

"What's the matter?" Chloe asks.

"Do you—"

"I'm sorry?"

"Do you need your—"

"What?"

The lady thrusts out her bosom with the shiny brass badge and draws out every syllable. "Your parking. Do you need it validated?"

"No, I parked on the street."

The people around Chloe stop, listen, and stare. The lady puts a smile and a frown on her face in a way that no one ever does, and Chloe's body sparks in anger. *That's not a real expression,* Chloe thinks. *She's just showing off.* Chloe turns her head hard to her right, to give one of the bystanders a dirty look, but the guy's back is turned. He's studying the directory.

She speed walks out the door, into the sun, and down the street. She waits until she's across the six lanes of Wilshire Boulevard before she turns around. The top half of the agency is still visible, a monolith of dark amber jutting up over its neighbors like a middle finger. She flips a bird back to the building and glances at the bright smattering of pedestrians on the sidewalk. No one noticed what she did. She can't act like that in public, making obscene gestures at buildings. It's how things unravel.

She leans against one of the Beverly Wilshire's front columns. The terra-cotta is hot and sandpapery on her shoulder. She closes her eyes, trying to make the last half hour of her life go away, but the memory of meeting Doug's wife keeps replaying like a looping GIF. She's looking for the flyer, and she can't find the flyer, and what did Doug's wife say? That her purse was ugly? How did that awful woman end up with someone as amazing as Doug?

Doug. Chloe keeps her eyes shut and touches her collarbone. She conjures an image of her boss in one of his faded T-shirts, leaning over her desk and whispering, *I'm sorry my wife was mean.*

"Are you all right?"

Chloe opens her eyes. There's a lady in front of her with a face full of wrinkles crisscrossing into matronly disapproval. She's close enough for Chloe to smell her coffee breath, to grab her silk scarf if she wants to. Chloe shuts her eyes again. *Go away, go away, go away.*

"It's hot out," says the woman. She reaches for Chloe. Her fingers touch Chloe's arm.

"Boundaries!" Chloe screams. She slaps the woman's hand away. But it's not enough. There's a wave inside her, and it's fiery and cresting, pushing her forward, toward the woman's chest until Chloe has shoved the woman back a step. Chloe wants to hit her. She raises her hand.

A picture enters her mind then: a vivid blip of a different old lady falling to the ground. A half-cried moan of "Why!"

Chloe stops. This surge, this continuing of anger, she's been trained to recognize it. She can choose to interrupt it. She can calm down. She lowers her hand and takes a deep, conscious inhale, but the woman—if only the woman would stop moving too—the woman spreads her hands across her neck, all imperious, like she's never been told to mind her own business, like she's never had to worry about getting punched in the face.

"You pushed me!" yells the woman. She turns to the crosswalk, where a man in a suit is watching. The lady points at Chloe. "She pushed me!" The man starts toward them.

One, two, three, Chloe thinks. She blows air through her lips, like she's blowing through a straw. She unclenches her fingers. *Four, five, six.* She holds up her hands. Her fingers are splayed. The woman flinches.

"I didn't," says Chloe. "You grabbed me."

"I was trying to help."

A young woman in a printed maxi dress joins them. "Is everything okay?"

The man reaches them. The lady starts explaining how Chloe looked like she was fainting, hanging on to the pillar. Chloe wants to run. But they'll chase her if she runs.

The bystanders' eyes are on the old woman. Chloe takes a sideways step. They don't notice. She backs up. She turns and walks at a normal pace. She doesn't look their way, doesn't jinx her head start. The Beverly Wilshire doorman smiles as she enters yet another marble lobby blasting cold air.

"Where's the bathroom?" she asks.

"Up those stairs and to your left," says the doorman.

Chloe navigates around the clusters of tourists snapping selfies in front of jewelry displays. She locks herself in an empty bathroom stall. Her phone chimes. "Shit!" she says and turns it off.

She waits. She slows her breathing. Someone in kitten heels enters and click-clacks across the tile floor. Chloe lifts her feet. She scrunches her whole body on the toilet and holds her breath as the person tries her door.

The person moves to the next stall over. Chloe digs a fingernail into the side of her thumb. The skin there is sore and raked over.

This thing, it keeps happening. When she goes outside, there's trouble. It doesn't matter how many warnings she gets, how many anger-management classes they make her take. It doesn't matter that her public defender got her latest expunged, that she has a clean slate. Even with all the help, she never knows how she'll react to provocation.

The bathroom door opens again. Chloe winces. She braces herself as the sound of footsteps approaches her stall. *Please,* Chloe thinks. *Please. Get me out of this. I swear I'll never lose my temper again.*

PART TWO
EMILY

CHAPTER THREE

EMILY

After Chloe stumbled out of my office, I closed the door and stared at my cell phone on my desk, lit up with a dozen notifications urging me to get back to work. But all I could think of was Doug.

He'd asked only once if I was pregnant, months before, on that first morning after Bella had gone missing. I'd just thrown up in the guest bathroom, the one I'd had tiled in abalone shell. I could see him approach in the mirror behind me. He ran his fingers through his messy hair and folded his hands at his waist, looking penitent. I dabbed toothpaste on my tongue and wondered again, in a flutter of panic, if he'd had something to do with Bella's disappearance. He asked if I was pregnant. I lied. I said it was impossible.

Admitting I could be pregnant would have made it real.

I spent the next weeks ignoring the little invader, the tiny alien inside my body, like some teen mom in denial, terrified of consequences, of bringing a child into our depraved world. For the first time in my life, I didn't have a plan. That was the worst part, that this man I'd married, who thrived on chaos and poor impulse control, had finally infected me, turned me into an improviser just like him.

But after Chloe left, I reached for my phone, propelled by some final rush of tenderness, an echo of affection. Doug and I had once been a team.

His phone went to voice mail after five rings. I hung up.

How? I wanted to ask him. *How did we get here?*

———

I was single for the whole year leading up to meeting him. I'd just turned thirty-six and was working a respectable client list at a small agency in West Hollywood when my dog, my snapping, haughty Pomeranian named Gucci, died.

She'd been my mom's. Bequeathing Gucci to me had been one of the many logistical obsessions consuming my mother on the hospice bed set up in my parents' living room. Her death wasn't peaceful. She spent her last days restless, wedged there between the La-Z-Boy and the overstuffed couch. Every few minutes near the end, she'd startle and strain to lift her downy head, whispering with an urgency that made me rush to her side, thinking she was about to confess some tragic secret.

"If you take the limo to the grave site," she said at one point, "you'll need a ride back to town."

"Mom, it's okay."

"It's not," she said. "Your father can't handle Gucci."

"I'll take her."

She turned her face away from me and reached unsuccessfully for the bedside rail. "You're a good girl," she murmured. "You be good." She fell back asleep before I could ask if she was being sarcastic, if that was her parting shot. I pressed back into the La-Z-Boy and closed my eyes. No. My mom wouldn't do that. She wasn't like me.

After the funeral, after lunch with my family and friends who'd made the trek up to Figblossom Valley from LA, I opened the door to my Range Rover and made kissing noises, summoning Gucci to the driveway of my parents' split-level ranch. She pranced to the foot of the lawn and panted at the edge of the asphalt.

"Come on," I said. Her face was fox-like and smiling.

She touched a front paw to the blacktop and sat on the grass. It was too hot. I shook my head. I'd been back a month and was sick of the daily miseries of life in my desert hometown: the burning tar underfoot, the untouchable steering wheels.

"Wally!" I shouted. My brother opened the front door and stood in his undershirt behind the screen. He'd gotten a haircut for the funeral, a flattop, buzzed on the sides.

"Where are Gucci's bootees?" I asked.

"Dogs don't need shoes."

"I gave them to Mom for her birthday."

Wally yelled to my sister-in-law inside the house. "Jessica? You see those dog shoes anywhere?" I didn't hear Jessica's answer, only the muffled sound of my dad coughing in his upstairs bedroom. Wally turned back with a shrug. "Sorry."

I swept Gucci under my arm. She weighed less than a baby doll and gave an appreciative moan when I plopped her on the passenger seat. She climbed onto my lap as I sped south on the freeway and lay there the entire three-hour drive south to LA.

I petted her. I needed her. She was my tether, my tactile reminder of what had just happened.

I'd grown accustomed to this euphoric feeling whenever I drove out of the Mojave, leaving behind the windowsill knickknacks and wall-to-wall mediocrity of my childhood. On this trip, though, it scared me, how quickly that familiar joy came rushing back. As I drove through the Cajon Pass, the world started to seem unreal. The sun dipped behind the hill, and the lack of shadow afterward made the puckered dirt on either side of the highway look two dimensional, the shrubs like cardboard cutouts.

It was as if my mother's life had been reduced to a movie, and I was now casually exiting the theater. I kept a hand on Gucci, smoothing her coat. *This poor, motherless pup,* I kept thinking, until I was finally overtaken by a reassuring wave of anguish. I was grateful for my tears, for my ability to experience an appropriate emotion.

Gucci and I spent the next few weeks protecting one another in our grief. I brought her everywhere, to work, to the store. I tucked her in my purse. She let out high-pitched yaps from under my arm and nipped at anyone who dared approach me.

She died, though. She was old. I was ready to pay the veterinarian $1,000 for a necropsy. It was unfair that I'd lost my dog, that I'd lost my mom. I wanted him to uncover foul play, some excuse for retribution.

But I couldn't afford the vet's fee. My credit cards were maxed out.

My finances came at me like whiplash. I'd almost forgotten that I needed to make money. I worked on commission. And I'd done well until that point. Agenting was lucrative. But my mother's death had distracted me. I'd looked away for what I thought was a reasonable amount of grieving time, and my career was suddenly in danger.

I came back from lunch one Tuesday to find my boss, Frank, a quick-tempered man with a bulbous nose, standing in the gray-carpeted hallway outside my office. "Fire sale on Emily's clients!" he bellowed as I approached. He paused his speech, waiting for my colleagues to poke their heads out of their doorways. Public humiliation was his specialty. "You know what your good doctor has been up to?" He wagged a finger at me. "She just had lunch, in Beverly Hills! With Gerry Handman and Faye Watts!" He was referring to my star client, my celebrity psychiatrist, Dr. Maryn. She'd just met with people from a major agency, an iconic one, based out of Century City.

My mother just died, you fucking asshole! I wanted to shout, but instead I let my upper lip curl into a snarl. Dr. Maryn was mine. I'd discovered her seven years before, scouring local news stations around the country for star commentators. There she was, a "special contributor" to the NBC affiliate in Saint Louis, standing amid the rubble of a collapsed apartment building as she simultaneously reported on the scene and counseled the survivors. Her compassion was outsize, and her hair was cut in a bright-red pixie. I loved the hair more than anything, a ready-made signature.

After I signed Dr. Maryn, I got her gigs on national news, appearing live via satellite after the latest hurricane or mass shooting. Within two years, she was headlining her own talk show. She now hosted and executive produced two additional reality shows. Her book, *Ten Hacks to the Life You Deserve*, was a bestseller for fifteen straight weeks.

"Emily!" Frank was now yelling. His jacket collar bunched around his neck as he pointed at me. "Where's your head at, girl? This is the major leagues!" My arms were bare in my silk shell. I could feel my exposed skin betraying me in a web of blotch and goose bumps. I brought my hands to my biceps.

"Frank, I just found out about the lunch." I looked to my colleagues, hoping for just one sympathetic glance, but every one of them avoided my gaze. Cowards.

I went into my office. It was small, a glorified cubicle. My desk was made of plastic. How was I supposed to keep pace with my most ambitious clients in this shitty workspace?

I leaned against the door and covered my face with my hands, cursing Dr. Maryn. She didn't care how much I'd hustled. She didn't care how many hours I'd spent demanding and pleading and cajoling on her behalf until I couldn't stand to hear my own voice anymore. I was alone. The world was a brutal place. It would only turn crueler if I let myself fail.

It wasn't a question of working harder. I'd tried that. It wasn't enough. What I needed was power. What I needed was to destroy my fucking boss, Frank, for screaming at me.

I grabbed a pen and legal pad and sat at my desk. I had to find an area for Dr. Maryn to grow. I sketched a map of everything I'd done for her, with each category spindling out to various subheadings and ancillary deals. Her television show led to her production company, which led to her book deal, which led to product licensing and massive fees speaking at conferences. It was all connected.

But there was one word, *TECH*, floating unconnected near the edge of the page like an abandoned satellite. I circled it. Dr. Maryn had a website, of course. She was on Twitter and had a mobile app. But she was using them the same way every celebrity did: for promotion, outtakes from her show, and a social networking element that no one ever used.

Tech was where we would innovate.

I flew to her vacation home in Saint Louis, a new mansion still smelling of paint, with front columns and a three-story foyer. Dr. Maryn and her husband, Stan, greeted me at the front door in matching Lycra. They were the same height, with the same short haircuts and rubbery divots above their lips. I heard the shouts and splashes of her grandkids in the pool out back. I knew the children. They called me Aunt Emily. But Maryn and Stan didn't invite me to the patio like usual. They didn't even offer me water. Instead, they led me to a seldom-used front parlor decorated like the lobby of a grand hotel. This meeting was their final courtesy.

I perched at the edge of my club chair and opened the pitch deck on my phone. "We're missing revenue," I said. Dr. Maryn looked alarmed. "Maryn, you are the face of mental health in America. Why not get a cut of everything? I'm sure other people have talked about building you more or different apps, but why stop there? We can build a whole fucking app store. The Dr. Maryn Store."

She raised one eyebrow, then the other. "I'm intrigued."

"I need more than intrigued. If we do this, we'll have to jump to a bigger agency. You know RFG Entertainment? Has its hands in everything. I've already got three of my clients on board."

Stan slapped his thigh and yelped. "This is the big time, baby!" Dr. Maryn called for her housekeeper and asked if I would like a glass of iced tea.

I stole eleven clients from my old boss, Frank, and brought them to RFG, my sparkling Beverly Hills firm with billion-dollar everything: film packaging, gaming platforms, celebrity branding. I didn't even bother with parting words for Frank or trying to see his face as he realized what I'd done.

I knew in my heart I'd screwed him over. That was all that mattered.

———

Dr. Maryn and Stan flew out to the RFG office to kick off the app-store development. My whole department was invited to the meeting, and I paused with my client just outside the door of the glass-walled conference room. I took in my new colleagues. The agents at the table looked exactly like my former coworkers—sharp eyed and clad in dark neutrals—but these here were impenetrable specimens. Their bodies were even more compact, more perfectly sheathed inside the agile fabrics of the one percent. I touched the break line on my jacket, a double-knit jersey blend of cashmere and wool, feeling like an exile returned from a land of cheap knockoffs.

Stan and I moved to our spots near the head of the table and watched Dr. Maryn make her entrance. She took over the room, waving and winking at the team members, who were all trying to catch her eye, hoping to lodge themselves in this famous woman's consciousness. She stopped for a one-on-one with my new boss, clasping his forearm and nodding in an unblinking display of active listening.

"Thanks, everyone, for being here," I said as people settled. "No one has made a celebrity app store before. We've got a lot of room to innovate."

Dr. Maryn stood and rapped her knuckles on the table. "For good luck!" she said. Her face brightened. "Shall we start with a brainstorming session?"

Stan gave Dr. Maryn's shirtsleeve a tug. "What about the interns?" he mumbled.

Dr. Maryn cupped her hand to her ear and gave the room a wide-eyed sweep, like she was addressing a group of preschoolers. "What's that, dear?" she asked.

"We talked about including interns."

Confusion hovered. Several lower-level employees sat up, glancing toward their superiors. I pointed at my assistant. "Interns!" I said. "Get them in here."

"Mail room too!" said Dr. Maryn. "I want to know what the kids think!"

After a few minutes, four interns shuffled in. A mail guy tried to bring his cart into the room and was given a harsh, whispered "No!" by a higher-up near the door. No one brought chairs. The extra people stood, shifting on their feet, for the next hour as the assistants recorded the ideas of the people sitting around the table: *therapy chat / anchor with pharmaceutical companies / confidentiality as marketing tool.*

I was participating, monitoring, noting who among the staff had the most useful ideas, when someone suggested branching out into cardiology, maybe even dentistry. Then I heard an unsettling voice in my mind: my mother's. My mom was always there with me, lingering in the background, visiting in conscious thought every so often, like a recurring dream.

What about the teeth? I could hear my mom asking.

She'd always wanted to know about the teeth. The guests on *The Dr. Maryn Show* were often missing theirs. It was one of the first items on the casting questionnaire: *How many teeth do you have, and where are they?* The show had an on-call dentist who'd do cut-rate fixes that lasted about as long as it took to get the guests' problems on tape. We'd treat the dysfunctional, the addicts and abusers, to stays in high-class hotels and all-you-can-eat craft services. In return, they'd spill their secrets for our national audience, unaware their dental work would last only slightly longer than Cinderella's pumpkin coach.

"Do they ever try to sue?" my mom used to ask.

I always laughed in response. "We make them sign over their first-born before we let them on the show." Sometimes I enjoyed her troubled, bewildered expression after I said such things. It was a sign of how far I'd come, watching this small-town lady from a simpler time grapple with what the world had become. I was in it. I was thriving.

"Emily?" Dr. Maryn was staring. So was everyone else. I'd been spacing out. I gave a vague nod.

"I'm thinking ahead," I said.

"And?"

I could feel the room sharpening, the junior agents leaning forward, these savvy little shits just discovering their ability to sniff out prey. Dr. Maryn stood behind me and squeezed my shoulder.

"Emily's a tough cookie," she said. "The best. Let me tell you about our trip to Kenya. We were doing an episode on one of those shoe handouts—you know the organization that gives moccasins to poor, shoeless children around the world? So we're in the back of a beat-up truck about two hours from Nairobi with this team of fresh-faced idealists, and we come roaring into this cement block village. And you know, the children in these places, they love it when strangers visit, so this mob of kids comes running out to meet us." Dr. Maryn put her hands up like a director mapping out a panorama. "The cameraman is filming, and the African sun is setting, and we're tossing out these plastic bags of moccasins, and the children are jumping and clapping, and we're all thrilled with how it's going. And do you know what Emily says to me? In the middle of this? She says, 'Shit. They're already wearing shoes!'"

The room erupted in laughter.

"She went up to the director to tell him," Dr. Maryn said. "He wouldn't listen, so she fired him on the spot. Took over the shoot. She yelled, 'Back it up, everybody! You kids go behind that building and take off your shoes. Then I want you to run toward us again in your bare feet!'"

———

Dr. Maryn and Stan took me to lunch after the meeting. We went to a farm-to-table restaurant on the border of Century City and Beverly Hills, the same place where Dr. Maryn had met with my competition. They sat me at the banquette and pulled their chairs together across the white tablecloth.

"I'm worried about you," said Dr. Maryn. Her tone had a touch of the overwrought compassion she reserved for the guests on her show. Stan picked at the label on his bottle of sparkling water. "I need you focused."

I opened my eyes wide. "Maryn, I'm one hundred percent here for you."

Dr. Maryn and Stan looked at each other. She reached across the table and put her hand on mine. "How's your personal life?"

She knew. She knew everything about me. She'd set me up with my last boyfriend, a CFO of a health care consortium who'd let me down easy after I'd spent four months showering him with access to film premieres and VIP rooms. He said he wanted a quieter life.

"Things are fine," I said.

"We think you could use a little stability."

Stan pointed at me. "You should get married. Doesn't matter to who. All you kids, you're holding out for 'the one.' There's no such thing. Just pick someone and settle down."

I gave a chuckle, pretending this was friendly advice from an older person, not a warning. "I'll get right on that," I said.

I met Doug soon after.

CHAPTER FOUR

I'd just negotiated my first victory for the Dr. Maryn Store. A pharmaceutical company agreed to sell their dosing apps exclusively with us in exchange for Dr. Maryn promoting their new children's antidepressant. It had been a delicate negotiation. We had to clear it with three legal departments: the network's, the pharma company's, and my agency's. RFG's head attorney was Gayle, a powerfully maternal woman in her midfifties who delivered the news to me in person, in my office. Not only had the deal gone through, but the pharma company had agreed to buy ad time on the show if Dr. Maryn prescribed their children's antidepressant on camera.

"Yes!" I shouted and jumped up from my desk.

Gayle crossed her arms and considered me. "Congratulations," she said in a monotone.

I stared at the empty doorway after she left, resisting the urge to chase after her, to demand, *Excuse me? Are you judging me?*

Of course on some level, I knew what we were doing was wrong. Not that it would get me arrested, but it could turn into a scandal if not handled properly. Even with legal cover, it would take only one kid with a bad reaction to the medicine, one investigative news segment, to hurt Dr. Maryn's credibility, make it seem like her loyalty was to Big Pharma, not her patients.

I sat back down and buzzed my assistant, Travis, a recent mail room graduate with remnants of acne around his nose. He popped his head in with an eager smile.

"Which market research firm do we use?" I asked.

"Doug Markham's firm, Beyond the Brand."

"Right. Ask them to design a study on how it would affect Dr. Maryn's likability if she started prescribing drugs on her show. Tell them we want to cover antidepressants, schizophrenia drugs, and all that."

Travis took a step backward and asked, "Can I get a pen?"

I stared at him. He froze. Why did these people have to make me act like a bitch?

"Don't ever come in here without a way to write," I said firmly. "Oh, and kids. Tell them to ask if people would have a problem with Dr. Maryn prescribing antidepressants to children."

I waved him out the door. *There,* I thought. *I'm handling it.* I could hear Travis at his desk outside my office, relaying the details of what we needed for the survey. He remembered everything. I buzzed him again.

"Good job," I said. "Can you get me an iced coffee?"

It was lunch. I pulled a salad out of my minifridge. I'd skipped breakfast that morning, saving my calories so I could enjoy two tablespoons of balsamic vinaigrette. Travis buzzed me. Doug Markham was on the phone.

"Doug Markham? Are you sure?"

"He said it was regarding the Dr. Maryn survey."

I looked down at my salad and sighed. I was starving. But Doug was the CEO of Beyond the Brand. He'd worked on a presidential campaign. He'd had a TED Talk go viral. I picked up the phone.

"Don't do it, Emily," was the first thing out of his mouth.

"I'm sorry?" I hadn't even said hello.

"Your doctor has the public's trust. Don't do anything sleazy with it."

Sleazy. I'd already had to suffer the silent moralizing of that fucking lawyer. I thought of hanging up on him, but he was quasi-famous. My overriding instinct was to appease.

"Dr. Maryn prescribes antidepressants all the time in private practice," I said. "I can't believe we haven't featured this aspect of her job before."

"Right. I get it. Let's talk about it over drinks."

———

I met him at a hotel bar near the Strip, a white Gothic-type place lined with gold-framed, mottled mirrors. A group of younger men was parked near the entrance, decked out in aggressively casual hoodies and retro sneakers. In what was becoming a familiar humiliation, they completely ignored me as I made my way past the host stand. It was hard to say exactly when it happened, my transition from attractive woman to well-groomed lady at the bar. I'd only just vowed to stop dating players, but the issue resolved itself without my having to do anything.

I saw Doug. I recognized him from his TED Talk. He was kicked back on a patent leather couch, looking more vibrant in person, alert, with a full head of dirty-blond hair and the rugged tan of an aging surfer. He didn't see me at first. He just sat comfortably in his skinny jeans and Paul Smith trainers, watching the scattered people at the bar, totally at ease without a phone or drink in his hand. I tightened my abs and smoothed the front of my jacket.

"Emily! How are ya?" He stood when I approached and opened his arms for a hug. I leaned in for an air-kiss. "What are you drinking?"

"Just a cranberry and soda," I said. "I'm heading out after this."

He laughed. "You don't have dinner plans."

I jerked my head back. "Oh, really?"

He gestured to my body. "Don't tell me you go out at night in a suit."

I had an impulse to tell him to fuck off. Instead, I smiled. "Okay, Detective."

Doug called the waitress over. "What do you want, wine?" he asked.

I ordered a rose hip negroni off the cocktail list. Doug asked for a Red Bull. I looked at him. He grinned and held up three fingers like a Boy Scout. "Twelve years sober," he said. In his TED Talk, he'd mentioned past substance abuse, hallucinogens. I nodded.

"I saw your talk. You were a Deadhead in college?"

"Actually, I was a cokehead." He leaned toward my ear and spoke in a low voice. "But that's not something I share with everyone." It was such a move, letting his bass notes resonate near my neck. Only the most skilled seducer, man or woman, would dare slither into someone's personal space like that.

The waitress came back. She was wearing a low-cut top and leaned forward as she handed him his drink. He winked at her. I sat up, shifting into attentiveness. There was another woman, in spaghetti straps, throwing him louche eyes from the bar.

He took my cocktail from the waitress and placed it in front of me. I looked more closely at him, trying to pinpoint his appeal. He was handsome, sure, but that wasn't enough to explain such overt flirting from these women. He seemed rich. That could have been it. There was also something simmering about him, the way he lifted his glass, leading with his forearm. He was masculine.

"Cheers," he said. The waitress glanced back as she walked away. He cleared his throat. "So in terms of Dr. Maryn. I'll gladly take your money to do this survey on giving kids the antidepressants. I stand to make a lot of money helping with all the ethics headaches that'll crop up."

"It's not about ethics," I said. "I'm worried about perception."

"You know what you are, Emily? You're a converted cynic."

"Excuse me?" I held up my index finger. He smiled, inviting me to turn my annoyance into something playful. The lounge turned darker, louder. A pretty girl at the edge of the crowd glanced at us and tugged at the hem of her micro mini.

He leaned into my ear again. "Cynicism doesn't come naturally to you, I can tell."

Oh yes, it does, I wanted to shoot back. I ruined anyone who messed with me. I mean *ruined* them. I wanted to tell him about getting a backstabbing sister kicked out of my sorority or how, in my assistant days, I'd turned the whole office against a credit-stealing rival. But I'd long since learned to keep those stories to myself.

"Growing up, we had these neighbors from Vietnam," Doug said. "And the dad was so into America, talking about freedom all the time. It was weird. Anyway, I think a lot of you guys in entertainment are like this. You're like converts to this kind of ruthless business style."

"Bullshit," I said. "Everyone loves to hate agents. You're like ten times more successful than I am."

"But I grew up with money," he said. "A sense of entitlement isn't a bad thing. I don't have to psych myself up the same way I see other people doing."

"That's it!" I sat up and squared off to him.

"What?"

"Your vibe. All these women checking you out. Don't tell me you don't notice."

His lips twitched. He was suppressing a smile.

"You have a feeling of ease about you," I said. "You look like you have an easy life."

I barely knew this man, but sitting beside him was a thrill, like I was a passenger on some ride to wherever his charisma wanted to go. Everything in my life was so painstaking, so carefully constructed.

There was nothing about me that wasn't deliberate. I wanted what he had.

I slid closer to him on the sofa, leaving just a few inches between me and the crook of his arm. "Have you done much television?"

He grinned and made a scolding motion with his finger. "I already have an agent." He pulled his phone from his back pocket and swiped through his photos until he came to a picture of something dark and spidery against a stark white background. "Here, check this out." He handed me the phone. "You're not the only one moving into technology."

I squinted at the screen. I didn't know what I was looking at. It was shiny, a domed strip of onyx sprouting a dozen thin and ominous-looking prongs. The whole thing assumed the vague outline of a bike helmet.

"I just bought a start-up," he said. "A wearables company."

"This goes on your head?"

"It's an EEG." He pointed to the small round disk at the end of one of the prongs. "The sensors pick up the electrical activity in the brain." I nodded, picturing a hospital EEG with its white wires and sloppy, gel-covered mesh. "We'll get people to wear these in their everyday lives," he said, "sell it as a wellness tool. Biofeedback, measuring their stress levels, you know? We'll pair it with an app. It'll give us a whole hell of a lot of data on people."

"Branching into tech," I said. "You and I are doing the same thing."

Doug tapped his index finger to his forehead. "Follow the money," he said.

He understood. The world had changed. The tech sector was gobbling up everything, making those of us in other industries seem like dinosaurs and ruining LA with rising real estate prices. Being comfortably rich wasn't a safe option anymore. For real protection, for power, for whatever the future looked like, I'd need the type of wealth that could separate me, insulate me completely. There were only a few ways to get there, and joining tech was the most logical. I raised my glass. "Here's to becoming super rich."

The waitress returned with menus. Doug ordered a mushroom flatbread and another round of drinks. He ignored her attempts at eye contact and grazed my leg with his hand as he gave the menus back. He looked at me for a moment without speaking.

"Don't do the children's-antidepressant thing," he said. "At least don't have Dr. Maryn prescribe it on the show."

"We'll have safeguards," I said. "Medicate only the kids who need it."

He shook his head. "You know something will go wrong with that, and then you guys will try to cover it up. You might even be able to. But it'll rot your soul."

But there was no reversing course, not after the network's ad sales had gotten involved. I swallowed against the muscles tightening in my throat. Morality was a luxury at this point.

He put a hand on my shoulder. "I'll make it disappear. I'll do a survey. We'll make sure it points away from drug placement."

"Okay," I said. I took a deep, involuntary inhale and missed my mother, with a sudden longing, a ferocity completely out of sync with the party happening around me. The bar was now standing room only.

Doug looked out at the crowd and raised his voice over the clamor. "I think we're the oldest people here."

———

Doug put his hand on my back as we made our way past the smokers in front of the entrance. I handed him my valet ticket and walked away to take a work call. When I came back, he kissed me.

"You're tipsy," he said. "Let me drive."

"Where?"

"My house."

"I have to get my car."

"Your car is fine. She can leave her car, right?"

Doug slipped the nearest valet guy a tip and opened his arm to shepherd me to the passenger side of his Porsche. I looked back, to the crowd around the entrance, imagining Dr. Maryn and Stan among them, sanctioning my decision to go home with this man.

———

He lived in Malibu, and his house was narrow, set into a small cliff dropping off the Pacific Coast Highway into the ocean. The entrance was on the top floor. I counted three bedrooms before we descended to a spare living room and kitchen decorated in standard-issue modern: Barcelona sofa, Noguchi table, Egg Chair. The style was overwhelmingly male and musky. It needed softening, a shag rug or mismatched pillows. The couch would have to go.

There was a sliding glass door leading to a balcony. I watched his reflection in the glass as he walked behind me to the refrigerator. He pulled out a bottle of wine. I turned. His counters were granite. Those would have to go too. I'd been lusting after a bright-blue stone from Brazil, azul macauba, that would be perfect for a breakfast bar.

He picked up a corkscrew and pointed toward the door. "I'll meet you on the deck."

Stepping outside was like boarding a boat. The ocean came right up under the balcony, the waves surging below the floorboards. I leaned over the railing and watched the sea-foam swirl around the pylons.

Doug came out with a glass of wine and stopped close beside me, injecting desire into the thin strip of air between us. He pointed over my shoulder. "Can you see the tip of that rock?" he said. "Where the water is breaking up a little?"

I saw a hint, a gleam, of some barnacle-covered magic in the distance.

"That's where the waterline is at low tide. If the conditions are right, I take my paddleboard out before work."

I waited for him to say something else, something about me. He wrapped an arm around my waist and pulled me toward him.

CHAPTER FIVE

I always stayed friendly with the men I dated. Former lovers were scattered through my network, creating sweet little pockets of intimacy and allyship. That was what I thought Doug would turn into: someone I could call on for favors. But we lasted, spending nearly every night together after the first few weeks. We formed our own unit. We'd stay up late during the week, having sex and then opening up our laptops and strategizing about the Dr. Maryn Store and his EEG project. We always woke early after an especially busy night, going out for an extra-long run before sunrise. It was exhilarating, jogging by all those dark windows, all those sleeping people.

I hired his company, Beyond the Brand, to help out full-time on the Dr. Maryn project. Sometimes he did research for us. Other times, he was just my sounding board. I'd never ventured so far outside the entertainment industry. I was incredulous the first time one of our press releases was vetted for accuracy. If we couldn't throw around terms like *miracle cure* and *magical properties* to describe FDA-approved drugs, how were we going to make them sexy? I considered handing off some negotiations to my colleagues in business development, but Doug wouldn't let me.

"They'll take the whole thing from you," he said. "Don't you dare tell me you can't handle this."

I made a generous deal for Beyond the Brand to sell Doug's EEG and app through the Dr. Maryn Store. His products weren't ready yet. He had to make the EEG smaller and sleeker, make it fashionable so people would wear it in everyday life, but it also had to function like a hospital-grade EEG. It was tricky. None of this was fun or glamorous. It was just hard work. That was our specialty.

Doug helped me the most with the tech consultancy we'd hired to develop the platform.

Erik, the project manager, was in his early thirties. He had fluffy, overly shampooed hair that would fill our morning meetings with the sharp scent of Pert Plus. I could never look at him without picturing him in a steamy bathroom, applying bits of toilet paper to his shaving nicks.

Erik was a pain in my ass.

He wanted to leave the Dr. Maryn Store open to independent companies so that any random person could list an app for sale on our site. I kept telling him no. We were selling exclusive deals with major brands. He never listened. Whenever I spoke, he'd look down at his phone.

I called Doug when I was frustrated. He let me vent. He even argued once for Erik's side. We were in his car, on the way to dinner, when he said, "Just playing devil's advocate here, but you guys are going to amass a whole hell of a lot of data."

That was our sticking point. Erik, and now Doug, loved to talk about all the data we'd be capturing. But Dr. Maryn couldn't sell any of it. She was a doctor.

"This is people's medical information," I said.

"But that's the beauty of making it open to third-party developers," Doug said. "If some app swoops in and steals people's psychiatric histories, you can say you didn't know anything about it."

He pulled up to the restaurant valet. A man in a red vest opened my door. I put a hand on Doug's arm. "Doug, you were the one who said we needed to protect Dr. Maryn's credibility."

"Are you talking about that pay-to-play scheme? With the children's antidepressants? You were going to endanger kids. Plus, it was so obvious. Anyone watching would know something was up as soon as Maryn started spouting off brand names. This, with the apps, the data, it's behind the scenes. A secret."

"And you called *me* sleazy!"

The valet opened Doug's door. He started out, but I gripped his arm tighter, feeling suddenly unstable. I'd thought Doug had been working off some sort of moral core, that he had a set of principles I could lean on, borrow from.

He squinted at me. "Actually, you're right," he said. "A flood of apps from wherever, it would end up being chaos. The Wild West. We'd want to be more deliberate."

He got out of the car, and I sat for a moment. "Miss?" asked the valet guy. Doug stood in front of me, spotlighted by his headlights. He made a shocked face, with his mouth open in a round O. I laughed. He was so sure of himself. And I didn't want to be alone anymore.

Erik went behind my back a week later. He tried going straight to Dr. Maryn, inviting her on a tour of his office, a playground of a space with lime-green love seats and supersize photographs of pomegranate seeds. I showed up, uninvited, and straggled within earshot as they strolled together at the front of her entourage, where he pitched her on his open-app-store idea. He broached the subject casually, like it was something he'd only just thought of.

"I love it!" said Dr. Maryn. Of course she did. She loved anything if she didn't have to do the legwork.

I stepped between them. "Erik, we discussed this."

Erik motioned for Dr. Maryn to continue walking. She stayed put, waiting to hear what I had to say. I smiled. I had him, the fucker. He was counting on me not to make a scene, but that was the only way to win these testosterone-fueled games.

"There are privacy issues," I said. "If you open it up to random app developers, we lose control of it."

He glanced at me before angling himself closer to Dr. Maryn. He was about to blow it. I could feel it. He lowered his voice.

"Think about all that data, Dr. Maryn. People's worries, their prescriptions and routines. It's a resource. You can't just not use it."

Dr. Maryn jerked her head back. "Wait, are you talking about selling medical data?"

Erik held up a hand, course correcting. "No. I mean, *we* wouldn't sell it."

"Because that's a violation," said Dr. Maryn. She crossed her arms and edged closer to me. I could feel myself expanding as we stared him down together. I knew how to ally myself with powerful people. He didn't.

———

After everyone left, I lingered in the lobby. Erik was vulnerable. But we weren't firing him, not yet. It would have been complicated to start over with someone else.

I texted Doug:

E dispatched.

He wrote back:

Take him out.

I stopped outside the door to Erik's office. He was sitting at his desk, his chin propped on his fists. He looked up at me with a hooded-eyed sullenness.

"You want to embarrass me again?" he asked.

"You did that to yourself," I said. "Let me buy you a drink."

We arranged to meet in a half hour at Shutters on the Beach. Doug texted me as I drove:

I'll join you later?

Yes

Erik was sitting in the lobby when I arrived, in an overstuffed armchair, finishing a martini. I asked the hostess for a table, and we moved to the French Riviera–themed patio, overlooking the beach path and its sunset joggers and bicyclists. I ordered a Campari and soda. Erik asked for a second martini. He gestured to a group of skateboarders practicing tricks on a wheelchair ramp.

"Look at this," he said. "You don't get this view anywhere."

I looked out in surprise. "I guess I take it for granted," I said. "I spend most of my time in Malibu."

He nodded and fell silent. The waitress came with our drinks. He picked an olive off the skewer and popped it in his mouth. His hair was sticking up in front, like a rooster's.

"Can I ask you a question?" he asked.

"Sure."

"Why are you always looking at my hair?"

"Seriously?"

"I'll be making a presentation, and your eyes always drift up to the top of my head. What's the deal with that?"

"You need to use conditioner," I said.

He touched his head. "My shampoo has conditioner in it."

"Doesn't work," I said. "Maybe if your hair were close cropped, but anything longer than two inches, you need a separate conditioner."

He chuckled.

"Now I have a question for you," I said.

"Shoot."

"Why are you making my life so difficult?"

"Don't take it personally," he said. "I can't abide inefficiency."

"What does that mean?"

He smoothed his hair with his palm. "All that data we'll be collecting," he said. "That's your product. That's your wealth. And you just want to let it sit there and do nothing." He put a hand to his heart. "I find it offensive."

"What about when you go to the doctor's office?" I asked. "Should we just make everyone's medical records available?"

"That's different," he said.

"How?"

"The rules change when you go online. This is about scale. Monetizing the population, that's the future."

He drained the last of his martini and looked around for the waitress. I slapped a hand on the table.

"So," I said. "You think your dermatologist should be able to sell information about that sebaceous cyst on your back?" Erik looked at me. His mouth opened. "The one that got infected after you tried to drain it yourself?"

"How do you know—"

"What about your therapist?" I asked. "It's okay for her to share details of your low-level depression? How is that pronounced? I can never get it right. Is it dis*thih*mia or dys*thee*mia?"

"What the hell?"

I pointed to his martini. "And you should really think before you order another martini, what with your elevated liver enzymes and all."

"Are you blackmailing me?"

I laughed. "I wish! To be honest, your secrets are pretty dull."

He stared. He made a motion to leave but stopped. I knew what was keeping him at the table: curiosity. "What did you do, hack my insurance?"

"Of course not. I have no idea how it works, but I think this was off your internet searches? All we needed was your IP address, which I got from your emails, and then Doug searched the logs of his clients' sites for it. You accepted their cookies, and voilà. I think it was even legal."

Doug appeared just then. He came in through the patio door behind Erik, like he'd been listening for the right moment to enter. He had on a zipped-up hoodie and jeans, and his hair was tamped down on one side. He looked good with unbrushed hair, wearing his power haphazardly. A woman passing our table startled at the sight of him and then smirked down at me in a show of soft-shouldered brutality. Doug ignored her and beamed at me, buoying me. He was mine. We were an army of two, and Erik was our first kill.

Doug leaned down to kiss me. Erik shoved his chair back and looked at Doug, incredulous.

"*You* did this?"

Doug pointed to Erik's empty glass. "What are you drinking?"

"This is unbelievable," said Erik.

Doug waved him off. "Relax. We were just trying to make a point."

"Which was?"

I leaned forward, put a smile on my face, and spoke softly, deliberately. "That if you go behind my back with Dr. Maryn again, if you fuck with me at all, I will fuck with you. And I'm better at it. I'm so good at it, in fact, that if you want to beat me at any kind of shit, you better make it your full-time fucking job." Erik's eyes widened for just a millisecond. Doug touched my arm.

"I think he gets it," Doug said.

Erik balled the napkin in his lap and threw it on the table. "Well, maybe I'll just quit."

Doug raised his hands. "Everyone, calm down. No one's fucking anyone. No one's quitting. Erik, we have a consolation prize for you, okay?" Doug motioned for the waitress. She raised her index finger to indicate she'd be with us and disappeared back into the main dining room. "You know the wearable company I acquired?" he asked.

Erik nodded. Doug pulled his phone from his pocket and flipped to a picture of the EEG. His designers had been working on it. It was sleeker and more discreet than the photo he'd shown me on our first date.

"This is our portable-EEG helmet. Our plan is to sell it to the public as a lifestyle tool, right? People can measure their stress responses, optimize their emotions. It'll be synced with an app that we'll put on the Dr. Maryn Store."

Erik looked at me and then at Doug. He nodded. "So you'll be collecting a lot of data yourself."

Doug turned to me and winked. My cue. I stood.

He'd asked me for time alone with Erik. I didn't know what they were about to discuss, not officially anyway. But of course, I understood. They were going to use Doug's app to rip off data from the store. All I needed was for Dr. Maryn's reputation to stay clean. Doug had promised me it would. And again, I technically had no idea why Doug and Erik wanted to be alone. That was how I rationalized my part in this side deal, this swindle that was about to take place.

A waiter approached our table. "I'll have a Hefeweizen," Doug said. I cocked my head. Doug looked up at me and winked again. He turned to Erik. "You want another martini?"

I didn't move. "A Hefeweizen?" I asked.

"When in Rome," he said and waved me off. "Beer's fine." From what I'd learned about sobriety, though, beer wasn't fine.

Erik sat up, attuned to the nascent conflict. I'd humiliated him more than once today. No doubt he'd gather whatever ammunition he could on me. I glanced to the ocean, to the streaks of dark purple signaling the end of twilight. The beach was empty except for a few straggling exercisers and a small group of homeless people setting up camp. I turned to Erik and held out my hand. "Sorry I had to be harsh earlier. Don't take it personally."

———

I waited at Doug's house for an hour and ran upstairs as soon as I heard his car pull into the garage. He pressed me into a wall and kissed me. His breath smelled like an Altoid. We stumbled into the bedroom and inhaled each other, the air between us entering our bodies all crisp and cool, like we were climbing a mountain together, ascending to higher and lighter-headed altitudes.

I waited until after sex to ask him about the beer. I ran my fingers up his chest. "I thought you were sober."

"It's about moderation."

Moderation. There was no such thing. My parents had both been smokers. I'd spent my childhood watching them cycle in and out of their pointless addictions, quitting one day, taping together torn cigarettes out of the garbage the next, until my mother got cancer.

I never gave into cravings. I'd thought Doug was the same, in control. "But in AA, don't you—"

"I'm not in AA," he said.

I sat up. I could have sworn he'd said he was in AA.

"I had a cocaine problem," he said. "I told you this."

I studied him. He stared back at me, his face neutral, deflecting. His eyes were clear. I'd dated a lot of men in Los Angeles and had been lied to in the most astonishing ways. "Your meetings—"

"What meetings?"

"When you leave for work early, you say you have a meeting. When you have to be back late, you say it's for a meeting."

Doug burst out laughing. "Em, I just bought a company."

"No." I shook my head. He'd been sharing all the details of his business with me. "These other meetings you go to, you act all secretive."

"There's no secret." He sat up to face me with a sudden, serious expression. "Listen. The science behind the EEG helmet isn't a slam dunk." He put a hand on my arm and rubbed my bicep with his thumb. "We're having issues getting the more fashionable versions to work. I didn't want to stress you out."

This made sense. And I was reassured, relieved by his answer. But a small part of me registered this relief as disturbing. I didn't want to admit I recognized the pattern: Guy lies. Woman confronts him. Guy laughs at her and comes up with a plausible explanation. Woman feels better and silly for doubting him.

"You want all the minutiae?" he asked. "I can give you that."

I sighed. I'd become so cautious, isolating myself on a dating field obscured by row after row of red flags.

I flashed to a memory of him ordering a Red Bull our first night together, of him holding up his fingers and saying he was sober.

The world turned hazy, as if my mind were being wrapped in gauze. I didn't want to argue. Doug and I made such a good team. I decided to believe him.

CHAPTER SIX

Doug wanted to meet my family. I held off for as long as I could, after I'd already spent an evening with his parents, who'd driven up from La Jolla. They took us to a steak house in Beverly Hills, a contemporary one, with striated onyx tabletops and lace metal place mats.

Doug's father was broad shouldered with silver hair, like a senior Ken doll. He greeted me with a bear hug at the entrance to the restaurant. His mother had an anemic handshake and was thin, bordering on frail. During dinner, she pushed her veal medallions around her plate and kept a nervous watch on a pair of celebrities two tables over.

"Do you know a lot of famous people in Hollywood?" asked Doug's dad.

I glanced at the couple. "I guess," I said. "I don't really think about it."

"Emily's been doing this awhile," said Doug.

His mother raised a single string bean to her mouth and paused before taking a bite. Her lipstick was immaculate. "I doubt I'd ever get used to it," she said. "We know Mitt, of course, from the club, but he blends in after a while." She lowered the string bean back to her plate.

"I must say," said his dad, "fame is a form of capital, isn't it?"

"Oh, absolutely," I said. "That's what Doug helps us with. We have metrics for things like how familiar a celebrity is to the public, how much the audience trusts that person. It's especially important for me, when one of my clients wants to license their name to a perfume company or whatever."

"Fascinating," he said. He poured more zinfandel into my glass.

"Easy, Dad," said Doug. His father winked at him.

———

My father and brother still lived in my hometown, a three-hour drive into the Mojave Desert. They never came to LA, at least not in the last decade.

We arranged to fly up on a Saturday. Doug had his own Cessna. It was a small plane, a four-seater prop, which he'd been trying to get me into. I kept begging off, saying I was a nervous flier. He didn't know this, but I'd dated two pilots before him and had suffered too many bumps and tosses and scary aborted landings. I hated small planes.

But I agreed to fly for this trip. It would mean we could zip in and out in one day. We wouldn't have to stay the night. Doug was so happy at the airport, bounding around with little-boy ebullience, introducing me to his flight-school buddies, showing me how to fill the gas tank on each wing. I helped him, hauling the heavy fuel hose over my shoulder.

"Manual labor looks good on you," he said. He climbed next to me on the wing and sucked a sample of gas from the tank into a syringe. "Purity check." He held the fuel-filled syringe up to the light before climbing down the stepladder and putting it back in his tool case.

"Don't you need to check the other tank?" I asked.

"Nope," he said. "I just filled it."

I knew, without a doubt, that he was supposed to check the tank on the other wing. Pilots had to do the same inspection every single time they flew. Doug reached up, motioning for me to slide into his arms. I stayed put.

"Why don't you check it?" I asked.

He looked at me a moment before saying, "Okay." There was tenderness in his voice, like he was doing it to placate me. It was my first inkling that this man was dangerous, that his carelessness could hurt me. And then I had the strangest thought.

He's going to die in a plane crash.

The idea contained a fleeting sense of certainty that disappeared as quickly as it took to flit through my mind. The only reason I remember it at all is because of what happened later.

———

We landed at the small airport outside town. I pulled up Uber on my phone. The nearest car was ninety minutes away. There was a card for a taxi company pinned to an empty bulletin board. I called it and braced myself for the ride.

The route to my dad's house was through the poor section, a desolate stretch of scrub and low-slung houses peeling paint in varied shades of human flesh. All the curtains were makeshift: dark blankets and cartoon-patterned sheets. And there were no yards, only the occasional chain link marking off a section of desert from the rest of the landscape.

Doug turned to look out the back window. "Whoa," he said. He'd never understand this. He was from a more benevolent California, from a coastal town carpeted in bougainvillea petals and Spanish tile. He started singing the "Dueling Banjos" song from *Deliverance* just as we passed Destiny Stimpson's old house.

"Stop," I said. "I used to know these people."

"Seriously?"

I swallowed back a sour taste and scanned for signs of Destiny or her family. The place looked empty, with bare, dirty windows and cinder block steps up to the raised front door. Destiny had been a tiny girl with an overbite and bangs that came down to her nose. In elementary school, we'd spent almost every afternoon together. Her mother would make us sandwiches, standing at the sink with her bra straps flopping down her arms, slopping mayonnaise and bologna onto white bread. She'd then send us out, unsupervised, to hike up the wash with red bandanas tied to our glitter batons.

I dared Destiny to do things. I'd tell her to give me half her sandwich or make a wild leap from the top of the riverbank onto the soft sand below. She always lowered her face before she did my bidding, peeking at me from under her uncombed hair. One time I got her to yell, "Druggies!" at the teenage boys smoking pot behind the gravel pits. They chased us. We ran.

By fourth grade, we were allowed to ride our bikes into town, and I dared her to steal from the dollar store. I hid behind the lone tree in the parking lot as she shoplifted candy and Beanie Babies, shoving them up the bottoms of her sleeves like I'd shown her how to do.

She smiled at me as she exited, just before the manager grabbed her arm. I held my breath as he ushered her back into the store. Then I left. I went home.

Destiny and her mom had to go to family court afterward, and my parents forbade me to play with her. I tried to make it up to her. Her desk in science was across from mine. I offered to let her cheat off me, but she could never manage it without calling attention to herself. By middle school, I was tired of feeling bad whenever I saw her. By then I'd assumed a spot within the elite of the school, the popular girls. Whenever Destiny said hi or smiled at me in the hallway, I'd ignore her. My friends caught on. They positioned themselves between Destiny and me. They called her Dirt Devil and asked in syrupy voices why her clothes never fit. I knew I was supposed to stop them, but I didn't. Destiny stared at me once in the middle of it all. Her expression was stoic, accepting.

I turned to Doug. "There was a girl in my class, Destiny. She gave birth by herself in a bathtub our freshman year."

He rubbed his palm over his chin. "Jesus," he said. "And you grew up here?"

"Not here!" I said. "On the hill."

The road divided, and we snaked into the foothills, through the ranches and subdivisions of Figblossom Valley's middle-class aristocracy, blanketed in unsustainable green. "The jewel of the jewel of the high desert," we used to call our front lawn. We were the first family in town to install Bermuda grass.

The taxi pulled into my dad's driveway. Our neighbor, Mrs. Gibbs, was taking out the garbage next door. Her hair was fully gray now, and she wore a housedress under her open bathrobe. She watched, expressionless, as we got out of the cab. I felt myself hardening in an LA kind of way, my sunglasses and lack of body fat radiating outward like a force field.

"Hi, Mrs. Gibbs!" I said. Cheer with an edge. The woman never forgave me for dumping her son. She hated me, actually. Everyone in this town did.

"You took a taxi from LA?" she asked.

"We flew," I said. Doug joined me at my side. "This is my boyfriend, Doug."

She hugged the front of her robe closed. "Your father doesn't need dinner, then," she said.

"Oh? No. Thank you for helping out, though," I said. "Say hi to George for me."

She looked Doug up and down. "George is vice president now. They just had another baby."

———

"I dusted," said my dad as I opened the door. He was sitting up, bright, on the living room couch, like he'd hoped somehow to spring to his feet. I went to him.

"This is Doug," I said. "This is my dad, Charles."

My dad gripped the end table and rose slowly. He smelled like shaving cream and mint and looked like he'd had a trim, no gray fuzz creeping down the back of his neck. I touched my cheek to his soft jowls. He patted my shoulder before collapsing back onto the couch, coughing.

Doug looked concerned. "Can I get you something?"

"He's fine," I said. My dad had COPD. He was always coughing.

I dug my foot into the carpet. It felt spongy. Floral slipcovers had been added to the couch and love seat. My mother had hated flower patterns. This was the work of Mrs. Gibbs? My sister-in-law?

My dad started breathing normally again. He looked up and crinkled his eyebrows at Doug. "What do you do again?"

"He owns a market research firm," I said.

"Ah," he said.

"We help companies get to know their customers," Doug said. "What they like about a product, that kind of thing."

"Can you get a job with them?"

Doug looked between my dad and me, confused. "With who?"

"With the company," said my dad.

"No, Dad, he has his own company. He's very successful."

I showed Doug the house, stopping in my childhood bedroom, now a storage space littered with my mother's old crafting supplies. I stood near a pile of boxes across from the closet.

"My bed was here. I had a canopy." I pointed toward the window, painted shut. "I used to sneak out to the roof at night and look up at the stars."

Doug lifted his head in surprise. "I can't really see you doing that."

"What?"

"Gazing up at the sky, contemplating the universe."

I shrugged. "It was a nice view. I wasn't precious about it."

I heard my brother Wally's voice coming up the path to the front door. I went to greet him and his family. Wally looked different, redistributed somehow and uneven, his bone structure still struggling for dominance, refusing to yield to the doughier parts of his face. My nephews, the eight-year-old twins, Asher and Jayden, were sporting identical buzz cuts. I bent to hug them. They each gave me a quick "Hi, Aunt Emily" and rushed into the kitchen.

My sister-in-law, Jessica, swept in last, all harried and laden with grocery bags. She'd updated her look, though. Her hair was blown out, less frizzy. "I like your eyebrows," I said.

She dropped the bags on the kitchen table and touched her face. "Oh yeah? There's a new salon on Main."

Wally called the boys into the living room. "Come on, kids," he said. "Let's meet Aunt Emily's latest."

"What is that supposed to mean?" I asked.

"Nothing, Em. I'm happy you have a new *lover*." He brought up his fingers for air quotes. Asher and Jayden laughed. Doug did, too, with his head thrown back, hard-dee-harring with a joviality so forced it almost seemed genuine.

"What's everyone drinking?" I asked.

"I'll have a beer," said Wally.

"Beer," said my dad.

"Nothing for me," said Doug.

"Oh, come on," said Wally.

"I have to fly later."

Wally pointed at him appreciatively. "I'm glad you watch it. You wouldn't believe some of the stuff we have to deal with."

"That's right, you're a policeman?" asked Doug.

"Dispatcher."

Doug gave him a solemn nod and held out his hand. "Thank you for your service."

My dad started coughing again, covering his mouth with one hand and clutching the arm of the sofa with the other. Jessica hurried into the living room with a mug of water and bowed in front of him. "Easy,

Chuck," she said. She spoke in loud, deliberate tones. "Remember what the doctor said? Use your stomach muscles. Hold your breath for two seconds . . . get under it . . . now cough."

I went to the kitchen as my dad let loose a series of productive barks and stood between the sink and the stove, the spot my mother had always occupied when she cooked. I hadn't been back since she died. I leaned on the counter. I hadn't known there was a proper way for my dad to cough.

I opened the fridge and took out two bottles of Amstel Light. Jessica swooped in behind me. "I can do that," she said. She took the bottles, delivered them to the men in the living room, and returned to unpack the appetizers with the efficiency of a professional cook. She pointed above the microwave. "Would you get the green bowl down?" I reached to one of the lower cabinets. "Actually, I rearranged some things," Jessica said with a tight smile. "The serving bowls are up there now."

I pressed my molars together and let her delegate. The house was now Jessica's domain. It demanded a nurturer, the sort of woman I wasn't. Sometimes I felt like the only one of my kind: the rare female born without the gene for caretaking. I'd always nursed a grudge against these mothering types, forever noticing, tending to the people around them, forever in everyone's service. They made me look selfish, unfeminine even, by comparison.

———

I opened a bottle of cabernet at the dinner table. Doug poured some for himself. "I love you folks up here," Doug said. "Just living your lives, thinking about dinner." He nudged me. "Kind of makes me wonder if we're doing it wrong."

Jessica and Wally traded looks. They glanced at me the next two times Doug topped off his drink.

"We decided to fly back tomorrow morning," I said.

Doug squinted at me. "We did?"

"Yes," I said with a gritted smile. "Remember? That's why it's okay for you to drink right now."

The table was silent for the next minute until Wally perked up. "Destiny Stimpson's out of jail," he said.

I gasped and threw my brother my meanest look, the one that had scared him when he was ten. My dad began coughing quietly, with his mouth closed, trying not to call attention to himself. Doug turned to me. "Was that the girl you knew?"

Jessica stood and started clearing the dishes. I moved to help her.

"Why was she in jail?" Doug asked.

"Oh, you know," said Wally, with a wave of his hand. "She's troubled."

CHAPTER SEVEN

Doug and I had been together almost a year when the Dr. Maryn Store was ready to go live. My agency cosponsored the launch party. I was chair of the planning committee. We took over the Hollywood Athletic Club, tenting the inside so that the rooms were uniformly white and billowing.

I gave the event a wellness theme and styled it like a Goop conference, with motivational speakers and swag bags full of CBD oil and singing meditation bowls. I was most proud of our aromatherapy motif. I'd had the party planners infuse each room with a different scent: eucalyptus for the reflexology space, cinnamon ginger for the bar, tea tree for the pop-up B12 clinic.

I chose lemongrass for Doug's wearable-EEG demonstration. His project was behind schedule. He'd blown through his first capital investment and was using the event to build buzz, attract more investors. Showing people their brain waves would be a novelty, a highlight of the party. We'd distributed a VIP sign-up sheet online, and it had filled up immediately.

An hour before the doors opened, I stopped to check on him. The atmosphere in the space was festive, with his team of hip, young workaholics clustered around a white pool table, pregaming their big perk of a night out. Doug stood apart from everyone, in a modal black T-shirt and jeans, gripping the back of a club chair.

I started toward him, but he didn't see me. He was focused on Sanjay, his biomedical engineer, as he snapped open a gray Pelican case. I stood close to a pillar and watched them. Sanjay adjusted his Buddy Holly glasses and lifted the new, portable EEG from its foam casing.

"Careful," said Doug. This version was even smaller than the last design, with a circular black headband and just three sensors reaching up toward the center. Sanjay called two brunettes over from the entourage near the pool table. They looked like models, twins almost, with pencil-straight hair and matching tailored lab coats over hot pants. They were both showing cleavage.

I frowned. The models had completely the wrong look. I'd had a hand in every detail of the party but had let Doug do his own planning.

Sanjay stepped forward to the model on the left and lifted the EEG over her head. "It'll feel a little tight at first," he said. The model on the right raised her hand.

Doug straightened. "Mia?"

She ran her fingers through her hair and asked, "Um, what does it do?"

Doug and Sanjay looked at each other before laughing. "I guess I should have gone over that," said Doug. He came around the chair and stood close to her. He pointed at the next Pelican case. "This is an electroencephalogram. Can you say that?"

Now it was the girls' turn to look at each other. They smiled. They were flirting, all four of them. I backed up toward the wall, my mouth filling with the faint taste of metal.

"Did you know your thoughts make electricity?" asked Doug.

Sanjay fired up a giant, old-fashioned desktop computer and connected it to a projector. The model's brain waves appeared in four purple lines on the drop-down screen above them. "The bottom one's the alpha," said Sanjay. "It tells us when the brain is at rest." The model raised her arms to adjust the helmet, exposing a sliver of midriff and making her upper waves turn squiggly.

Doug leaned his forehead toward Mia. "It's called neuromarketing, like reading your mind. We'll be able to tell if people are bored by a product or, you know, turned on."

"Doug!" His name came shrieking out of me. He turned. His expression opened in delight, with zero hesitation. It was too slick a move. Any normal guy would have had a moment of awkwardness after ogling a gorgeous woman in front of his girlfriend. I scowled as he walked toward me.

"Did you hire go-go dancers?" I asked.

Doug looked back at the women. "Those two? They're demonstrating the product."

"They look like strippers." Sanjay and the models glanced over at us.

"They're wearing jackets."

"It's not the Maryn brand." The models were staring at me now, stone faced. I pointed to them. "Girls, what else do you have to wear?"

Mia shrugged. "Leggings."

"Travis?" I yelled for my assistant. "Travis!"

Doug put his hand on my shoulder. "Em, let's think about this."

I looked at the time on my phone. We had forty-five minutes. I went to the hall outside the library and yelled, "Someone find Travis!" I waved the models over. "What size are you?"

"Zero," said Mia. I glanced at her body. She had boobs. The bottom of her waist sloped outward into an unmistakable pair of hips.

"Size two," said the other model.

Travis came rushing up, out of breath and wearing a walkie-talkie earpiece.

"Travis, I told you to shadow me."

"I'm sorry," he said. "Would it be easier if you had a walkie?"

I recoiled. "I'm not wearing a fucking walkie! You think that's my role? For random people to ask me where the bathroom is?"

"I'm sorry," Travis said. His cheeks were red. "I just—" I held up my hand to shush him and looked at Mia, the model, up and down.

"You're not a size zero," I said. Mia flicked her eyes to Doug and back to me, pleading. "The dress has to fit, Mia."

She sighed. "I'm size four."

I pulled my corporate card out of my wristlet and handed it to Travis. "Where's the nearest department store?"

"There's a Ross."

"God dammit!" I looked it up on my phone. It was a half mile away. "Run," I said. "Buy all the little black dresses you can, sizes two and four."

"Got it." Travis pivoted and sprinted to the exit.

"And tasteful!" I screamed after him. I turned around. The models, Sanjay, and the group of hangers-on were staring at me.

Doug put his arm around my shoulder. "Easy," he said. Mia stood, pouting at us a moment before following Sanjay to the other side of the room.

"I'm not apologizing for that," I said.

"It was a little harsh," he said.

"Tonight has to be flawless."

"I get it," said Doug.

I took a breath and shook out my hands. "I have to check on Maryn."

"Wait," he said. "I have something for you." He reached into the inside pocket of his suit jacket. "It's not worth it if you don't take the time to celebrate."

He pulled a long jewelry box out of his inside pocket. Inside was a watch. It was gold and exquisite, just delicate enough to be feminine, just expensive enough to say, *Don't fuck with me.*

"Most guys would have done earrings, right?"

"I love it," I said.

"Look on the crown." A sapphire, my birthstone, was embedded in the knob. I slid my index finger over the tiny stone, pebble smooth and soothing. "I had it customized," he said.

It was perfect. Tonight was perfect. The Dr. Maryn Store was taking off. His EEG would be next.

We were about to start making real money.

I pictured us in a mansion. I could see the house so clearly, in overhead drone footage: a sprawling Tuscan on an ocean bluff with a lap pool and fifteen-foot hedges.

"We are so fortunate," I said. My voice broke. I looked up at the ceiling to stop myself from crying. A bass line started up in the bar, and interior floodlights switched on, illuminating the tenting in pale violet.

"I better get changed," I said.

———

My job, once the party started, was to monitor my most lucrative client. While everyone gave themselves over to the glitter and commotion, I maneuvered through the motley crowd of lifestyle vloggers, TV stars, and insurance CEOs with a single objective: manage Dr. Maryn. She was easy to find, in her shimmery gold pantsuit. She cleared space with her laughter, throwing her whole body into it.

At one point I saw Erik, the tech consultant, weaseling his way toward her with a martini in his hand. His hair was slicked back. Before I could run interference, I heard Dr. Maryn shout out, "Erik!" She summoned him with outstretched arms. "The man who made it all happen!"

Erik tripped and almost fell into her before recovering and planting a kiss on her cheek. I moved closer and turned my back, listening in on their conversation. "Actually, you should thank your girl, Emily," he said. He was slurring his words. "You know, I was skeptical that a

Hollywood agent would be able to head up something so complicated, but she and Doug really got in there."

Dr. Maryn paused. "Doug?" she asked. "Emily's boyfriend? What does he have to do with the store?"

Fucking Erik, getting sloppy, saying whatever popped into his head. I never uttered a word without careful planning, without thinking how I could leverage what I said for greater purpose. And then along came this undisciplined moron, exposing me in the name of making conversation.

I scanned the room. Doug was on the opposite side of the hall, near the bar, with Maryn's husband, Stan, who was wearing a suit with a too-long tie. Doug had his arm around Stan's shoulders and was leading him to a cluster of attractive young women. The whole group then disappeared into his EEG room together. I glanced at Dr. Maryn, hoping she wasn't watching the scene, but she was.

Doug came back out by himself. He smiled at me and winked. I turned to Dr. Maryn. She was staring at me. Her eyes were narrow and assessing.

———

I sighed at grotty palm trees and billboards as Doug and I drove back to his place after the party. La Brea Avenue was lined with litter. The whole of LA seemed ugly. Everything did.

"That was a great night," he said. "We really raised our profile."

"Who?"

"Me. You." He reached for the back of my neck and massaged it. I touched my knuckles to the cool passenger window. I swallowed. I normally had no problem putting people in their place.

"It's funny," I said. "Being an agent is basically a service position."

He took his hand back and put it on the steering wheel. "Everyone's gotta answer to somebody."

"Right, but your clients are companies," I said. "Mine are people."

"I deal with people."

"But you don't have to follow their triathlon times or remember the names of their pets."

"You do that?"

"I represent some pretty big egos." I trailed off. Doug had an ego. "I have to appear devoted. To them. Like my whole point in life is to make them happy."

Doug stopped behind a line of cars waiting to get on the freeway. "Doesn't that feel like you're shortchanging yourself? Like, is your sole purpose to flatter famous people?"

"Doug. You're not hearing me."

He frowned. The cars ahead of him moved forward. He shifted and sped up.

"When you're with me," I said, "for something to do with my work, you're an extension of me."

He blanched. "Are you scolding me?"

"Think about my position."

"I'm supposed to start kowtowing to your clients now?"

"No!" He was making this harder than he needed to.

"Then what?"

"The way you were cozying up to Stan. It was bad, Doug. Maryn was pissed."

"Stan wants to invest."

"You looked like a pimp."

He let out a pained laugh. I didn't care if he was hurt. He'd created a pocket of exclusion at the party, too trendy, with too many models. It was a place for the young, for men. Stan was welcomed there as a tourist, but Doug's room had nothing to offer Dr. Maryn.

"I know the pretty girls are fun to talk to," I said. There was spite in my voice.

"That's what this is about?"

"Dr. Maryn—"

"You're jealous? Seriously? Em, this was my first product demo, and you almost derailed it."

"How?"

"You had a temper tantrum!" He shifted hard as he moved to the left lane. We jerked forward and lagged a second before accelerating. He leaned on the gearshift and clenched his jaw, unable, for a moment, to make his Porsche work in concert with his testosterone. This was the first time I'd seen him angry.

"I yelled at my assistant," I said. "That was nothing."

He threw a few quick glimpses my way. "You know, I almost didn't give you that watch," he said and anchored his eyes on the road, letting his words land, letting them pierce me. They were a threat. Our life together wasn't guaranteed. I hadn't realized until just then how much I was depending on ending up with him. The Tuscan mansion disappeared from my thoughts, and I pictured myself repeating the bleak endings of all my past relationships: packing, crying, moving back into my condo, all lonely and raked and wounded. That was my truth, the square one I kept returning to.

"I'm sorry," I said.

Doug grimaced and shook his head. "You have to think before you explode like that. It wasn't you."

CHAPTER EIGHT

I could tell the house was empty the next morning before I opened my eyes. On Sundays, Doug normally got up first and opened all the windows. I'd wake to the stirrings of my senses, smelling, tasting the salt and sound of the waves. He'd make coffee, and we'd stay in bed for hours, making love, reading the paper on our phones, recovering from our work lives.

But today the air was still. I went downstairs. The coffee maker was cold. I checked my phone. There was nothing from him.

I thought of texting him, but I couldn't. He was punishing me. Contacting him would be giving in. I'd said I was sorry the night before. I winced at the memory of my apology, like it was some shameful fragment of a drunken evening.

I took a shower and stayed under the water long after I'd finished washing my hair and body, thinking, considering his point of view. He'd said he'd been supportive, and he had. He'd spent a tremendous amount of time on the Dr. Maryn Store. Now he must have felt like it was his turn.

But his help also included billable hours.

I clenched my jaw around a slim thread of paranoia. There was, indeed, a transactional element to our relationship. It was measurable, even. All I had to do was look up the invoices he'd sent to my agency, whatever side deal he had going with Erik.

I turned off the water, wrapped myself in a towel, and picked up my phone from the sink. Still nothing from him. There was movement in my periphery, out the bedroom window. I turned and saw dorsal fins. A pod of dolphins was playing in the kelp bed past the wave breaks.

I looked at my phone again. Still no word.

Fuck this, I thought. I put on my bikini, went to the side balcony, and reached through the cascading bougainvillea to the bungee cords holding my kayak. I unhooked it and lowered it to the sand.

This was it. This was the life I wanted. I could have it on my own. I almost ran back upstairs then, to check my phone again. But I didn't. I held the boat steady with both hands and pushed it with a running start into the shallows. I hopped on and paddled hard, straight toward a cresting wave, piercing the top of it. The water was mellow on the back side of the surf. All I could hear was the swirling of my paddle, the clomp of my hollow boat. For the first time that day, I felt a sense of peace.

I looked to the shore. A woman in a bikini was standing on the balcony of the ramshackle clapboard bungalow three doors down from Doug's place. The house had been vacant since I'd met him. It was a teardown, a leftover from the sixties or seventies. The woman crossed her arms. Even from far away, I could tell her hair was overprocessed, the color of urine. It was hard to tell if she was staring at me.

A burst of air and liquid sounded behind me. There was a dolphin surfacing just a few feet away. I whistled and patted the water with my hand. It came closer, lingering a moment, inspecting me as best it could before ducking under the kayak. "Oh," I said. The thing probably weighed four hundred pounds. It popped up along the other side of me. The skin around its eyes was crinkled.

"I know," I said and reached for its rubbery body. "I know you can knock me over." I patted the water again after it disappeared into the deep. It didn't come back.

———

Doug returned while I was kayaking. He took the boat from me after I paddled to shore and began dragging it back to the house. His hair was damp with sweat. I planted my feet on the sand. "Well?"

He put the bow of the boat down and lifted his chin. "Well, what?"

"You're going to make me ask?"

"I'm confused."

"Where were you?"

"I told you," he said. "At the gym." He took off his shirt, balled it up, and tossed it onto the kayak. "I'm gonna take a dip."

"You didn't tell me."

"I sent you an email," he said. "I didn't want to wake you with a text."

He swam out and rode a wave. I sat at the edge of the waterline, making a drip castle with the wet sand. The blonde from three doors down came back out to her deck. She watched Doug.

I went into the house. My phone was on the breakfast bar. I checked my email. There was nothing from him. I checked the spam folder, the promotions tab, nothing. I had a growing sense that I was scrambled, like static between radio stations.

I was dating a liar.

His drinking, his "meetings." There was always some dysfunction lurking, peeking through his personality at odd intervals. But this outright lie, this petty challenge, scared me.

He came into the room and froze. "Is everything okay?" he asked in a voice I'd never heard. It was tiny and pitiful: a caught-in-a-lie, faraway cry from some hidden place I'd never be allowed access.

What do you want? I should have said. *Why are you with me?* But I didn't ask him anything. I was too afraid of the answer—Doug was with me because he knew I wouldn't confront him. Or rather, *as long as*

I didn't confront him. This was a test. If I said nothing, we could keep going on in his beautiful house, with our beautiful lives.

But no, I thought. I stiffened. I raised my chin. I had my dignity. If only the lie had been about something important. I cleared my throat, not knowing where to start, not wanting this conversation.

"A dolphin came right up to me when I was kayaking," I said.

"Oh yeah?" he said. His smile was bright, relieved. I inhaled, flooding with an unexpected mix of giddiness and reassuring clarity. I could see through Doug finally, like I could see through everyone else.

"I want a dog," I said.

He was silent, considering. "Like your mom's dog?" he said. "What was that?"

"Gucci was a Pomeranian," I said. "I want something bigger."

CHAPTER NINE

Bella was my beautiful, my wiry, my watchful Doberman pinscher. I met her when she was five months old, living with her brothers and sisters in a giant chain-link kennel at the edge of a dusty field in Ventura County. The other puppies were frisky. They jumped and pawed the fence with yelps of, *Pick me! Pick me!* But Bella was silent, standing alert in the back corner of the cage. All I could see was her eyes. They were calm and judging.

The Doberman breeder, an overly tan lady with dirty fingernails, suggested one of the livelier dogs. "Shy pups are tricky," she said.

I nodded, keeping my gaze on the animal staring back at me. With most dogs, sustained eye contact would have been taken as a gesture of dominance, a signal to either look away or turn aggressive. But Bella continued observing.

The breeder looked troubled. "See the others?" she asked. "They're playful."

I thought of telling the truth, that I didn't like to play, that I knew this dog understood. "I think she's picked me," I said. The breeder gave a respectful nod and went in with the leash.

Bella came out slowly, shaking. I knelt in the dirt and opened my arms. She folded into me, trembling, not quite comforted. "It's okay," I whispered and smoothed her coat with long strokes.

"You're sure you don't want to see another dog?" asked the woman.

Bella rested her chin on my knee and glowered up at the breeder. "I have to take her," I said. "No one else will want her."

I brought her home that night. Her muscles were tight, on high alert, as I walked her into the house. Doug bounded to the top of the stairs, calling, "How's the dog?" and stopped short at Bella's rumbling growl. I took hold of her collar.

"Easy," I said. "This is your daddy." She went silent and sat up next to me in sentry position. "Here," I said. I tossed Doug the treat bag. "Give her one." He held out a bone-shaped biscuit. She crawled to him low on her haunches, like a stalking cat, and snatched it out of his hand.

"She doesn't act like a puppy," he said.

"She just needs to get used to things," I said.

CHAPTER TEN

It was the beginning of summer, about two months before our wedding, when I heard Bella barking on the balcony. I yanked her collar and looked over the railing. The young blonde woman from a few doors down was on the beach, staring up at us. Her sunglasses were reflective, catching the glare of the sun. I put a hand over my eyes and said, "Hello."

She scowled and turned around, adjusting the side straps of her thong as she walked away. She spent the rest of the summer outside, lying on her balcony, her R&B playlist buzzing low over the beach like a mosquito. I asked her to use headphones once, expecting a scratchy response, a voice hoarse from too much partying, but she said nothing. She just switched it off and went inside.

"I bet she's a kept woman," I said to Doug.

"Do people have kept women anymore?" he said.

"I came home early last Tuesday, and she was out there. Friday morning, she was out there."

"Maybe she's rich."

"No one in Malibu spends that much time on their deck. This is a novelty for her."

———

He visited her late one Saturday when he thought I was asleep. I heard the front door open and shut, letting in a rush of traffic noise. I stepped onto PCH just in time to see him letting himself into her place, and I stayed there, barefoot, at the edge of our tiny driveway. The cars and trucks sped close, but I barely registered their blasts of air as a million understandings exploded inside me. I was outside. I was standing on gravel. The gravel wasn't real. The gravel was real. It hurt my feet. Her house was in front of me. He was with her inside that house.

My jaw locked into place, like it was tightening around an invisible rod of iron.

"Mine," I whispered.

I went back inside and did a search of his drawers as Bella jerked on the doggy bed, the sound of my rustling invading her dreams. I went to his side of our walk-in closet and slid my hands under his folded sweaters.

I ran down the stairs. I threw aside cushions. I flung open kitchen cabinets. I didn't know what I was looking for until I found it: a lease for the ramshackle house. The agreement was in the office filing cabinet under *Real Estate*.

Doug opened the sliding glass door. The tide must have gone down far enough for him to take the beach. I'd always thought his solitary walks were evidence of something soulful.

He paused in the living room, taking in the mess.

"Emily?" he said. He stopped in the office doorway. "What are you doing?"

I held out the document.

"Oh," he said. He froze. His eyes darted, his pupils tracing the shape of a diamond, betraying the fact of some inner logic. *If cheating equals lease in my hand,* I could see him thinking, *does lease in my hand equal cheating?* If B then C and so on.

"You don't have some lie prepared?" I said.

"Is that the bungalow lease?" he asked. "I need to double-check it. It was a studio, but I turned it into a one bedroom."

My head snapped back. I reached for the words. I reached for the facts. He kept talking.

"I was just over there, by the way. She has a job at a nightclub. Not a kept woman."

"Are you sleeping with her?"

"Anna? Jesus, Em, she's our tenant."

I looked back down at the lease. No mention of Anna.

"It's one in the morning," I said.

"Her toilet was backed up."

I had the urge to flee.

"I told you." He hadn't told me. "I stayed in that house before I moved in here. The rent was cheap, so I kept it. We're charging her an extra thousand a month."

All I needed was my car keys. I didn't need my purse. I didn't need my shoes. I just needed to get out of there.

"I know it's shady," he said. "Subletting like that. I couldn't resist."

"I trusted you!" I screamed. "How could you?" It was involuntary, the way I went on, repeating the laments of the jilted throughout time and fiction. My crying did something animalistic to my vowels. He stood there quietly, letting me have my catharsis, confessing nothing.

"You're so fucked up," I said.

He shrugged carefully. I pounded my fist on the wall. Bella woke and came hurtling down the stairs with an explosive series of barks. She lunged at Doug.

"Bella, nein!" I caught her by the collar and gave it a hard yank. "Sitz!" Bella sat.

Doug put his hands up. Any other day, he'd have complained about the dog, about my decision to do Schutzhund training and the fact that he didn't have time to learn German. He'd have said he hated feeling like an enemy in his own house.

"Bleib," I commanded. Bella stayed while I went to the pantry for a doggy treat. Doug followed me. Bella growled.

"Nein!" I said.

He leaned against the counter. His forehead was creased, worried. "What are we going to do?" he asked. As if it were up to me to figure out.

"Are you a sociopath?" I asked.

"I don't think so."

"You don't *think*?"

"I took a quiz."

"She has to go."

He bit his lip and looked down.

"Today," I said.

———

There is a space between the conscious and the unconscious, a space where you can choose things that aren't really choices at all but more like pointing yourself in a certain direction, like how you steer a car without even thinking about it. It's where you tell yourself things like, *There is more than one definition of love,* and you keep on the same way you were before.

I know. I'm making it sound like I was brainwashed. Like I didn't actually *decide* to marry a man who'd cheated on me so flagrantly. Like it didn't take superhuman strength to bring all the bucking, rebelling cells of my body to heel.

I had to choose: upheaval or status quo.

The wedding was three weeks away, a destination wedding in Punta de Mita. Our guests had already bought their plane tickets. Dr. Maryn was giving a speech. I couldn't cancel. It would have been a scandal. Doug was well known enough that it might have made the news. It could have killed my career.

And the truth is I wanted Doug. Our life together, the money we were beginning to make, the compound we would buy, the space, the security. At least 90 percent of the time, Doug was exactly what I wanted. The other ten would simply require managing.

You can handle this, I told myself. It was a short declaration and took only a second to say, with the same number of syllables as *one Mississippi.*

CHAPTER ELEVEN

Doug was in top form at the wedding, playing emcee during the photo shoot on the beach in Punta de Mita, overruling the photographer's suggestions. At one point, he had all his groomsmen lifting me like Madonna in the "Material Girl" video.

Wally objected. "I'm not touching my sister's hips!"

"Then give us some jazz hands!" Doug shouted back.

Everyone posed with their joyfully splayed fingers in the next several pictures, and I pushed away my rising bursts of jealousy as Doug put his arm around Charlene, my sorority sister with the big boobs. A little later, I'd started over to him, to interrupt his side conversation with my anorexically thin friend, Magda, when a dozen or so young children in matching blue polo shirts came running onto the beach.

"Em!" said Doug. "Let's get a picture with them."

"Cute!" yelled someone in our group. "Genius!" shouted someone else. The photographer called the children over, and soon Doug and I were swarmed with adorable kids. I let a little girl of about five or six touch the raw silk fabric on my gown. "Bonita," she said, smiling up at me, angelic. I touched her face and smiled back. The photographer clicked away and called out, "Perfect!"

We heard the yelling before we knew where it was coming from. Some commotion on the edge of our collective vision.

"Señor! Señor!"

A man in a white polo shirt was running across the beach so fast he kept pitching forward, almost losing his balance. He waved his arms in front of him. "No! Señor, no pictures!"

He reached us and didn't even try to catch his breath. "No pictures, señor," he said. "Security!"

"Security?" said Doug. "What happened?" We looked around, matching the man's alarm as four men in dark suits with machine guns flanked our party.

"A government conference, señor, at the hotel. These are the children of the politicians. They are the rich! They are like you!"

Doug got boisterous laughs out of that story for months afterward, across dinner tables, in the backs of golf carts, even speaking from a podium at a charity event. He'd always look to me for a moment of meaningful eye contact after each retelling. I never knew if our locked gaze was just for us or something more performative. Either way, we were our best selves in public.

I turned my focus outward, toward some constantly shifting point on the horizon, accepting every invitation, going out four or five nights a week, sometimes with Doug, sometimes alone. There were dinners and concerts and benefit concert dinners. We showed up at movie premieres even though neither of us worked in film.

We named ourselves Team Markham and ran the LA Marathon for children's literacy. We did the AIDS bike ride from San Francisco to LA. We rode every Saturday morning, pedaling slowly, in unison, to the top of Topanga or Trancas Canyon. I always kept up with him, competing, forcing my burning legs to comply. We didn't stop or even speak until we'd reach the scenic overlooks. Then we'd rest, sitting on the guardrail and watching the tourists in their rental cars and khakis like they were a separate species.

Doug traded in his Porsche for a Tesla. I sold my condo and my Range Rover and bought a hybrid Mercedes. I also took charge of redecorating the house, making weekly trips to the Pacific Design Center. The showpiece was our sofa. I insisted on custom upholstery, a gray linen velvet threaded with real silver that glowed at sunset.

I was determined to live my best life.

Doug and I took Dr. Maryn and Stan out to dinner a few times a month. Those were magical evenings, a blur of blended silk and burrata salads with the outsize personalities of Maryn and my husband joining forces across the table, creating a supernova of frenzied charm. They'd lead the laughter, order one-last-rounds, ask nearby tables if they wanted a taste of the cult wine we'd brought in.

Doug introduced Stan to biking. Stan lost weight and began outfitting himself in spandex and corporate logos. Normally, I would have tried to discourage a friendship like that, with my client's husband. But I trusted Stan. I liked knowing where Doug was when he was with him.

I didn't notice or really think about it when Dr. Maryn began begging off our dinner invitations. She was a busy woman, a star. She still met me for lunch every few weeks.

Most importantly, I had Bella. She let me cry into her fur at night when I was alone and wondering where the hell Doug was. Bella always took my side when he came home late. Or didn't come home. I'd flinch at the sound of the garage door opening, and she'd spring into action.

I started doing it on purpose. If he didn't have a good explanation for why he was late or why he hadn't answered his phone for five hours, all I had to do was tense my shoulders. Doug couldn't see it, but Bella could.

"Pfui!" I'd scold as she barked at him.

———

At work I was promoted to vice president of client ventures, overseeing RFG's expansion into gaming, AI, VR—any industry we could get our people into. Two weeks into my new position, Ron Faulman, one of the managing partners, called me in to meet with him. Ron was in his sixties. He wore a gray beard and dressed like a dandy in immaculate three-piece suits. His father had started the agency, the *F* in *RFG*. His office was a time capsule, lined in dark oak. He asked me to shut the door.

"I want to give you a heads-up," Ron said. He leaned back in his leather chair and interlaced his fingers. "There's going to be a review of vendors, looking for improprieties, nepotism." I moved to the edge of my seat. "It'll be company-wide," he said. "But I imagine we'll take a look at Beyond the Brand."

I didn't react. I couldn't. I'd given a ton of work to Doug's company. He'd been handling all the research for Dr. Maryn. His portable-EEG helmet was almost ready to launch too. He was practically a partner in the Dr. Maryn Store.

"Did someone complain?" I asked.

"Emily, come on. We're living in a new climate."

I raised my eyebrows. It was always a new climate. There was always some crackdown, some whack-a-mole righting of wrongs, happening somewhere in the entertainment industry. I'd successfully dodged most of them. I allowed my underlings to claim their overtime. I made no sexist or racist comments. But RFG had spent a massive amount of money on market research for the Dr. Maryn Store. I knew how it looked. The money went straight to my husband and straight back to me.

"This sounds like score settling," I said, trying to think of who had issues with me, who might be an enemy. "Can you tell me who said something?"

He shrugged. "Don't bother trying to find out. You'll drive yourself crazy. Just assume everyone is gunning for you right now, at least until you're settled in the new position."

I nodded. I couldn't believe I hadn't seen this coming. I rose to leave. "Can I just ask one thing?"

"Shoot," said Ron.

"Is Dr. Maryn aware of this?"

Ron held up his hands. "See? You're making yourself crazy. Fix the problem. Then you won't have a problem. Okay?"

I got home before Doug that night. I waited on a stool at the breakfast bar until I heard his car. I poured him some bourbon as he came downstairs.

"Thanks," he said. He looked at me, curious. "Is it my birthday?"

"No," I said. "I'm trying to soften the blow."

He narrowed his eyes.

"I'm going to be a little less hands on with the store now," I said.

"What does that mean?"

"I won't be in charge of hiring research companies like I used to."

He shrugged. "You're vice president. You can do what you want."

"Someone said something," I said.

He looked up and took a step back from me. "Emily, RFG is one of my biggest clients. From before I even knew you."

"The climate has changed," I said. "It looks like I'm self-dealing."

He grabbed his highball glass from the counter and made like he was going to throw it at the wall. Bella grunted from her spot next to the couch.

"Nein," I shushed her. "I don't know who complained."

Doug dumped the drink in the sink. "You're gonna let some punk bully us?"

"If I fight, I'll be swinging blind. It'll make me look powerless."

"Jesus, Em. Show some loyalty."

I stood. I met his eyes. I'd sacrificed so much for this relationship. "You want to talk about loyalty?"

Bella stood, alert, but I didn't need her tonight. I played the wounded-wife card sparingly. When I did, it was effective.

Bella went missing the next week. I came home on a Tuesday night, expecting to hear claws scampering across the tile-floored entryway.

"Bella?" I called.

I checked to make sure the bathroom doors were open, that she wasn't trapped. I walked down the stairs to the living room.

"Bella?"

The house was empty. I went onto the balcony, an indistinct worry gathering, tightening around me. She wasn't there. The gate to the beach was open. I ran down the stairs to the sand.

"Bella!" I yelled. "Bella!"

I looked under the deck, at the pile of belly-size stones the ocean had dumped against the house foundation. I didn't see her. I looked up the coast, hoping she hadn't found her way to the road. The homes all blocked access to PCH, except for a state-mandated walkway about ten houses north. I ran to it. The gate was locked from the beach side, an illegal padlock placed by some anonymous neighbor. The people who lived here didn't like intruders.

I peered down the coast. I could see for a half mile at least. There was no Bella, but there was no way off the beach. She had to be somewhere. I ran down the shoreline.

"Bella!"

The older couple next door joined me on the sand. They hadn't seen her. They offered to look farther north. I ran south. The tide was coming in. Doug appeared on the beach just as the water started to lip the houses.

"She'll come home," he said. He tried to put his arm around me.

"She'll drown." I rolled up my pants and let the ocean swirl around my calves.

"How did she get loose?" he asked.

"The gate was open."

He ran home. I didn't follow. I checked under more houses, maybe she was hiding, taking shelter beneath a stairway. A tall, solitary wave pelted my thighs. I braced myself against a pylon. I could hear Doug, just barely, shouting over the ocean. I looked back to our house, a quarter mile away. He was at the railing, motioning with his arms for me to come in.

Another wave hit me.

"I need to check the houses!" I screamed even though I knew he couldn't hear.

The ocean knocked into me again. It tugged at my legs, letting me know it had the power to drag me, crush me. I let go of the pylon. I had to check a few more houses, exhaust all options. Another wave came, and then one right after, throwing me onto my hands and knees. I flattened myself on the rocks as the water washed over me, digging my fingers into the space between the stones.

My neighborhood had turned treacherous.

I was able to scramble to the staircase at the next house over, crawling flat and sideways. I climbed to the middle step and imagined Bella trying to do what I'd just done, her paws slipping on the rocks as the water engulfed her. I leaned my head against the railing and looked out to sea for any sign of her, a dark head above water, dog-paddling away from death. She wasn't there. It was getting dark.

Doug was still on the balcony, silhouetted by the sunset. He pointed to the house above me, suggesting I go up, drenched and shivering, and introduce myself to complete strangers. I could hear children's voices and the clinking of plates inside. I swept my fingers under my eyes and looked at them, black with mascara. My knees were bloody. There was no way I'd humiliate myself by knocking on their door.

I stood. I would have to swim home. I took off my wool pants and balled them up. I held on to them as I waded into the ocean but let go after diving under a breaking wave. The water was opaque black on the other side of the waves, and I panicked a moment, kicking at the surface, imagining some unseen creature waiting to drag me under. I turned north, toward the house, and tried the breaststroke, but the current was against me. I might as well have been treading water. I pushed harder. I thrashed my arms in a series of freestyle sprints. I did sidestroke, backstroke, exhausted when I finally neared the house. The water around me had turned thick, like wet cement. I had no idea how to get to shore. There was danger of losing control, of washing up against the house. Doug climbed down to our bottom step. He'd changed into his bathing suit. The ocean crashed against his waist. I rode a wave halfway in and tried to come to a stand, like a landing skydiver, but I stumbled. The water caught me, tossing me like a towel in a washing machine.

"Here!" shouted Doug. He was on top of me. He grabbed me under the arms, in a lifeguard hold. A wave broke over us, bringing the water to our chests, but he held steady.

"I got it," I said.

"No, you don't."

I let him guide me in, hating the fact that I needed help. I leaned on him as I climbed the stairs and then slumped against the rail at the top. He brought me a towel. I didn't have the energy to take it from him. He wrapped it around my sopping shirt and shoulders.

"Let's get you cleaned up," he said after a few minutes. We went to the bedroom. He started the bath. "You want a fizz bomb?" he asked. I shook my head and stood at the door to the bathroom, watching the water run.

"We'll find her," he said.

My mouth filled with sour liquid, pouring from the base of my tongue. I pushed past Doug and fell to my knees in front of the toilet, barely making it before I threw up.

"Jesus," Doug said.

"Get out."

"Did you swallow seawater?"

"Go!"

I hurled again, unable to control the sounds of tortured puking. When I finished, Doug was sitting on the bed. There was something unnatural in his posture, too casual.

"Did you leave the gate open?" I asked.

His face lost all tension, all tone. His voice came out flat. "You were the one on the beach this morning." I covered my mouth. He was right. I'd taken Bella for a run. She loved the sand, always digging, always barking at imaginary threats in the water. But I'd closed the gate. I'd locked it. I always did.

He wasn't done. "I can't believe you'd even think of asking me that!" He didn't need to add that last bit. It was an overreaction, blunt-force defensiveness. I wondered, briefly, if he'd done something to Bella. But I put the thought away.

I'd married a charming, successful, somewhat messed-up guy. I hadn't married a monster.

———

I threw up the next morning after slicing open an avocado. My retching was more violent this time, producing nothing but yellow bile. I flushed and wiped my face with a washcloth. Doug was standing in the doorway, frowning at me.

"Are you pregnant?" he asked.

"No," I said.

"When was your last period?"

I shook my head. It had been a while. I didn't want to look at my calendar in front of him, though. I didn't want to be pregnant.

I called in sick and printed posters, using a portrait I'd had taken of Bella, meant to be ironic, with a Sears-portrait-style mottled background. Doug helped me stuff the flyers in our neighbors' mailboxes and staple them to utility poles. I posted on Facebook and Nextdoor. We never found her.

I felt the loss in my chest, a persistent, hollow ache, and took to making a fist at the top of my sternum, digging in, trying to soothe myself. Doug offered to get me a new dog. But I didn't want a new dog.

I was pregnant.

I'd picked up a home test at a pharmacy on my way to work and done it in a bathroom stall in my office, holding the stick horizontal on my thigh, watching the moisture wick across the window, before throwing up for the third time that day.

I told no one. I kept my life exactly the same, forcing my face into a mask of competence while my insides lurched to the rhythm of early pregnancy. A month went by. I dreamed of insects, of being invaded, playing host to a parasite. I learned to puke silently, sneaking to bathrooms on different floors of my office, away from my colleagues. Another month passed. I started to feel it, a tightening, a tug at the top of my pelvis. I ignored it. I dreamed I left a baby alone on the beach and watched from the balcony as it floated away.

My nausea subsided at three months, replaced with cravings for heavy Italian food. When I was four months pregnant, Doug texted me at work:

Need favor.

No.

Favor was a code word. He'd promised my time to someone.

She's a dancer.

Definite no.

Please?? Last time I swear.

———

There were no immediate, drastic changes to my life after Chloe entered it. That afternoon, after she fumbled her way out of my office, I actually had a moment of pity. Then I more or less forgot about her. It would take months before I learned who she was, how destructive she could be.

PART THREE
CHLOE AND DOUG

CHAPTER TWELVE

CHLOE

Chloe has been waiting, hiding, huddling on a toilet in the Beverly Wilshire bathroom for almost an hour. The air-conditioning is blowing on her shoulders, and her arms are purple. She can't feel her lips. But she doesn't move. It's been fifty-five minutes since she shoved that old lady on the street. If they called the police, there would be squad cars and witness interviews. "There she is!" one of them would scream if she walked outside right now. She can't afford that, not when things are finally going her way.

Two women with Valley girl–sounding voices enter the bathroom, complaining about some coworker. One stands at the mirror. The other goes to the next stall over. Pins and needles prick at Chloe's right foot. She reaches down to massage it. The women fall silent. They can tell, suddenly, they're not alone. They stop gossiping.

Chloe stands and stretches. How does she keep ending up like this—on the verge of getting caught? It was the old lady's fault. She shouldn't have touched Chloe. And Chloe wouldn't have reacted that way. She wouldn't have pushed her if it hadn't been for Doug's wife.

The women in the bathroom trade places. Chloe unzips her bag. Doug's wife's card is on the top of the pile. She runs her finger along the embossed lettering: *Emily Webb*.

Emily Webb is a mean girl, Chloe thinks and pictures what she must have been like in middle school, making fun of other girls' purses. *That poor old lady.* Chloe would never have pushed her if Emily Webb hadn't been so awful.

The women leave. Chloe takes a breath. Surely things have calmed by now. She heads to the lobby and peeks out the main entrance to the hotel. The sidewalk is empty, no lingering commotion. It's like it never happened.

She crosses the street to her old Toyota Celica with its maroon paint mottled white with sun damage. It's like a sauna, the inside of her car. Chloe sits for a minute with the windows closed. She breathes in the burning air and feels safe and solid. She's back in her own surroundings. She rolls down her windows and turns her phone back on. Doug's cell number is saved in her contacts list even though there's no reason for her to have it. Chloe is tempted to text him, give her version of what happened in case he's talked to his wife. She wonders if it would be weird for her to do this. She'd have to start with something breezy like, *Your wife is really sweet!* or *Thanks for setting up the meeting!*

Her phone rings. For a minute, she's elated, thinking it's Doug, that she summoned him simply by thinking about him. But then she sees the name of her Common Parlance castmate, Dylan, on the display. She starts the car. She doesn't have to answer. The group does everything by consensus, so it's not like Dylan is in charge, but he more or less founded Common Parlance, and he's been texting all day.

"How did it go?" Dylan asks.

"Horrible. She insulted my purse."

"Meow!"

"There's no meow. I was nice the whole time."

"I should have come with you," Dylan says. There's a decisiveness in his voice. She doesn't bother reminding him he didn't have the choice. Doug set the meeting up for Chloe alone. "Did you give her a flyer for the Grove?"

"Of course I did," Chloe says. "She won't come. Anyway, LA isn't the place for us. We should move to New York."

"Chloe, forget New York. New York is done. If we go anywhere, it'll be Detroit or Boise, Idaho. Somewhere we can actually do some good."

Dylan assumes this speechifying air at least once per conversation. She pictures him standing on his coffee table, using his free hand to gesticulate to an imaginary group of admirers. She moves into the right lane, following signs for the 10.

"I'm getting on the freeway," Chloe says. "Let me call you when it's less windy."

She merges onto the highway, matching the speed of the fifteen-mile-an-hour traffic. She slows to ten miles an hour, then five. Her hot car is no longer a comfort. She presses the AC button and waves her hand in front of the vent, but her air conditioner hasn't worked in months. The hint of breeze blowing past her window is cruel, a tease.

The traffic stops just as the first trickles of sweat begin their trek down the front of her chest and soak the seam at the lip of her tank top. "Shit," she says. She'll be drenched soon and has nothing to change into. She rips off her top and drives, shirtless, back to her day job.

———

Chloe steps off the elevator into Beyond the Brand's lobby just as the LED panel on the front of her desk morphs from periwinkle to magenta. Jo-Ann, the office manager, is at reception covering for Chloe. Jo-Ann tucks the front wisps of her gray bob behind her ears and smiles.

"How was your audition?" Jo-Ann asks.

"It was more of a meeting than an audition," Chloe says. She glances down the hall to Doug's office. His door is closed. The light is on, though. Chloe can see the glow in the frosted glass above the doorway. Doug is here.

Jo-Ann grabs her cane and limps to the orange-lacquered cabinet behind the desk.

Chloe starts to follow her. "Let me do that."

"No, no," says Jo-Ann. "I need the exercise." Jo-Ann yanks open the cabinet and leans to her right, shifting her weight onto her good leg. She reaches for a clean headset with her left hand.

Chloe sits. She counts the colors in the lobby: the slate couch and violet pillows, the splashes of orange leading to a large, open warehouse of an office with communal tables and rounded corners everywhere. It was part of a reality show, the redesign of the office. Doug didn't have to pay for it. His wife set it up.

"Do you know Doug's wife?" Chloe asks.

"Emily?" Jo-Ann hands Chloe a headset. "Of course."

Chloe wrinkles her nose. "I'm not sure I like all these colors together."

Jo-Ann takes a salted caramel out of the bowl above Chloe's desk. "Did you change the booking for the Warner preview?"

"Yep," says Chloe. "And I fixed the questionnaire."

Jo-Ann tosses the caramel to Chloe. "You get a prize."

"Thanks!" Chloe says. She unwraps the candy and pops it in her mouth, settling back into the normal rhythm of her day. Beyond the Brand is a cheerful place. Most of the employees are upbeat and interesting, just like Doug.

Chloe hears his voice. It's muffled, on the other side of his door. He's with at least two other people. The meeting spills out into the hall with exclamations of "Great!" and "We'll get you more titles tomorrow."

Chloe runs her fingers through her hair. Maurice, the innovation strategist with the shaved head, appears from around the corner. He stops. "Hey, you," says Maurice. "How'd your meeting go?"

"How did you know about my meeting?" Chloe asks.

"People talk," he says.

Who talks? Is Doug talking about her? "People talk way too much around here," Chloe says. Jo-Ann and Maurice let out deep laughs.

Their chatter draws more guys out to reception; Jeremiah, the IT manager with the crazy full beard; Roderick, the statistical-modeling fellow in ironic pinstripes; Tom, the recruiter with the fleshy fingers; even Teddy, the mail room guy with the hair growing out of his ears.

Chloe is back in friendly territory now. She's surrounded by men. Men buoy her. They anchor her. It's like a promise, their attention, that she's special or meant for something special, and she floats inside their gaze, riding the currents of the way they look at her, lapping up their compliments and small favors.

The same scene plays out multiple times over the course of each workday with a revolving cast of male coworkers and sometimes Jo-Ann. The conversations are light and usually centered on the salacious side of current events. Sometimes they ask her what Fefu Fornes, the pop star, was like. "So sweet," Chloe usually says before changing the subject to the "real art" she's now doing. They love to tease her about her performances. "So what, you're a mime?" is a running joke. "I'm not a mime," Chloe always whines and aims a rubber band at whoever says it.

Today, the talk has turned to yet another *LA Times* article about millennials.

"What's with the participation trophies?" says Tom, the recruiter. He has a wreath of silver hair above his ears, the only man in the office who's let himself go naturally bald. "Chloe, did you get a prize just for showing up to soccer practice?"

Chloe blinks back a quick firecrack of anger. Questions are snares. "I think I'm technically Gen Z," she says. Tom peers down at her with a thin-lipped smile, like he's registering some silent advantage. She shrinks. "I mean, I moved around a lot."

It's like a magic trick then, the way Doug suddenly appears at Tom's side, rescuing her. He always does that, shows up in the middle of things and catches everyone off guard. "Am I interrupting anything?" Doug asks and leans back on his heels in an expansive gesture. Whenever he talks, it's with a twinkle and nudge of good-natured condescension.

Chloe's eyes go to his arms. They're muscular and tan, and he's wearing an army-green T-shirt she's never seen before. His hair is messier than usual. She tries picturing what he's like at three in the morning, exhausted or wasted, dropping all professional pretense. Tom clears his throat and shuffles aside.

Doug points to Chloe. "How was the meeting?"

She searches his face for hidden malice, any sign his wife told him about her freak-out looking for the flyer. His expression is open and sincere. "It went great," Chloe says. "Your wife is so sweet."

"Your wife?" Jo-Ann purses her lips and looks from Doug to Chloe. She excuses herself from the conversation.

Doug leans over the counter. He lowers his voice. "How did it really go? You can tell me."

Chloe and Doug share a smirk, a flash of understanding that of course it didn't go well. It never goes well with wives, because wives are shrews who hate younger women and nag their husbands and never want anyone to have any fun. The rest of the crowd drifts away.

"Seriously! She's putting me in touch with her commercial department."

He nods. His voice and face are gentle. "You made it out unscathed, then? I'm impressed." She's never heard him speak so softly, so without his layers of glib and swagger. Is this what he's like in his personal life? Does his wife have access to this?

"*I'm* impressed," says Chloe. "You're in a power couple."

She leans onto her elbows. He glances down her shirt. Married men have always been off limits, but Chloe can't remember why anymore. Nobody here cares. FOD, they call the staff members he has affairs with. Friends of Doug. Things like right and wrong, they lose their meaning the longer Chloe stays in LA.

Take Doug's wife. All Chloe did was ask her a simple question about the Calder in the lobby, and she had to be so snotty. *What do you think?* That's what Emily said. It's like the woman doesn't care if she hurts people's feelings.

Chloe stares up at Doug. He seems amused, almost giddy. She can still back down, flub another moment, and embarrass herself for the umpteenth time today. Or she can decide. She can focus the tangled buzz of seduction hovering hot over her skin. That's what Emily would do. Everyone else, they take. It's time for Chloe to do the same.

"To be honest," she says, "I felt a little guilty going to the meeting."

Doug draws his head back and studies her. *Crap.* She's flirting too hard. But wasn't he just hitting on her? Isn't he always hitting on her? He looks down each empty hallway before fixing his eyes on her like he's watching her but also letting her in on a secret. She loves it when he looks at her like that, like he sees something in her.

"Now, what on earth would make you feel guilty?" he asks.

Chloe lets her lips work their way into a tiny smile.

"What do *you* think?" she says.

CHAPTER THIRTEEN

DOUG

Doug raises his eyebrows at Chloe, hesitating, letting the uncertainty build. She lowers her face and blinks at him like a cartoon doe. He wasn't actually planning to sleep with this girl. For Christ's sake, he just introduced her to his wife. He's not a complete asshole.

"What do I think?" he asks, not quite making fun of her. "I think you found some confidence this morning." She sits back in her chair, deflating, just a bit.

"Doug!" His assistant, Harper, bounds down the hall to reception, her mass of auburn curls a lesson in controlled drama. "Emily is on line one," Harper says. Chloe glances up at her with a skittish smile. A play for acknowledgment. Harper ignores her and waits for Doug to follow.

He drums on the counter above Chloe's desk and adopts a stern tone. "We'll continue this later, young lady."

"Bye," she says in a squeak.

This girl. She shifts so quickly from statuesque to flustered. It's exquisite, actually. Her flashes of panic when he pretends she's in trouble for breaking the printer or parking in the wrong space. And her relief when he tells her not to worry about whatever transgression he's just made up. She locks eyes with him and grins like she's in on the joke. Like she's just as far beyond the reach of the silly rules as he is.

Doug shuts his office door and stares at the blinking red light on his desk phone. He blows a faint whistle and presses the speaker button.

"Why aren't you answering your cell?" Emily asks.

"Well, hello to you too."

"Can you keep your ringer on? For me?"

He pulls his iPhone from his pocket. Two missed calls and a text.

"Doug, you have to stop sending me these people. They're depressing."

"What did you say to her?" he asks.

"Nothing! The girl's a wannabe. She almost started crying."

Doug fights the urge to click into his wife's snideness. Her dismissal of everyone who isn't as shellacked as she is.

Chloe isn't like Emily. She's unspoiled. Normally, a beautiful woman like her would be impossible to flatter. You try. You toss a compliment her way and watch as nothing happens. Just a flicker of hard acknowledgment. Maybe a laugh if she needs something from you. But once, when he told Chloe, "You don't act like it, but you must know you're gorgeous," she swelled and beamed like the accounting gals do when he admires their printed blouses.

He pulls up Chloe's Instagram. There are new pics of her and some arty-looking twentysomethings in the desert, staring into the lens with album-cover impassiveness. He wonders if he should pay her more. Jo-Ann lowballed her when she hired her. They laughed about it at the time, how little Chloe was willing to accept.

"Doug, are you listening to me?" He takes his wife off speaker.

"I'm listening!" he says.

"My job is just as important as yours."

He switches to Harper's Facebook. His assistant just put up a new profile picture. She's biting her lower lip.

Oh Jesus, Doug loves women. He loves them. The hush of their skin, the rise of their hips. The broadcasting, broadcasting, always broadcasting. Bra straps, bellies, and vanity, and lace. There's a woman out there for every kind of sex. Pillowy ones you can sink yourself into and sophisticates you think you'll be able to screw head-on, but they turn on you last minute with all their demands. He likes the uncomplicated ones the best. The fun ones.

Doug lowers his voice into the receiver. "You know what I'm thinking about?"

"How would you like it if I asked you to hire someone who knows nothing about marketing?"

"Market research," he says.

"Same thing."

"Now you're just trying to piss me off. Seriously, do you remember that first night together? We were at the valet, and you went off to take a call."

She sighs. He pauses. He waits for the silence to turn visceral.

"I was eavesdropping on you," he starts. "I could tell from your tone it was a business call. An unfriendly one. I heard you say, 'What is that supposed to mean?' like a shot across the bow. I thought, *This woman is going to eat me alive.*"

She was a pit bull. He needed someone like her. The women before were too defenseless. Too hurt by his misbehavior.

"What time are you coming home?" she asks. An unusual question. They've taken to socializing separately during the week.

"Why?"

"Let's have dinner."

"Are you pregnant?"

"I'll pick up Italian."

"Are you pregnant?"

"Love you."

Emily hangs up. He spins his chair and looks out his window onto Rose Avenue. A barefoot, shirtless homeless man is dancing in front of a store window. Doug opens the camera app on his cell and videos the guy. He texts it to Emily:

I see potential—can u meet with him?

Fuck off

He laughs and wonders if having a baby will soften his wife. She's been hiding her pregnancy from him. For most couples, this would be a sign of something terribly wrong. But he and Emily are a match.

Doug strides to his whiteboard and uncaps a marker. *Brain Trainer* and *Connected Thought* and other terrible names for his portable-EEG project are scribbled in Maurice's handwriting. He clenches his jaw. The project is so far behind schedule he's going to have to drum up more money. But he doesn't want to think about it right now. He erases the board and writes *TIME!!!* at the top.

He's been kicking around a theory for a while now. Vertical Tasking. Which is just like multitasking, except you're doing only one thing at a time. How many ways can you exploit a moment? Altruistically, monetarily, sexually. How can you leverage time?

The idea overtook him in college one morning as he surfed Mission Beach near his parents' house. He'd just duck dived under a wave when the ocean calmed suddenly, sizzling into stillness like a hot tub with its jets turned off. The marine layer started coming in fast above him. Doug watched the fog surround him and meld with the sea, until he couldn't tell where the mist ended and the water began. It felt like he was floating on something vaporous and sweet.

The strangest notion filled him then—this idea that time was a three-dimensional object. He had only to dig into the moment, into time itself, and for a split second, he'd experience everything that split second contained.

He paddled hard to shore, ditched his board on the sand, and ran to his car. He scrambled through his glove box for a pen. He wrote on the back of his insurance card, *Live in the NOW* and *Be present.*

No. He closed his eyes and concentrated on what he'd felt only a few minutes before. If this was going to be anything, it had to be something original. Something he could sell. *Infinity inside the finite,* he wrote.

Total garbage. He brought his forehead to the steering wheel and cried. It was a full-belly cry, overloaded with mucus and tears. He was supposed to be in class that morning. He was on academic probation. They were going to expel him for sure this time.

He wiped his nose and looked to the water. The whitecaps were back, stretching all the way to the horizon.

And that was when he heard it. His own voice, still and small, in a barely audible chant of the words that saved his life. "I will stop smoking pot," he said to himself. "I will stop taking acid."

It's a great story. It's his origin story. He gave up drugs after failing to describe a transcendental experience and went on to build a company that turned the mystical, the raw data of human behavior, into actionable information. It's how he opened his TED Talk on holistic entrepreneurship.

The story wasn't true, of course, not totally. But it made for a good TED Talk.

He did give up drugs for the first time when he was twenty. But that was because he crashed his dad's BMW into a utility pole. The first thing he did after stumbling out of the car, bleeding from his forehead, was dig his key in a little baggie of coke. There was a homeless man across the street, staring, shaking his head at the sight of him.

Harper knocks on his door. She pokes her head in. "Do you want to talk to the phone-bank kids?"

He looks at his watch. Almost dinnertime on the East Coast.

"Harper, you need to get me earlier for these."

"You told me not to get you before quarter of."

She glances behind him, to the back window, where his computer screen is reflected. Harper's profile picture is still up. He walks to his desk and shuts his laptop. "Did you set up a whiteboard in the conference room?"

Harper nods. He selects a dry-erase marker from his board, orange, the color of inspiration, and follows Harper down the hallway. Chloe straightens at her desk as they pass. He winks at her and crosses to the oversize conference room.

The phone bankers are already wearing their headsets, ready for the coming blitz of robodials. Doug centers himself in front of them. He doesn't need to be here. Anywhere else, the project manager or an outsourcing firm would brief the employees with a PowerPoint and wish them luck. But accessibility is Doug's hallmark. Let people see you. Let them think your position is within their grasp.

He writes on the whiteboard, *Market Research*.

"What does this mean to you all?" he asks. The operators' faces stay blank.

"Everyone, take your headsets off," Doug says. "This is real talk right now. I want to know something. Why do you think you're here?" The pause lasts long enough to feel uncomfortable. Doug shrugs. "Why are we interrupting families at dinner?"

A kid in the front, early twenties, with spotty facial hair, raises his hand.

"You," says Doug. "What's your name?"

"Xavier, sir."

"All right, Xavier Sir, what are we doing?"

"We want to get people's opinions on the new stadium?"

"And why do we need that?"

Xavier thinks. He draws out his words. "Because we want to figure out the best way to sell it to the public?"

"Very good!"

Doug writes *DATA* in large letters and turns back to the kids with an exaggerated slump, like he's accepting defeat. "I gotta be honest with you. These types of surveys are on their way out. Everyone's familiar with tracking cookies, right? A long time ago, I turned Beyond the Brand into a tech company, a big data broker, to survive. So why on earth, why now, would I have you contacting people by telephone?" Doug mimes dialing an old rotary phone. The kids laugh.

The door at the rear of the conference room opens. It's Chloe. She slinks into the back row, all supple and seductive. He raises his chin, giving her half a nod. Harper, in the front, glances back at Chloe and shoots Doug a worried look.

Xavier raises his hand again. Doug spins back to the whiteboard. He writes *High Touch* and caps the dry-erase marker with a flourish. He turns to his audience. He looks directly at Chloe.

"When you're dealing with something controversial, there's no replacement for the personal touch." He points at Chloe with his marker. "That's where you come in."

Chloe covers her mouth. Doug raises his arms like he's about to burst into song. He addresses the crowd at large. "Think of yourselves not as data collectors but as ambassadors for the stadium."

The phone bankers are attentive, rapt. It's incredible, energizing a whole room like this. It makes Doug wonder sometimes if his personality is too big for ordinary life, if there's too damned much of him to go around.

He glances up at Chloe again. She touches her neck. He should tell the crowd about his EEG. Even though it's not ready yet. They finally got the prototype to work, but it's not syncing with the app. But these kids should know that they're at the start of something revolutionary.

That they're listening to the man who will usher in a new age in market research, gathering data directly from people's brains.

"How many of you know about the brain—"

His phone vibrates against his leg. He clutches his pocket. The first notes of "The Imperial March" from *Star Wars* ring out.

Jesus! This is why he never has his ringer on! Does she really expect him to be at her beck and call like this? Doug looks up to the last row. Chloe—sweet, pliant Chloe—runs a finger over her lips.

He takes his phone from his pocket and waves it above his head. He shouts like an old-time stand-up comedian: "Sorry, folks! It's my wife!"

CHAPTER FOURTEEN

CHLOE

Chloe stands on the balcony of Morel's Steakhouse, overlooking the Grove Mall. Her castmates from Common Parlance are with her: Dylan, Sheralyn, and Howie. Their performance is scheduled to start in fifteen minutes. Chloe leans over the railing and peers down at the nearly empty cobblestone paths.

"Careful," says Dylan. He's shorter than Chloe, with a closely shorn beard that tempers his vaguely elfin features. He touches her arm. She lets him guide her a step back from the railing.

"Slow shopping day," says Chloe.

The fountain in the center sputters to life, and a dozen water spouts arch and sway to the tinny strains of a Frank Sinatra classic. A few patrons stop to watch. Chloe places her hands on the railing and swings her hips. "It's not affecting anyone," she says.

"Sure it is," says Howie. He's the actor in the group. Everything about him is crisp and camera ready, from his square jaw to the clean-lined edges of his buzzed Afro. He gestures toward a family of four standing at the edge of the fountain. "See how they stopped to watch?"

Sheralyn is on the other side of Howie, thick armed and tattooed, with an asymmetrical black bob. She leans in front of him and catches Chloe's eye. Howie had a callback this week for an NBC pilot. Whenever he gets close to leaving them all behind, he contradicts everything they say.

"Yes, but you'd think the fountain would make it more festive," Sheralyn says. "The folks down there look passive."

Chloe is hit with resentment. What Sheralyn just said—that was the point Chloe was trying to make. People always do that to her, say what she wants to say more clearly.

"There's no sense of the public square in LA," says Dylan. He checks his phone. Chloe peeks over his shoulder. No one has texted him. He looks up from his screen at her. She grants him a moment of sustained eye contact, a second of encouragement, before looking away. He has a crush on her. "We've got ten minutes," he says.

Chloe squints at the scattered shoppers, hoping for some patterns or murmurations to emerge. There's enchantment in the way a mass of people moves. It's outside words, almost outside consciousness. At the last Venice Beach performance, she improvised morphing into a skateboard and its rider all at once, gliding through the throngs of tourists and eccentrics, clearing a path with pure impulse.

Chloe spies a couple in complementing plaid shorts across the walkway. They ponder a restaurant menu. The wife pivots to the mall at large, inspecting the movie theater's art deco facade. She raises a hand and pauses before committing to a recognizable gesture. Chloe rolls her shoulders forward and imitates the woman's airless indecision.

She looks farther up the cobblestone and starts at a tiny patch of bald on an otherwise full head of hair. Doug! No, it's not him. Doug is slimmer. He'd never wear a denim shirt.

"I'll stop by," he said.

Or maybe it was, "I'll *try* to stop by."

She can remember him saying both as he hopped on the elevator with a private wave in her direction. Chloe sighs. It's every time now. Every time he passes her desk, there's some secret, charged exchange.

Starting an affair is complicated, though. There are plans to be made, and she has to be alone with him to make them. Sometimes she worries she's been imagining it all. That maybe the bell-peal sounds of his voice down the hallway, on the phone, teasing, talking business, aren't a telegraphing of desire for her but an overflow of charisma.

If they could be by themselves for a minute! *This is so tawdry,* she'll say when they're finally together. Then he'll kiss her and pay the bar tab. He'll whisk her to a hotel room.

Seduced. Chloe runs two fingers along her bottom lip. *I'm being seduced.*

"What on earth are you thinking about?" asks Howie. He's staring at her.

Chloe smirks, savoring her tiny victory. Howie never shows interest in her. He's too much of a careerist. She tilts her head in his direction and whispers, "Sex."

"I can tell."

Dylan claps his hands together. "Okay, five minutes, guys. Let's spread out, cover the whole mall. And we're agreed we're not going to start acting like zombie-shopper people?"

"But they're all shopping!" Sheralyn bursts out. "And they're all zombie-shopper people."

"It's trite. They covered that in *Dawn of the Dead.* We're not a bunch of communists."

"I'm a communist," says Sheralyn.

"Let's not get hysterical," says Howie.

"But everyone looks unhappy," says Chloe.

"Y'all think consumerism is this country's biggest problem, don't you?" Howie waves an imaginary wand over their heads and speaks in a spell-casting monotone. "Look past the suburbs from whence you came. There is more to life than hating your parents."

"Screw off," says Sheralyn.

"Let's move," says Dylan. "Chloe, why don't you head to the Gap?"

Chloe starts off and sees Doug, finally, coming out of Nordstrom with a shopping bag. Of course he's here. It's not so much relief she feels but confirmation.

She puts on her mask. It's expressionless white neoprene and covers the top half of her face. Her body switches on as soon as it touches her skin. It gives her power, the mask. She's a blank, with no history. No thoughts. She is only instinct.

Doug jogs over. "Hey! I like it," he says. "Very mysterious."

She says nothing. She remains still and fills with intention. Dance, it's not all about movement. She lets her casual stance transform into a pantomime of informality. The outline of her arm cuts a form in the air. She takes the shopping bag from his hand and slides it to her elbow in slow motion. She lets her other hand rest an inch off her hip, just like the mannequin in the Athleta window.

"Oh, right," Doug says. "You're performing. Carry on." He backs up. She opens the shopping bag. It's a disappointment, the cold-brew coffee machine inside it. Doug is supposed to be here for her alone. No multitasking.

She raises an index finger and improvises an aimless turn away from Doug. He's still looking. She can feel his eyes on her back. She reaches for the strap on her tank top and flicks it off her shoulder.

There's laughter near the entrance to the movie theater. Shoppers are gathering. Probably around Howie. He's a crowd-pleaser no matter how many times they tell him to lower his profile. The people near Chloe drift toward the commotion. Doug wanders with them.

Stay, she wants to call out. *Watch me.*

Whatever hammy thing Howie is doing is getting applause. She walks over and sees him in the fountain, trying on clothes. He puts an oxford shirt on backward. People laugh. They'll laugh at anything.

"Oh my God, what is he doing?" says a girl. She's the same age as Chloe, with flat-ironed hair and a pastel cardigan. Her boyfriend is holding a Victoria's Secret bag.

"Dude!" says the boyfriend.

"Dude!" shouts Chloe. She feels the boyfriend notice her, a quick glance at first and then a longer one.

Howie lets an extra-large pair of pants fall around his ankles like some clown from a hundred years ago. The crowd keeps laughing, and Chloe joins in, reflecting back the cadence of the surrounding voices. She lets her laugh morph into a mechanical bark.

"Guffaw!" she crows. "Caw!" She slaps her knee and doubles over.

The girl starts looking at her. "What is this?"

"What is this!" Chloe imitates in a high-pitched whine.

The girl looks up at her boyfriend. "Is she serious?"

Doug's face appears over the boyfriend's shoulder. She locks eyes with him as she nestles close to the guy. "This is so tawdry," she whispers and lifts her mouth to the boyfriend's. She feels the guy react, respond, for just a second.

"What the hell?" says the girlfriend. The guy steps back from Chloe and raises his hands like he's under arrest. The girl yells, "Did she just kiss you?"

It's obscene then, the glee. It starts out like a private joke between Chloe and herself until it bubbles and pops and forces her face into the wickedest smile. The girlfriend yanks her boyfriend toward her. Doug is still watching. Chloe covers her bare teeth with her hand as the boyfriend says, "This is fucked up," and leads his girl away.

CHAPTER FIFTEEN

DOUG

The bar is dark and smells like beer and fresh-cut citrus. All the stools are occupied by the scruffy and postcollegiate. Doug hands out gin and tonics to Chloe and her castmates, Sheralyn and Dylan, standing near the service area.

"You guys were great," Doug says. He hands Dylan a glass. "I thought I was going to see a bunch of mimes."

A stool opens up next to where they're standing. Doug motions for Chloe to sit.

"I'm okay," she says.

"Chloe, sit," says Dylan. He maneuvers to the other side of her as Chloe sits and swells between the two men. She leans back against the bar. Doug runs his eyes down the length of her arched torso, sheathed in scratchy-looking spandex. She needs new clothes. He hasn't decided yet if he's going to sleep with her. If he does, he'll take her shopping.

He notices Sheralyn next to him, breathing in sharp, like she's taking a sip of air. She has that short-banged, alternative look that comes back in style every few years. Her arms are tattooed in various permutations of red hearts and Rosie the Riveter. *Probably into kink,* he thinks.

He leans over to her. "I'll save you the next one." Sheralyn flashes him an edgy pout.

Chloe props an elbow on the bar. "My favorite thing we did—do you remember this, Dylan? We formed a line in front of a store to see if we could get anyone to stand with us. We couldn't make it too straight, or else they'd walk right by. Did you know when people line up, they naturally stagger?" She lets her face fall into something beatific. "It's amazing, the way people arrange themselves."

Doug puts a hand on the bar behind her and lowers his voice. "I wasn't expecting you to be this deep."

"I know," says Chloe. "It's like a parlor trick. I say something halfway interesting, and people are like, *It thinks!*"

Two girls with facial piercings move in from the periphery. One of them whispers in Sheralyn's ear.

"But what you were saying before," Dylan says. "About mimes. Mimes are an idiom. You already know what to expect. We start with a blank slate each time. We don't force anything."

"Except for Howie," says Sheralyn.

"Was that the guy in the fountain?" says Doug. "He was funny."

Dylan and Chloe trade a glance in the silent language of the young and judgmental. No one speaks for a moment.

"Doug's my boss," Chloe says. Doug becomes aware of a sensation, as unfamiliar to him as it is unpleasant. He feels uncool.

"Love it," says Dylan.

Little prick. Doug stands straighter and scrolls through a mental set list of jostling, dominating questions. *How much do you make? What kind of car do you drive? Are you fucking Chloe? Because if you are, you're going to stop.*

"You know anything about market research?" Doug finally asks.

"Me?" asks Dylan.

"Beyond the Brand, that's my company," says Doug. "We were voted one of the top ten innovative firms by *Adweek*."

Dylan lowers his head and wriggles his bottom lip. He looks like he has a wad of chewing tobacco in there. Doug opens his phone and finds the picture of his latest EEG prototype, a thin black band with just two wire sensors.

"I'm bringing a new wearable to the market, a portable EEG."

Dylan takes his phone and raises his eyebrows. "This goes on your head?"

Doug continues, talking up his project like he always does, projecting confidence that it will actually turn into something. "People are going to be able to measure their brain waves, monitor their stress levels as they go about their day, as they shop. And that's going to give me a whole hell of a lot of data."

Dylan swishes his lips. He's definitely chewing something. Nicotine gum, maybe. He parks it on the upper right side of his mouth. "Do you know how the tech works?" he asks.

Doug chuckles. "You mean the zeros-and-ones part? No. You don't have to be a geek anymore to work in this stuff."

"Hey!" shouts Chloe. She waves Howie over from the entrance. He squeezes a path to them. "Where were you?"

"His agent was here," says Sheralyn.

"You're not going to introduce us?" asks Dylan.

"She couldn't stay," says Howie. Dylan watches the entrance for a few seconds.

"Doug's wife is an agent," says Chloe.

"We know," says Sheralyn. "Doug, you're famous around here."

"Famous? What have you been saying about me, Chloe?"

"You're all she talks about," says Sheralyn. The pierced girls trade nasty smirks.

Chloe smiles up at him. She seems unaware she's in the presence of people who hate her. These kids' lives are so populated. He's almost forgotten the crisscrossing social circles of his twenties. All the time spent with people he couldn't stand. He checks his watch. He'll stay for another ten minutes.

"I don't talk about you that much," Chloe says.

"Doug has a plan to monitor our brains," Dylan says to Howie.

"Not you individually," says Chloe. She sits up. "It's like data on everyone, all together. It's really cool. Like, when people are at a store, their Bluetooth and GPS will let the app know if they're in front of the milk or orange juice or whatever. And the EEG will be measuring their brain waves at the same time. And when you put all that information together, Doug will be able to tell if people *like* a particular brand of orange juice or if they're just so-so about it."

Doug beams at her. This is just her day job. She doesn't have to care about what he does. He touches the small of her back.

"It's a little more complicated than that," he says. Chloe blinks and looks down.

"Can I opt out?" asks Sheralyn. Her voice is husky and confrontational. She lifts her chin in a gesture of defiance.

"Why would you want to?" He matches Sheralyn's hard stare, generating a crackle of heat. Sex is *everywhere*.

Chloe slips her fingers over his hand on her back. He returns his attention to her. "Let's get out of here," she whispers.

———

Chloe's car is junky and dirty. Her face in the driver's side window is a lesson in juxtaposition: fresh and beautiful versus apparent inability to qualify for an auto loan.

He drives behind her, following her up through the winding eucalyptus groves and cliffside homes of Laurel Canyon and down the other side of the mountain. The boulevard widens as they reach the Valley, as if to accommodate the flat sun glare and pale stucco apartment blocks. Chloe speeds through a yellow light. She pulls over to wait for him across the intersection. She does it again a few blocks later. Doug taps his fingers on the steering wheel at each red light, wishing he knew Chloe better so he could call her and tell her to start using her brains.

He calls his wife instead. She doesn't answer. He leaves a voice mail, reminding her he has a client dinner tonight. But his voice is too smooth and natural. He only speaks like that when he has something to hide. Emily always knows. She has a tell. A tiny expiration of breath. A flicker of a pause before she changes the subject. Doug sees signs for the 101 and thinks of taking it home to her.

Emily had her first OB appointment that morning. She didn't know they'd be doing an ultrasound. She FaceTimed him and held the phone up to the screen so he could see the squirming black-and-white outline of their baby.

"Wow. Wow," was all he could say as he sat at his desk. He put his hand on his screen and held it there, pretending he was touching his wife's belly. "Turn the camera so I can see your face."

"No," she said. He could tell she was tearing up. "I need to figure out how to process this."

"Ah yes, my lovely and emotionally stunted wife."

Her laugh was throaty. *Emily,* Doug thinks. He has an urge to call her again. Maybe she'll pick up.

Chloe stops at the next red light and sticks her head out the window with a cheery thumbs-up. He flicks his finger against his forehead in salute. He should go home. He rests his hand on the blinker, almost signaling left, the direction of the freeway. He'll pick up a bottle of champagne on the way.

But then he remembers that Emily won't be able to help him drink it. She might not even be up for sex after such a big day. The light turns green, and his car edges forward, straight, like a horse on a well-worn trail ride following the beast in front. A block later, Doug isn't thinking about Emily at all.

———

Chloe scoots ahead of him into her apartment. She picks up throw pillows and sweeps something terry cloth underneath a blue futon. Everything else in the apartment—the carpet, the walls, the vertical blinds—is uniformly off-white.

She disappears into the galley kitchen. "Do you want something to drink?" she calls.

"No," Doug says. He follows her.

"No?" She turns to him.

He keeps walking. "No, I don't want anything to drink." He smashes his body into hers, pushing her up against the counter. She lets out a cry of surprise and moves a resistant hand to his chest. He pulls his head back. "Are we doing this?" he asks. He wonders if Chloe is planning to waste his time.

"Yeah," she says. "I just—you move kind of fast."

Doug stifles an eye roll. He could be home with his wife right now. But he has to suppress his impatience. These girls are so easily offended.

"Sorry. You just drive me crazy, seeing you every day," he says. He lowers his face to her shoulder and slowly moves his lips to her ear. He feels her start to melt, just a little. "Sometimes, you're all I think about." He exhales onto her neck. "You're so fucking beautiful." She tilts her head back and gives a soft, appreciative moan.

The front door opens. Doug lifts his head and looks at Chloe. He hears the sound of someone padding along the carpet to the edge of the kitchen.

"Oh my God," says a familiar raspy voice.

"Who is that?" he whispers.

"Sheralyn," she mouths, never taking her eyes off him. "She's my roommate."

Doug coughs but doesn't turn around. "Hi, Sheralyn," he says.

"Hey."

Sheralyn shuts herself up in a room off the small hallway, which is a shame. He'd love an audience for this. Chloe is one of the prettiest girls he's been with. The urge to show her off intermingles with his desire for sex. He undoes the drawstring on Chloe's pants, angling his movements out to some invisible witness like they're a couple of porn stars in a montage of skin and curves and burning points of contact.

"Jesus, you're fucking hot."

"Shhh," Chloe whispers. "She'll hear you."

"So?"

They smirk and bring their faces to each other. Two rascals making mischief. It's what she wants. She's a total exhibitionist. He knows this instinctually. That's his skill. Figuring women out. It's what makes him a good lover.

They move to her bedroom. He undresses her. She has a scar across her thigh. It's long and raised and pink. He starts to ask her about it, but then he's struck by a sense of repulsion. He doesn't actually want to know where it came from. He listens for her roommate.

"Do you think Sheralyn wants to join?" he asks.

Chloe lifts her head and peers at him over the length of her torso. "That might be weird," she says.

"What, you never had a threesome?" He keeps his tone nonchalant, a trick he picked up long ago, from his buddies in college. A girl will do anything as long as you make it seem like no big deal.

"Of course," she says. "But Sheralyn and I aren't really—"

Doug moves up next to her and kisses her before she can finish her sentence. The whole time they have sex, he imagines Sheralyn with her ear to the door, listening.

He lies next to Chloe afterward and runs his fingers down the length of her bicep. Her goose bumps transfer to the surface of his own skin.

"You're electric," he says.

"That's what I feel like!" she says. "I can barely stand it."

He hears Sheralyn moving in the kitchen. An unexpected shame begins to stir underneath his exhaustion.

"I just wish everyone would stop trying to make me feel bad about it," Chloe says.

"What?"

"Oh, I don't know. Men are okay for the most part." Chloe blinks up at the ceiling. He has no idea what she's talking about. She jolts up to a sitting position. Energized. "Like at the office. Jo-Ann is nice. But all these women have problems with me for no reason."

Doug slides a hand up her thigh. "So what," he says. "You want me to fire all the meanies?"

"That's what it is! They're mean, but they can't be open about it. I know they talk about me behind my back."

"Whoa," Doug says. He shakes his head. "Chloe, do you know what de facto discrimination is?" Her face is blank. "I can't show any favoritism at the office, especially now that we've slept together."

She opens her mouth wide. "Oh no! I wasn't asking for that. I just wish I had more woman friends."

Doug breathes out and studies her. He considers whether it's worth saying anything. This situation between them isn't going to last long, he can tell. But she's young. A little lost. He sits across from her on the bed and pushes the hair from her face with two hands. "Listen. You're very pretty, obviously. Actually, you're more than that. You're probably disturbing to some people."

Chloe shifts her weight. Settling in. Hungry and attentive.

Doug continues. "For most folk, life is about coming to terms with their limitations. I'm sure some women, they find a niche, right? They get what they can and convince themselves it was what they wanted all along. But then you come along, and you're an absolute. You are what beauty is. You're like a walking reminder of inequality."

Chloe lowers her face and pinches a fold in her sheet. "I can't say anything like that, though. They'd tear me to pieces."

"Don't start feeling sorry for yourself. You're what everyone wants to be. Jesus, you're what I want to be. Use it. Make them look up to you."

She shakes her head slowly. "I don't know how to do that."

He's ready to launch into his standard advice to young people. That your life is a story you tell yourself. That you can make it whatever you want. But then he glances around her room. At the water spots on her cheap throw rug and the clothes spilling from the milk crates lining the opposite wall. Her closet has no door, just a giant tapestry falling to about six inches above the floor. Underneath is a clutter of cardboard and procrastination.

He gestures to her closet. "Well, you could start by getting your shit together. No offense."

"I didn't know you were coming over."

It's deeper than that. She thinks it's okay not to own a dresser. "How old are you again?"

"Almost twenty-five."

Almost young enough to make the way she's living excusable. What do these kids call it? Adulting? But there's a lack of self-respect in this room. She moves her face in front of his. He avoids her eyes.

She asks, "Are you mad at me?"

He needs a minute. He needs to decide if he's doing this. These girls have a way of becoming dependent. Chloe breaks away in a huff and reaches for her bra at the bottom of the bed.

"Of course I'm not mad," he says.

"But you think I'm a slob."

"Do your parents give you money?"

She gives a caustic laugh and fastens her bra. "I was raised by my grandparents."

"Do they help you?"

She pulls some cotton underwear out of the banker box next to her bed. "I don't need any help."

Oh yes, she does. She turns from him and starts dressing. He reaches from the bed and snaps the elastic on her bra.

"Ow!" She jumps back. He stands.

"I'll buy you a dresser," he says.

"You don't have to do that."

"I do," he says. "I do have to do that."

She pouts. "So you'll be my new daddy?"

"Whoa," says Doug. He grabs a handful of her ass. "That's what you want?"

Chloe brings her lips near his. She presses into his body. He kisses her, fully aware that he's sinking into a mess: a steaming, sloppy, luscious mess.

CHAPTER SIXTEEN

CHLOE

It's been three weeks. Everyone at the office knows. How can they not? It isn't that they can read Chloe's mind. But when she's at her desk and thinking about Doug grabbing her neck or kissing his way down her stomach, the images shimmer so brightly it's like it's all happening in real time, and her skin and lips and trillions of tiny blood cells are reduced to a single function.

They crave.

They crave in the direction of Doug's office. They crave when she hands smooth, cool bottles of water to visitors in the lobby. When she runs her hands along the curving Lucite counter above her desk. Her fingertips, the shape of the walls, the muted clicking of dozens of keyboards all resonating in the same frequency: sex.

He tried to leave her last night at two in the morning. He mumbled something about his wife. But Chloe's body was still humming. She convinced him to take a Viagra, and he stayed another forty minutes. She asked him to wait until she fell asleep before he left. The two times they spent the night together, she didn't have her usual dream.

But he woke her a few minutes later, clearing his throat as he put on his shoes. Soon after she had the nightmare, the same one as always: an old lady on the ground, shielding her head. "Why!" screams the woman in a garbled tongue. It's always the scream that wakes her.

Chloe stands up at her desk. She's restless. She looks toward Doug's office even though he's not in there. He hasn't come in yet. She sits back down and lays her head on her desk, like the teachers used to make her do in school. The elevator bell chimes. She jerks up. Elise, the vice president, in a sheath dress and sweepy blonde bob, gets off and sends a vague nod in Chloe's direction.

Chloe checks her phone. It's eleven. She pulls up Doug's Twitter. No posts today. She goes to his Instagram and scrolls down. His account is mostly business related—conference pictures and promotions for Beyond the Brand. But about four pages in, there's a wedding picture of him and his wife on a beach. Chloe clicks on it. The bride seems out of place. Emily's expression is too hard for her breezy surroundings. Her smile looks plastered on, and she has her fingers pressed into Doug's arm like she's holding him hostage. Chloe brings her phone close to her face and examines Doug's strained smile. He's not happy.

"Chloe, have you checked the voice mail?"

Chloe looks up. Jo-Ann is standing over her. Her perfume is astringent. It cuts through the musk Doug left on Chloe's T-shirt.

"I'm sorry?" says Chloe.

Jo-Ann points to the blinking message indicator light. "The Volvo focus group participants were supposed to call if they had to cancel."

Crap. Chloe dials into the mailbox. "Are we missing anyone?"

"We're supposed to have ten. We only have eight."

Holy crap. Chloe's insides start churning. The clients are already set up in the viewing room. She punches in the password, praying for this not to be her fault. She and Jo-Ann listen as two cancellations play on speakerphone—a woman with a kid home from school and a man with car trouble.

Chloe brings her arm in front of her stomach. "I'm so sorry," she says. "I usually check the messages first thing." Jo-Ann leans onto her cane and starts back to the client room. Chloe follows. "Is it too late to get alternates?"

Jo-Ann shakes her head in irritation. She ignores Chloe and closes the door to the observation room. Chloe stands there a moment before she heads back to her desk. She wants to hide under something. She wants to smack her own face. It's awful, the sense of being in trouble.

Doug isn't here; that's the problem. It's like she needs him now to function. The easiest tasks—like answering the phone with a cheerful "Beyond the Brand!"—have turned into some kind of performance, a private one, meant only for him. When he's not here, it's like there's no point to any of it.

Jo-Ann and Tom, the recruiter, come back from the direction of the viewing rooms.

"They're going ahead with eight participants," Jo-Ann says. "But we need to talk about how to handle this going forward."

Tom smooths the silver wreath of hair above his ears and brings his thumbs to his suspenders. "It's a lot of work putting these groups together, Chloe." He lands on her name like a punctuation mark. She lowers her head.

The phone rings at Doug's assistant Harper's desk. The back of Chloe's neck tingles. "Hey, Emily," Harper says, emphasizing each syllable of Doug's wife's name.

Tom continues, overenunciating as he speaks. "The participants have to be able to reach us. That's why I give them the main number."

Harper laughs at something Doug's wife says. "The size of a sweet potato!" Harper exclaims. "I love the food comparisons."

Where *is* Doug? Chloe texted him earlier, but he hasn't responded. There's no one she can ask. It's technically none of her business. Harper lowers her voice into gossip-sharing mode. Chloe strains to listen.

"Can I count on you?" asks Tom. He smiles at her with a practiced-looking warmth. All Chloe wants is for him to shut up or go away. She can't hear anything Harper is saying.

"Of course. I'm so sorry."

Tom's smile shifts to the left. "Let's shake on it," he says. But Chloe doesn't want to touch him. She glances at Jo-Ann, who's clicking away on her phone. Chloe reaches up. He flicks his thumb over her knuckle as they shake, in some bumbling message of dominance.

———

Doug comes to her performance later that afternoon. The group is hiking this time, on a dusty trail in Griffith Park overlooking LA on one side and the Valley on the other. They're wearing formal clothes with their white masks today. They wanted to pop among all the midriff-baring athleisure wear.

But no one pays attention to the group. The other hikers came to exercise. They came to show themselves off. It reminds Chloe of the time they imitated everyone in a café and buried themselves in their phones. None of the other patrons ever bothered looking up. People in LA are jaded.

Chloe stops in the shade of a lone tree overhanging the trail and looks back. Doug is following behind Sheralyn, who stops and says something to him before smacking her sequined hip and jogging up toward Chloe.

"I think we need to stick with tourist spots," Chloe says.

"Yeah, this isn't working," says Sheralyn. "We're just walking."

Chloe lets Sheralyn go on ahead. She decides to work against the action around her, provide a counterpoint. She faces the edge of the trail. She kicks her leg out over the cliff in slow motion and pauses, midstep.

A man's voice, a British accent, cuts through the air. "Did you hear that?" Chloe turns. There's an older guy standing in the knobby brush, near the tree. He looks like a broken-down rock and roller with long gray hair and deep creases in his face.

"Did you hear that?" the guy asks again.

His jeans and button-down are covered in dust, and his eyes are sick, like they're looking at her from a sick place. She wonders if he's trying to hit on her. She gets so many guys coming up to her, all the time. Maybe this is how the disturbed do it.

"I don't hear anything," Chloe says.

"Sure you do," says the guy. The way he's smiling, it's like he recognizes her, like he's some sprite from a fairy tale, malevolent but all-knowing. She mirrors his stance, leaning her torso to the right. The guy moves closer, kicking his leg as he steps in slow motion, just like she was doing before. It's like they're performing together, like they're in a trance.

"Chloe!" yells Doug. He rushes up the trail toward her.

She hears someone else running from above. It's Dylan. He shouts, "Chloe, move away from the edge."

"You called me," said the guy. For a moment Chloe believes him, that she conjured him, that she has that power. He's only a few feet away now.

Doug reaches them. He stands between her and the guy. "We're good, thanks," he says.

Dylan is there too. He motions for the guy to leave. "Go. Now."

The guy cocks his head and watches Chloe with a quizzical expression. *He knows,* she thinks. *He knows about me.* The guy holds up his hands and shrugs. "She called me," he says before turning back to the scrub brush. Doug and Dylan keep their eyes on him as he disappears over the hill.

Chloe drops her mouth open. The interaction was so pure, so divorced from the everyday. She doesn't know what to do with it, with the excitement and the energy of that guy, of the two men on either side of her. It's like she's about to explode.

"That was so real!" she squeals.

"Freaky," says Dylan. "Are you all right?"

"Of course," she says.

Doug grips her arm. "Chloe, that guy was about to push you."

"No, he wasn't," she says.

"He was dangerous," says Doug.

Chloe shifts her head to the side and squints. "No," she says. "He was fine. I can tell when someone's about to be violent."

"We should get going," says Dylan. He turns to head up the path. Chloe starts to follow, but Doug's hand is still on her arm. He pulls her toward him. His face is serious and intense.

"What's your plan, Chloe?"

"What plan?"

"This . . ." Doug gestures to the group ahead of her. "You really think there's a future here?"

"I thought you liked it."

"I do, but you put a lot of time into it. Are you making any money?"

Chloe breaks off eye contact and stares out at the LA Basin. The air is clear today. She can see downtown rising in the distance, a cluster of skyscrapers reflecting the afternoon light. She's only just landed. She's only just stopped obsessing about where she's been. She can't even think about what comes after.

She smiles at Doug. "You could always give me a raise."

Doug laughs. He pulls her toward him. "Come away with me. Tonight. I'll take you somewhere."

She wonders about his wife. How he can just leave like that. She wants to ask but doesn't want to bring her up. "I'll have to go home and get my clothes."

"Nope," he says. "I'll take you shopping."

———

Doug drives her north to Oxnard, a coastal town carpeted in strawberry and bell pepper fields, and pulls into a sprawling chain hotel on the water. "It's not fancy," Doug says as they stop at the top of a U-shaped driveway. "I can't risk the usual spots."

Chloe looks to her right, down a sandy path into the dunes, shrouded in fog and succulents. She and Doug can go for a walk later. They can hold hands without worrying if anyone sees.

"It's perfect," she says.

They change into their swimsuits and bathrobes and follow the signs through the pool area to the hot tub. It's chilly. All the lounge chairs are empty except for a lone woman wearing a pantsuit and lanyard. The woman glances up from her laptop as they pass and runs her eyes down the length of Chloe's body.

Chloe opens the separate gate to the Jacuzzi and slips into the water. It hurts at first. It forces the air from her lungs, it's so hot. Doug picks up her bathrobe off the ground and drapes it over the fence.

"Cannonball?" He pretends to take a running leap.

Chloe laughs and screams. "No!"

He turns the bubbles on and slides in next to her. She flicks foam onto his shoulder. Two women and a man in business clothes and name tags stop outside the pool area. They look so uncomfortable in their conference wear, so much less alive than she and Doug.

"You know that guy, Tom?" Chloe asks. "The recruiter?"

"Tom, sure."

"You don't think he's a little weird?"

Doug lowers his chin into the water.

"He creeps me out," she says.

"I've got a lot of employees," says Doug.

"Yeah, but he gave me this freaky handshake."

"I'll give you a freaky handshake." He swims up on top of her. Chloe looks toward the three conventioneers. The man, a trim older guy with salt-and-pepper hair, makes eye contact with her. Doug reaches between her legs. His expression is neutral, giving nothing away to the people outside the fence. His lips hum with energy. She guides his hand to the inside of her bikini bottom. Doug gushes, "You're incredible."

She is. She's incredible. It's like she's a lightning rod. She *feels* everything. And she's learning how to maneuver around her history, her awful bursts of rage. She can see past all that now, just in glimpses, to where there's this exquisite undercurrent. Once she clears anger out of the way, she can see beauty and joy and aching and sex and grief all intertwined and streaming through everything and everybody, but most people never even bother to look for it.

Doug looks. He sees it in her. She didn't realize it before, how badly she needed someone to notice her.

Two men in khakis and polo shirts amble along the fence. Chloe peels off her bikini bottom under the bubbles and grabs Doug by the hips.

"Oh Jesus," he exhales into her ear. She straddles him. "You're fucking amazing."

She is. She's fucking amazing. She rocks on Doug's lap, just enough so that any passerby would wonder if what they think is happening is really happening. She sneaks a look behind her. The polo shirt guys are standing at the fence, watching them.

CHAPTER SEVENTEEN

DOUG

Doug tightens his hand around his office doorknob. He doesn't move. He's been successful, so far, at staving off the panic. It's been gathering. Just outside himself.

Today is yet another field test of his EEG and app. Today, it has to work. He's burned through two capital investments. He's leveraged 49 percent of the project. He shakes out his hands as he walks toward the elevator, enraged at his team. They don't communicate problems to him. Sanjay, his biomedical engineer, has created something beautiful—what should be a flawless mindfulness tool—that will usher in a new age of data collection, direct and unfiltered, straight from the consumer's mind.

But they can't get it to work right. There are too many moving pieces. And Erik, the Dr. Maryn consultant, his partner in crime. He's in charge of the app portion, but he doesn't talk to Sanjay. No one talks to each other. All they do is cover their asses.

Doug has been doing the same, of course, with Emily. All he tells her now is that there are delays. He doesn't get into it. She's been patient. Hasn't pressured him, even though she went to huge lengths to get his

EEG an exclusive on the Dr. Maryn Store. They were supposed to be a team. Equals. But now he's practically her subordinate. It sucks. He has to manage up to his wife.

He approaches Chloe at reception and looks down at his watch, hoping to sneak by without acknowledging her. But she perks up with an expectant smile. He flashes her a quick grin. It's every single time now. Whenever he sees her, he has to relay some private signal. Even today, when he's preoccupied, when he's worried about whether or not he'll be able to tell his board the goddamned EEG is finally going to pay off, Chloe expects him to keep up the sexy subterfuge. If he doesn't, she'll send him a ??? text and ask if he's mad.

It's been two months since they first slept together. Two months of being her audience, of replacing her cheap wardrobe with Phillip Lim and Marc Jacobs, of doing her from behind in brutally lit department store dressing rooms.

Funny. He had no idea the degree to which semipublic sex would come to feel routine.

But he has a business to run. He's slept with a lot of employees in his career. He can tell when it starts affecting the staff. People get restless. They look for signs of favoritism and start showing up later and later until a 9:00 a.m. office turns into a 10:00 a.m. office. That one girl, Tamra from research, would take advantage of the newly lax workplace, oblivious that she was at the root of it. She'd stroll in around ten thirty the mornings after Doug had been with her, her eyes smeared with heavy makeup. Doug would mouth the word *slut* when he saw her. She used that detail later in the lawsuit, which was unfair, considering it made her giggle.

He presses the call button on the elevator. He's supposed to go to another one of Chloe's performances later but doesn't want to. They're all the same. But then he thinks of Sheralyn. Of her tattoos. She keeps flirting with him. Overt and raunchy.

The elevator arrives just as Harper, his assistant, catches up. She's wearing a white blazer with a popped collar, *Miami Vice* style, and has both Doug's and her laptop bags slung over her shoulder.

"I won't need my computer," Doug says as he holds the door open for her.

Harper swipes her curls away from her face. "I'd rather bring it now than have to go back for it."

"You know me so well," Doug says. It's true. Whenever he doesn't bring something, he usually ends up needing it. At least one woman here is trying to make his life easier. "You're one of the good ones, Harper."

Harper offers him an exasperated eye roll and walks past him onto the elevator. His thoughts turn back to sex. Harper would want it private. Sensual. Under the covers. Just the two of them in heated isolation.

"Bye!" shouts Chloe from the other side of the glass. He gives her a wave with the back of his hand. The door closes. Doug looks over Harper's neck. He tries to picture having sex with her again, but nothing comes. He looks to the ceiling and blinks back his growing anxiety.

"Are you okay?" asks Harper.

A pained moan bursts from him. "Not really."

"But we're getting all this advance press," says Harper.

The elevator lands at the lobby. Doug motions for Harper to go ahead of him into the main hall. He isn't sure he should talk to her about this. He isn't in the habit of discussing potential failure. But Harper is a stellar employee. She needs a mentor. He's neglected his staff over the last two months.

"It's the first truly portable EEG," says Harper. She stops at the building exit and looks into his face with a sincere expression. "Doug, you've done something incredible."

He grabs the door handle and leans toward her. "Think about it. We spent a lot of money, more than we should have, to make it small, portable, something people would want to wear. Why?"

Harper cocks her head. "To get the data, right?"

Doug taps a finger to the side of his nose.

"But it's not going well?" she says.

"Yes. And why do you think it isn't going well?"

There's a flash in Harper's eyes. She's excited. This kind of talk—insiderish, strategy focused—she loves it. He'll let her sit in on more meetings.

"Is it not working?"

"The EEG is. The app isn't. But that's not the real problem."

She looks out in front of her, like she's searching the air for answers. "Are you running out of money?"

"Very good, Harper!" He starts to laugh, but then the dread comes searing across his chest. It's sharp, and it hurts. He reaches his hand across his collarbones and rubs them.

Harper frowns. "What are you going to do?"

"One thing at a time," he says. He opens the door for her. "Cross your fingers the field test goes our way."

The morning is moist and chilly, cold enough to warrant the hoodie Doug thought of bringing. They walk two blocks up Main Street, to a stark art gallery of a clothing boutique. Sanjay, his bio-medical engineer with the heavy nerd glasses, is set up at a card table inside the entrance with Erik, who's buzzed his hair on the sides, leaving a wave on top.

"You got your hair cut," Doug says.

Erik jerks his hand to his head. "You like it?"

Doug ignores him and motions to a freckled young woman sitting on a folding chair. She's wearing ripped jeans, and on her head is Doug's EEG, now a sleek, concentrated semicircle of sensors fastened near the base of her skull. Doug can barely see it. Her hair is almost completely covering it.

Doug smiles at her. "I'm Doug."

"I'm Becca."

"You've got my baby on your head, Becca. How is it? Are you comfortable?"

"It's tight, but I'm getting used to it."

Doug turns to Sanjay. "Is it supposed to be tight?"

"We don't want it sliding around," Sanjay says.

"People aren't going to want to wear something uncomfortable."

Sanjay shakes his head, annoyed. "I thought we were focusing on the app today."

Doug puts his hand on Becca's shoulder. "So you know your brain is full of electric activity, right? That's what the EEG is going to measure."

Becca nods. Doug points to the interior of the store. "We have Bluetooth stations set up all around to pinpoint your location—if you're in front of the jewelry, the jeans, we'll know. I want you to browse, like you're really shopping, okay? Try on shirts, check the price on the earrings—can you do that, Becca?"

Sanjay boots up the desktop computer he's hauled to the store for this test. It's specialized, medical-grade equipment, registering the signals sent from the EEG. Erik pulls out his iPad and opens the waveform app they're planning to put on the Dr. Maryn Store. Doug watches Becca as she starts into the store. She stops at a row of dresses and lifts one up. Doug turns to Erik and Sanjay.

"How can you tell where she is?" Doug asks.

"It's all encoded," says Sanjay. He toggles to a window full of computer script. "See? P3657 means she's at the perfume counter."

Doug glances to Becca as she lifts a small card to her nose. He points to Sanjay's computer. "That looked like a hit there, when she smelled the sample?"

"Could be," says Sanjay.

He glances at Erik's iPad. The waveforms are unchanging. It's supposed to match what's happening on Sanjay's computer.

"Becca?" Doug calls across the store. "Can you try another scent?"

Doug looks between Sanjay's computer and Erik's iPad. Again, there's a hit on the computer but not on the app. Doug points to the iPad. "Which layer measures smell?"

Erik's eyes go wide. He looks at Sanjay, whose eyes are shut tight for the length of about ten blinks. "Smell is processed in multiple places in the brain," Sanjay says. He motions to Erik. "Erik? Do you remember you were going to combine the different data into categories? One for each of the five senses?"

Erik shakes his head at Sanjay. "You were supposed to send me the code for that last week."

Sanjay speaks through gritted teeth. "I did."

Again with the ass covering. Doug balls his hands into fists. He can't figure out who to believe. He's late to tech. To all this. He should have majored in computer science. He points into the store. "So you're telling me that woman there is smelling a perfume. Becca, did you like that scent?"

"Yeah," Becca calls out. "It's jasmine."

"And you're telling me the app has no way of knowing whether she likes it or not?"

Sanjay lets out a slow exhale. He stares at Erik. Erik clears his throat. "It's complicated," says Erik.

Doug suppresses the urge to scream at Erik. He needs Erik. Erik knows too much. He lowers his face to Sanjay's. "We spent too much time on the design!"

Sanjay stands. "Do you have any idea what I did? We have something that looks amazing. That people actually want to wear. And it's accurate! I did all that!" He shakes his head in disgust as Erik slumps on the table, head in his hands. "It's not my fault your boy wonder over here can't get his act together."

Doug is out of options. He points to Erik. "Now," he says and exits the store. Erik follows. It's sunny, but Doug doesn't notice the warmth on his arms. "What the fuck, Erik?"

"I'll get it to work," Erik says.

Doug studies him. Erik looks back, all wide eyed and sincere and with the complete lack of uncertainty that typically signals incompetence. Doug has managed people his entire adult life. He's never ceased to marvel at the way certain workers fail to deliver. Maybe Erik is spread too thin. Or lazy. Or out of his league in some malignant mix of Peter principle and Dunning-Kruger effect. The why doesn't matter. Doug needs to contain the damage. He'll have to hire someone else. A programmer who understands the minutiae of biofeedback. But he can't fire Erik. He needs him for the data mining.

Doug rocks back on his heels. He's going to have to come up with an extra salary on top of what he's already paying. "Get me something I can show my board," Doug says. "Do you understand?"

Erik keeps his eyes on him and gives him a slight nod.

"Fake it if you have to," Doug says. "What's the excitement waveform?"

Erik grimaces. "Beta waves? I think?" Doug glances through the glass doors of the boutique. Both Sanjay and Harper are staring at them.

"Let's walk," he says. They start around the block. "I specifically picked board members who don't know anything about science. No one is going to look too hard at the tech. Do a little research. Say the beta waves, or whatever waves it is, went wild when she smelled the perfume."

Erik runs his fingers through his hair. "What about Sanjay?"

"Sanjay's finished," says Doug. Sanjay is too competent. Self-righteous. He won't stand for what Doug's about to do. "We need to talk about next steps. Isn't that what you want?"

Erik stops. He stares at Doug, thinking. "You're ready to do that?"

The nuclear option. Doug and Erik plotted it out long ago, as a hedge, after Emily left them that night at Shutters on the Beach. The original plan was for Doug's app to start siphoning data off the other apps from the store. It was elegant. Almost impossible to detect. But Doug can't get his EEG to market until the app starts working. And he can't get it to work without more money.

Erik and Doug have an agreement, a contingency plan. Erik will simply steal the data from Dr. Maryn's store. Doug knows where to sell it and who will pay. The newspapers describe it as a "shadowy world" of illegal data brokers, but really, it's some of the same people who deal in legit information.

All he'll need is one, maybe two data dumps. That'll give him enough cash to keep going.

"I'll be in touch," says Doug. They separate. Doug starts down the street.

"Hey!" Harper yells. She's chasing after him, struggling with the two computer bags.

"Let me carry them," he says, struck by a surge of chivalry. His decision to steal Dr. Maryn's medical data makes him feel strangely virtuous. It's not that he *wants* to do anything illegal. He takes the bags from her. "Harper, I need you to go through all the emails between me and Erik. If you see anything talking about or even joking about something like 'the nuclear option' or 'medical data'—I think at one point I said something like 'I know a guy'—if anything sounds even remotely shady, I need it deleted. Not just off your computer but off the backups, the archives, everything. Talk to Jeremiah in IT about how to do that."

Harper stops. Doug starts forward but turns back when she doesn't follow.

She lifts her chin. "Why?"

"You really want to know?"

She shakes her head. "Doug, people can tell when emails go missing."

"Who?" He steps toward her and peers into her face. "Who can tell?"

"It's a red flag," she says.

"I have a right to organize things the way I want, Harper," he says. "I'm asking you, as my assistant, to do that for me."

He hands her computer bag back to her. She lets him walk ahead. He breathes out hard. He wants to circle back to Harper. He wants to tell her he's not a bad guy. Whatever she's thinking right now. She has the wrong idea.

He continues walking. His muscles twitch. Itch. An impulse appears. A visceral set of memories: Doug in a crowded dive bar, pressing himself against an anonymous female body. Doug at a seedy kitchen table, burying himself in a big fat fucking pile of drugs.

Cocaine.

It's incredible, how fast the urge comes on. It's been, what? Five years? Seven years since his last relapse?

Emily.

He pulls out his phone and hovers his thumb over his wife's name at the top of his favorites list. He needs her to talk him through this, through the deal with Erik. But she asked to be kept out of it. Doug expels a single breathy laugh. As if plausible deniability would protect Emily if he got caught.

He texts Chloe:

Meet me in the garage.

Tell Jo-Ann you'll be gone for the rest of the day.

She's already there when he arrives, leaning against the walls of the elevator vestibule with her arms crossed over her chest. She's pouting.

"Jo-Ann's getting fed up with me," she says.

Right. Things are getting sloppy. He scans the empty garage for his employees.

"Actually, go back upstairs," Doug says. "Come to my place after work."

CHAPTER EIGHTEEN

CHLOE

It's dark by the time Chloe pulls to the shoulder of PCH across from Doug's house. A truck rumbles close, just as she's about to open her door. He told her not to park near his driveway. She waits until she sees no headlights. Then she stands at the white line, waiting for another break in the fifty-mile-an-hour traffic, and makes a panicked dash across the road.

Doug greets her with an extended kiss in the front hall. His breath smells like brown liquor. She follows him down an unlit hall, down the stairs to the living room. She walks the perimeter of the shag rug and considers the glinting silver sofa in the center of the room. It looks like a museum piece, not something anyone would actually sit on. There's a screen door leading to a balcony. Chloe can hear the sound of the waves tumbling just outside.

"Where's your wife?" she asks, even though she knows from Emily's Instagram that his wife is in Atlanta, with dozens of other hyperpolished ladies at some women-and-media conference.

"Away," Doug says. He hands Chloe a glass of wine and points her toward the outside. She walks out to the railing. *Holy crap.* The house is on top of the water. She inhales deeply. She imagines swimming out toward the full moon and letting the dark sea swallow her. It's almost painful, her capacity to appreciate such beauty. It's raw. She wants Doug on the balcony with her right now. She wants him to see her seeing all this.

Doug opens the screen door. "You like?" he asks. He moves up close behind her.

"Look." She points to the moon. It's full and hovering just over the horizon, shining a rippling half cylinder of light onto the black Pacific. "That must be what they mean when they say 'moonbeam.'"

He takes her waist in his hands. She turns to face him, expecting him to pounce, to gobble her up. But his kiss is supple. Chloe leans in, trying to increase the pressure.

"Ah, ah." He pulls back with a kindly expression. His voice is tender. "We have all night."

This is odd, this softness. They're normally hard on each other, with slamming, laughing, devilish sex. He strokes her arm lightly. "Come upstairs," he says. Chloe studies him. "Come on, silly."

She follows him up to a lived-in-looking master with an unmade platform bed. On the dresser is the same wedding picture from Instagram, with Doug and his wife on the beach. Next to it is an eight-by-ten framed photo of a Doberman pinscher. It looks like a yearbook photo.

"This is your room?" Chloe asks.

"Yep."

"Are you sure we should do it here?"

He brings his lips to her ear in a seductive rumble. "I can't remake the bed in the guest room the way my housekeeper does."

He closes the drapes. It's slow and deliberate, the way he does it, like it's part of some plan. Chloe tilts her head and wonders, briefly, if he's going to kill her. There's no fear to the thought. It's just one of many things that cross her mind in any given period.

He guides her to the bed and pulls the covers over them for an episode of intimate, claustrophobic sex. He keeps his face close. She keeps breathing in his carbon dioxide. She turns her head to the side and pushes the covers away. He starts to gather the duvet back over them.

"I'm a little hot," she says.

He puts his hand to her cheek and smiles. "Okay," he says. She tries to squirm out from under him, for a change from missionary position, but he resists. She takes his hand and closes his fingers around her hair. He doesn't grab. He doesn't pull. He just stays on top of her. He forces the eye contact the whole time. It feels like they're in a sensory-deprivation tank.

She doesn't come. He offers to go down on her.

"It's okay," she says and sits up.

He lies back and brings his hands under his head with splayed elbows. He looks vulnerable, feminine even. "Did you like that?" he asks.

Chloe notices an unshaven strip of hair on her shin and runs her finger up it. "It was cool," she says.

It's so sudden then, the way his face goes dark. His eyes flicker to the closed curtains. She's lost him. She can feel it. It was a test, the quiet sex. He was trying to be real. He gets out of bed and opens the drapes.

Chloe swallows. If it were another day, at her place or at a hotel, he'd be dressing, readying himself to leave. But he's already home. And his wife is away. They have all night. She can get him back. If he wants to be close, she can do that.

"Doug, can I tell you something?"

It's terrible, the way she's always on guard. Stopping up all the bitty fragments of her story that keep threatening to skitter from her lips. She won't tell him everything, of course. She'll say nothing about how lucky she felt when she was hired at Beyond the Brand, how she could answer honestly on the background check that she'd never been arrested. The judge had expunged what happened with Fefu Fornes. And the other incident, she was a minor then.

He lies back down. "What is it?"

She knows she can't share that it made her feel special, the fact that she was the only woman in her anger-management class.

"I had a pretty rough childhood," she says.

The sound drops out of the room then. Chloe can't hear anything, not the ocean outside, not Doug laughing. He's laughing now. He's laughing at her.

"Oh, honey," he says. He sits and puts a hand on her back. "Of course you had an awful childhood. Why else would you be here?"

The room comes into focus. Chloe tunes into its edges. The walls, the pillows, the sharp lines and shadows. Doug's not making fun of her. He understands. Everyone has problems. Maybe that's what Chloe can be, just a regular person with problems.

"So then, why are *you* here?" she asks.

He pauses a moment before deadpanning, "My father was a serial philanderer. He left our family when I was five. He left us six times."

It's startling. It's awful.

"But he always came back!" he says.

Chloe and Doug laugh in each other's faces.

Surely it isn't this easy? She'd been assuming there would be a moment, a horrible moment when she'd have to fess up about why she's no longer a backup dancer, about where she's from. And her mother's twisted face and all the midnight escapes and terror of waking all those different fathers.

I got out, she thinks and fingers the raised scar on her thigh. It's so thick. She can pinch both sides of it. She barely remembers, now, how much it hurt.

"What happened to you?" Doug asks. "Wait, let me guess." He points to her scar. "You were a cutter?"

Chloe blinks. She smiles. This is funny too. He thinks she's predictable. He thinks he can put her into a category.

"My mother tried to kill me."

Doug goes quiet. He rubs his forehead with his fingertips and slides his back up against the headboard. Chloe waits for him to respond, to tell her he's glad she said something about her past.

"Anyway, I should have majored in computer science," he finally says.

Her lungs fill with a sharp gust of air.

"Those tech guys, man," he says. "They're changing the world."

He heard her. She knows he did. But he doesn't want to know about this stuff. No one does.

"Bullshit," says Chloe.

His face turns hard and cautioning. It's the reflex of a powerful man, someone who doesn't like to be challenged. Chloe brings the side of her thumb to her teeth. *One, two, three,* she thinks. She bites off a flap of skin. *Four, five, six.*

He frowns. "Are you counting?"

Doug's not any better than her. He needs to know that. She sidles up next to him and brings her fingers to the soft inside of his elbow. She pinches him.

"Ow!"

"Sorry. I didn't mean to do it that hard."

He draws his head back and stares at her. "Don't do it again."

Chloe pulls her knees up and hugs them tight. Doug doesn't say anything else. But his wife is away. They have all night. She lies back and follows a crack in the ceiling to the wall above the dresser. The Doberman in the portrait is staring at her.

"Is that your dog?" Chloe asks.

He sighs. "Was. If you run into my wife, don't mention it."

"Why?"

"It was vicious. I had to take it back to the breeder who sold it to her."

CHAPTER NINETEEN

Doug

Doug is sitting at the small conference table in his office with Maurice, his innovation strategist with the shaved head. Eva, his fiftysomething communications vice president, needs a place to sit. Harper knocks lightly on the door. She rolls in an extra chair. No one asked her for one. Harper just knows what's needed. She's wearing a deep, purple V-neck with a choker necklace. The kind that was popular twenty years ago.

Eva leans across the table to connect her laptop to the projector, exposing the elastic waistband on her basic black trousers. She's wearing a quilted blazer. Harper starts out the door.

"Harper," Doug says. "Do you want to stay for this?"

She gives him a surprised smile. "I'd love to." She moves to the back of the room. He winks at her as she leans against his awards shelf. His first instinct was to shut her out, lead her away from everything to do with the EEG. But he already got rid of Sanjay. A firing spree would only attract attention. Better to keep her close, monitor her, practice his denials on her. She keeps asking questions. When they were putting together the board packets, she asked, "Is this real?" about his claims the EEG would deliver the information on a customer's color preference or their moods relative to the time of day.

"Of course it's real!" he insisted last week. "What are you accusing me of?"

There's a magical indignation he inhabits when he lies. A small window of uncertainty where he's free to maneuver. Because whoever doubts him, well, that person doesn't 100 percent *know* he's lying. And what if he were really telling the truth? What right would anyone have to suggest otherwise? Just the thought of someone not believing him fills him with outrage.

Eva shuts off the light and projects a video onto Doug's whiteboard. An animated universe appears, twirling to the tune of a cheerful pop orchestra. Galaxies and constellations part to reveal a pixelated Planet Earth. The image zooms down to street level in a cartoon city as the coy, husky voice of a female narrator glides over the violins.

"What if we could simulate our world? Create an avatar of each person . . . where we know their tastes . . . their wants . . . their desires?"

The picture pans to a busy sidewalk, paved in flowcharts and spreadsheets. Blocky stick figure people, made up of swirling numbers and code, rise from the various database schemas and join the rush of pedestrians.

"Not long ago, customer data was flat, inert. But with Beyond the Brand's patented consumer insights, we're leveraging multiple data points to create a complete, interactive profile of—"

"Stop there," says Doug. He leans back in his swivel chair and clicks a ballpoint pen in the air. "'Leveraging multiple data points'—it sounds too much like corporate speak. We're collecting more intimate information than our competitors. That's what we want to get across."

Eva handwrites on a legal pad. Maurice types into his MacBook.

"Harper," Doug says, "do you have any comments?"

She stands and folds her arms across her chest. "Um . . . I'm wondering about the story," she says. "You know, does this capture the story of what Beyond the Brand is doing?"

"Very good," says Doug. He gives Harper a nod. She's been paying attention. It's all about the mythmaking, the corporate story. That's how companies stand out. That's how TED Talks go viral.

The phone on Doug's desk rings. Harper jumps up and heads to her workstation. He hears her say, "Doug Markham's office," on the other side of the door.

"And let's have a man for the voice-over," says Doug.

———

Harper slides into his office after the meeting. "I'll take that chair back," she says. She rolls the extra seat toward the door. "That was Erik Powell on the phone. I sent you an IM. I'm not sure I understand what he was asking."

Doug looks up from his computer. "What did he say?"

"He said we made out the check wrong?"

The air around Doug stills. "What check?" His words come out like a whipcrack.

"The invoice he sent you last week. I forwarded it to accounting."

"He sent it to *me*?" He stands. He strides to the door, flings the chair in her hands out of his way, and heads to her desk. He shakes her computer mouse, bringing her home screen to life.

"Show me," he says.

"What?"

"The invoice."

Harper opens her email and clicks to Doug's inbox. "He said the check was supposed to go to him personally," she says. "Not his company." Doug leans forward. Erik's invoice is official, professional looking, requesting $75,000 for "services rendered."

"Jesus," he says. He turns to Harper. "Why didn't you come to me about this?"

Harper lifts her chin, steeling herself. She looks him straight in the eye. "Because if I did, you'd ask why I was bothering you about accounting stuff."

Doug points to her computer. "Delete it," he says. "Tell accounting to cancel the check. It's an error. And delete your message to me and all traces of this invoice. I want it off our servers."

He storms back into his office. *Goddamned Erik.* He's a loose cannon. Doug knew it from the beginning. That's why he thought the guy would be useful. That's why Doug showed up that night at Shutters, when Emily took Erik out. But these rule breakers. These drunks and egotists. They're easy to manipulate. Impossible to control.

He pulls out his personal cell phone. "You sent me a fucking *invoice*?" Doug says when Erik answers.

"Where's my money?"

"You want us to get arrested?"

"I want to get paid for my work."

Doug flinches. He clenches his jaw. Is it actually freaking conceivable that this guy who oversees multimillion-dollar projects doesn't know how back-channel payments work?

"Erik, I have to get paid first; then that money has to clear; then I pay you. But the trick is, it all has to be untraceable. Got it? That's why we set up our accounts."

"It's been weeks, Doug."

"If you're impatient, call me. Don't fucking threaten me with an invoice."

Erik is silent for a moment. "I thought you'd find the 'services rendered' part funny."

"You're an idiot," says Doug.

"I know. I have another drive for you. Chock full of good stuff."

There's a knock on his door.

"Don't screw me like that again," says Doug. He hangs up.

Harper opens the door just enough to poke her head in. "Doug?" she says. "Can I talk to you a minute?" She sounds small, suddenly. Meek. He's never heard her speak without confidence. He waves her in. She's carrying a folded piece of paper.

"What's up?" he says.

"I have an opportunity," she says. "At a start-up." She runs one hand down her thigh, like she's wiping sweat off her palm. "I wasn't sure if I was going to take it—"

Doug jumps up. Harper startles. "You're quitting?" he says.

"It's a great opportunity."

"Harper, I'm about to promote you."

She takes a breath. "Thank you," she says. "This has been a . . . good place to work." She pauses and shakes her head with her mouth open. "I have a letter." She starts to put the paper on his desk.

"Jesus Christ!" He grabs the paper from her and squeezes it into a tight ball. She can't leave. She's been keeping his secrets for so long now. He doesn't even know how much she knows. "How about some goddamned loyalty?"

Harper takes a step back. "I'm feeling uncomfortable right now."

Uncomfortable. That's his lot in life. Making sure people under him are comfortable. He comes around his desk and sits on the edge. He attempts a smile.

"I'll promote you," he says. "Today. I'll make you a manager. You want to work in PR?"

"Doug, it's not—"

"Fifty percent raise. That'll bring you to what? Ninety thousand?"

Harper breathes in and straightens herself. He's emboldening her now. He can tell. She's ready to negotiate. They all come around when you mention money.

"Come on, Doug," she says. "We've gotten two huge influxes of data. No one knows where they come from. They just go into this pool, this swirl of information. Jeremiah said you guys were opening up 'new categories,' which, I'm sorry, but are you selling people's medical information? I mean, is that legal?"

Doug looks Harper over slowly. He lingers on her waist before bringing his eyes up to meet hers. "Did you delete the invoice?"

Harper spreads her hands out to the sides, like she's trying to steady herself on the air. There's confusion in her now, overtaking her momentary show of defiance. "I'm not really comfortable with that."

Comfort. Again. Now she's using it against him. "It's your job, Harper."

She stammers. "My job is not . . . this isn't what I . . ."

He pushes off from his desk quickly. She starts for the exit, but he's faster. He sprints past her and presses his hand against the door. Shutting it. Keeping it shut. She stops short with a tiny "Oh!" and brings her hands to the sides of her nose in prayer position. She backs away from him to the middle of the room.

"You think you're gonna go whistleblower on me?"

"You're scaring me."

Of course he is. People like Harper think the world is supposed to be fair or kind. They know nothing of risk. Of what it means to own a business. They never have to resort to savagery.

He leans forward and spits his words at her. "I will annihilate you!"

She's shaking. He lets her stand there a moment before opening his door and motioning for her to leave. She turns from him as she passes. It's not like he enjoys frightening the shit out of people. It's just something he has to do every once in a while.

He sits back down at his desk and pretends to work at his computer. He glances through the doorway and watches as she gathers her pictures and tchotchkes.

"Don't touch that computer," he says.

She lowers her head, hiding her face from him. Is she crying? Her beautiful curls are masking everything. He feels bad now. He feels like he's sinking. He'll have HR follow up. They can offer her a small severance.

Chloe texts a few minutes after she leaves:

Did Harper just quit????

Get in here.

Chloe barrels into his office, all out of breath and eager. "I have to tell you something," she says. "I never liked Harper."

He closes the door. "Have you ever been hate fucked?"

Chloe cocks her head to the side. "Sort of?"

"Stand over there."

He points to the middle of the room, where Harper was standing. He holds the door shut with his hand and watches Chloe prance away from him. She peeks over her shoulder. Playing seductress.

"Take your shirt off," he says. She does. Her bra is gray, the sheer demicup he bought her. "Take your pants off." She's wearing flowered cotton panties.

She puts her hands on her hips and shimmies. Even in mismatched underwear, she's a show-off. It's not what he wants. He wants her dirty. He wants her humiliated.

"I'm sorry," he whispers. He charges. He grabs her by her hair and pulls her to the floor. "I'm so sorry."

CHAPTER TWENTY

DOUG

It's been a week since Harper left. Doug paces his office with his phone in his hand and switches from his browser to his email app. Jo-Ann has sent two more résumés. Neither has included a picture. He needs a personal touch in his new assistant. He needs someone to ask if he's okay when she sees him pacing his office with his phone in his hand, searching online for his most recent drug dealers, the ones from before his last stint in rehab. When was that? Seven, ten years ago?

Things are getting murky. Doug has been here before. He knows when he's inviting chaos. Hunting distraction.

One of his old dealers is in jail. Another owns an auto-repair shop in Alhambra. The guy's profile picture shows him cradling an infant with a muscular arm.

Doug fights the urge to text Chloe, to tell her to come into his office. They've been screwing a lot more. At work. In the bathroom. It was mostly after hours at first. A bit of rebellious fun that fast became a daily compulsion. She's his go-to now. Warm and malleable. Chloe is comfort food.

But this behavior is dangerous. He knows this. He's been sued. The last one, Tamra. It almost went to court. Almost went public. She didn't want to sign the nondisclosure.

Plus, he has a baby on the way. Jesus. He needs to behave. Emily is what, seven months along now?

He texts Chloe:

Let's go. Your car. Pick me up at Rose and 4th.

"I'll drive," he says as she pulls up to the sidewalk in her Celica. He opens her door and moves to let her out of the car. But she just climbs over the center console to the passenger seat. "Where are we going?"

"A quick errand," he says.

He takes the 10 freeway east, speeding out of the coastal mist into the stark sunlight. Doug reaches for the sunglasses he's hung from the collar of his crewneck. Chloe takes hers out of the Mulberry tote he bought her. He gets off at the exit for Garfield Avenue and drives through tracts of nondescript warehouses.

Chloe sinks into her seat. She looks disappointed. "Is this Monterey Park?" she asks.

"Alhambra," he says. He should have told her where they're going. There's nothing sexy about fixing the air-conditioning on a car. Still, he has to take care of this. He has to set her up not to hate him when he breaks it off with her. If he can give her enough financial help, she'll be grateful.

He pulls into the lot of a yellow cinder block garage.

"Time you got some AC."

"Really?" She opens her mouth wide and clutches a hand to her heart like some lucky game show contestant. "Oh my God, thank you!"

The mechanic, Doug's old dealer, comes out. He shakes Doug's hand. "Hey, man, how you been?"

Doug explains what they want. The mechanic checks under the hood and addresses Chloe. "When was the last time you added coolant?" She looks startled and glances to Doug.

"Do you think that's the issue?" Doug asks.

The mechanic clicks his tongue against the back of his teeth. "Hard to say. We can do a diagnostic with new fluid, but it'll be about two hundred to even find out what's wrong."

"Just call when it's fixed," says Doug.

Doug and Chloe sit silently in the Uber on the way back, an old Lincoln Continental driven by a white guy in his sixties who looks like he's done time as a taxi driver. Doug feels hopeful. He doesn't know if the mechanic is still dealing, but the guy was friendly. A good sign. Not that Doug is planning to start doing drugs again.

"Thank you for this," Chloe finally says. She's looking out the window. Her voice is high pitched and tight. "Do you think it's really just the coolant?"

Doug frowns at her. "When was the last time you had your car serviced?" She inhales and grips both thighs. "This stuff isn't that complicated, Chloe."

"I know. My brain just goes into lockdown around money and logistics. Like, say the word *taxes*, and I'm the Batmobile. *Vvvt, vvvt, vvvt.*" She mimes closing a zipper around her head.

"Taxes?" He's finding it difficult to hide his exasperation. "You do your taxes, right?"

"It's just, I claimed more than my fair share of dependents."

"How many?"

"I'm only supposed to do one, but I did three."

He shakes his head. "The IRS doesn't care about that."

She squeezes the bridge of her nose with her thumb and forefinger. There's something deeply off about this girl, more than the run-of-the-mill issues of the disorganized. Is it new, or is he just now noticing? She closes her eyes.

"Are you breaking up with me?" she asks.

The Uber driver looks at Doug in the rearview.

"What are you talking about?" Doug asks.

"The air-conditioning. That's like a booby prize?"

Doug squares his body to her. She's not wearing her seat belt. "You know, Chloe. You'd be better off if you weren't smart."

The air of burgeoning conflict dissolves as Chloe's face opens, all eager and expectant. "What do you mean?" she asks. Jesus, this girl loves talking about herself.

"Look, I'm no saint," Doug says, "but you're carrying on like a bimbo. You know that, right?"

She nods.

"If that's all you want, fine," he says. "You'll do well in LA. But you need to understand something."

She touches his leg, near his crotch, and presses firmly. He squeezes her hand and moves it to the seat. He looks at her. "Chloe, you don't have the same margin of error that I do. Do you get that?"

She slides toward him, waiting for an objection. This is difficult. He wants to be done with her. She swings a leg over his, straddling his thigh. "I need someone to tell me things like this," she whispers.

"Easy," he says. He gestures to the driver. "This guy's going to give me a bad rating."

She pouts. "We did it in the other car," she says.

"That's because we used your account," he says.

The driver speaks up in a gravelly voice. "Don't mind me. I've seen everything."

Chloe lifts her shirt, exposing her apple-size breasts. He reaches for them reflexively. They move onto an exit ramp. He pulls her shirt down as they stop at a red light. Pedestrians cross ahead of them. A twentysomething skateboarder. A mom in yoga pants pushing a stroller.

"Do you promise not to give Doug a bad rating?" she asks.

"Cross my heart, darling," says the driver.

Chloe lowers herself to the floor. "But maybe you're right," she says. She brings her mouth close to his crotch. "Maybe we shouldn't."

She thinks she's fucking with him. That's what she thinks. He grabs the back of her neck with his right hand and unzips his fly with his left. The driver meets his eye again in the rearview mirror. They stop at another red light. There's a line of people on the sidewalk, waiting to get into an onigiri stand, and Doug is overwhelmed by the stench of mildewed floor mats and linen-scented air freshener.

Chloe looks up at him. "You okay?"

He redoes his pants and addresses the driver. "You can let us out on the next block."

"Okay, Chief," says the driver.

They're a half mile from the office, farther than where they usually separate. They make a game of it normally, looking around for familiar faces before Chloe gets out of his car. "Do you see anyone? Do you see anyone?" they say like cat burglars on an adventure.

This time, they don't look. They don't scan the cluster of customers outside the bibimbap place. The driver says, "Thanks for the show," as Chloe opens her door.

He hears her say, "Hi!" before his foot hits the curb. On the sidewalk are Angela, his dragon-nailed accounting lady, and Ellen from HR with the frizzy hair. He, Chloe, and the two women freeze.

Doug nods. "How are you, ladies?"

"Good!" they say in unison.

"Glad to hear it." He gives them a salute and heads to the corner. Chloe follows, and he can hear the silent shock of his employees behind him, yawning and gaping into a giant *OMG!*

He presses the walk button. Chloe stands close. "God dammit," he says. He slams the signal with the base of his palm.

CHAPTER TWENTY-ONE

CHLOE

How does gossip travel? In whispers? In bathrooms? Text message chains? Do dirty details float invisibly through the air and wiggle their way into the ears of every person but Chloe? For the next two days, she hears nothing from anyone directly. Her affair with Doug is announced in some backstage area where Chloe has no access. One by one, her coworkers emerge from behind its curtain with a subtle change in demeanor.

Maurice, the innovation strategist with the shaved head, has always been one of her regulars, stopping by once or twice a day for a chat. Now the most he'll offer is a grim smile. Jeremiah, the bearded IT manager, is different. He's begun loitering near her desk, leaning on the counter above with a voice heavy in leer and innuendo.

Elise, the sweepy-haired vice president who usually ignores Chloe, stops at the mailboxes next to her desk in the afternoon. She glances at Chloe and seems like she wants to say something. She doesn't, though. She fiddles with the stacks of bills and junk mail.

"Hi," Chloe says in a hopeful whisper.

Elise sighs and gives Chloe a low, "How's it going?" She doesn't wait for Chloe to answer. She just walks away.

Chloe stares after her, marveling at the fact that Elise paid her any attention at all. The mood of the entire office has shifted. *It's so weird,* Chloe thinks. *It's all because of me.*

She texts Doug:

I think everyone knows.

He doesn't respond. She texts him again a half hour later:

????

Take it easy.

People are acting weird.

Don't be ridiculous.

Teddy from the mail room comes by to pick up the outgoing envelopes. "Thanks," says Chloe. He doesn't respond.

Doug texts:

I have a job for your group. This Friday.

What is it?

Party in Bel Air. Dr. Maryn's house.

Chloe texts the other members of Common Parlance. They can make themselves available but want to discuss it first. Jo-Ann appears around the hallway with Brooke, the marketing manager. Brooke's lipstick is deep purple.

"Hello, Miss Chloe," says Jo-Ann. "Brooke is going to need the conference room at nine tomorrow."

Brooke gives Chloe a tiny gasp and a wide-eyed stare. "Your skin is glowing," she says.

Chloe touches her face. "Mine?"

"What kind of moisturizer do you use?"

"Oatmeal, I think. It's from Rite Aid."

"See?" says Brooke. She turns to Jo-Ann with raised hands. "Chloe is just one of those girls. She doesn't need makeup. She doesn't even need good moisturizer."

Chloe hesitates. There's nothing in Brooke's face to suggest she's making fun of Chloe. But still.

Jo-Ann purses her lips. "Are you going to mark Brooke down for the conference room?"

"Oh, right." Chloe pulls up the reservation system on her desktop. "Jo-Ann?"

"Yes?"

"I have to leave at four. I have a meeting."

Jo-Ann shrugs her shoulders. "Whatever you need, Miss Chloe."

This is the fourth time today Jo-Ann has called her Miss Chloe. It feels like Jo-Ann is mocking her too. Which isn't fair. Not at all. Jo-Ann, Brooke: all these people are acting like they have a say in Chloe's relationship with Doug. But they know nothing. Nothing! They've never seen the pleading frenzy in his eyes in the second before he comes. They have no idea how his body jerks as he falls asleep and how, when he wakes in the middle of the night, he squeezes her and says, "I need you." These women have never loved Doug.

Oh God. That's what it is.

Chloe loves him. She loves him so much. It's a pure thing, completely divorced from all these judgmental people. It's potent and at the same time so fragile it's like a living piece of herself cradled in the palm of her hand. She texts him:

I have to talk to you.

He shows up from around the corner, instantaneously. He nods at her. He feels it too. There's no way this thing can be one sided.

"Gearing up for Friday?" he asks.

"Friday?"

"The party."

"Oh yeah! We're meeting this afternoon about it."

Doug calls to Jo-Ann, who has started back to her office. "Did you hear? Chloe's group is performing at Dr. Maryn's party."

Jo-Ann pauses before turning around. "Really? Chloe, why didn't you tell me?"

"It wasn't a sure thing until yesterday," Doug says. "The synchronized swimmers they'd booked ended up canceling."

Chloe's whole body turns warm. She doesn't even try to hide her smile. Doug is a genius. This explains why they were in the same Uber. He's working everyone. And he's asking her to join him in tricking the rubes.

Chloe says, "We went—"

"We saw the meeting planner the other day," says Doug. "What do you guys say in entertainment? Good in a room? Chloe's good in a room."

———

Chloe meets the other members of Common Parlance at a brew pub on the way to Culver City. Sheralyn is at the bar already, waiting for the bartender to notice her. She's added Day-Glo-orange streaks to her hair.

"I like your hair," Chloe says as she sidles up next to her.

Sheralyn raises her eyebrows. "I've had it this way for a week."

The bartender finishes loading a tray of shots for the waitress. He points to Chloe. "What'll you have?"

Sheralyn lets out a grunty laugh.

"I think she was first," says Chloe.

"Oh no." Sheralyn bows to Chloe and unfurls her hand like a court jester. "After you."

Chloe orders a glass of pinot grigio. Sheralyn raises her chin high as she asks for a beer. *It must be hard,* Chloe thinks, *not being pretty.*

Her phone chimes. A text from Doug.

Prepare something for this one.

Don't wait to feel the vibe. Maybe write some jokes?

Chloe and Sheralyn join Dylan and Howie at a high top. The table is sticky. Chloe runs her dry cocktail napkin over the surface, leaving tiny shreds of paper behind. She tells her castmates about the offer.

Sheralyn starts off. "So, what? You want us to be the entertainment at a rich-people party?"

Chloe gives a vigorous nod. "Basically."

"I was a Power Ranger at a birthday in Beverly Hills a few years ago," says Dylan. "It was humiliating. The kids kept roundhouse kicking my shins. The parents just laughed."

"No one is going to kick you," says Howie.

"Have you seen *The Dr. Maryn Show*?" says Sheralyn. "It's degrading."

Chloe bites her bottom lip in an effort to suppress her first few stirrings of desperation. She'd been so taken with the brilliance of Doug's plan to have them perform. And his explanation of why they were in an Uber together. She forgot that her castmates were an ornery group.

"This could be amazing exposure," says Howie.

"Watch, they'll make us use the servants' entrance," Sheralyn says.

Chloe touches Sheralyn's arm. "No offense, Sheralyn, but you're way too class conscious. LA is actually pretty equal."

Sheralyn points her forehead at Chloe, like she's peering over the top of reading glasses. "Just because rich middle-aged men flirt with you doesn't mean LA is *egalitarian*."

"What is that supposed to mean?"

"Meow!" says Dylan.

"It's not meow," says Chloe. "I didn't start anything."

Howie paws at Sheralyn's shoulder. "Is it meow?" he asks.

"Screw off." Sheralyn slaps the table. "Anyway, what's up with Doug? Is he our manager now?"

"Seriously, Sheralyn," says Dylan. "Chill."

Sheralyn throws up her hands and crosses to the bar. Chloe stares down at her fingers, at the patch of rough skin on the side of her thumb. She scrapes at it. They *have to* agree to the party. Doug's already told everyone at the office.

She searches her mind for arguments, for a plan, for some way to make things happen for herself. She looks over at Sheralyn, waiting again for the bartender, and bites off the last bit of scab on her thumb. It hurts. She's bleeding. She blots the cut with her napkin. Howie gives her hand a troubled glance. Dylan drains the last of his beer.

"I think the issue is, how do we all see the group?" says Dylan. "There's a risk of self-parody if we start doing these kinds of events. Like we're holding up a mirror to society, right? And if we do this, show the elite what we really think of them, there's a danger that they'll lap it up and not get it."

"You're overthinking it," says Howie. "This is an opportunity. We take it."

Sheralyn calls out, "Should I get a pitcher?"

Chloe picks up her almost empty wineglass. She approaches the bar with urgency. Her roommate straightens and hardens as Chloe nears.

There's always been something resolute in Sheralyn, like she's never been afraid to stick up for herself.

"Are you mad at me?" Chloe asks.

"Nope." Sheralyn signs her credit card slip and doesn't look at Chloe. She lifts the pitcher.

"Are you sure?"

Sheralyn stops. "But I'd love it if you stopped having sex in the living room."

Chloe nods. Sheralyn brings the pitcher to the table. Chloe watches Dylan pour a round. Doug said Sheralyn wouldn't be able to hear when they did it in the living room. She knew it wasn't true, but she believed him. It always feels right to go along with what he wants. But Doug isn't here right now. Chloe moves to the table and stands close to Dylan.

"Is this a paid gig?" asks Howie.

Chloe brightens. "Oh yeah! Ten thousand dollars."

Sheralyn shakes her head.

"That's a lot of money," says Dylan.

Sheralyn looks away. "Fine."

"Um," says Chloe. They turn to her. She's embarrassed to say it. "Doug asked that we plan the performance a little?"

Dylan and Sheralyn stare at her.

"I don't have a problem with that," says Howie.

"We're not planning anything," says Sheralyn.

CHAPTER TWENTY-TWO

CHLOE

It's early evening when Chloe caravans with the other members of Common Parlance up Dr. Maryn's long driveway lined with cypress trees. Chloe blasts her air-conditioning even though the temperature is dropping. She can't believe she has AC. Doug had the mechanic personally deliver the car to her apartment.

Dr. Maryn's mansion comes into view. It's a blocky Tuscan with a fountain and front courtyard fenced in wrought iron. They drop their cars at the valet. Dr. Maryn's husband, Stan, told them to dress in "stage blacks," and now they look like a pack of wedding photographers as they approach the front door. Chloe glances down at Dylan's tuxedo pants. His satin stripes are coming loose. She touches the sheer sleeves of the top Doug bought her. The fabric is light and airy.

A maid in uniform gestures them inside. The foyer is round, three stories high with a life-size mosaic of a koi pond tiled on the floor. Chloe steps onto one of the trompe l'oeil lily pads.

"If you don't mind removing your shoes?" says the maid. She leads them to a vaulted closet under the grand staircase and points to a tidy stack of satin drawstring bags. "You can put them in these." She produces an electronic label maker from her apron. "Can I have your names, please?"

Chloe glances around for smirks among her group, ready to hiss *stop it* at the first snarky comment. Dr. Maryn sweeps into the foyer with her famous spiky red pixie cut. Her husband, Stan, trails after. He peels an orange and fills the room with the scent of citrus. Dr. Maryn looks each member of the group up and down, before landing on the baby-blue remnants of Chloe's last pedicure.

"Where are your bathing suits?" Dr. Maryn asks.

"No, hon," says Stan. "The swimmers couldn't do it. This is the improv troupe."

Dr. Maryn's face freezes. "You hired an improv group?"

Stan pops a section of orange into his mouth. "Which one of you is Chloe?"

"Here," says Chloe. She raises her hand and waves. A delighted smile breaks over Stan's face. Chloe crinkles her eyes in response. Dr. Maryn stares down at Chloe's feet again.

Dylan steps forward. "We're not really improv," he says.

Dr. Maryn tilts her head to the side. "Then what are you?" Her manner is more severe than what Chloe remembers from the few times she's watched the woman's show.

"It's more of an open-ended approach," says Dylan.

"Doug set it up," says Stan.

"Ah yes." Dr. Maryn spits her words out in a singsong. "Where would we be without Doug?" She points to Chloe. "Darling, what's your name again?"

"Chloe."

"Chloe, I'm going to need you to cover up those feet. Teresa?" The maid steps forward. "Please find a pair of socks for this young lady." She gestures to the rest of them. "You can start outside."

The members of Common Parlance don their masks, a mix of blank white and ornate Venice Carnival disguises. Dr. Maryn gives them a distracted frown and says, "Oh, mimes," as they venture in their bare feet to the front courtyard. Her manner softens and turns convivial as the first guests arrive. She and Stan trade air-kisses with the newcomers and usher them around a lit pathway to the backyard.

Howie stands near the valet in a smooth gold mask that covers his entire face. His posture is erect and overcorrected. Chloe, Dylan, and Sheralyn form a receiving line next to him, standing up straight and formal, like they're all servants in a nineteenth-century manor house. They offer exaggerated greetings to the new arrivals.

Dr. Maryn returns and stops at the sight of Dylan holding both hands of a confused-looking woman in a lace cocktail dress. She waves the group over with a wide, animated face, like she's about to let them in on a secret. "I need you all to be less interactive, okay?"

"Sure," says Howie. "Whatever you want."

"Not everyone likes to be touched. Why don't you pretend to be waiters for a bit? You can carry some trays." She motions for everyone to follow her along the stepping-stone path to the backyard.

"This is some bullshit right here," Sheralyn mutters.

Moisture from the grass seeps into Chloe's sock. She stops and lets the rest of the group continue. Everyone else at the party gets to keep their shoes on. It doesn't make sense for them to be barefoot or in socks. She looks back down the path. Stan is near the driveway, leaning over a young woman about Chloe's age. He feels like a friend. Maybe she can ask him for their shoes back. She returns to the portico and waits for Stan to break off his conversation and notice her. He doesn't. She moves to the front door of the house and opens it. The foyer is empty and quiet except for the muffled sounds of jazz piano drifting in from the outside. She tries the closet, thinking she can quietly pass out everyone's shoes, but the door is locked. Chloe peels off her wet socks and lays them next to the doorjamb.

A bearded man and a brunette poke their heads in. They're dressed almost identically in thin leather jackets and dark ripped jeans. "Are we in the right place?" asks the woman.

Chloe checks to see if her mask is straight, and she doesn't know why, but she gets the urge to speak in a robot voice. She goes with it. "Please take your shoes off. The tile is new."

"Right on," says the guy. They keep their shoes on and walk through the house to the party.

Chloe stays in the foyer, watching stray newcomers navigate their awkward moment of first entry: a stop, a flicker of confusion at the sight of this masked woman in front of them. Many look vaguely familiar, like former character actors or low-rent versions of Steve Jobs.

A lanky man enters, leading with his limbs, and Chloe is suspended in time. She knows him, his shaggy brown hair, his stooping height. Chloe presses herself into the foyer wall. This man's name is Alonso. He's a choreographer. And he fired her two years ago from the Fefu Fornes shoot. He stops. He notices her.

"Hi." She barely gets the word out. Does he recognize her? She should have moved from LA right after that. She should just leave now, skip town, get out.

"How are you?" he asks as he passes.

She hears Doug. He's outside. His baritone ricochets through her body. Doug is an ally. She pushes herself from the wall and shakes out her hair. She hasn't been alone with him since that Uber ride. There's so much she needs to tell him. She wants him to know how hard she worked to convince the other members to do this gig. She wants to warn him that Dr. Maryn reacted all weird and bitter when Stan mentioned Doug's name earlier. She wants to lie with him and not talk at all, just listen to him breathe.

Doug strides into the foyer. Even something as simple as entering a room, he stands out. Chloe notices someone else, though, at his side. A petite woman with streaks of honey-blonde highlights. Chloe knew about this. She knew his wife would be here tonight. It's the first time she's seen Emily since the woman insulted her purse. Chloe was even planning to make a joke about purses, to lighten things up, but Emily doesn't look right. There's something different about her body, about her stomach. Her shirt stretches like a sling around some low-hanging roundness.

Chloe's palms grow hot and twitchy. It always starts in her hands, the shame.

There've been hints. Words like *eating for two* and *ultrasound* have occasionally floated from the direction of Doug's office, from Harper before she left. These words, though, they lingered only a moment in some ethereal, troubling form before dissolving back to nothingness.

"What's this?" asks Emily, motioning to Chloe's mask.

"What's this?" Chloe asks back and points to Emily's belly.

Doug puts his arm around his wife's shoulders and points her in the direction of the door. "I think the party's out back," he says.

"When are you due?" The question bursts from Chloe. She's shouting. "When are you due?"

Emily turns and lifts her chin. Her face looks haughty and confused, like she's unaccustomed to being asked a direct question. "Excuse me?"

"Are you pregnant?"

"Okay, let's get going," says Doug. He grips his wife by the hips and tries pulling. She doesn't move. She peers hard at Chloe, like she's trying to see under her mask.

"I know you," she says.

"Of course," says Doug. "This is Chloe, my receptionist. I think she's supposed to stay in character."

Emily looks at Chloe's top, the beautiful black suede blouse with the three-quarter chiffon sleeves. Chloe can feel Emily expand, like she's outraged and it's making her grow in size. Emily looks from Chloe to

Doug, from Doug back to Chloe. She points at Chloe's shirt. "That's Prada, isn't it?"

Doug gives an awkward chuckle. They're all silent until Dr. Maryn appears in the doorway. She grimaces at the sight of Chloe and claps twice. "Performers in the backyard, please. What are those socks doing there?" She notices Doug's wife and changes her tone back to gregarious. "Emily!"

"Maryn!" says Doug's wife. The two women hug. Dr. Maryn touches her belly.

"Oh boy, you're getting there!"

Chloe can't move. If she moves, she might dislodge whatever is holding back the churn and froth of her humiliation. *You knew he was married,* she says to herself. *You knew he was married.*

Dr. Maryn turns to Chloe with a combination of glare and smile and speaks in elongated vowels. "Pick up those socks please, thank you."

Chloe glances to Doug for support. He pulls out his phone with a sudden industriousness. "Hold on; I have to deal with this," he says and walks out the door. Chloe is now alone with the two older women. Dr. Maryn crosses her arms and edges closer to Doug's wife. Chloe feels their eyes on her as she makes her way to the socks, as she bends to pick them up.

"Here," says Emily, coming toward her. "Let me help you with that."

It's a trick. It has to be.

"I got it," Chloe says.

She shoves past them to the outside. Doug is far away, on the other side of the driveway. She starts toward the backyard. The socks are in her hand. She tucks them under a rosemary bush, delighting at the thought of Dr. Maryn discovering them later. But then she realizes it'll be the poor gardener, not that awful woman, who sees them. She scoops up the socks and tosses them high into an avocado tree. One lands on a branch. The other drops to the ground. She balls it up and throws it at a window.

"What are you doing?"

It's Doug. He's come up behind her. Chloe raises her arms and lets an old sense of mischief overtake her. "Unbound," she says. "I am unbound."

Doug moves in close and speaks in a murmur. "I'm sorry," he says. "I didn't think about how hard this would be for you."

"You knew he was married," she says in the same robot voice she used earlier.

"What?"

"You knew he was married."

"Are you performing right now?"

Her life always comes back to this, this playing on a knife edge of terrible impulses. It used to scare her when she was a kid, the urge to grab the marker from the teacher and scribble profanities all over the dry-erase board. There was nothing stopping her, really, just another part of her same self: a flimsy force field forever threatening to give way.

You knew he was married. Chloe stands on her tiptoes. *You knew he was married.*

She steps up to Doug like she's about to kiss him. She moves her mouth to his shoulder. She bites down. Hard. Doug hesitates at first. She feels him take a millisecond to understand what's happening before his hands are on her throat, her chest. He shoves her. She lands on the ground. A thread of fabric is stuck in her teeth.

"What the fuck!" He looks behind him to see if anyone is in view. "What the fuck!" He lifts his collar and moves his hand under his shirt. "I'm bleeding!" Chloe stays where she's fallen. "What the fuck is wrong with you?" He holds his shoulder as he steps over her.

Chloe waits on the path. She doesn't think of counting. She doesn't think of breathing deeply. She hears laughter ahead of her. There's a party happening. She moves toward it.

The backyard is magic. There are so many lights, in all different styles, strung up between the trees: paper lanterns, stained glass, bent copper, and crystal chandeliers. They hover above like a thousand Tinkerbells, waiting for their cue. Waiting to spring to life.

Chloe walks deeper into the party. Emily is to her left. She is standing near a firepit with several people, including Alonso, the choreographer. Chloe turns her back to them. They're talking about her. They must be. Chloe's life is over.

She keeps walking. On her right, behind the bar, is Dylan, in a plague mask. He cuts up lemon slices. Sheralyn stands near an empty section of lounge chairs, in a spangled butterfly mask. She poses in a series of Hollywood affectations—fish lips, shoulder popped forward. Sheralyn then brings her hands to her head and hip like a pinup from the 1950s.

Chloe turns from Sheralyn. She watches the partygoers. It's grotesque, the scene around her. The people here are sharp, so sharp. They'll cut you with their sharpness for the crime of stumbling into their territory.

She notices a famous actress dead ahead, next to the pool, in an off-the-shoulder shirt and skintight, patterned pants. The woman is surrounded, protected by a semicircle of revelers. And she exudes no vanity, no self-regard. That's what Sheralyn's act is getting wrong. The celebrity in front of her is all about power.

Chloe heads toward them. The members of the star's entourage give Chloe the once-over and look to the actress, to see if they should let her come close. The movie star lifts her face to Chloe with a polite smile and says, "Hello."

Chloe doesn't respond. Instead, she kneels. She sinks down to the woman's feet and starts bowing in a cartoon version of prayerful devotion. This. This is what's really going on. Chloe's showing them all what they look like. And she forgets about biting Doug, forgets about his wife being pregnant, forgets about Alonso. Chloe focuses only on her play worship of this idol in front of her. She toys with the irony of it, letting in just enough emotion to make her supplication feel dangerous. Nonsense words come chanting out of her in a torrent of euphoria. This truth, this expression of it, it's the only thing she's ever wanted.

The movie star lets out a bark of a laugh. "I get it," she says in a dry tone. "Very funny."

There's a splash in the pool behind the actress. The guests lift their heads in unison, like a herd of worried gazelle. Howie has stripped to his boxers and is shouting from the deep end, "Common Parlance proudly presents: synchronized swimming!" He raises both arms above his head in ballerina fifth position and sinks down.

"Who is that?" the movie star asks her companions.

A woman in a sequined Nehru collar motions to Chloe. "He's with her." The actress straightens her shoulders and sighs. Everyone goes quiet. Howie thrusts his legs above the water and points his toes before slapping them into a dolphin kick.

"Maryn?" the actress calls across the yard. She darts her eyes in Chloe's direction.

Dr. Maryn speeds over and guides Chloe to her feet with a sweep of her arm. "Come with me, dear. Actually, let's get all of you together. Would you mind gathering your friends at the front?"

Chloe looks to the lounge chairs. Sheralyn is sprawled across a glass table, pretending to be passed out. Dylan is deep in conversation with a guy in a hoodie. Chloe tells Howie to get out of the pool.

"Why?" he asks.

"They're kicking us out," she says.

———

Teresa, the maid, is waiting at the top of the driveway with their shoes. Chloe slips on her sandals and watches the valet guys sprinting up and down the street. She wishes she could trade places with them.

"I told you it would be a disaster," says Sheralyn.

A valet pulls up with Dylan's Honda. Dylan starts toward it but then stops. He scratches his beard. "Tonight was a message," he says. "It's working. We're doing something right."

A round of laughter reaches them from the party, the place where they're no longer welcome. Nothing is "working." The people in there aren't thinking about them at all.

She hears a scream, a howl, from right next to her. It's Howie. "Thirty-five!" he yells. He raises an arm and slaps the roof of Dylan's car. "I'm thirty-five! And I have nothing!"

The valet guys stop moving. Scattered partygoers stare. A valet pulls up with Howie's car and parks behind Dylan's.

"I can't do this anymore," Howie says.

Dylan rushes to his side. "Get a drink with us. Let's talk it out."

"Not now." Howie hustles to his car and speeds away, fast and reckless.

Chloe texts Doug:

We got kicked out.

She's almost forgotten that she bit him. Her insides jumble and twist. She's never seen him mad like that before. It feels like their first fight. It feels like a milestone. She texts him again.

Sorry about earlier.

The parking guy brings her car.

"Will you come for a drink?" Dylan asks her.

"I can't," says Chloe. She looks back at Sheralyn, who jerks her face away.

Dylan follows her to her car door and puts his arm in front of the opening. He looks pained. There was a time when she thought Dylan was the way forward, that art was the way forward. The first time they met, he was performing at Echo Park Lake, not long after she'd been fired from Fefu Fornes. He and Sheralyn were in their masks, picnicking on a checkered blanket. Chloe watched them for a half hour as they ate and chatted and lay back and counted the clouds. It was like they were pantomiming relaxation while simultaneously relaxing. She sat down with them, thinking, *This is real life.* They offered her a deviled egg.

Dylan leans in close. She can feel his breath on her cheek. "Come," he says in a creaky whisper. "We need you."

Chloe shakes her head. "I don't know what I'm supposed to want anymore." She slips into her car and thinks briefly, with a hit of longing, of Dr. Maryn's husband, Stan. He gave her that kind look in the foyer. She checks her phone. Doug hasn't texted back.

CHAPTER
TWENTY-THREE

DOUG

Doug runs ahead of Emily into the house when they get home from Dr. Maryn's party. He hurries to the master bath and examines his shoulder in the mirror.

Emily knocks on the door. "Doug?"

"Be out in a second." He runs his finger along the top arch of tiny bruises. The teeth marks are unmistakable.

"Why won't you let me see it?"

He told her he walked into a tree branch. "Where are the Band-Aids?"

"Look in the second drawer. My side." She tries the door handle. "You locked it?"

He covers the bite with three slim bandages. Emily sits up in bed as he slips from the bathroom and grabs a white T-shirt from his top drawer. Her boobs are bigger now. They rise up out the top of her maternity negligee. He crawls next to her, kisses her cleavage, and waits for her to start an argument.

He screwed up. Chloe's group was a fiasco.

"You're so great at parties," he says. "I love that I never have to worry about you socially."

Emily's top lip curls. She sips from the water glass on her night-stand. "Do you mind sleeping in the guest room?"

He puts a hand on her thigh. It's incredible how tight her quads are. If it weren't for her stomach, you'd never know she was pregnant. "Of course I'd mind," he says. She moves her leg from his grasp. She has a right to be mad. Jesus, he's been wasting his time on Chloe: a girl with zero discipline. She doesn't know how to behave. He reaches his arm around Emily's waist. "You're too big!" he says. "I can't reach the other side!"

Emily sighs. "I want to sleep," she says. "I want to be alone. Who is going into the guest room, you or me?"

If he hadn't been assaulted earlier. If he hadn't been unnerved by the way Chloe snarled, she actually snarled, before sinking her teeth in his shoulder, he'd be cajoling his wife into a good mood right now. He'd be under the covers with her, and they'd be talking shit about everyone from the party. Their usual routine.

"I'm sorry, Em."

"Okay."

He hugs a pillow to his chest and starts out of the room. He stops at the top of the stairs. Emily warned him about Chloe months ago, when he introduced them. Oh Jesus. He needs his wife. She's the one who makes them work. He trots back to the bedroom. She moves quickly, hiding her phone under the covers.

"I need you on my team, babe. Are we a team?"

"Whatever, I'm just not feeling well."

The guest room is musty. Lonely. Cold. The bed looks like it hasn't been touched in years. Doug plugs his phone charger into the open outlet and blows on the thin layer of dust covering the dresser. His phone chimes. And chimes again. He mutes the volume as a third text from Chloe comes in:

Please tell me you're okay.

Please don't be mad at me.

I have anger issues, but I'm dealing with them!

He rubs his eyes with his thumb and forefinger. Suggesting Chloe's group seemed like a perfect solution after they were spotted in the Uber. It all fell into place, with Stan asking him for help finding new entertainment. Doug has always been a sucker for serendipity.

But Chloe is an embarrassment. The whole lot of them. How could they *not* do a terrible job? They're . . . he hates even to think the word because he believes that anyone can improve, that no one is hopeless.

But Chloe and her friends are losers.

He swipes his phone to the home screen. Another text from her.

I'm really stressed out.

Of course she is. She can't manage her life. People like that are in constant misery. Still, he has an impulse to text her back. To tell her not to worry.

But no, he thinks. *No.*

You can't go off half-cocked and start feeling sorry for everyone. You'll get annihilated. Empathy is a tool, not a personality trait.

PART FOUR
EMILY, DOUG,
AND CHLOE

CHAPTER

TWENTY-FOUR

EMILY

Yes, I saw the bite. Of course I did. Doug would never have been able to keep something like that from me. By that point, at eight months pregnant, I was in a state of constant vigilance.

My belly had taken over, making it so I couldn't run, couldn't walk up the steps to my bedroom without losing my breath. The baby was merciless, kicking me over and over, stomping, poking, swiping its tiny extremities across my bladder. "Enough!" I'd sometimes explode in a harsh whisper, clamping my hands over my stomach.

I hated being a woman, sentenced to these months of lumbering, viscous indignity. And I resented my husband. I'd lie in bed in the mornings and watch him pull on his gym shorts, seething at the sight of his unburdened physique, the ease with which he could simply escape if he wanted. I hadn't understood, until then, what it meant to be vulnerable, and I found myself dwelling in fear, imagining my plodding waddle from a house fire or active shooter. For the first time ever, I wanted protection.

If we'd had a normal relationship, a loving one, I'd have shared these thoughts with Doug. But I couldn't bring myself to be open with him, knowing he'd use my vulnerability to his advantage. It didn't matter that I said nothing. The more pregnant I got, the more dependent I became. And then he simply intuited how trapped I felt, how unlikely I was to leave. His behavior turned reckless, spending nights away with the flimsiest excuses. He'd even brought a woman into our bed. I could smell her on my pillow.

She'd used my razor.

That was when my reflux started, at my discovery of another woman's body hair clogging my Oui Shave single blade. I gulped back the acid scalding my throat as I sat at the edge of the tub, scraping out the hair. It was still wet. I saved the bits in a Ziploc bag.

At that point, the logistics of a breakup—the packing and moving boxes and potential nastiness—the idea of these was paralyzing. I was about to have a baby. I couldn't just leave him. Divorce required careful planning.

I started by turning on location tracking for his phone. He spent a lot of time at an apartment building in Van Nuys. I began documenting everything, saving screenshots of his locations, making notes in a Word file when he didn't come home.

The morning after Dr. Maryn's party, when Doug went for a jog, I took the towels out of the bathroom, betting he'd take the Band-Aids off his shoulder when he showered. I didn't know what was underneath them. All that mattered was that he didn't want me to see it.

"Em!" he yelled from the bathroom. "Where are the towels!"

I brought in a fresh one and stopped when I saw the bruise. I hadn't expected it to be so incriminating, so mouth shaped. He lifted his hands to the sides by way of apology.

"I'm an idiot," he said.

I didn't respond. I left the bathroom and sent myself an email describing it. I wrote, *Bite probably from receptionist, Chloe. She is unstable.*

———

It had to have been Chloe. I knew her story now. Her shirt gave her away. There was no way she could have afforded this season's Prada.

I'd watched her in Dr. Maryn's foyer as she'd bent to pick up a pair of socks. Her hair fell forward. All I needed was one strand of that hair, just enough to test her DNA against the gunk from my razor. I moved to help her. Plucking it would be quick, a little strange of me, but I didn't care. She'd say *Ouch!* and I'd make up something about wayward grays.

She skittered around me, though, out the door, before I could get close. I looked at Dr. Maryn, and we laughed.

"Maryn, you have to let me help you with the entertainment," I said.

She held up her hand. "That's Stan's department," she said. "I have to keep him busy."

She walked me through the house to her backyard, which overlooked Los Angeles. Her new decorator had done well, mirroring the expanse of city lights below with row upon row of hanging lanterns. I stood for a moment, taking in the various social groupings. The most famous person there that night, an actress client of mine starting her own lifestyle brand, was safely surrounded by my colleagues. I spotted a guy, behind the bar, in a mask just like Chloe's. I approached him and asked for a cranberry and soda.

"I'm not really the bartender," he said.

I nodded and waited. I pulled a swizzle stick from its dispenser and pointed it at him. "That girl, Chloe," I said. "She's your friend?" I thought back, almost with a tinge of nostalgia, to when I'd met her, that tender, deluded afternoon when I'd actually thought Doug had stopped cheating on me.

The masked guy didn't answer but started making my drink. I raised my voice, just a touch, and asked, "Does Chloe live in Van Nuys?"

Stan was nearby. He perked up and rushed over like a good host, heading off uncomfortable scenes. He said he wanted me to meet some people and led me to a group near the firepit that included Alonso, a theatrical-looking choreographer. We stood together for a while, making small talk about my due date and gawking at the train wreck of Chloe's performance group. I made a joke about being married to the moron who'd suggested them.

"This is LA," I said. "I could stick my finger in the air and find better talent."

"And that one is twisted," said Alonso, pointing at Chloe. I startled as she bowed low in front of my actress client. Any other time, I'd have been on top of Chloe, grabbing her by the arm and escorting her away from the celebrities. But Alonso had information.

"Really?" I kept my tone nonchalant, not letting on that I knew Chloe. He would clam up if he sensed a desire for anything but idle gossip.

"She worked for me," he said.

"What happened?"

"Oh, she was always late, and she got a third warning from the stage manager. Now, the stage manager was snarky, but then it was like, bam!" He made a cymbal-smash motion with his hands. "Chloe slapped her across the face. No one did anything at first. We were all in shock. But then Chloe just dove at her. It took five of us to calm her down."

I kept my expression casual, fascinated, while something like a low-pressure system blew through my body. The people around me, the architecture of my world, froze in place as Chloe, on the other side of the yard, kept bending and scraping.

My peers and I could do anything to one another—steal clients, destroy reputations—as long as our behavior fell within the genteel confines of passive aggression. We had to remain cool. We weren't allowed to hit each other.

I glanced around for Doug but didn't see him. I wanted to hiss in his ear, *You brought a lunatic into our lives!* He found me soon after. His body relaxed in relief as he spotted me and navigated across the crowd to the firepit. He moved behind me as Chloe and her group passed us on their way out. He rubbed his shoulder. Something had happened. I'd never seen him shaken before.

"This is a major fuckup," I said.

He nodded. "I'm sorry. I've seen them perform. Normally they're really good."

"I have to find Dr. Maryn and apologize."

"Do you want me to come?" He touched his shoulder again.

I had an edge over him for just a moment, an opportunity to extract a favor. "I want you to cool your friendship with Stan," I said. "I can tell Maryn isn't happy about it."

He nodded.

I left him and walked down the side path, to the edge of the front courtyard. I backed up against the rosemary bushes and watched as Chloe exchanged intimate words with the performer who'd made my drink. She got into her car, a wonderfully tragic sedan with fading paint and a missing front hubcap.

I had no real plan then. I just knew that she lived in Van Nuys, couldn't afford a presentable car, and had a propensity for attacking people. I had no experience with violence. I tried to imagine what it would feel like to shove someone or shoot them, but I couldn't get past the embarrassment, the tackiness of it. As she pulled away, I remembered how nervous she'd been in my office and how eager she'd seemed after I'd started showing interest in the conversation.

Chloe didn't have to be a threat. She could be a weapon.

CHAPTER TWENTY-FIVE

CHLOE

The digital clock on Chloe's bedroom floor reads 6:57 a.m. She's had three and a half, maybe four hours of sleep. Her head is thrumming, and she closes her eyes, hoping to get back to the dream she was having. She usually doesn't remember her dreams, only the recurring one with the old lady screaming. But just now, before she woke up, Doug was in front of her. He picked up a pair of socks for her and told his wife and Dr. Maryn to stop being so mean.

She opens her eyes. She pulls her covers back and reaches for her phone on the floor. The battery is dead. Her empty screen reflects her image back at her, scolding her. Of course she isn't allowed to see whether Doug texted. She left her one and only charger in the car.

She wanders into the kitchen. Sheralyn's phone is plugged in on the counter. Chloe switches it out for her own phone just as her roommate's bedroom door swings open. Sheralyn appears in a long tank top and boy-short briefs. The tops of her arms are red and pimply.

"That was so messed up last night," Sheralyn says. She looks down at her unplugged phone.

"Your battery was almost full," says Chloe. "I hope you don't mind."

Sheralyn shakes her head and moves past Chloe to the coffee maker. She opens an airtight bin and spoons fresh coffee grounds into the basket. An apple appears in the center of Chloe's screen.

"We're almost out of coffee," says Sheralyn.

"I'll get some," says Chloe.

"Yeah, right."

Sheralyn presses the brew button on the coffee maker and disappears into her room. Chloe's screen goes black. *Come on, come on,* she thinks as the icons load onto her home screen. She starts as she sees a red bubble indicating a new text. She opens the messenger app. The text is from Dylan:

Let's take time to decompress. Meet in two weeks?

She closes out Dylan's text and opens her conversation with Doug. At 10:15 last night, she texted:

I have anger issues, but I'm dealing with them!

At 10:43, she texted:

Hey!

At 10:45:

Can you call me?

At 10:55:

Sorry for the lash out. R U okay?

At 10:58:

Sometimes I don't know my own strength lol.

At 10:58:

Sorry about performance too.

At 11:43:

Seriously, please let me know u r okay.

At 1:30:

I get that u r mad but please let me know things are alright.

Please, oh please, she thinks. She pets the phone like it's a living thing. All she needs is a tiny answer from him. Just a word.

Chloe hears Sheralyn's shower. The coffee carafe is filled halfway. She pours herself a cup and steals a splash of Sheralyn's milk from the refrigerator. She opens the cabinet. Sheralyn has labeled her sugar carton with a giant Sharpied *S!!!!* Chloe opens the spout and pours a spoonful into her coffee. She heads back into her bed and pulls the covers up to her chin.

This feeling, it's disturbing. It won't stop, the sense that she's owed an answer. She wants it clear, in words, what last night's consequences are, what Doug is thinking. She wants to be able to argue back. She picks up her laptop off the floor.

She googles *bite*.

Then *bite person*.

bite boss
bite boss boyfriend
affair not texting me back
doug markham
doug markham bite
doug markham dr maryn
dr maryn husband
stan dr maryn
dr maryn emily webb
emily webb
emily webb agent
emily webb pregnant
emily webb hometown
emily webb bitch
emily webb bitch agent
i hate emily webb

It was disgraceful, the way Emily started to help Chloe with the socks, like she was pretending to be kind. But Chloe is the soft one, the nice one. She opens her bookmarks and clicks on Emily's Instagram. *Shit.*

The account is now private. She types Emily's name into Facebook. There is no longer such a person. Doug's wife has blocked her.

Chloe jumps up. She paces her room. Did Alonso recognize her? Does Doug's wife know? She sinks to the floor and imagines Doug and his wife in bed, the bed that Chloe's slept in. She pictures them laughing at the rabid girl getting kicked out of the party.

She opens her messenger app. No. She's been texting too much. She's starting to look crazy. She opens her email. She starts writing *I hate you I hate you I hate you* but thinks better of it.

From: ChloeChloe123@gmail.com
To: dmarkham@beyondbrand.com

Subject: Hey

Hey,

I just want you to know that yesterday was kind of a shock for me. I DIDN'T KNOW your wife was pregnant. (Congratulations by the way!)

Honestly though, it was hard for me. I found out something about myself. I didn't really know what jealousy was before this. I mean I THOUGHT I knew what it was, but last night it kind of overtook me, and I know this will sound crazy, but biting you was the most NATURAL THING to do at that moment. It's almost like it wasn't me that did it—it was this thing OUTSIDE of myself. And I've never experienced anything like that before.

It makes me wonder if jealousy is something different. Maybe it's not really an emotion like sadness or happiness. It feels more like something from the atmosphere and you're not supposed to disturb it or it'll get mad and take it out on people or something.

It's making me see why people are mostly monogamous—like maybe marriage is there for a reason.

So I think you should just be with your wife. That's what I think now.

I want you to know that I cared about you and was falling in love with you. That's why I did what I did.

Love,

Chloe

She reads it over. She deletes the *falling in love* part and types *I love you I love you I love you* after her signature. She holds her breath and deletes the *I love you*s. She hits "Send." The click of the touch pad recoils through her like a rifle shot.

Sheralyn knocks and speaks through the closed door. "I'm going to the store now," she says. "Don't bother buying coffee."

"No, don't," says Chloe. She rushes to her door and opens it. Sheralyn's hair is wet. "I'll go. I'm sorry. I just broke up with Doug."

Sheralyn steps back. "Was that his wife last night? The pregnant lady?"

"Yes!" says Chloe. "And I'm so not a home-wrecker, you know? Can you read this email I just sent?"

It's like Sheralyn's a hippo, the way she doesn't move, the way she fills up the doorway. Chloe brings her the laptop. Sheralyn's eyebrows draw together as she reads. "You're gonna get fired," she says.

"That's not even what I'm worried about."

Sheralyn hands back the computer. "You think you're gonna end up with him?"

Her words. Chloe would never say those actual words out loud. Not yet, anyway. "His wife is awful," says Chloe.

"Do you have enough for rent if you get fired?"

Chloe lifts her chin. "I have money."

"Do you have five dollars for coffee?"

———

Doug doesn't respond to her email. Chloe doesn't leave the apartment. She can't. She waits. She checks her phone. She sleeps three hours

Saturday night and sits up in bed at first light Sunday morning. She checks her phone again.

Nothing.

Doug. Oh, Doug. Oh, fucking Doug.

She put so much work into that email! She typed it and retyped it. She was honest and raw, and the whole time she kept thinking, *Am I doing the right thing?*

She clenches her teeth and pounds open their text conversation. She writes, *Do you know how much courage it took to send that email?* and holds her finger over the send symbol. No. She deletes it. He'll never know how much courage it took. No one will.

Chloe is alone.

She drops her phone and bends to the floor, sobbing.

———

She wakes at 5:00 a.m. on Monday. She stands at her window and watches the brightening strip of indigo peeking through the apartment buildings across the street. It's a workday. She texts him:

Weirded out. Should I come in today?

As soon as the message sends, she's flooded with a sick, sticky sensation. She should have stopped writing two days ago. But then her phone chimes. It's him:

Relax

He told her to relax one night as he massaged her with the lavender oil from a hotel gift basket. She kept thinking she should be doing something, arching her back or reaching up to kiss his neck, but he whispered, "Relax. Just relax."

CHAPTER TWENTY-SIX

DOUG

Doug closes his office door behind him. He pulls his wallet out of his pocket and drops it on his desk. He doesn't sit.

What did he plan to do? He's forgotten. It's not as if he's never known this feeling. The sense of being underwater. When simple things like reading the *LA Times* and going for a run become tinged and hot with missing the person you were sleeping with the week before. He has feelings, for Christ's sake. He's not a robot.

He grips his chin with his thumb and forefinger. He likes Chloe. He gave her a polite grimace as he passed her desk a few moments ago. She blurted, "Hi!" and then, "Hi!" again, all breathless and desperate. Just that small interaction has softened him. He'll give her a good reference.

He waits until noon and asks her to meet him near the community center at Virginia Park. Open space is better than a restaurant. She'll have room to get upset if she needs to. He's been through this. Better to get it all out in one shot rather than let it fester. He finds a shady spot near the splash fountain and watches the children run through the water spouts, their shouts muted by the gurgling water. "Bat! Bat!" screeches a toddler as she slaps a puddle. Cute. His baby will be doing that in what? A year? A year and a half?

He looks at his watch. Chloe is late. His sympathy for her drains as he watches her pull up to the curb and put on lip gloss. His shoulder is still sore.

Chloe steps out of her car. She's wearing the black blouse he bought her with the asymmetrical neck. The shirt is severe. It streamlines her face, taking away some of that apple-cheeked innocence. She's still gorgeous. Perfect, actually. She walks toward him, grinning, unsuspecting. Like it's an ordinary day.

"Do you want to sit in the sun?" she asks. "I have a blanket in the car."

"Sit," he says. "This is going to be a difficult conversation."

She sits close to him. "I'm sorry about the bite."

"You mentioned."

"I've been thinking about your wife."

"Please don't bring up my wife again."

Chloe's eyelids flutter. She shakes out her hair. It's as if she has no sexless gestures in her repertoire. She faces him with a look that's half-seductive, half-steely.

"So what's the deal?" she says.

He clenches his jaw. In a different era, he could simply kick her to the curb. Leave her penniless on the street to die of consumption or syphilis or whatever. She's a lucky girl to be living in twenty-first-century America.

"Understand that I'm not firing you or encouraging you to quit," he says. "But if you choose to go, HR can help you with options."

She sniffs. "How much?"

"Excuse me?"

"How much is the severance?"

"You'd have to discuss that with HR."

She nods into space. He stands.

"Do you have any more questions?" he asks.

Her body jerks. She looks down.

"I've kept you too long. Don't want Jo-Ann wondering where her receptionist has gone to."

"Are you going back to the office?" she asks. He doesn't answer. He doesn't have to. He's her boss.

A sensation takes over as he strides to his car. It grows as he sits in the driver's seat. He starts his engine. Before he even puts his car into drive, he feels like he's in motion. His body pulses with an unbearable urge to *consume*.

Gobble, gobble, he thinks. That was what he and his buddies used to say before a big night of shrooms and pills and coke. Gobble up the drugs.

He searches his phone. What was that other girl's name again? He can picture only her dark bangs and tattoos. Marilyn. No. Karyn. No. He has the contact information of everyone in Chloe's group. He scrolls through his address book. Sheralyn. That's right. Sheralyn the raunchy. He texts:

Hi there

He waits for the pulsing ellipses to indicate she's writing back. Nothing. He thinks back to her pouts at the bar after the Grove, the way she slapped her ass on the trail for him. Sheralyn will sleep with him. Whether she'll do it because she hates Chloe or because she's easy, it doesn't matter. If he has any instincts, any sense of certainty, it's this. He knows which girls will screw him. He tries again:

This is Doug.

Doug who?

Chloe's friend

Is everything ok?

Not really. Can we talk?

What's wrong?

Better in person. Are you home?

Wow.

I guess.

OK.

He shuts off his phone before getting on the 405 north. Emily has been tracking him. He checked their cell accounts after she was so sneaky this weekend, stealing a look at his shoulder. He almost turned off the location-tracking option when he saw it but decided to let it stay. He didn't want to tip her off.

———

Sheralyn greets him at the door to her apartment in high-rise jeans and a boxy white T-shirt. "Hi," she says. She raises her arm to the door's edge, standing in the narrow open space between him and her apartment. The thorny edge of a rose tattoo peeks out from the top of her crewneck.

"Hi."

"What's happening with Chloe?" she asks.

Doug shrugs. "I was going to ask you the same thing."

She studies him a moment before backing into the room. "You want to come in?" She walks ahead of him. Her movements are slow. Her body is meaty. Dirty. Pleading for violation. "I made banana bread," she says.

He coughs. "I'll just have some water if you've got it."

She gestures to the futon. "Have a seat."

He stops. The coffee table is a mess of bubble wrap and manila envelopes. The futon is crowded with mop-headed baby dolls.

"What's this?" he asks.

Sheralyn turns on the tap and calls over the sound of the water, "I sell them on Etsy."

He picks up one of the dolls. It's made of cloth, a rough muslin. Arts-and-crafty looking. Something you'd expect to find collecting mold in an empty nester's basement. He holds it up as she comes back into the room. "This is exactly what I pictured you doing for a side gig," he says.

She smirks and hands him a mug of lukewarm water. There are no coasters on the coffee table. He sets the cup down on a piece of junk mail. Sheralyn sweeps the dolls to the side and sits. "Chloe thinks she's going to end up with you."

Doug raises his eyebrows. "She said that?"

"No. She'd never say it outright, but I know how she thinks."

"And how is that?" He sits close to her. Her reaction is subtle. A slight recline. A sliver of an invitation. He wonders if she'll let him tie her up.

"I see how Chloe looks at herself in the mirror," Sheralyn says. "It's never quick or like a simple once-over before she goes out, you know? She gets drawn in. She's always swaying and tracing her fingers along her collarbone, like she's got some kind of movie going in her head."

Doug nods. "You don't like her."

"I don't like anybody."

He slides his knee toward hers so it's touching. "Not even me?"

Sheralyn jerks her leg away. Her voice grows agitated. "I can't stand these girls. It's like they read some fairy tale and they think they're going to win some prize. Chloe totally pictures herself as this fair-maiden type; I can tell. Like she's waiting to get plucked. I mean, have some agency! I have zero respect for her right now."

Doug sits back. He pumps air through his closed lips. "That's really harsh, Sheralyn."

"Whatever. She's boring. I don't like talking about her."

"Then let's stop."

He puts a hand on her thigh. She looks down at it. She's deliberating, he can tell. In a second, she'll think, *Why not?* and have sex with him. He knows this.

"What are you doing?" she asks.

"You know what I'm doing."

He moves in to kiss her. She ducks underneath him and scrambles to stand. "Dude, what the hell?"

Rejection. It's part of the dance. He lets it in. Lets it singe him slightly. He leans back and offers a little-boy pout. "I thought you liked me."

Sheralyn winces. "This is weird."

He smiles. "Why?"

"You're married."

"So?"

"You were just sleeping with my roommate."

He shrugs.

"I think you should leave." Her voice is flat. Her eyes are blank. She's serious.

He's miscalculated. These girls. They're different now. The signals aren't the same as they used to be. But he can't leave with her thinking she's won. That he's some kind of creep. He's not a creep. He stands, stooping just a little. A small gesture of submission. "I'm sorry," he says. "I just—"

"You were trying to see what you could get away with."

He nods. "I'm an asshole." He scans his surroundings. He needs an opening. The envelopes on the table. She's handwriting the addresses. He picks up another doll and inspects its seams. "Who are your customers?" he asks.

She sighs.

"Seriously, Sheralyn. Do you know what I do for a living?"

She sighs again but starts talking. "Well, I thought it would be mostly kids, but there's a lot of middle-aged people."

"Really?" he says. His curiosity is piqued. "What percentage?"

Sheralyn shakes her head. "I'm not sure."

"Do you want my help?"

"Um—"

"Pro bono."

"This is still really weird."

"I feel bad," says Doug. "Let me make it up to you."

———

Doug waits until he's safely parked in his office garage before he turns his phone back on. He steps out of his car. His phone vibrates as his messages and voice mails begin to load, but Doug doesn't look at them. His attention is on this kid in front of him, a twentysomething wearing a black T-shirt and fanny pack. The kid is hovering outside the elevator vestibule. There's something unnatural and nervous about the way he's standing. He glances at Doug before burying his head into his phone.

"Good afternoon," says Doug.

The kid meanders away from the door and lingers in the middle of the parking lot. Doug presses his key fob to make sure his car is locked and enters the vestibule. He looks back as he hits the call button. The kid is staring after him. Doug enters the elevator and frowns down at his phone.

He has eleven new voice mails. Four from his main office number. One from Jo-Ann. Two from Stan. There are texts too. From Jo-Ann. Stan. Eva, his PR lady. He opens the one from Jo-Ann and sees the first few words:

DON'T COME IN

The elevator door opens.

Doug sees the camera first, hulking, gray, and mounted on the shoulder of a burly guy in cargo shorts. The guy twists his hand around the lens. Doug peers into the dark glass circle, trying to make sense of this machinery pointed at him. Something dangles above. Doug looks up to see a fuzzy oval, a microphone, held aloft by another stone-faced man, also in cargo shorts.

"Welcome back!" shouts a woman.

It's Dr. Maryn. She's standing in the middle of his office. Her arms are spread wide as if she's inviting him in for a hug. A second camera is pointed at her. She looks giant and out of place, like a redheaded Barbie storming a Lego village. Stan is off to the side. He makes eye contact with Doug and then looks at his feet.

Doug swallows, tasting only the briefest hint of fear before he moves past it. He locks into the front lines of his personality.

"Maryn! Stan!" He crosses to the center of the room with a cheerful smile. It doesn't matter what he's done. What they might know. He needs to stay upbeat. "What's with the cameras?"

Dr. Maryn smiles back and salutes him with a gun finger motion. "Gotcha journalism! We're bringing it back. I'm talking old-school *60 Minutes* Steve Kroft–style exposés. What do you think?"

"I love it!" says Doug. There's no time to digest the meaning of Dr. Maryn's words. "Let me show you around!"

He holds an arm out, gesturing for them to walk ahead of him, but Dr. Maryn stands in place. She nods slowly. Stan looks uneasy. Doug glances at his frozen, gawking employees. Chloe is turned around in her chair at reception. Her hands cover her face. The open floor plan was a mistake.

"Question for you," Maryn says in a deadpan. "What do a schizophrenic diabetic and a bipolar cancer patient have in common?"

Doug offers a conciliatory laugh.

"They're both my customers," she says.

"Aha," he says.

"They trusted me with their information."

"Maryn, I think you've—"

Dr. Maryn wheels around to address the employees on the other side of her. "You know what my privacy policy says?" She stalks the crowd, like his staff is her studio audience. "It's three sentences." She counts off on her fingers. "We don't share information. We don't sell it. Ever."

The room is silent except for the whir of the camera zooming in on Doug's face. He fights the urge to peek at it. He needs to speak, to make a show of strength. "That's only two sentences, actually."

Stan snorts. Dr. Maryn shoots him a look.

Doug's phone is still in his hand. He grips it tighter. He needs to call Erik, find out what the hell is going on. The cameraman moves closer. Doug clears his throat. He can't tell the guy to back up. He can't ask Dr. Maryn to leave. These things will make him look weak. He has to project confidence.

"I'm sick of the bullshit, Doug." Dr. Maryn crosses her arms in slow motion and sits on a programmer's desk. The people nearby scoot their chairs away.

Doug waits. Maryn waits too. She's toying with him. Doug won't give in. He can't. He hears another woman behind him. A soft murmur. "Rick, go to a two-shot."

Dr. Maryn stares him down. She's milking the theatricality; that's what's happening. There is a tone being set here. And he's not controlling it.

"Maryn," he says, adopting a hyperreasonable tone. "Let's talk."

Dr. Maryn turns her head and raises her eyebrows at the woman behind him. Doug can see a flesh-colored earpiece in Dr. Maryn's ear. The other woman, the producer, Doug guesses, is dressed in black jeans with a walkie-talkie clipped onto her belt. She brings a ChapStick-size microphone to her lips. "Stay here," she murmurs.

"I can hear you," Doug says. The producer scowls at him. He turns to Dr. Maryn and raises his hands. "Maryn, come on."

He's savvy enough not to ask them to put down the cameras. Not while they're filming him. It will only make him look guilty.

"I was just at your house. What happened this weekend?"

Dr. Maryn clasps her hands in front of her. "You know, Doug, I think the world of your wife. Because of that, I let you make a deal to put your app on my store, ignoring the fact that you're a year late with it and you're a dozen sexual harassment lawsuits waiting to happen. I was even ready to overlook you bringing mimes . . ." She waves a dismissive hand toward the reception desk. "You brought MIMES to my house! But when I start hearing about your secret payments to my tech consultant, your influxes of data . . . well, Doug, that's the kind of thing that makes me wonder."

Harper. It was Harper.

"Maryn, are you worried about the data we collected? That's for you!" Doug lies. Oh Jesus, Doug is so fucking good at lying. "That's a favor I'm doing for you!" He doesn't know where he's going. He just has to keep talking. Move forward. Deflect. "Erik hired me to curate your suggested apps to users. I tossed him a bonus. Is that the money you're talking about?"

Dr. Maryn looks to her producer. The producer tightens her lips. This might be a fishing expedition. They might not know anything. He just needs to introduce enough uncertainty. Boring, wordy uncertainty. No easy sound bites.

"I thought you knew," Doug says. "I mean, when your customers get offered apps based on their interests, who do you think does the background work on that?"

Dr. Maryn narrows her eyes at him, still playing like they're in a standoff. But he's fighting. He's surviving. He thinks of everything he'll have to do to make it look like he was working for Erik: create phony work orders, dedicate a server to the Dr. Maryn Store data, backdate downloads—is it even possible? Erik. He needs to talk to Erik.

Dr. Maryn lifts her face. "I don't believe you."

"Let's do an audit, then." It's a good line. A solid line. He's so conscious of the cameras. He's coming off as powerful.

Dr. Maryn points at him while looking at her producer. "I still don't believe you," she says, but now she seems distracted. She drops her arms, drops her performance. The cameramen and sound people relax, just a bit. "Where is Erik?" she asks the producer.

The producer turns to a younger crew member. It's the kid from the garage, the one with the fanny pack. "Try him again," the producer says. The kid pulls a phone from his bag.

The camera trained on Doug lowers even more while its operator stretches his neck. Doug sneaks toward Chloe's desk; maybe he can make it to his office, shut his door. But the other camera whips around and catches him. Doug's cell phone rings. He ignores it.

"So what now?" Doug asks.

"Are you going to answer that?" asks Dr. Maryn. Doug blanches.

Dr. Maryn turns to the producer. "What do you want to do?"

The producer gestures toward Doug. "Is this something you want to preserve?"

"Guys," Doug says. "I'm right here."

The producer gives Dr. Maryn a pointed nod. "We should get the . . ."

"Yep," says Dr. Maryn, clipped and officious sounding. She turns her back to Doug and brings her hand to her forehead. The boom operator and the rest of the crew come to attention. Dr. Maryn takes a few hyperventilating breaths before spinning around.

"You betrayed my trust!" she yells with her finger in the air. Her face is red and raging. "You stole my data! And did God knows what with it!"

Doug freezes. He's caught. Trapped. Just for a moment. Then he recovers. He smiles, points to the elevator, and speaks calmly. "Nice talking to you, Maryn," he says. "Now would you please get the fuck out of my office?"

———

Doug turns to his employees after the last of the TV crew has shuffled onto the elevator. His staff is stunned, staring back at him. Everything he built is about to collapse.

Chloe stands. She says, "Doug . . ."

He puts a hand up. "Not now."

Chloe is a weakness. She's a mistake. He's made so many. But he has to survive. He has no choice. He checks his phone. It was Erik who called. He looks up. His staff is still watching. He texts Erik:

Call u back in five.

He raises his hands and addresses everyone. "Listen, people, what you just saw was a travesty. A cheap media stunt. We have done absolutely nothing wrong. I want you all to take the rest of the day off, okay? We'll have a company-wide meeting tomorrow morning." There is movement, packing up. He starts toward his office and stops. He turns back to his staff. "And remember your nondisclosure agreements!"

Doug rushes to his office, dialing Erik. "I offered to let Maryn audit me," Doug tells him. "I was helping you with suggested apps for the users, okay? That's the story."

His call waiting beeps. "Shit," he says. No interruptions. Not now. He and Erik need to plan. Doug almost doesn't look at who is on the other line. But he does. It's like a gift from God that he looks and sees Stan's name.

Doug tells Erik he'll call him back and answers Stan's call. "Stan, what the hell?"

Stan's voice is hushed and intense. "This is all my fault," he says. "I had an affair. She blames you."

"Tell her I didn't make you do that!"

"It's too late," says Stan. "I can't really talk, but I feel terrible."

Doug waits for him to say more. He doesn't. "That's it?" Doug says. "You feel bad?"

He hears Stan sigh into the phone. Doug holds his breath. Stan has more to say—he knows it. "This didn't come from me, okay?" says Stan.

"Okay."

"They're recording Erik right now. They're taping your conversation."

Doug hears a tone. It's high pitched and piercing, and it drowns out the sound of him pounding his fist on his keyboard. He catches only pieces of Stan's next words about Erik using the Dr. Maryn Store to blackmail people. Catfishing. Sting operations. The details don't matter. Doug is the only one who matters.

"Are the police involved?" Doug asks.

"Not yet."

———

Doug sails up PCH. There's no traffic tonight, just speed and cliffs and darkening ocean. He calls his lawyer. He calls two of his friendliest board members. He explains that Dr. Maryn's tech consultant has had a breakdown of some sort. The guy is an alcoholic, spouting lies and nonsense. They need to separate themselves, defend themselves.

He pulls into his garage, next to Emily's car, and sits. He listens to the silence. He doesn't want to go inside. Emily must know by now. He waits for her to burst into the garage.

But she doesn't come up.

He enters his home. The lights are warm and dimmed. There's jazz on the speakers downstairs. It's like he's entered a parallel world. Traveled back in time. Emily is in the kitchen. He can hear her. He starts down the stairs and watches from the middle step as she moves from dishwasher to cabinet and back again, putting away silverware and cereal bowls. Her yoga pants are folded under her waist, giving her a taut overhang of pregnant-belly midriff.

"Hey," she says. "Are you hungry?"

She thinks this is just another day.

"I could eat."

He moves to a stool. She takes last night's poached salmon and zucchini spirals out of the refrigerator and arranges them on a plate. He takes a bite and shivers. Emily. He has a wife. He has a family unit. "Hey," he says and grabs her hand across the counter. He makes her stand still for just a moment. "I love you," he says.

The last thing he wants to do right now is tell her about Dr. Maryn.

CHAPTER TWENTY-SEVEN

EMILY

I gasped. I lay my elbows on the breakfast bar and held my forehead in my hands. "Oh my God," I said. I repeated it over and over. Doug ran around the counter and touched my back.

"Is the baby okay?"

I slapped his arm away. "Maryn is my life! She's my friend!"

"I need you to talk to her," he said.

"And say what? *I'm sorry my husband hacked you?*"

"I didn't!" Doug opened his mouth wide in horror, in an exaggeration of innocence. "Erik messed up," he said. "I'm handling it. It's my word against his."

That fucking optimism of his, it was relentless, completely unsuited to the situation. He picked up a zucchini spiral with his fingers and popped it into his mouth. "You know, I think Erik's an alcoholic?"

"What are you, twelve?" The baby jerked inside me. I felt acid rising, coating my esophagus. I opened the cabinet and took out a family-size package of Tums. "She's going to have you arrested," I said.

"She hasn't gone to the police yet."

"How do you know?"

"Stan told me."

"Don't talk to Stan!" I screamed. "You fucking moron! Don't talk to anybody!" All this time, I'd assumed my husband was operating with some baseline of competence. But his carelessness was a disease. It infected everything.

I wondered if there was any way to salvage Dr. Maryn for myself. I'd have to leave him, disavow him, play the victim. If only she'd come to me first. "Oh my God," I moaned again. I doubled over as I realized what it meant, that she'd left me out. She didn't trust me.

Doug gripped my arm. "Stop it," he said. "This is damage control. You talk to her, then you shore up your other clients."

I pulled away. "She humiliated you. It's going to be on television."

"Nope." He reached for his fork and stabbed off a piece of salmon. "First, I didn't sign anything allowing them to film me or my office. Second, I made the whole thing sound boring."

"Are you seriously that naive?"

"I'll get an injunction." He shoveled the salmon in his mouth and breathed hard through his nose as he chewed. "There was one point I offered to do an audit. I was bluffing, but I think I'll look good there if it ends up on the air. I'll come off as strong."

This rich prick, so sure of himself. All he'd ever had to do in life was show up. "How did you get to be so successful?" I asked.

"Enough," he said and held up his hand. "I'm your husband."

I'd have to call Maryn soon with the news I was divorcing him. I'd have to leave him that night. Even then it might not be enough to convince her. Doug threw his fork at the wall behind me. I watched it bounce to the floor near my foot.

"Jesus, Emily, you're gonna choose some midwestern quack over your family?"

"You don't know what I'm thinking," I said. I put a hand under my belly. My life was about to explode. I had to proceed logically, carefully. "Am I financially liable for any of this?"

"No," he said. "My lawyer said you'll need your own lawyer, though."

I'd stayed out of the swindle. Not knowing the details was supposed to protect me. His end of the bargain was to not fuck it all up.

"How did you pay him?" I asked.

Doug winced. "Pay him?"

"Erik. Did Beyond the Brand write him checks? How did it work?" He wouldn't look at me. He picked at his zucchini with his fingers.

Dr. Maryn, her customers, and God knew who else were going to sue. We were facing financial ruin. And yet Doug was standing there, so calm, eating with his fingers. Someone had paid him for all that data, I realized. I wondered how much money he was hiding.

"We need to set up a trust for the baby," I said.

He shook his head. "This isn't the time."

I raised my head and spoke in a firm voice. "I don't think you're in a position to argue right now."

His movements were quick, speeding around the counter and pushing his face next to mine. He grinned like a drunken frat boy. "You're threatening me? Don't go claiming innocent spouse all of a sudden. You were there when I made the deal with Erik."

"What are you talking about?"

"At Shutters," he said. "You were at the table with us."

"No. I got up and left."

"You think Erik will testify to that?"

I should have recorded the whole conversation at Shutters, taped myself leaving. But that was back in the beginning, when I'd trusted him—when I'd loved him. I could feel my tears rising.

"You're gonna cry now?" he said. "Emily, keep it together."

"You're a fucking asshole."

He shrugged. I could leave him. I could stay. Either way, he was going to be the end of me.

I wish you were dead.

What if he were? He'd be out of my life. He'd be punished. Plus, Dr. Maryn would never air video of herself browbeating a dead guy. She might not even sue. And there was hidden money. Of course there was.

I wished I'd thought ahead, wished I'd known that I was supposed to have spent my marriage preparing for this moment.

I moved into the kitchen. I was restless, ready to get started on something. On what, I wasn't yet sure. All I knew was that I was powerless. That had to change. I looked toward the office. Doug's laptop was open on the desk. It was password protected. I could install a camera, a pinhole one in the recessed lighting. I could log his keystrokes.

I needed time.

"Doug," I said. I made my voice gentle. "If I help you, we have to work together. You have to protect me."

He looked at me a long time and nodded, softening. I let him slide up next to me. I let him put his hand on my belly. "I'll protect you both."

CHAPTER TWENTY-EIGHT

CHLOE

Chloe is late to work the day after Dr. Maryn ambushed Doug. It made her think, the big scene. She has something to say. She's been rehearsing her speech all morning.

When she gets in, the office feels eerie, abandoned, even though the open workspace is full of people. No one looks her way. No one talks to each other. And the reception desk is empty, which is weird. Jo-Ann always finds someone to cover for Chloe.

Chloe looks down the hall. The window above Doug's office is dark. He's not in yet. She sits at her desk and conjures an image of him in her mind. He was so brave yesterday, dealing with Dr. Maryn. She touches her lips. She can practically feel the heat of his skin next to hers. It scares her sometimes, what she can do with her imagination.

Her phone rings. It's him. She's summoned him for real this time. She digs her phone from her purse and looks at the display. It's not Doug.

It's her grandfather. She holds her phone to her chest until the ringing stops.

Her mother must be dead. Or dying. Her grandfather only calls when her mother is dying. Chloe tries to remember what her mother looks like, but the only things she can recall are the sounds of rage and weeping. A red bubble appears next to her voice mail icon. She presses the callback option. Her grandfather's hello is scratchy. Chloe pictures him in the small, porchless house she grew up in even though he and her grandma moved to an apartment years ago.

"Hi, Simon," says Chloe.

"The cops called," says her grandfather. His tone is accusing, like this is somehow Chloe's fault.

"And?"

"Your mom was in the hospital."

Chloe breathes out. "Was." Whatever happened, it's over and done with.

"Did she fall?" Chloe asks.

"Something like that. It's a shame. I had her coming to meetings with me and everything."

Chloe is exhausted suddenly. Her insides feel grimy.

"You don't need to call me about this," she says.

"You all right, Chloe?"

Chloe slumps in her chair. "No," she says. She waits. He doesn't speak for a bit.

"Well, you take care of yourself," he finally says.

She hangs up and touches her collarbone, trying to get back to imagining Doug. But it's like her brain has been hijacked by images of this mother she hasn't seen in years, sprawled on a sidewalk or heaped unnaturally across a bottom stair.

Jo-Ann comes from the direction of Doug's office, wearing an expression of hard worry. She stops and looks through the outgoing mail on the counter above Chloe's desk.

"I'm sorry I was late," says Chloe.

"What?" Jo-Ann looks down at her, like she's just noticing her.

"Traffic was really bad," says Chloe.

Jo-Ann shakes her head at Chloe, but not like she's mad. It's more like Chloe is an irritant. "It's fine," she says and starts in the direction of her office.

The elevator chimes. Chloe sits up. She has so much she wants to say. Doug knows she's deep, that she's smart. She wants to help. She rehearses her speech under her breath.

The elevator doors open to reveal Tom, the bald recruiter. "Talking to yourself?" he asks. She slouches back down.

"So you bombed at the party, huh?" says Tom.

Chloe shrugs. "It wasn't the right scene."

"Well, at least you're not a criminal," he says, keeping his eyes on her face, waiting for a reaction. Chloe looks down. Tom rocks forward on the balls of his feet. He seems satisfied. "Nothing like a scandal to keep things interesting," he says as he walks toward the bullpen.

Chloe stays focused on what she wants to tell Doug. She's thought a lot about *The Dr. Maryn Show* in the last twenty-four hours, how it's exploitative. When he finally does arrive, ten minutes later, she says, "Hi!" He nods at her.

That's it, the nod. That's all she's ever going to get from him ever again. She stares at his back as he stops in the kitchen doorway and talks in a low voice with Eva, the PR woman in the pleated pants.

There's stuff going on here. It's almost exciting. Doug finishes up with Eva and starts toward his office.

"Doug," Chloe says. "I have to tell you something."

He stops. He turns his face to hers. His eyes are bloodshot.

"I was thinking about *The Dr. Maryn Show*," she says. "So many people who go on TV there are unemployed and, like, poor, right? I mean, there's no more work in the factory or wherever, and society doesn't need their labor anymore. But the world, it's not done with them. These folks have been moved to the scrap heap for people like Dr. Maryn to pick over. Because they still have value, you know? Not their work, no. But their stories, their misery, are still worth something. And Dr. Maryn is monetizing it. She's actually selling pain!"

Doug's eyes never move from her face as she speaks. But it's like he's not even looking at her.

"Anyway," Chloe says, "I think what you did isn't any worse than what Dr. Maryn does every day."

He blinks. "I can't do this right now," he says. He walks away.

Talk to me! she wants to scream. If only he would push back, tell her she's too flighty or impulsive, that her comments are stupid. She fights the urge to rush him, to push him into the wall. She hurries back through the open office area, through the accounting-department cubicles, to the single-stall bathroom in the rear of the office.

She slams the door with her back and slides to the floor and runs her palm down her body to the front of her jutting hip bone. Doug always loved touching her there. She lets out a series of sobs and touches her other hip. Then she quiets. She thinks she hears someone. She listens. But it's only the low hum of the air shaft above. No one is there. No one is watching her. Chloe is alone. Totally and utterly alone. She panics a moment, wondering if she's even real, and opens her mouth into a soundless scream.

Someone knocks, finally. "Chloe?" Jo-Ann calls through the door. "Are you in there?"

"Just a second," says Chloe, grateful for Jo-Ann. She stands and splashes cold water on her cheeks. She opens the bathroom door.

"What is the matter?" asks Jo-Ann.

"I'm sorry," says Chloe. "Do I look like I've been crying?"

Jo-Ann recoils. "You should go home."

"Are you mad at me?"

"Why would I be mad at you?"

Jo-Ann has been so nice to her. And Chloe has no one. "Can I tell you something? You have to promise not to tell anyone, though."

Jo-Ann's expression hardens.

"You know Doug, right?" says Chloe.

"You mean the president of our company?" Jo-Ann's voice is deep and direct.

"Well, you know Doug and I have been dating. I mean, I don't know if you'd call it dating, but—"

Jo-Ann puts a hand up. "I'm going to stop you right there," she says.

"But I—"

"Go home. I'll give you an extra sick day."

———

Chloe pulls out of the building's underground lot and makes a right, toward the freeway. There are two signs for the 10. East will take her home. West will take her to the ocean, to PCH. Why shouldn't Chloe drive up the coast? It's not like Doug owns the Pacific. The sun is kinder in Malibu. She has a right to go wherever she wants.

Still, it feels forbidden, this highway, approaching this neighborhood. The traffic slows as she nears Doug's house, a tower of white stucco. The windows look like arrow slits. The traffic stops. She pulls out her phone and takes a picture of the houses past Doug's place: a wall of skinny Tudors and Cape Cods, all blocking the ocean view. She posts on Instagram. She adds a caption. *The rich think they own the Pacific.*

A car horn sounds off behind Chloe, long and blaring. She checks her rearview mirror. The honker is a white guy with a mane of gray hair. He's driving an Audi. She gives him the finger and speeds to the next cluster of stopped cars.

Doug's wife is rude and entitled like that. Thoughts of Emily come back; they always come back, like the intermittent whine of a trapped mosquito. Emily insulted Chloe's purse. Chloe closes her eyes and voices her retort. "Well, I think *your* purse is ugly." No. Too blunt. "Well, you're a fucking bitch!" No. Too childish. She looks up Emily's Instagram again. It's still set to private.

The driver in the Audi pulls to Chloe's right. He motions for her to roll down her passenger window. She stares straight ahead.

"Get off your phone!" he yells.

"Fuck you!" she screams back and shakes her middle finger at him. He cuts in front of her. She lowers her window and sticks her head out. "Suck a dick!"

The traffic again comes to a standstill. The guy is right in front of her. What the hell does he care if she looks down at her phone? These people. These people who don't know how to mind their own business. Chloe opens her car door. She marches to the driver's side of the Audi. She knocks on his window.

"Congratulations. You moved twenty feet, asshole."

She raises her hand, ready to smack his car. The man's expression turns resolute and warning. He shouts through the glass, "You want to start something?"

Chloe's anger swerves away from the man in front of her and ricochets along the stream of chrome and neutral faces, searching for an outlet. She can still see part of Doug's house. She wonders if anyone is home. She pictures his wife padding about, all pregnant and vulnerable.

Chloe storms back to her car, lifts her phone from the center console, and opens her browser. When is Emily due? There are no search terms to enter. She can't ask at the office. She opens her Twitter and posts, *D is an asshole.*

She thinks of breaking into their house, of rummaging through papers and finding the due date on some doctor form. It won't be hard to get in, not from the ocean side. Chloe could break the sliding glass door.

The traffic starts moving. She drives through the downtown and makes a right into the hills at Pepperdine. She concentrates on the winding road, on the sheer face of stone across the canyon. It's frightening, how powerful a car is. How easily it can turn uncontrollable.

She could poison Doug's wife.

That's the only way to do something like that. She pictures sneaking into their house and squeezing a medicine dropper of colorless, odorless liquid onto the woman's food. It makes Chloe laugh then, the image in her head, because she realizes she's picturing Emily's plate set out like a pet bowl.

Too bad Emily isn't a cat. Chloe comes to a straightaway and tweets as she drives. *Meow, says his wife. Meow meow.*

———

Chloe gets to work early the next morning and finds Jo-Ann in the kitchen, refilling the tray of prepackaged snacks. "How was your day off?" Jo-Ann asks, except it doesn't sound like a question. It sounds like she's reading an item off a list.

"Good," says Chloe. "I drove to—"

Jo-Ann turns her back to Chloe and limps stiffly into the hallway. Chloe stares after Jo-Ann, the snub echoing in the empty air. She walks back to her desk and pulls up her Twitter. She counts seven followers from the company before she lowers her face to the keyboard.

It's not that she didn't know they'd see the tweets. It's that she assumed things couldn't get worse than they already were.

And then, as the first few coworkers trickle in, Chloe can't really get a handle on what's happening. It's quite possible that nothing is happening. If a casual observer were perched on Chloe's shoulder, it wouldn't see anything unusual in Roderick the statistical-modeling fellow's hesitating at the sight of her and would think his sullen glance at his watch as he passes was the gesture of someone concerned with the time. And

Jeremiah from IT. A casual observer wouldn't pick up on the difference between his regular cheerful hello and today's cold eyebrow raise.

A casual observer wouldn't notice the sharpness of Elise the vice president's cheer as she greets everyone in the lobby but Chloe. Or the fact that Teddy, the mail guy, drops his bundle of envelopes in her inbox with more force than usual. It's not a full slam, and a casual observer might excuse it as an accident, but then the way Teddy glares at Chloe, like she's personally done him wrong. A casual observer might think, *That's a little weird.*

The casual observer can't be sure, as the morning wears on, whether there's an uptick in people turning away as they pass, like there's some silent agreement to punish Chloe because she finally went too far. By this time, the casual observer has begun focusing its attention inward, to Chloe herself. It notices every breath, every flinch, as her veins and tendons tighten, stretch thin like guitar strings.

And that's when the most curious thing happens. This casual observer, this thinking part of Chloe, begins to lift from the turmoil and materialize into its own distinct being: an entity of pure thought.

The pure thought is detached. It puzzles over certain colleagues and their intermittent circling of Chloe's desk, the way their stares grow brazen and carry highly specific levels of malice. Chloe hasn't done anything personally to any of these people, so it's interesting, why they seem so angry. Perhaps this one guy's sneer as he eyes Chloe's torso is an unleashing of hidden misogyny. And maybe this other lady's wince of disgust at entering Chloe's space is a jealousy situation. But the source of the animosity doesn't really matter. It all results in the same predatory energy.

Time to go, says the casual observer. It nudges Chloe in the direction of her computer and watches as she looks up the balance in her bank account. One hundred twenty-seven dollars. Not enough to leave. Not enough to walk out the door.

Chloe has to sit there and take it.

She decides to return a few dirty looks. That was how she used to do it. When was it, yesterday? This morning? It's a simple exchange, a touch of rudeness in response to rudeness. It's how people protect themselves. She furrows her eyebrows at a junior account exec, a guy her age. She's met with a scoff and "Why are you glaring at me?" Someone else nearby makes a tsk noise.

They won't let her fight, thinks the casual observer. It watches Chloe's face lock into place as her coworkers search her demeanor for weakness. And when Brooke, the marketing manager, comes through with a group Chloe used to eat lunch with and says, "Lo, how the mighty fall," the casual observer notes how Chloe stares straight ahead, like she can't hear their cackles.

You've made your point, the casual observer wordlessly warns them. *Now it's time to stop.*

But they keep at it.

Lunch comes and goes. Chloe doesn't eat. She doesn't visit the bathroom. She's stuck to her chair, and her insides are getting tighter, but then Tom the recruiter approaches. His smile is almost friendly.

"Hi," says Chloe under her breath. For the first time that hour, she lets a touch of life back into her face.

Can you believe how everyone is acting? she wishes she could say.

Tom jerks his chin up. "How's show business?" he asks.

There's no mistaking it. Everything anyone says now has more than one meaning, and because it all *sounds* innocent, none of it is legally actionable. And who knew they all had this way of speaking in their arsenal? Teddy throws the afternoon mail even harder on the counter. It's a threat, an unveiling of hatred, backed by the full force and venom of every single one of her coworkers.

A desperate sliver of Chloe's consciousness springs to life then and begins dancing about, waving its arms and begging silently, frantically, through Chloe's frozen face and out the top of Chloe's scalp. She begs them all to ease up.

And then Doug. Oh, Doug. He comes to work near the end of the day and flashes her a low peace sign: a coded gesture, signaling under duress. It's exquisite, the way he shuts his door. Two soft clicks of the latch—a sweet, percussive melody that only Chloe can hear. And the music part of her flits into the air and winds its way to the frosted glass above his doorway and tries to peek in.

If only she could talk to him. All she wants is to talk.

CHAPTER TWENTY-NINE

EMILY

No one at my agency gave any hint they knew about Dr. Maryn's confrontation with Doug. I'd test them. I'd mention her name and watch for hitches and hiccups in my colleagues' faces, looking for a sign that I was being plotted against. The most I got was patronizing sympathy and conversations redirected to my impending motherhood. I was asked, sometimes, in astonished tones, "You're working right up to delivery?"

They wanted me out of there.

Three weeks from my due date, I had to fight to be included in a multidepartment strategy session. As soon as I sat down, though, my cell phone vibrated into the oak conference table. My brother was calling. I glared at the intrusion of his contact information on my screen. I turned off the ringer. A few minutes later my assistant, Travis, slunk into the room and whispered loudly enough for the people nearby to hear. My brother was on the office line. My dad was in the hospital.

The faces around me gaped open in a collective demonstration of concern. More pity. People in my industry loved glomming onto these episodes of humanity. But 80 percent of them would forget me after I walked out the door, and the other 20 would be angling to exploit me.

I growled at Travis in the hallway. "Don't you dare spring personal information on me like that in public."

"Your brother said it was the only way to get you out of the meeting."

"You work for me, not my brother."

I tried to stalk ahead of him, but the increase in stride set off a sharp pain in my pelvis. I was too pregnant. I slowed. By the time I reached my desk, my brother had hung up. My first call back went to voice mail. He picked up on the third ring the second time.

"Dad has pneumonia," said Wally.

"No cancer?"

"They don't think so," he said.

"We have to get him out of there," I said. "Get him to Cedars or UCLA."

"Why?" There was a challenge in Wally's voice. I pictured him widening his stance at the door to my dad's room like a nightclub bouncer.

"Our father is three hours away from the best hospitals in Southern California," I said. "He's not staying at Desert Adventist whatever the hell it is."

"Hey. My sons were born here. I had my appendix out here."

"For some things the local place is okay, but when Mom was sick? Did we go there? No, she came to UCLA."

"It didn't help."

"Mom was at your wedding," I said. "She got to meet your kids, you prick."

He hung up. I covered my mouth with my palm. I called back his cell. My sister-in-law answered.

"Hi, Jessica." I kept my voice calm and even. "Is my dad awake?"

Jessica covered the mic with her hand. I listened to her and Wally's muffled back-and-forth. "She's your sister," I heard her plead. Wally responded in grunts.

"There's a mute button," I said. Neither of them heard. She passed the phone to my dad.

"Hey, Em." His voice was filled with fluid.

"What happened?"

"Had a little trouble last night."

"We're going to get you out of there, okay? We're going to have you transferred to Cedars."

He spoke in a weak falsetto. "If you think it'll help."

I called my dad's primary care doctor, then the attending physician at Desert Adventist. I called Cedars and the insurance coordinator at Desert. Medicare wouldn't pay for a medevac flight. We had no way to transfer him.

I hung up, keeping my grip on my landline receiver. I ached to call Dr. Maryn. She was connected, friends with the chairs of hospital boards. She'd have sorted this out in an hour. I coughed back a burning spurt of acid reflux as I recalled my last phone call with her. It had been in this same spot, at my desk, the morning after she'd stormed Doug's office.

"If you would just meet both of us for a sit-down," I'd pleaded, hoping we could talk our way out of it. "We can explain everything."

She was silent. I pressed the receiver hard against my face and told her there'd been a conspiracy against Doug and me. "Right after I got promoted," I told her, "some asshole accused us of double-dealing."

"That was me," said Dr. Maryn.

My muscles went slack. "Maryn, you could have come to me." My voice came out dry, chapped.

"I'm sorry, Emily, but I can't let my agent's personal problems become my problem."

She stopped speaking again, creating a vacuum with her silence. No one in my life, not even my family, had ever dared put it to me that succinctly.

"I don't have personal problems," I said.

"Emily, please, I'm a psychiatrist."

It wasn't an invitation to confide in her, not in the slightest. And so I didn't. I didn't tell her that the worst thing, the idea I never thought about, but at the same time, I always thought about, was that I was convinced he'd killed my dog. Of course, I didn't *really* think that, not all the time, but wasn't it unhealthy? That I could think that about my husband?

"Look, can we just talk?" I had to keep trying. "Face-to-face?"

"Emily, you have a lot on your plate." Her tone was intimate, full of the condescending warmth she reserved for the guests on her show.

Bitch. I made you.

"Please, Maryn. I'm begging you. Don't use that footage of Doug."

"I'm not sure what our plans are," she said, fending off my need for information. It was the most I could get from her.

She laid out her timetable. Out of respect for "our history together," she agreed to wait on switching agents until after I started my maternity leave. She'd even let me announce we were parting ways. I had until a week after the birth.

I'd heard nothing from her since. She was back in Saint Louis, on hiatus. I pretended things were normal as I struggled to think of how I could part ways with her and remain sane looking. Agents don't fire their stars. Agents don't have creative differences with their biggest clients.

I was going to have to quit, totally. The only way it made sense was if I announced I was becoming a stay-at-home mom. I'd been an agent for seventeen years. It took that long to get where I was.

The baby kicked hard on my bladder, forcing me back to the present. My throat felt coated in lava. I shook two Tums from the bottle in my drawer and lowered my face toward my belly. "You better be worth it," I whispered. I googled independent air ambulances to transport my dad to LA. We would have to arrange for a private helicopter.

I called Doug.

"How much is it?" he asked.

"Forty thousand."

"Jesus, I'll fly him myself."

"It needs to be an air ambulance."

"We can't be throwing around that kind of money, not right now."

Liar. I had logs of his keystrokes. I had video of him logging onto his offshore accounts. He'd made enough money from the data sales and who knew what else, skimming from his company, probably, adding embezzlement and tax evasion to his list of crimes. He was hiding cash in Belize, the Seychelles, and the Cayman Islands. I had his account numbers, his usernames and passwords.

I'd expected hiding money to be a complex process, full of subterfuge and nesting dolls and crypto keys and locked metal briefcases. But when I tried it myself, I saw that the banks were user friendly, with simple log-in pages. All I had to do was google *start a shell company*. There were any number of places I could choose to open one: Switzerland, the Dominican Republic, Cyprus. I went with Nauru, a small, lonely atoll between the Marshall and Solomon Islands. It was so remote there was no Google Street View, only satellite images. It took just half an hour for me to become the anonymous owner of Nauru's newest corporation, EWM LLC.

My call waiting beeped. It was my brother. I answered.

"When are you coming, Em?"

"Tomorrow. Doug will fly me up in the morning."

———

The table next to my dad's hospital bed was cluttered with Styrofoam cups and empty applesauce containers. An ice cube the size of my pinkie nail was melting into a tear in the laminate. I moved a dirty sheet off the chair next to him and sat.

"Julia Gibbs had a stroke," my dad said. His face was gray. He wore a nasal cannula. "She's in the ICU. They won't let me visit her."

"Dad, you have enough to worry about. Just concentrate on you."

He blinked up at the water-stained ceiling. I looked at the floor. The wastepaper basket in the corner was overflowing. Unacceptable. I scanned the bed rail for the call button.

"It's awful, Em," he said.

"What is it?"

"Getting old. People keep dying. Even the ones I barely know. You count on seeing familiar faces around town, but they're all disappearing."

I said nothing. I just sat. I rested my hand on his forearm.

———

Doug didn't spend more than five minutes at a time in my dad's room. He kept jerking to his feet and pacing before asking if we wanted anything from the cafeteria. Once, my sister-in-law, Jessica, said she'd like a coffee, but forty-five minutes later, he still hadn't returned.

"I'm sorry," I said to Jessica. "I should never have married him."

She turned to Wally with raised eyebrows. My father said, "Shit," from the bed. I found Doug two floors above, sprawled on a pleather couch in some surgical waiting room, reading a celebrity magazine.

"Penny Marshall died," he said.

"That's an old issue," I said. He tossed the magazine onto the end table. I glanced over at a small group in the corner, three generations of a family. "They think my dad can go home tomorrow."

Doug sat up. "That's great!"

"I want to stay tonight."

He stood and shook his head. "No," he said. "That won't work."

"Doug."

"Tomorrow is my mom's birthday."

"You go. I'll rent a car," I said.

"What if you go into labor?" His voice was getting louder. The family in the corner was staring at us. I motioned for Doug to come out into the hall and stopped short at the nurses' station. There was a woman, a patient, shuffling across the floor with an IV pole, her face a map of bloat and exploded capillaries. She stared at me. I stared back. I recognized the stoic hurt in her eyes. I'd never forget that look.

"Hi, Destiny," I said.

"Hi," she whispered. She glanced at my belly and looked away before shuffling off in the direction she'd come from.

Doug was behind me. I went on my tiptoes and whispered into his ear. "Do you remember that girl I told you about? Destiny Stimpson? She buried the baby in the dumpster?"

"Your preschool friend? I thought she had the baby in the bathtub."

"Would you lower your voice?"

"There was a bathtub baby *and* a dumpster baby?"

"She put it in the dumpster after the bathtub."

His lips twitched. I shoved my finger in his face. "Do not fucking laugh." I looked back. Destiny Stimpson was gone. "I'm staying tonight. It's only a three-hour drive."

"You want to give birth at a rest stop?"

"Then stay till tomorrow."

"I've never missed my mom's birthday."

"My father is in the hospital!" I stopped trying to control my yelling.

"And my mother is old!" He was louder, topping me. "I don't know how many birthdays she has left!"

I peeked over at the nurses. They were going about their business, pretending not to notice us. "We stay till visiting hours are over," I said.

227

Doug helped me into the passenger seat of his Cessna for the flight home, his hands under my butt, boosting me up through the door. "This is humiliating," I muttered.

He climbed into his seat and took my hand. "We'll get you on the board of the American Lung Association."

I sighed. "Why would I do that?" I asked.

"Some good has to come out of this."

"Does everything have to be momentous? Can't I just be sad for a while?"

"We need to think bigger," he said. He had no idea how much I hated him. "What would the Kennedys do in a situation like this?"

"Oh my fucking God."

"They've had so much tragedy, but do they sit around and mope? No. They run for office. They start foundations." There was a light in his eyes. An energy that seemed to come from an external source. I wondered if he was high. He pointed to the observation deck, to a family dressed in cheap, spangled tube tops and XL graphic tees. "Look at those people!" he yelled. "That's not us!"

He started the propellers without shouting *clear prop* out the window.

"Doug, have you taken anything?"

"Of course not."

"Seriously. If you're on drugs, I need to know."

"Don't be ridiculous."

I'd married a bozo. He was going to get me killed. I grabbed the window strap as he taxied to the end of the runway. He sniffed and requested permission to take off.

"I'm uncomfortable flying with you right now," I said.

Air traffic control gave him the go-ahead. He gunned it. I closed my eyes and imagined us sliding sideways off the runway, nose-diving once we were airborne.

Of course, I realized. *He can die in a plane crash.*

CHAPTER THIRTY

DOUG

Doug's parents' kitchen smells like sausages and maple syrup. His mom sits at her usual spot at the breakfast table with the *Union-Tribune* splayed out before her. It's early, but she's already wearing lipstick and earrings, her chunky gray bob set and styled. Doug kisses her cheek and hands her a bouquet of sunflowers. He takes his place across from her, in the spot he sat as a child.

"Emily says happy birthday."

His mother pours him coffee and places the pot back on the warmer. "How is she feeling?"

"She's huge," Doug says. "I'm trying to get her to the gym."

"Leave her alone," his mom says.

His dad comes in and sets his mug down. His mom tops off his coffee. An effortless interaction. They don't even need to speak. Doug tries to remember why he was so anxious to leave La Jolla after college. Life is uncomplicated here. You make money. You work out. You live in a nice house. It's no different from what he's doing in LA. But LA is harsher. It's full of strangers.

"How is her father?" his mom asks.

Doug shrugs. "They're sending him home today."

"Poor thing."

Doug's dad smirks at him, showing off the tiniest gleam of white, capped teeth. He's eighty-two and radiates good health and good life choices. Emily's father is, what? A decade younger? It's disgraceful, how badly the guy has wasted his body. Doug has only seen those oxygen tubes slumming it in the sadder Vegas casinos.

"Dr. Maryn," says his dad. "Where are we with that?"

"Haven't heard a peep."

"What about that guy? That tech guy."

"Erik? He's an asshole."

"A real cocksucker," says his dad.

A chalky taste hits Doug's tongue. It's been weeks since the confrontation with Dr. Maryn. But the memory, the shame of this woman invading his office, interrogating him in front of his employees, it keeps attacking at odd intervals.

He wants to ask his dad what to do about the girl, Chloe. But he can't talk to his parents about it. He needs them to know he's not a screwup anymore. He decided not to fire her, not to stir up more drama. Besides, her crazy tweets were a useful distraction. He's even sensed his employees taking sides, rallying around him.

"What did you tell your people?" his dad asks.

"That her tech developer had a breakdown, turned criminal. This is fallout from that."

Doug's dad raises his mug of coffee for a toast.

"What about the injunction?" asks Doug. Doug's lawyer was ready two weeks ago to file a motion to stop Maryn from releasing the tape.

"No," says his dad. "Media people don't respond well to that kind of thing. You'll just provoke her. Keep it boring. It'll stay boring."

Doug props his chin on his hand. His dad's advice is like a bedtime story. He wants to close his eyes and rest.

"This will blow over," says his dad. "If she actually thinks there was a security breach, on her own company, it'll look bad that she's sitting on that news right now."

Of course. His dad is right. Dr. Maryn can't do anything without implicating herself. A feeling makes itself apparent to Doug. Fear combined with relief. He didn't understand until just now how afraid he's been. But maybe this can stay private. And whatever is wrong with him, and yes, something is definitely wrong, it won't be amplified in the news or social media. He won't be publicly weakened. And then the women. His old employees. They'll have no reason to think they'll get away with violating their nondisclosures.

There will be no pile-on. No unraveling of his entire life.

Doug lowers his head onto the counter and hides his face in his arms. He starts crying, sobbing. He can't control it. His parents rise from their stools. His mother puts a hand on his shoulder.

"Why don't you skip church," she says. "We'll see you at the club."

———

Doug flies back to LA later that afternoon and circles the Santa Monica Airport. It's peaceful in the air. He doesn't want to land.

Strange. On some level, he's grateful to Dr. Maryn. She's a sign. You have to pay attention to what the universe throws your way. That other girl, Sheralyn. He's helping with her doll business, but she still won't sleep with him. These are messages: evolve or devolve.

His muscles relax away from their battle-ready position. Yes, he has a problem. But he can fix it. He's been given another chance. All his trips to rehab, the promises to his parents, the way he betrayed every ex-girlfriend. They were dress rehearsals for this. A genuine crisis. This time he'll change for real. He has to.

———

He stands at the top of the stairs when he gets home. He listens. Emily has on new age music. The breathy voice of a lady guru sounds through the ceiling speakers.

"Take a cleansing breath, iiiin through your nose and oooouuuut through your mouth. Imagine a pool of light in front of you . . ."

Doug takes off his shoes and creeps to the living room. Emily is reclining on the floor against a pile of cushions. Her stomach dwarfs the rest of her tiny frame. She opens her eyes at the sound of him.

"Keep going," he says.

"I can't visualize anything," she says. "I think I was born without an imagination."

He turns off the stereo and sits cross-legged in front of her. "Keep it simple. Just focus on your breath for ten minutes." She sighs. The look in her eyes. He doesn't remember her ever showing so much contempt for him. It's all the time now.

"I can't keep apologizing," he says. He takes her hands in his. What he's about to do is healthy. Bringing the darkness into light. Everyone struggles. It's how you deal with it that counts. "I need to go away for a little while."

She says nothing, but the room turns vivid. More real. It's what he's been craving. Intimacy. Honesty. Emily brings a pillow to her stomach.

"Sweetheart." He edges next to her so they're sitting side by side. "I think I might be a sex addict."

She scoots back to face him. "You want to do this now?"

He swallows. "This is hard for me to talk about."

"What is your problem?" She raises her voice.

"I'm doing this for us. For the baby."

"Are you fucking your receptionist?"

"Of course not. It's porn. I can't stop watching."

Emily leans forward onto her hands and knees. Doug tries to help her stand.

"Don't touch me!"

He backs up and looks at the floor. "There are places in Utah," he says.

She shoves her finger in his face. "You son of a bitch," she says. Her voice is low and shaking. "I'm having a baby."

"Emily, it's—"

"Shut up!"

He closes his mouth.

"I am going to need your help. Do you understand?"

"Okay."

"Physical, practical help. And whatever this is." Emily waves her hands at him dismissively. "Fucking table it. Give me six weeks. Can you do that?"

"Okay."

"If you really have an issue, hire a sex worker. You have my blessing."

CHAPTER THIRTY-ONE

DOUG

The hookers are an amazing idea. Doug can't believe he's never thought of it before.

Once the first day, and then twice the next, and then, fuck it, for a few hours every weekday morning, he enters this hermetically sealed gorging on time and flesh and oh, sweet Jesus, his desire. It turns into a thing that he can breathe in and push against and mold into the shape of himself at his most basic. He was a prude before, and he didn't know. Dancing around the edges of true sex with sorry facsimiles of affection. Now it's him and only him getting serviced in luxury hotels, in midrange motels, and then, fuck it, in the front seat of his Tesla on Vermont Avenue.

He's free finally. Free from context. From whatever the hell other people want him to be doing. No more cajoling. No more failed passes.

It's a Thursday morning in a nondescript hotel, and he has two girls today. He tells them to wait. He has a surprise for them.

The lighter blonde, the tougher looking of the two, stands at the foot of the bed and squints at him. She puts her hands on her hips. "We're really not into surprises."

"Relax," Doug says. "It's just drugs."

The mechanic, his old dealer, calls up from the lobby. Doug tells him the room number, and the whole transaction takes ten seconds. Things have changed. Doug didn't even need to take out cash. He just Venmo'd the garage.

He moves to the head of the bed and rubs the palm-size baggie between his fingers, savoring the slight crunch of powder beneath plastic. He opens the Ziploc and taps a tiny pile of cocaine onto the glass-covered bedside table. He stares at it like he's a kid and this is a birthday cake with mounds and mounds of sweet icing. He cuts three lines with a credit card and turns to the women.

"Here," he says.

The women look at each other. The darker blonde says, "I have to pick up my kid later."

Doug motions to the lighter blonde to come closer.

"Not my thing," she says. "Do you have any weed?"

Fuck these girls. They're not going to ruin his good time. He rolls up a five-dollar bill and chases the line down the surface of the table like it's an escaped animal. He lies back on the bed. The surface of his skin crackles with energy.

———

Afterward, he has to work quickly. He has six or seven minutes before his mood changes. If it happens in the room, with the hookers lingering and making small talk, his satiety will solidify. It will turn heavy and invite in a sense of gloom. Or guilt. Whatever. He doesn't have time for that.

"I'm going to take a shower," he tells them. "If you're gone by the time I come out, I'll ask for you again." He gathers his clothes and his watch and locks the bathroom door behind him.

———

On the freeway, on the way back to work, he marvels at how easy it is to remove the morning from his mind. It's like a trick, like he's escaped from the inside of a balloon without letting out any helium. He even throws his baggie of coke out the window because he's done. Done with this little experiment, and thank God he's stopping before he gets hooked again.

"Goddamn!" he screams.

They give him space, the hookers. He can be there for his wife now, through the birth and afterward. He can finally love her the way he's supposed to because he doesn't have to spend emotional currency on anyone other than her.

Doug hums to himself as he descends to his office's underground parking lot. But then he brakes before turning into his spot. Someone is there. A bony vulture of a person hunched on the concrete block. She lifts her head as he edges the grille of his car to just a few inches from her face. She stands and grips her elbows, trembling. He shuts the engine off.

Chloe is turning into a problem.

CHAPTER THIRTY-TWO

CHLOE

Chloe stands in front of Doug's car. It's okay that he won't look up from his steering wheel, that he keeps his hands at ten and two o'clock. She's prepared for a standoff. This is the most resolve she's felt in weeks.

There was a break today in the ostracism, a few moments when no one was paying attention, resuming their routines in starts like the first trickle of shoppers returning to a bombed-out market. Chloe tested it, the normalcy. She sat back in her chair and let her face muscles relax. When no one reacted, when the gaggle of ladies near the elevator didn't let out a flurry of outraged clucks and there were no taunting double entendres like *I guess there's no such thing as bad publicity*, Chloe bolted to the garage to wait for Doug.

The thing she can't do anymore is sit at her desk and let it morph again. That's what it does, the ostracism. It shifts and sways to the cadence of everyone's daily moods like octopus tentacles smacking her in the back of the head and letting her regain her composure before poking her ribs and jabbing her from the other side. The most aggressive stare her down. They look at her in mock surprise and say, "You're still here?" But the worst are the ones who ignore. Even when Chloe is feeling brave, when she tries to say something as simple as hi, they look away.

It's not about the tweets anymore. Chloe knows this. Nobody stays mad over the same thing for that long. She's unearthed something, some self-perpetuating madness. If she were just a little less available up there in reception. If she could close a door so that the know-your-place people and the I-never-liked-you people and the moralists and power trippers had less access.

The elevator opens behind her. Chloe turns to the glass vestibule to see Clive from client services stop at the sight of her. Clive's eyes move to Doug. He shoulder checks the door as he slips back into the elevator.

Doug gets out of his car. "I can't be talking to you like this, Chloe."

"Clive is a good person," she says.

"This isn't the time."

"You can tell the nice people because they seem embarrassed by the way they're acting."

Doug's words come out slow and forceful. "I'm sorry if you're unhappy working here."

"Would you stop? I'm not going to sue you."

His face closes in on itself. He wipes his nostrils with his knuckles. "Okay, we're done," he says.

This is it. This is her only chance. She reaches for his arm as he moves past her but pulls back before touching him. "Please," she says. "I'm dying." She has to tell him how bad things are. If he only knew, he'd put a stop to it.

Doug slumps in exaggerated annoyance and spaces his thumb and forefinger a teensy measure apart. "You have this much capital left with me."

"Call off your dogs," she says.

"I don't know what that means."

"The people in there. Teddy is the worst. I think he wants—"

"I can't force anyone to like you, Chloe."

No. He's not allowed to pretend that this is okay. "You do nothing," she says. "It's like a weapon, the way you don't do anything."

He sighs. But he's listening now. He crosses his arms. "Chloe, you started this. I didn't tell you to post insane tweets about me."

"I didn't use your name."

"And I didn't fire you."

She places her palm on the cement bollard behind her and leans. Doug is right. If any other employee had done what she did, he'd have gotten rid of them. A shiver of elation spreads up the back of her neck, like it was poised there, ready to spring at the smallest hint he still cared.

"Tell me what to do," she says.

"You're a grown-up."

"Can I go on unemployment if I quit?"

Doug cocks his head. He raises an eyebrow. "So it's my understanding you no longer want to work here?"

Oh God. Oh no. He's trying to trip her up. She wants to scream that she doesn't have any money. Why is he being like this? But losing her cool, that will be the end of her.

"I wasn't saying that," she says.

"What do you want?"

"My group. We submitted the invoice to Dr. Maryn's husband, but he's not paying us."

Doug makes a show of considering. "So you want money?"

She gasps. He wants to trap her, harm her. If she only had the right words: magic words, legal words. "I'm a human being," she says.

"I can't help you if you're going to act like this."

He swings open the vestibule door. *No, no, no, no, no, no.* This is her only chance. She catches the door before it closes.

"Doug, I'm sorry." He presses the elevator button. She runs to his other side and presses a fist to her chest. "My heart," she says. "It's agitated."

"You're making a scene."

"I'm not!" She holds her hands up. "See? No scene."

The elevator door opens. There are two people inside. No one from Beyond the Brand. "Going up?" says an old guy from a law office. Doug waves them off. The doors close.

"Here's what I can do," he says. "Since I set it up, I'll give you all the money you should have gotten from Stan. What is it, two thousand each?"

"Twenty-five hundred."

He raises his eyebrows.

"We asked them to rush the check," she says, "but they're not even calling us back."

"Okay," he says. He hits the button again.

When the elevator opens, there's only one person: Elise, the vice president. Her mouth drops open. Doug moves in next to her. Chloe steps forward. He puts his hand up.

"You're on the next one."

———

Common Parlance meets that night. Dylan and Sheralyn are at the rehearsal space when she arrives. She almost cries at the sight of them together, splayed out in their sweats and leggings on the dusty floor of the dance studio. The rat-a-tat of a flamenco class pounds above their heads. This is her world.

"Holy crap." Chloe drops her bag near the door and sits across from them. "You have no idea how awful my life is right now."

Sheralyn gives her a pat smile and inches closer to Dylan. There's a languidness, a confidence Chloe has noticed in her lately. "What did you do?" asks Dylan. He has a flicker of boredom in his voice.

"Chloe's got a scarlet letter," Sheralyn says. "*T* for *tweet*."

"That place I work at, it's toxic," says Chloe. "I have these candies on my desk, and people come by and say things like, 'Sweet on the outside but rotten on the inside,' and they'll, like, stare me down when they say it."

Dylan frowns. There is concern on his face.

"I'm not crazy," says Chloe.

"No, I don't think that," says Dylan.

Chloe gets a whiff of relief. Dylan's a really good guy. She should be with someone normal and kind. Sheralyn glances Dylan's way. She sidles up closer to him.

"So what are you going to do?" Sheralyn asks. Her tone is higher and lighter than Chloe's ever heard, like she's doing her best imitation of a girly BFF. Chloe studies her face. Her eyeliner is different, with deep purple applied directly on her bottom waterlines.

"You should quit," says Dylan.

"I talked to Doug," says Chloe. "He's going to give me the money for the party, so that's something. I'll pay you guys when I get it."

"How much?" asks Sheralyn. Her smile is serrated. Chloe searches the floor in front of her for a way to say, *What's your problem?* "How much is he giving you?" Sheralyn asks again.

Chloe shrugs. "Ten thousand, I'm guessing."

"Wow!" says Sheralyn. "That's how much he's giving Dylan to distribute. Do you think we're getting double the amount?"

Blind white panic ricochets through Chloe's body. Sheralyn hates her. Everyone hates her. She'd scramble out the door if she weren't paralyzed in place.

"You talked to him?" asks Chloe.

Dylan stands and slaps his thighs. "We should get started. Howie's not coming. He booked a commercial."

"Jesus," says Sheralyn. "We should just kick him out."

"But I have good news. I wanted Chloe to get here before I said anything." Dylan gives Chloe a reassuring nod. "The party wasn't all bad. There was this guy there, Gill Summerland. He's an investor in this immersive theater company in Brooklyn. They have a whole warehouse where they stage shows. I'm flying to New York next week to meet with him."

Dylan focuses in on Chloe, like he's trying to gauge her reaction. New York. Of course. But surely Chloe can't just leave Los Angeles. Surely it's not that easy. Dylan winks at her.

Sheralyn's phone chimes on the floor. A text notification pops up. The sender's name is Doug. Sheralyn snaps up her phone, but not before Chloe reads the top of the message: Put 2K of the $ into Pinterest doll ads.

"Give me that," says Chloe.

Sheralyn holds the phone close to her chest. "No," she says.

Chloe stands. "Is that from my Doug?"

Sheralyn gets up. "He's not *your* Doug."

"You're texting with him?"

"Hey," says Dylan. He steps between them.

Chloe can feel herself coiling. Sheralyn puffs up her chest and stares Chloe dead in the eyes. Sheralyn is relaxed. This is familiar territory for her. There's no rage to Sheralyn. She's just tough.

"Are you fucking him?" says Chloe.

Sheralyn points at her. "You are crazy," she says.

"Guys! Stop!" says Dylan.

Chloe's heat fizzes to her face, making her eyes sting. She points at the rose tattoo under Sheralyn's collarbone and stutters an impotent, "You are not my friend." It's all she can manage to say.

Chloe walks out of the room. On the drive home she thinks over and over, *Why? Why would she do that? Why would he?* People are horrible. It's the only possible answer. Tom the recruiter. Teddy from the mail room. They're animals, all of them, gnawing her alive.

She gets home before Sheralyn and finds herself at the door to Sheralyn's bedroom. She kicks it, denting the hollow wood at the bottom. The door opens. The floor is covered with bins of mophead dolls, neatly organized according to size and hair color. There's a stack of empty FedEx boxes on the bed. Chloe pounds on the pile and scatters the cardboard. It's not enough. She stomps. The boxes are too light. They only make her more angry.

She picks up a yellow-haired doll with black stitches for eyes and red dots for cheeks. She shakes it and says, "Please don't hurt me," in a high-pitched ventriloquist's whine.

"I'm not going to hurt you," she responds in a deeper voice.

The doll's face stays expressionless. Chloe covers it with her palm and pulls. Nothing. She pinches its neck and twists the head sideways, but the best she can do is a button-size tear in the seam. *Not good enough.* She looks around the room. There's a pair of pinking shears on the dresser.

She wraps both palms around the handle and plunges the scissors into a bin. But the point is too dull. It just goes around the dolls. She opens the blades and digs into a belly. She snips off an arm, then a foot, and noses, and knees, and heads, and shoulders. She cuts all the dolls from one bin, then another and another, until her hand starts cramping. She stretches it out and massages her palm. She switches the scissors to her other hand and cuts until she's too tired to continue. Then she stands and wonders what she looks like, surrounded by these scraps, these shredded babies, such strange confetti.

There are two bins left. Chloe cracks her knuckles. It would be so easy to quit, to escape the horror she's made of Sheralyn's room. But she can't. It wouldn't be fair to the destroyed dolls to leave the rest intact.

CHAPTER THIRTY-THREE

EMILY

I decided to have a C-section. I couldn't stand the thought of Doug coaching me through some exceptional labor, a spectacular labor, and me all sweaty and panting and pained. I was done sacrificing my dignity. The operation was scheduled for 6:00 a.m., a week before my due date. We had to be at Cedars-Sinai by 4:30. I couldn't sleep that night. I felt like I was floating between worlds. I wandered around the house and took a selfie in the kitchen, trying to solidify a memory of myself before baby. I posted it to Instagram with the caption, *Calm before the storm.*

Dr. Maryn liked it two minutes later. My body started in joy at the sight of her handle. Then I remembered. We had an agreement. This was her reminder she'd be coming to collect, like some modern-day Rumpelstiltskin or wicked witch, setting off an hourglass countdown to the end of my career.

I deleted my post and blocked her.

There was a wall of sheeting set up on the operating table, blocking my view of my abdomen. I couldn't see or feel when the baby was removed from my body at 7:04 a.m. I don't remember how much it weighed. They brought it around and held it next to my face. The baby looked like all the pictures of newborns I'd seen, scraggly and coated in slime. They told me I could hold it later, after my medication wore off.

Its cry was pitiful. I knew that babies were supposed to wail after they were born, but it sounded so despondent. "Why is it crying?" I asked.

The nurse furrowed her eyebrows at me. "Because she's a baby."

They took her away. Doug followed them. I was rolled into the luxury maternity suite. The room was colorful, with a cherry blossom comforter and leather couch. It didn't feel like a hospital. A makeup artist came to help me get ready for my first new-mom pictures. I asked my hairstylist for a neck massage and closed my eyes as she balanced the base of my skull on her fingertips. I almost forgot where I was until Doug rolled a plastic bassinet into the room.

I held the baby. I had expected to feel something once I had her in my arms, some lightning strike of affection, but we were strangers to each other. My instinct was to show her respect. She was an independent being. I wanted to introduce myself slowly.

"Hi," I said. I held her on my lap and looked into her eyes, wondering what she could see. Was my face blurry? I'd read that newborns have short fields of vision. I bent close so she could get a better look at me. "Do you remember me? I'm that lady that was carrying you around."

A nurse was in the room with us, wearing bunny-print scrubs. There was always some extra person, hovering. She butted into this first moment with my child with a panicked, "You're her mommy!"

My voice rose, thin and tight. "Can we have some privacy, please?"

A lactation consultant came by a few hours later, a woman in her fifties wearing pleated khakis and an oversize blouse. She started off gushing at the baby in my arms. "Ooh, what a cutie! Hi, precious!" She raised her eyebrows at me. "What's her name?"

Doug and I looked at each other. We couldn't decide on a name.

"We're thinking of Myrtle," I said. "It was my mother's name."

"Nope," said Doug.

"We agreed!"

"Em, your mother's name is dated. I was fine with it until I saw this little baby here."

He was never fine with it. I was never going to be able to name my daughter after my mother. What had brought Doug and me together, what I'd thought was love, turned out to be a momentary aligning of objectives.

Now he was just in my way.

"Myrtle the turtle," Doug said. "Myrtle wears a girdle. Do you want her to get bullied?"

The baby clenched her tiny fists and raised them up above her chest. I felt a vibration as she let out a loud, burbling poop.

Doug reached for her. I clutched her close.

The lactation consultant put a bright smile on her face and said, "I think someone needs a diaper change." I started to give her the baby, but she held up her hands. "Why don't I come back later," she said.

Doug and I fell silent. Neither of us had ever changed a diaper.

———

We decided on a name, Grace Myrtle Markham, and brought her home.

The afternoon she turned a week old, I sat in the rocker in the nursery and watched the nanny we'd hired change the baby into her Gucci onesie with the interlocking *G* logo on the front.

"Emily," Doug said. He was standing at the door to the baby's room. He had a gift basket of bibs in his hand.

The nanny handed the baby to me. I felt a sharp pain in my incision as I pulled her to my chest and shoulder. Grace nestled her face into the crook of my neck. "Did you see that?" I said to Doug, delighted. She'd been such a lump that first week. Just this tiny movement, this small awareness from her, was exciting.

Doug held up the gift basket. "It's from Dr. Maryn," he said. He read from the card. "'Eagerly awaiting your announcement . . .'"

The nerve of that woman, disturbing our tranquility like this. "Throw it out," I said. "Get it out of this house."

The nanny asked if I needed anything else before she left. I told her she could go and stared out at the slip of ocean visible from Grace's room as I rocked her. The light was mellow and cast a picture on the floor in the shape of a slanted rectangle. Grace fell asleep in my arms.

"Doug," I called into the baby monitor. He came back to the room. "Can you take her?"

He scooped Grace from my arms and laid her down in the crib. She started to fuss. He turned on the zoo-animal mobile above, quieting her. The music was plinking—an eerie, bygone melody. I flashed to an involuntary image of us mourning our child, the mobile transforming into a brutal memento. I thought of a tiny coffin I'd once seen on the news. Something about babyhood felt so close to death.

"Did you write up the announcement yet?" Doug asked.

I shook my head. "Maryn is asking me to dig my own grave," I said. "It's cruel."

"Here," he said and helped me up from the rocker. I put a hand over my incision and rested on his arm. It felt like my insides were ready to burst out of me. I leaned on the railing as I descended to the kitchen and then sat at the breakfast bar, my nausea swelling as I turned on my laptop and composed an email to my colleagues. I wrote that I'd decided not to return after maternity leave, that I was doing it for "personal reasons." I wrote that I was excited about "this new chapter" of my life and hoped they would be too. I said I'd do everything possible to make this a smooth transition, and I implored them, *Please, don't hesitate to contact me with questions.*

I was going to have to send a personalized version of this same email to each of my clients. All because of my fucking husband and Dr. Maryn.

I hovered my finger over the "Send" button. I retched. I didn't press it. I couldn't. This was suicide.

No, I thought. I was ceding too much control. Dr. Maryn wasn't in charge of my whole damned career. If she wanted me gone, she was going to have to fire me. And I doubted she'd do it while I was tending to a newborn. Her company was listed in the top ten places for new moms to work. It was a gamble, but I had three months' maternity leave. I could figure something out.

Doug came downstairs. "Did you send it?"

"No."

I let out a breath, feeling strong for the first time since my C-section.

"Just get it over with," he said. "Then we can move on."

I ignored him and attacked the stairs. I didn't hold the railing. The first thing I had to do was get back in shape. After the first two steps, though, my whole body felt slammed, my incision tugging at the rest of my torso. I forced myself to keep going. My legs shook. By the top, I was dizzy and sweating. Doug came up behind me.

"Are you okay?"

I waited to catch my breath. "Yeah."

"We need to do what Maryn says."

"We don't, actually."

Grace began crying, a hiccuping whine. I went to her room. I knelt by her crib and put a hand over my stomach, longing for her, agonizing over the absence of her body inside mine. She'd been protected in there. She'd been abstract. I hadn't really understood until she was outside me: her cries, her skin, what it meant that this creature was fully human.

Grace started wailing. I pressed my forehead to the slats of the crib and cried along with her.

If only I could rid myself of this memory—it was incessant, creeping around my thoughts like an invasive species. If I could just forget everything to do with Destiny Stimpson and her baby, born in a bathtub and buried in a dumpster. All my life I'd avoided thinking about it. But now I couldn't stop the flood of pictures in my mind: Destiny's baby sinking into the garbage, pricked by the sharp-edged packaging, melting into rotting food.

How long had it been in there, suffering? How long had it taken for it to die? I asked my mom the day after they found its puny body. She said she didn't know. She turned her head away. My mother refused to look at me again for months.

"Emily, what are you doing?" Doug was standing in the doorway, watching me. These awful hormones. They were intrusive, turning me into someone I didn't recognize.

"Fuck this," I said. I stood and shook my head, shook away my guilt. I leaned over the rail to pick up Grace, not caring how much it hurt my abdomen, and held her close. Her warmth, her weight, was like an opening, a tunnel through the expanse of my universe to some alternate dimension of pure love.

"You're a lucky baby," I whispered. I inhaled her powdery scent. She was alive. So was I. We would start from there. Motherhood wasn't going to work for me if I spent it worrying about unlucky children.

CHAPTER THIRTY-FOUR

CHLOE

Someone is hammering at Chloe's front door. She sits on the carpet in her empty living room and backs up against the wall. There's no furniture to hide behind. Sheralyn took everything when she moved out.

Chloe watches the person's feet, two shadows in the late-morning light seeping through the bottom crack. The knocker knocks again. Chloe sneaks to the peephole. Her mailwoman with the close-cropped hair is there, waving an envelope.

"Certified letter," she says.

"Just leave it out there," says Chloe.

"You have to sign for it."

"Can I see it?"

The woman holds up the envelope. Chloe hones in on the orange flash of Doug's company logo in the corner. She pauses. She needs a lawyer.

The mailwoman turns to leave. "It'll be at the post office for seven business days."

Chloe opens the door as far as the chain lock will let her. "Wait."

"I'm not arguing with you. You sign for it here, or you can pick it up at the post office."

"Can I open it first to see what's in it?"

"Honey, it's certified mail." The mailwoman points at the return address. "These people sent you a letter, okay? They need your signature to confirm you got it."

It's harassment, showing up at her home like this. They keep calling. She's had messages from Jo-Ann, from the human resources people.

"Last call," says the mailwoman.

"Just give it to me." Chloe yanks the pen from her hand and signs. She slams the door and scans her bare living room. It echoes, the emptiness. She isn't quite sure, but she thinks she misses Sheralyn. She misses having someone around.

It was disappointing, Sheralyn's reaction to the dolls. She didn't yell or get angry. She just backed out of her room, away from the corner where Chloe was crouched, and ran out of the apartment. It was weird, how scared she acted, because by then Chloe wasn't mad anymore. She'd even put down the scissors.

Chloe sits on the carpet and carefully opens the letter.

Dear Chloe, reads the greeting. She winces. It's so formal, so spiteful. They have a taste of her now. It's like they still need feeding.

She keeps reading. Since the management at Beyond the Brand wasn't able to get in touch with her after her "abrupt departure," and since she now has over ten consecutive "unexplained and/or unexcused absences" from work, they decided, for their "mutual benefit," to "terminate" her employment "effective immediately."

Terminate. Another threat.

There's a check in the envelope for $1,157, the whole pay period, even her unused sick days.

Good luck in your future endeavors, says the last line of the letter. At last, a kind word. She runs her fingers over the laser printing and clasps the letter to her chest and rocks, sobbing, comforted in the arms of extreme emotion. Something else—a force, a feeling—is in charge.

She's been numb since that last day at the office. There was a company-wide email. She wasn't cc'd on it, but she could hear "Aw!" and "Omigod!" sprouting from the open workspace. Chloe kept her head down while they exclaimed, "The baby!" and "Did you see the baby?" to each other in high-pitched treacle.

"Go," said a voice that Chloe had never heard before. It was low and calm and female, and it didn't care whose fault any of it was. "Go," it said in regular intervals until she rose like a patient under hypnosis and found her way back to her apartment.

Chloe's crying subsides. She leans forward, her forehead almost touching the floor, and tries to summon back the sadness, but it's done with her for the time being. She lies on her side and fingers the indent in the rug from Sheralyn's futon.

She can't have another day like yesterday. Today she has to do something.

Food. The first thing is food. The clock on the unconnected DVR says 12:30. She hasn't eaten today. She walks to the kitchen. A clear plastic bread bag is crumpled on the counter. Inside is a stale end slice. She takes a bite. She can barely chew. She's out of peanut butter. She's out of butter. The hummus has been gone for a week.

She needs to go shopping. She has to make a shopping list. Chloe pulls the second-to-last Post-it from the magnetic dispenser on the refrigerator door and opens the drawer next to the silverware. It's empty. The pens are gone. She slams the drawer shut and marches to her bedroom, where her phone is charging. Sheralyn's voice mail picks up after the first ring.

"It's me again. Did you seriously take all the pens? I have to write things down, too, you know!"

She gets a text from Dylan:

I have your check.

What check?

The $2,500.

She isn't expecting the $2,500. But of course, Doug promised it to everyone.

Are you back from NYC?

They pushed the meeting. I go next week.

$2,500 plus the $1,157 she just got plus the $8 in her account adds up to $3,665. She's never had that much money all at one time.

Want me to drop off your check?

That could work. She and Dylan can have sex. She lies back and tries masturbating. Nothing. It's like her soul is gone. She turns onto her side and blinks, and suddenly her alarm clock says 3:30. She can't tell if she fell asleep or lay still for a few hours. She needs to eat. She texts Dylan.

Can you mail me the check?

K. What happened with Sheralyn?

Chloe sits up. She should go out. Order a chicken wrap. Maybe a veggie burger. She needs to shower.

Doug. Dylan. She feels warm, thinking of both of them. These guys make things happen for themselves. She needs to be more like them. A doer. She tries Doug's Instagram again. His account is gone. His Twitter is still deactivated. She puts her phone down. She needs to do more than check the same websites over and over. She can't have another day like yesterday and the day before and the day before and the day before.

She needs to get out of her apartment. She has to diversify. *Diversify.* That sounds like something a doer would say. What was it Doug's wife said to her? She had a great look. She should do commercials.

Emily's agency is huge. They have offices in New York, even. Why shouldn't Chloe reach out? Successful people network. Successful people exploit their contacts.

Chloe reaches into her closet. She digs through the floor full of empty backpacks and canvas totes until she finds her old yellow hobo bag. Doug's wife's card is in the inside pocket.

> From: ChloeChloe123@gmail.com
> To: Ewebb@rfg.com
> Subject: Hi there!
>
> Hi Emily,
>
> I'm not sure if you remember me, but I met with you a few months back about my group, Common Parlance. If you remember, we do site specific performance art. Also, more recently, I believe we ran into each other at Dr. Maryn's party in Bel Air where my group was the entertainment for the evening. I hope you enjoyed it! Congratulations by the way on your new arrival!!
>
> I remember that you thought I might be good at commercials? I've given the matter some thought, and even though I have deeper artistic ambitions, I

would definitely be interested in doing something like that. Additionally, my performance group might be moving to New York soon, and it would be great to have representation on both coasts. Would you please let me know who I should contact about this? Or would you mind forwarding this to the right people?

I hope you're doing well. Congratulations again on the birth of your child.

Sincerely,
Chloe

CHAPTER
THIRTY-FIVE

Chloe

From: ChloeChloe123@gmail.com
To: Ewebb@rfg.com
Subject: RE: Hi there!

Dear Emily,

I was hoping to have heard back from you by now, but I know you're probably really busy. Are you on maternity leave or did you go back to work? I guess that's always a hard choice for a new mom to make.

Anyway, like I mentioned, I hope to start doing commercials. Oh and added bonus—I just whitened my teeth! I used Crest Whitestrips and have a before and after picture in case they're looking for something like that.

Thanks. I hope to hear from you soon.

Chloe

———

Chloe is a half hour late to meet Dylan for happy hour on Melrose. He just got back from New York. The plan was to race out of her apartment the minute she woke, but she kept stopping for long intervals to check her email and examine her bone structure in the mirror. She's lost weight. It accentuates her cheeks and jaws. Her looks are reassuring. Whatever's happened, she's still gorgeous.

She parks on the street outside the restaurant and opens her phone. Doug's wife hasn't responded. She reads over the last email she sent, and the one from the day before, and ones from two days to two weeks before that. They're perfectly fine. She sounds normal, cheerful even. But maybe sending so many seems desperate.

She's not desperate. It's important that Emily know that.

From: ChloeChloe123@gmail.com
To: Ewebb@rfg.com
Subject: RE: Hi there!

I realize I've been sending you a lot of emails! If it's too much, just let me know. While I'm really looking forward to getting into commercials, I also have a couple thousand dollars, so it's not like I need the money right away, but then again, money doesn't grow on trees!

Warmest regards,
C

Dylan is sitting on the terrace, at one of the rustic tables. His chair and the empty one beside it face out toward the street. A bottle of white wine sits in an ice bucket.

"Sorry," Chloe says. "Traffic."

"You like pinot grigio, right?" Dylan asks and butters a palm-size baguette slice for her. Instead of his usual Old Navy T-shirt, he's wearing a short-sleeved oxford tucked into jeans. His beard has grown out a bit.

"Thanks. I didn't have breakfast," says Chloe.

"You look thinner." His eyes linger on her face with a searching concern. Yes. He's a good option now that she's single. He must have been nervous, waiting for her to show up.

"How was New York?" she asks.

"Very instructive."

The waiter comes over. Chloe tries to read the menu. It's difficult, though. She can't quite see past the contrast of black type on the pale-yellow page. "You go first," she says. Dylan orders the mussels. "That's what I'll have." She hands the menu back to the waiter.

"So New York," says Dylan.

"New York," says Chloe.

They hold each other's gaze, and between them passes either a highly charged understanding or a wish for something like it. When it's time to look away, though, Dylan stays locked in on her. His expression turns determined. Why does he have to be so intense?

He lifts his hand and lets it fall next to hers, just barely touching. "Can I ask you something personal?"

"Depends," says Chloe. It's easier for Chloe to picture herself with him when he's not around.

His pinkie moves first, hooking hers. His other fingers follow, crawling in stop-motion across her hand like a sweaty tarantula. Chloe puts her hand on top of his and speaks as gently as she can. "I think we're better off as friends."

She's said as much a thousand times before in small gestures and changes of subject, minor blows that always land with him pausing, staring into space for a fragment of a second. About 5 percent of her likes putting him off, knowing it won't change his feelings, knowing he'll make another attempt. Today, though, he scowls. He yanks his hand away.

"Hold on," he says and pulls his phone from his back pocket. "I have to take this." He gets up from the table. The mussels come. She pours herself a glass of wine and dunks the rest of her bread into the broth.

"More wine?" she asks as he sits back down.

"No thanks." His tone is upbeat. He scoops two mussels onto his spoon and inspects them. "So New York was good. They pitched me on a gaming project."

"Like what?"

"Virtual reality, but open ended. It could be a livestreaming kind of thing. Could be a scavenger hunt, an escape room. Gill, the guy from the party, said he wanted to capture our spontaneity. I'm going back next week."

But they're not supposed to be about video games. They're about live performance. The public square. They're not supposed to cheapen what they do. "You're going by yourself?"

"I'll talk about bringing you along when it's time to produce something."

"How long?"

"They offered me a six-month contract."

"You took a job?"

"Technically, I'm just a consultant," he says.

Chloe wasn't expecting this. She was expecting everything to work out. The plan was to move to New York as a group. "You went behind our backs."

Dylan pushes his plate away. "You went behind my back going psycho on Sheralyn."

"I didn't."

"Whatever. She's gone. Howie's gone."

"We can find new people."

"Me!" Dylan slaps his chest. A couple at a nearby table looks their way. Dylan frowns and lowers his voice. "I can find new people." He tightens his lips and looks up to the heavens like he's asking permission for something. He takes a breath. "The creative vision for the group was my idea. You all acted like you came up with it."

"We did everything by consensus."

"That was my idea too! I'm a leader, Chloe. I'm done pretending I'm not."

Chloe touches his arm. He pulls away. It's a troubling prospect then that she hones in on. Dylan doesn't want to sleep with her anymore.

He keeps talking. She can barely hear him. "I don't want this to end badly," he says. "And I want you to keep going. Out of all of us, you're the most capable of carrying on the work."

It's like he's talking to her across a canyon now, with the lights of civilization twinkling behind him. She knows she should join him there. All she has to do is assemble some combination of sentences, pull from a sanctioned list of behaviors. That's all people do anyway, repeat the same phrases back at each other and reassure each other they're sane.

"Chloe? Are you okay?"

She smiles at him. "Yeah, why?"

"You just had a weird look on your face."

"Oh," she says. She laughs. Dylan is quiet a moment before laughing along with her. He motions to the waiter for the check. Chloe can't be sure, but it seems like his hands are shaking.

———

There's traffic on the way home. Chloe waits in the correct lane to get on the freeway. She waits to take her turn. And this guy, he's driving an Alfa Romeo. He speeds in from a faster lane and tries to cut her off. She honks and pulls up close to the car in front, but the guy keeps going, edging ahead of her, daring her to ram him. She honks again and angles her chin so he can see clearly.

That's right, she thinks. *I'm fucking gorgeous.*

He pulls in front of her. She leans on her horn. She keeps it up until they reach the light at the top of the ramp.

"Dick!" she screams.

The guy wiggles five cheery fingers in the air before speeding away. It's the classic LA diss, the gesture of impenetrable happiness. She's nothing to him. Nothing at all.

———

From: ChloeChloe123@gmail.com
To: Ewebb@rfg.com
Subject: Doug

Dear Emily,

I had an affair with Doug the whole time you were pregnant. I got fired. Doug is a very bad person. But I bet you don't give a shit. Nobody gives a shit about anybody. People are awful, and I'm sure you're no different.

Hugs and Kisses,
Chloe

CHAPTER THIRTY-SIX

EMILY

I was waiting until I got stronger, until I felt like I could parent Grace by myself, before I would decide what to do about Doug—leave him, figure out a way to get rid of him, or even stay married and accept a low-grade unhappiness. Our daily routines, feeding our daughter, rocking her to sleep, had begun blunting the worst of my hostility toward him. He even seemed like a good dad. He had a short attention span, sure, but he would dance with Grace and sweet-talk her in baby language.

Dr. Maryn had been quiet. There was no news of the tape or legal action, no more cryptic messages. It was almost as if there were no problem. If it hadn't been for the deluge of gifts we received from Doug's colleagues, I might not even have noticed the fact that I received nothing from my workplace.

And so I found myself on the couch with Doug, under the same blanket, watching a mob movie, the kind of thing he liked. Grace was asleep upstairs. The faint sour smell of her spit-up was still on my shirt.

I brought the fabric to my face and inhaled. Doug put his arm around my shoulders and pulled me into him.

What if we could stay like this? I wondered. When people talked of the ups and downs of marriage, I'd assumed they meant some pattern of fights and making up. I hadn't realized it was possible to come back from such profound disgust.

My phone lit up from the side table.

"No," said Doug. "Turn it off."

"Wait," I said. It was my work email. I moved to the chaise. The room turned cold after I read Chloe's first sentence. Doug paused the TV.

"Are you watching this with me or what?"

"Give me a second," I said. I ran up to our bedroom and read the whole thing three times. It was incredible. I now had solid proof.

What I would use it for, I had no idea. Destroy my family? Confront Doug? I pictured him receiving the news with a shrug. I'd already consulted a lawyer, hoping the hair from my razor would avenge me in a court of law. But I'd learned that California was a no-fault divorce state. An affair meant nothing, no leverage.

The TV was still on pause. I went downstairs and sat at the other end of the couch. He picked up the remote.

"Where are we with Grace's trust?" I asked.

"You want to talk about this now?"

"You keep putting it off."

He pressed play. The sound of gunfire erupted from the speakers. A tracksuited man on the screen fell to the ground. I went behind the entertainment center and unplugged it.

"Em! What the hell?"

"Dr. Maryn might sue. We need to protect Grace, set up an irrevocable trust. There could be a class action. Fuck, Doug. You could get arrested."

"Fine," said Doug. He stalked to the office. "You want a trust fund baby? Go ahead and set one up yourself."

I followed him. "Why are you turning this into a fight?"

He stopped in the doorway and faced me. "Because I'm not Bill Gates!"

Doug sat at his desk. I walked to the sliding glass door. The night was dark, but I could still make out the whitecaps moving past my reflection. The water was soothing, something I always associated with unlimited funds.

Doug called me into the office. He was logged onto Merrill Lynch.

"Look," Doug said. "We've already started Grace's college fund. I don't want her to have to worry about paying for school. Now, here is what we have so far for retirement . . ."

"We went over this for the prenup."

"Then why are we having this conversation?"

I steeled myself. There was no turning back after I said it. "What about your slush fund?"

His face froze. He stared at me with a sick-looking smile. "You just tipped your hand," he said.

"Stop."

He leaned back in his chair and squeezed the leather piping between his thumb and forefinger. "What, were you biding your time until you could sic a forensic accountant on me?"

"What if you end up dead?" I asked. "What's going to happen to that money?"

He expelled a lungful of air and looked away. "You're so entitled, Em."

"Bullshit," I said. "I bought all this furniture."

"Could you afford that?"

"Could *we* afford that."

"The couch was eighteen thousand dollars," he said.

"That's how much they cost."

"You have three ten-thousand-dollar purses upstairs."

"I can't show up for work with a cheap purse!"

"You're lucky I feed you."

My lips caught fire. My face muscles twitched. Everything that he was, that he'd done. "If you're not paying for shit," I screamed, "what is the point of you?"

The baby monitor chirped to life. Grace started up her tinny wail.

"God dammit!" I said.

I went to the coffee table and picked up the video screen. Her eyes were glowing in the infrared. She'd freed one arm from her swaddle and was pawing the air with her fist. Doug came up behind me and put a hand on my shoulder.

"Should you go up?" he asked.

"No. She might go back to sleep."

He put his hand on my back. He spoke softly. "We'll take care of her. She'll be fine."

Grace's cry shortened into a series of hard, staccato howls. We went to her. We sat on the floor and took turns feeding her until he got bored and went back downstairs. I gave her the last of the bottle and moved to the rocking chair, waiting for her eyelids to droop so I could put her down drowsy but awake, like all the baby books instructed. She didn't close her eyes.

"Go back to sleep," I whispered. She kicked at my thigh. I closed my palm over her foot, breathing in a sensation of contentment and peace, wondering how long the feeling would last.

Dr. Maryn had advanced and retreated. And now where was she? No matter how hard Doug tried to convince me or himself that things were fine, I pictured her waiting, patient, getting the timing just right. *What is she doing right now?*

I stopped rocking.

Dr. Maryn was editing. She was in postproduction, which takes months. She hadn't called the cops, hadn't begun legal proceedings, because she didn't want to spoil the surprise. She was making a television show.

Grace grunted and wriggled her face. I almost dropped her. I almost ran to my computer in a panic, in an effort to rally the few people who might stick by me.

But we were done. Or Doug was. There was no stopping this.

I put Grace on my shoulder and patted her back. I did the math. I had some retirement. But not enough for Grace and me to live on for long, and certainly not enough to leave her any inheritance. Doug's life insurance was worth a million. If he died, that money was mine whether or not Dr. Maryn sued, whether or not her app-store customers started a class action. If he could somehow die, a million would give me time. His offshore accounts held about four million. If I could get that money—I'd have to move the cash, hide it on other islands until everyone forgot about us.

Grace burped. "You just burped," I said, narrating her experience back to her, following the directions from the baby books. She made a soft siren coo up and down an octave. I repeated the notes back to her, just as the baby books had taught me, laying the foundation for later language development. I stared into her face. She looked away.

The world was so different from the time when I'd grown up. And it was becoming more precarious day by day. I'd tried to buffer myself, expanding into tech, marrying someone set to revolutionize his field, but I'd failed.

I leaned my face next to her ear and whispered, "I wanted to give you the chance to be mediocre, but it looks like you'll have to work just as hard as your mommy."

I put her on the floor, on her stomach, her legs splaying out behind her like a tadpole. She rolled her face to the side and rested her cheek on the teddy bear–skinned rug.

"Come on, Grace," I said.

The baby books called this tummy time. According to the development charts, in four weeks, Grace was supposed to be able to lift her head forty-five degrees from this position. But hitting benchmarks wasn't enough. She had to be advanced.

"Pick your head up, sweetie," I said.

Grace ground her face into the carpet. "Eeehhhh," she mewled. "Eeeehhh."

"You're working so hard," I said, praising her effort. That was what books said to do, focus on the effort, not the result. "I can see how hard you're working."

She groped the rug with her forearms and pushed at the air with her feet as a rush of images, all the terrible fates that could befall her, flickered through my mind: poor and scrounging, homeless. In every one she was lost and lonely.

"You can do this," I said.

Her chest and face stuck to the floor. She wasn't going to make it. "Heeeehhhh!" she cried. I resisted the impulse to comfort.

"Please, Grace," I whispered, my desperation rising.

"Waaaaah!" She cried and strained and swam and crawled and flailed like a turtle racing to nowhere.

Doug lowered the volume on the TV downstairs.

"Please, sweetie."

Her wails turned guttural.

"You have to. It's called a work ethic."

Her face was red. She was sweating. She raised her head a fraction of an inch and pecked at the floor.

"Good!" I said.

"Wah! Wah! Wah!"

"Keep going!"

I heard Doug running up the stairs.

"Lift your head!"

"Pick her up." Doug was standing in the doorway.

I held up a hand. "Hold on," I said. "She's almost got it."

"Pick her up!"

She was so close. He barged past me and took her in his arms.

"Dammit!" I yelled. "I was working on something!"

"Shhh," said Doug. He cradled Grace and swayed. "You need a time-out," he said.

"You want her to end up like Chloe?"

He pointed past me. "Get out."

"You ruined my life!" I lunged for Grace.

He held her above his head, away from my grasp. "Out!"

———

I ran downstairs and held on to the edge of the breakfast bar. I thought of marching back upstairs, snatching Grace. All I had to do was buckle her in her car seat and start driving.

But he'd never let me take her.

I had to calm down, come up with a plan. I took my phone from the end table and reread Chloe's email. I scrolled through the half dozen other messages she'd sent. You'd think the emails would have grown in hostility, but aside from the most recent, she seemed intent on ingratiating.

I grabbed my purse and went to my car in the garage. I reached for the ignition but crumpled. I covered my face with my hands. If only he'd been competent, if he'd have let me in. I would have welcomed the job of fixer, of making his women, his problems, go away.

But he was the problem now. His blithe malignance, his negligence, his scandals. He didn't even see it. That was the saddest part. He couldn't see that he was evil.

He was destroying us. He would ruin Grace's life. I looked at Chloe's email again. She'd included her phone number at the bottom. I called her.

"Hello?" she answered.

"It's Emily."

She said nothing. I told her to meet me at Tom's Diner in Brentwood.

CHAPTER THIRTY-SEVEN

DOUG

Doug keeps a tight hold on Grace and listens, bracing himself for Emily's reentry, for some *and another thing* to top off her litany of complaints. Her car starts.

"Keep going," he whispers. The rumble of the garage gate drowns out the sound of her motor. "Go, go, go." The gate closes. Doug walks to the hallway with Grace nestled in the crook of his arm. Emily is gone.

He looks down at his daughter. Her skin is smooth and pudgy. "Cutie-pie," he says and lifts her close. He sinks his lips into the baby fat on her cheek. Grace smiles and cocks her face to the side. A flirt already.

He turns to the empty space around him, expecting someone to take the baby now that he's had a complete moment with her. All the women in his life. Emily. His mother. The nanny. They're always taking over.

He brings Grace to the living room. He dims the lights and uses his free hand to set up the Portishead album from his vinyl collection. He holds her upright as the noir downbeat kicks and starts dancing. He sings along to the mournful soprano's lyrics and kisses Grace's forehead and wipes her spit-up from his shoulder.

It's perfect. It's exactly how he imagined fatherhood. Playful and hip. If you can call Portishead hip anymore. It doesn't matter. What matters is they're doing joy. And yet, he's certain if Emily were here, she'd have some kind of problem with it.

What did she say to him? *What is the point of you?* What the hell.

He has another instinct to hand Grace off. His legs take him in a circle around the room. He's conscious of his changing mood. He thinks of going out, taking Grace for a drive. He'd have to put together her diaper bag, though. His muscles tighten in a quick surge of outrage at the fact that he can't simply walk out the door.

He pulls her activity gym from the corner and lays her down under its cushioned arches and zoo animals. "Stay there," he says. Grace pants and waves her hand near a stuffed giraffe. He opens the sliding glass door and peers over the edge of the balcony. Low tide. The beach is walkable.

Ten minutes. He'd be back before Grace even noticed. He glances at her. She's found a way to flick her foot against the gym, shaking and jingling the whole contraption. He smooths his eyebrows with his thumb and forefinger and reaches into his pocket for his house keys. He moves to the kitchen. In the cabinet, behind the rice and dry pasta, is a can of baking soda. He unscrews its false bottom and digs half a key full of cocaine from the plastic bag hidden there. Just a maintenance bump.

Oh Jesus, he loves cocaine. His sinuses go numb as the drippings collect on the back of his tongue. The kitchen takes on an astringent quality, cold and blue and scrubbed completely clean.

Grace is on the other side of the counter, all fluffy and warm, batting away at her zoo animals. It's not as if he's unaware of what he's doing. Where he's choosing to be. He's been through this before. He actually considered quitting completely, but he can't afford a month of bad moods right now. He reaches his key back into the baggie but then stops.

This revolving carousel of compulsions. He's always assumed they were confined to his periphery. *But what if,* he wonders. What if they're the central facts of his existence?

He agreed to give Emily six weeks. He won't even have to mention the drugs. He'll tack the cocaine withdrawal on top of the sex-addict rehab. His own secret detox.

Coke is embarrassing anyway. Those two hookers who turned down the lines he cut for them. They shared this look, like he was some kind of middle-aged hairpieced dude they'd be laughing at if he weren't paying them to be there. What do the kids do now? Molly? Oxy? Anyway, he's cut down on the sex workers too. He's getting tired.

His cell phone rings. It's Emily. He declines the call. She tries the landline. He walks to the office and picks up the cordless phone.

"What now?"

"Did you give Chloe any payouts?" she asks.

Grace starts to cry. "Em, I can't deal with this." He presses the receiver between his ear and shoulder and steps to the living room. He picks Grace up and bounces her.

"Is she in her crib?" Emily asks.

"Where are you?"

"Did you make Chloe sign a nondisclosure agreement?"

He shakes his head. "I'm hanging up now." Doug holds Grace to his chest as he presses the phone's off button. He stares out the screen door. The ocean is choppy tonight. Emily knows something, obviously. But that's not what bothers him. It's the caginess. How calculating she's become. He has to be able to trust his wife.

What is the point of you?

That's what she said to him.

CHAPTER
THIRTY-EIGHT

EMILY

I waited on PCH behind a line of cars turning left onto Sunset and startled at the sound of breaking news on the radio, a new development in some local scandal. I held my breath and listened for my name, for Doug's name, even though the story had nothing to do with us.

I turned off the stereo. My phone lit up. There was a text from Chloe.

Traffic. B there in 20.

"Shit," I said.

I deleted her text and covered the screen with my hand as the cells in my body gathered into a low simmer. I looked back at my recent calls. There it was, third from the top: evidence that I'd contacted her.

Of course, I'd done nothing wrong by calling her. It was a perfectly reasonable response to her email. That in itself wasn't against the law.

I opened my browser and started typing *burner phone* into the search box. No. I stopped. That wouldn't do. I thought about trying *prepaid phone*, but these web searches were recorded somewhere. Weren't they?

I wasn't planning anything then. I was only thinking. But I had enough sense not to do any of that thinking on the internet.

The car behind me gave a nudging beep. I turned and pulled into a gas station parking lot. Tourists were gathered on the corner, waiting to cross to the beach. I closed my eyes. Who used burner phones? Criminals. And where did they buy these phones?

I touched the air with my fingers, anchorless without the aid of a search engine. I drove up Sunset, scanning every minimall and storefront. I saw a sign for an office-supply store and parked in the underground lot. The woman at the entrance told me they were closing in ten minutes.

"Where are your cell phones?" I asked.

She walked me to a long, low aisle of smartphones with indecipherable deals stickered on the shelf below them. I thanked her. She started back to the front door.

"And, um . . . ," I started. I froze as she turned to me.

"Yes?" she said.

Do you have any prepaid phones?

It was a simple question, an easy one, but my throat was stiff, my vocal cords refusing to cooperate. It was as if my voice had developed its own conscience. And it knew, no matter how I tried to convince myself differently, it knew I was planning a murder.

Nothing about it would come naturally, I realized. If I was going to make myself capable of this, I'd have to work at it, like I worked at everything else. I flexed my fingers and conjured up a swirl of enticements, motivations to kill, in a word cloud of demented self-help aphorisms: I had to get out of my comfort zone. I had to lean into it. I could feel my blood thickening, stopping up access to anything but pure resolve.

The saleslady was still looking at me. The question grew, inflated behind my lips. I let it burst.

"Burner phones," I said. "Where are they?"

CHAPTER THIRTY-NINE

CHLOE

The diner is bright. The windows are enormous. Chloe watches from the parking lot as Emily slides into a vinyl booth and pulls her phone from an expensive tote bag, plastered all over with some idiot's initials.

Emily Webb. She looks different. Still skinny, but her jawline is broader, and there's a ruddiness peeking through her tinted moisturizer. The woman's ponytail is immaculate, though, and her nails, Chloe can see from here, her frigging *nails* are perfectly shaped and shiny. It's like a costume Emily's wearing, a low-maintenance new-mom costume.

Chloe bites a piece of ragged cuticle from her thumb. She flings open the restaurant door and plops her yellow purse, the one from their first meeting, on the table. The plan is to open with the bag and demand an apology, but Emily doesn't even look at it. Chloe picks it up and sets it down again.

"I didn't think you'd show up," says Chloe.

Emily lifts her menu with a puncturing sigh. "I was the one who asked you here. Sit."

The waiter comes to their table. He's young but has the belly of a middle-aged man. He calls them "ladies." Emily orders an iced decaf. Chloe asks for pomegranate juice.

"Anything else?" asks the waiter. Chloe glances at Emily. She wants food. She wants someone to eat with.

Emily says, "That's all."

"No food?"

"That's all," Emily repeats a little more forcefully. The waiter catches Chloe's eye. He winks at her and brushes his hip against her shoulder as he leaves. This sets off a minor flurry of panic in Chloe. The waiter is just like Dylan. Just like Doug. There's no salve, no kindness, in Chloe's world anymore. There's only sexual tension.

Emily leans forward. Chloe crosses her arms. These people. They're pigs, rooting around in everyone else's vulnerability.

"Why did you send me that email?" asks Emily.

"I'm sorry." Chloe tries to control her stammer. She didn't come here to apologize. "I just thought you needed to know."

"You were mad I didn't get back to you, right? About the commercials?"

"No, I—"

"I'm on maternity leave. You don't think to give me a few weeks before you try to wreck my life?"

Chloe wasn't expecting this. She doesn't know what she was expecting, but definitely not Emily saying something so reasonable. Emily is the bad guy. Emily's the one married to Doug. She's the one who's friends with Dr. Maryn. Emily made fun of her purse.

"I wasn't trying to wreck your life."

Emily pushes on. "You need money? Is that it?"

Chloe can feel her face getting smaller, sharper. "I'm not a whore," she says. Emily jerks her hands off the table. It helps, seeing this move, seeing that her anger still has an effect. Fury is the only power Chloe has left. Emily lowers her head and looks at her lap. The waiter comes back with their drinks.

"Are you sure you don't want food?" he asks.

Emily doesn't answer. She moves slowly, stirring milk into her iced coffee. She reaches into her purse and unpeels two Tums from their paper tubing. The waiter raises his eyebrows at Chloe. Chloe shakes her head.

Emily doesn't look up until the waiter is gone. When she does, she seems defeated. "Chloe, we're the same. We're both in a bad situation."

Chloe inhales. She wishes it were more satisfying, seeing this woman just a little bit weaker.

"Doug is the worst thing that ever happened to me," Emily says. "He's a criminal, Chloe. He took over my life. You know, I'm actually jealous of you?"

Chloe brings a hand to her mouth. This is her problem! Women are jealous of her. "No one ever admits that," she says.

"You're young enough to start over! I know it doesn't seem that way, but Chloe . . ." Emily looks off to the side and lets her eyes scan her surroundings, like she's searching for a way to express herself. "You're really fucking talented. I mean, you're electric."

Chloe tilts her head to the side. What Emily's saying, it's like the intro to a song Chloe only half recognizes.

"When you started bowing in front of that actress, I was thinking, this girl is *fearless*."

Sometimes Chloe forgets why she came to LA, that she wanted to dance, to be an artist. "We got kicked out."

Emily offers a sigh. "People are so uptight."

Chloe pauses. She considers. It's a risk, what she wants to ask. "Did you know that guy?"

"Who?"

"The one you were talking to at the firepit."

Emily throws her head back with a gentle laugh. Her eyes settle on Chloe's face. Her voice is empathetic. "You want to know if he told me about the stage manager?"

Chloe's muscles loosen their grip on themselves. It's like she's defrosting. This thing was so secret, the fact of what happened, how she lost it. The memory begins trickling through her, becoming part of her again.

"Why did you attack that woman?" asks Emily.

"I got mad," Chloe says.

Emily nods. She understands.

"I get so mad, sometimes," Chloe says. She brings the inside of her thumb to her mouth and chews.

"Where are your parents?"

"They're not—I was raised by my grandparents."

"Can you call them?"

Call them. Emily Webb has no idea. Chloe picks up a paper napkin. She starts shredding it. Emily doesn't seem that terrible anymore.

"I keep thinking about this man," Chloe says. "At Doug's office. He was wearing a jumpsuit, like he was a maintenance guy. I'd never seen him before, but he kept walking by my desk and, like, staring me down. At one point, he pointed down the hall to Doug's door and said, 'Whose office is that?' I said, 'Doug Markham's.' Then he said, 'Who? Who?' He kept making me repeat Doug's name."

Emily doesn't move, doesn't blink. "Doug hired him to intimidate you," she says.

"You know this?"

"I know how these things work."

A stream of relief courses up Chloe's body, just under the surface of her skin. Emily reaches into her tote and hands Chloe a packet of tissues. Chloe never carries tissues. Her purse is filled with junk. She wipes her eyes.

"You can't let people treat you like that," says Emily.

"But how do I do that?"

It's so easy for Emily, for everyone here, living their lives without predation. Why can't Chloe be like them? She watches a muscular waitress deliver drinks across the dining room. Someone at the table says something to make her smile.

"Look at me!" Emily bobs her head to get Chloe's gaze back in line with her own. She taps her finger on the table with an urgent voice. "You have a moral obligation to protect yourself. You let yourself take these hits, right? And you think if you keep your eyes open, see it all happen, you think you can handle it, but it doesn't work like that. You get twisted inside, and the worst part is that you watch that happen too. You watch yourself turn horrible."

Can you read my mind? Chloe searches Emily's face. There's a flicker of a response. A pulse. A pixilation.

"Tell me what to do," Chloe says.

"Fight back."

"That just gets me in trouble."

Emily reaches across the table. She puts her hand on Chloe's arm.

"You won't get into trouble if you're calm," says Emily.

Chloe nods.

"I can't be your friend unless you're calm. You understand?"

"I think so."

Emily's eyes crinkle. It's the first time Chloe's seen anything resembling happiness on the woman's face. And the part of Chloe that once would have said, *Don't trust this woman. Get away from this woman,* it sounds only the faintest warning, a light pluck on some faraway string Chloe barely picks up over her ache and loneliness. "Did you hear that?" she wants to ask, but she doesn't. It's not something a calm person would say.

"Emily, can I ask you a question?"

"Of course."

"Did you ever have a dog?"

CHAPTER FORTY

EMILY

I wanted Doug tortured. I wanted him pinned to the wall with a pitch-fork. Whatever reservations I'd had were gone. Doug deserved to die.

My upper lip curled, involuntarily, as Chloe searched my face. She sat back with a satisfied smile. She was sharper than I'd realized. "I shouldn't have said anything," she said, her tone innocent and caring. "It's just that when he told me about sending it back, it was weird. It didn't feel right."

I reached for my phone. Bella was back from the dead. I wanted to call the breeder immediately, find out where she was. But I stopped myself. I dug into my purse for more Tums, giving myself a moment to think, to recognize the opportunity Chloe had just handed me. I was so close to earning her trust.

"Her name is Bella," I said, my voice breaking.

"I'm sorry."

"He made me think I'd killed her." I kept wincing, tasting bitter-ness. I looked Chloe in the eye, in a careful display of my pain. "He helped me put up posters."

"He's a bastard," she said.

"It's the lies," I said. "If someone can lie like he does, what else is he capable of?"

"Do you think he really stole all that data? Like Dr. Maryn said?"

I sat back and shook my head, closing in on myself. "I can't talk about it." She leaned forward. I glanced around, assessing the other people in the diner, and lowered my voice. "You know Doug. He acts like this fun-loving, laid-back guy, right? But he's not. When it comes to his business, he's deadly fucking serious."

Chloe gave a slow, glassy-eyed nod. "I know what you're talking about," she said. Her face was losing some of its color. "Have you ever stared power in the face?"

I held my breath and kept still.

"The strangest things happen when you bump up against it," she said. "You become desperate. Like you want to escape or fight back, but there's nowhere to go. I mean, the people in the office. They would say the worst, sneakiest things, or they'd ignore me or look at me so mean, and I just had to take it. I couldn't defend myself." Her eyes filled. She pressed her fingers flat against her lips and whispered, "It felt like they were going to kill me."

"Doug did that to you," I said.

The waiter sauntered up to the table. "You ladies want anything else?" His voice was loud and smug, taking pleasure in interrupting our intimate moment. The gnat. The fly. I pointed behind the counter and spoke firmly. "Go over there and come back when we call you."

Chloe watched the waiter walk away and turned to me, beaming. "How did you do that?"

"You'll see," I said. I pulled the two burner phones I'd bought from my purse. They were flip phones, with no GPS tracking. "Do you know how to text on a numeric keyboard?"

"You're giving me a phone?"

"Doug and I share a Verizon account. He checks who's calling me." She opened one of the phones. "You want to stay in touch with me?"

"Of course!" I touched her arm again. I wrapped my fingers around it. She put her hand on top of mine.

"My God, you're so skinny," I said. "When was the last time you ate?" I raised my other hand for the waiter to come back.

———

I waited until Chloe started in on her burger before excusing myself to make a phone call. I stepped out to the sidewalk and called the breeder. She answered in a sleepy voice. It was after 10:00 p.m. I didn't care that I'd woken her.

"This is Emily Webb," I said. "You sold me a Doberman about two years ago?"

"Excuse me?"

"The dog, Bella. I just learned that she was returned to you?"

"Who is this?"

"Emily Webb. I think my husband gave you back my dog."

There was silence on the line. The breeder spoke in hushed tones with someone else, another woman.

"This was the nervous pup, right?"

"Yes," I said, my chest tightening. I wanted to scream, *Tell me where she is!* "Bella. You took her back?"

The woman blew out a long stream of air. It felt like she was blowing right into my ear. "I took her back," she said. "And then I couldn't get rid of her."

I covered my mouth, suppressing a moan, and doubled over. I could barely get the next words out. "Is she dead?"

"Oh Lord, no," said the breeder. "What kind of operation do you think I'm running? She's out at the ranch. My daughter's fostering the rejects."

I couldn't hold it in anymore. I started crying. "I want her back," I said. "I'll pay you anything."

"All right," said the breeder. "Take it easy. Just tell me when you want to come get her."

I swallowed. I couldn't do it, not right away. I couldn't let Doug know that I knew. "I'm not sure," I said. "Can you hold on to her? For a few weeks?"

"Okay, wait a minute." The breeder started talking again to the woman in the room with her. She came back on. "We can do that."

"I'll pay for her food in the meantime."

"Hold on a second."

The woman in the room with the breeder spoke louder, more insistently. I heard her say, "You have to tell her."

"Okay . . . okay," said the breeder. Her tone was strained and polite. She was hiding something. "Hold for just one more second."

The phone went mute. I watched the traffic on Sunset, there was confusion at the spot where the lanes split, half of them leading to the southbound freeway, the other half going straight ahead. Every minute or so a random driver would find themselves stuck in the wrong lane and block traffic as they tried to right their error.

The phone unmuted. A different voice came on, a deeper, more confident one. "Emily? That's your name?"

"Yes," I said.

"Your husband is Doug?"

"That's right."

"You're still married?"

I gave a laugh. "Let me guess," I said. "He had an affair?"

The woman didn't speak for a moment. "You should know we don't normally let people return dogs," she said. "We made an exception because he told us you were dead."

CHAPTER FORTY-ONE

Doug

Doug dims the lights in the living room. Grace is asleep in her swing. He wanders into the kitchen and opens the cabinet again. He stares at the baking powder. Just one more hit of coke. But it's late. He'll be up all night if he does that. There's a couple of Vicodin in the medicine cabinet, but he doesn't trust himself with that either. Not while he's in charge of Grace.

He pulls a Lalique rocks glass out of the lower cabinet. It's heavy and reassuring, carved to resemble a Grecian urn. He pours himself three fingers of Blanton's and brings his drink to the balcony.

What is the point of you? That's what Emily said.

Sometimes the point is just this. A drink on a back deck with a nice ocean view. There are worse things to organize a life around. He sits on the lounger and stretches out. The ocean gives him a hint, a sizzle, of stillness. He puts his drink down and listens. That was such a strange thing that happened to him, all those years ago when he was about to get kicked out of college. Like the sea was talking to him.

He hears a chirp. Then a chime. He sits up. He looks out into the darkness, confused. What kind of bird or being would make such a noise? He hears them again. He can't place the sounds, until he realizes they're not from the natural world. They're coming from inside the house. Two different devices, his phone and laptop, are sounding the same alarm. He looks back. His laptop is open on the breakfast bar, push notification after push notification rolling down his screen. He picks up his bourbon and sips.

There's only one app allowed to chime on his laptop. Google Alerts. The tones mean his name has appeared somewhere on the internet. He hears them again. His name is popping up all over. He sips his drink.

The garage gate rumbles above. He puts his hands over his ears. But he can still hear Emily's car pull in. The thud of her door slamming. He can't hear her footsteps over the waves, but he knows she's checking the baby's room and wondering at the empty crib.

His phone and computer sound off again.

"Doug?" she calls from the top of the stairs. He reflexively starts responding, *Down here,* but stops himself. He has fifteen, maybe twenty seconds before she comes down. He wants those moments to himself.

"Doug," she says. She's leaning out the sliding glass door with her feet still in the living room. She waves her phone at him. "Have you seen it yet?"

CHAPTER FORTY-TWO

EMILY

Doug acted like he couldn't hear me, like he was in a trance. His phone was vibrating on the counter. "Doug," I repeated, louder. "Come inside."

He puffed up his cheeks and let the air flap through his lips and walked to the balcony railing. He had a crystal glass in his hand, an expensive family heirloom. He lifted it over the edge and let it go, let it fall to the beach.

"Dr. Maryn dropped the video," I said.

He looked back at me with one raised eyebrow. "No kidding."

"Come."

I led him to the breakfast bar and sat him on a stool. He opened his browser.

"Go to YouTube," I said. The thumbnail was clickbaity: a woman running away from the camera. The title read, *GOTCHA! A NEW SHOW FROM DR. MARYN* . . . Doug clicked on it and was met with the smash of a gong and trumpets as the video player flashed fat white lettering against a rippling blue background.

*THIS FALL . . . DR. MARYN . . . TAKES ON THE PARASITES . . .
THE DEADBEATS . . . THE SWINDLERS.*

Sound effects of scraping metal and crashing cymbals punctuated
clip after clip of Dr. Maryn ambushing people in business suits, pencil
skirts, and hard hats. Timpani drums rolled in, tribal and unrelenting,
as a lady in an evening gown escaped through a parking lot, screaming, "Shred the file! Shred the file!" A man in a yellow vest hid his face
behind a traffic cone.

Finally, Doug's promotional video, the data animation with its
swirling digital shadow humans, began playing. He leaned toward his
computer, his eyes close to the screen, like he was searching the computer's innards. Erik's voice came in low and penitent over the footage.
"I gave him a new hard drive every two weeks."

Doug gasped when he saw Harper, her curls filling the frame. She
looked into the camera with sincere, sorrowful eyes. "He told me to
delete everything."

"Bitch," Doug whispered.

The giant text was back now, propelling outward in 3D motion,
each phrase given its own hit on the snare.

*THE ONE THING . . . YOU DON'T DO . . . IS MESS . . . WITH
DR. MARYN.*

Doug covered his mouth as he watched Dr. Maryn storm his office,
the video cutting to shots of his alarmed employees and then back to
Dr. Maryn with an outraged hand in the air.

"You betrayed my trust!" she shouted. "You stole my data!"

The video cut to a close-up of Doug, his Adam's apple pumping,
his eyes darting straight into the camera lens. He shook his finger at the
screen. "No," he said. "I only looked at the camera once, right when
I came into the office." He hit the space bar, pausing the video, and
looked at me, incredulous. "She rearranged the footage."

I stared at him, narrowing my eyes. "Yes," I said. "They do that in
television."

Doug hit the space bar again to reveal another shot of Dr. Maryn planting her hands on her hips, triumphant and furious. The drums beat faster. Then Doug was back on camera, panting. He was panting. The video ended with a flourish, with the word *GOTCHA!* spun from a small, faraway font to chunky and full screen.

Doug jumped up, toppling the stool. "What about the part where I told them to get the fuck out of my office! Why didn't they show that?"

I laughed. "Are you serious?"

"Em, this isn't what happened." He leaned over his laptop and typed *twitter* into the address bar.

"What are you doing?"

"The video was doctored."

"You're pissed they didn't show you swearing?"

He ignored me and logged onto Twitter, reactivating his account and breathing hard through his nostrils. I watched him, wondering if I should let him publicly implode. I'd be able to point at him finally, turn to some shadow audience, and say, *Do you see what I've had to put up with?*

He clicked on the *What's Happening* box and started punching out the words, *Totally fake video . . .* I put my hands over his and squeezed his fingers.

"Stop," I said.

"They edited it to make me look scared!"

"And tweeting about it will make you look crazy. We need to hire a crisis-management firm." Doug tried to free himself from my grip. I held his hands tighter. "No typing," I said.

"Fuck this!" he yelled and tore away.

"Quiet," I said. "You'll wake her." I glanced at Grace, asleep in her fuzzy swing, her little fist pressed to her ear. Every minute it was becoming clearer: I needed to save her from her father.

He sat down on the bottom step to the upstairs and buried his face in his arms. "The police will come," I said. He let out a moan. "How did you pay Erik? The Belize account? The Seychelles?"

He lifted his head and scowled. "You have been spying on me, haven't you?"

"We need to act. Now."

He sighed and let his face go slack. "An account in the Caymans."

"That account is toast. Don't touch it again. I set up a shell company in Nauru. We can transfer the rest there for the time being." He glared at me. I wasn't having it. "What else are you gonna do?"

He stood, his face a complete blank. "You really are a piece of work, Em." He started to move past me toward his computer. I grabbed his arm.

"Don't do it now!" I said. "Go to a café or the library tomorrow morning. Use their Wi-Fi. We'll have to destroy both of our computers."

It was pitiful then, watching him turn from me and walk up the stairs, his shoulders slumped. I almost felt sorry for him, for what I was about to do to him.

I went to Grace's swing and slid my hands underneath her in one smooth movement. She didn't wake up. I was getting better at this mothering thing. I brought her upstairs to her crib and took a pillow and blanket from the closet. I lay down on the floor next to her and slept soundly.

Doug was gone when I woke the next morning. I texted him.

Are you doing it?

Yes.

The nanny arrived at eight. I showered and changed and kissed Grace goodbye. I told the nanny that I was going for a hike.

"If there's an issue, call Doug," I told her. "Cell service is spotty where I'm headed."

I made sure my burner phone was in my purse and checked that my iPhone was on. I turned on its location services. Then I hid the iPhone under the mattress.

CHAPTER FORTY-THREE

CHLOE

Chloe sits up in bed and opens her blinds. It makes the room happy, the way the light filters into it. Things are different today. She's been having this awful sense until just now that there was a hole inside her, all bottomless and sucking her down. But this morning it feels filled in.

She looks on top of her dresser, the one Doug bought her. Her flip phone, the one Emily gave her, has been charging all night. She opens it, carefully, like she's unfolding a secret valentine. And then it's magic, what happens next. A text comes in. She wasn't expecting to hear from Emily, not this soon.

Did you see the video?

Chloe is smiling, she realizes. She decides to keep the smile on her face. It's easier. The last thing she needs is to give in to the fear lurking around her edges. She'll start worrying if she does that, and she'll never make it out of her bedroom. She taps out the letters on her numeric keypad.

Video?

Dr. Maryn

Chloe picks up her laptop off the floor, searches for the video, and watches, scanning the screen for signs of herself. She's only visible in one wide shot.

Doug looks terrified.

She waits for another text, but this phone is so basic she doesn't even get the blinking ellipses. She has no idea if Emily is typing or what. She types again:

Are you okay?

No.

You want to talk?

I'll come to you.

Chloe throws on leggings and an old tank top. She rushes past the unopened mail scattered across the living room floor to the dishes piled up in the kitchen. She picks up her detergent bottle. It's empty. It's been empty for the last week and a half. She sniffs. Something smells. She opens the cabinet under the sink. Her garbage is overflowing.

Her intercom rings. Emily is here. It's so soon. Chloe hasn't even started cleaning. She shoves her dirty dishes, her mugs and glasses, into the cabinet under the sink. Displaced spray bottles of Clorox and Fantastik clatter onto the linoleum. "Crap," Chloe says. She pushes them back. A can of Comet tips over, spilling gritty powder under her feet. Emily rings again. Chloe shuts the cabinet and buzzes Emily up.

Emily sweeps in. She's wearing sunglasses and a baseball cap and jeans with a soft, long-sleeved T-shirt. Even in this casual outfit, Emily looks rich. She has a Starbucks tray with two coffees and a white paper bag. She stops in the middle of Chloe's empty dining room and looks around the apartment. There's one lone picture on the wall, above where the futon used to be, a print of a thick-brushed painting announcing Chloe's senior-year dance recital. It's crooked, Chloe realizes. She starts toward it. Emily brings the coffee to the kitchen.

"Don't clean on my account," she says. She opens the lid of a coffee cup and looks into the white bag. "Milk and sugar?"

Chloe straightens the picture. "Sure," she says.

"They only gave me Splenda," Emily says.

Chloe moves into the kitchen. She opens the cabinet next to the fridge and pulls out the cardboard Domino Sugar carton Sheralyn left behind, Sharpied with a giant *S!!!!*

Emily points to the writing. "What's that?"

"My old roommate," Chloe says. "Did Doug see the video?"

"He's in a rage about it," Emily says. She bristles. "He's scaring me, actually." She stirs sugar into Chloe's coffee with a plastic spoon and then holds up the spoon. "Where's your garbage?" Before Chloe can tell her to leave it on the counter, Emily opens the cabinet under the sink. She stares at the plates and toppled cleaning supplies.

"Chloe," she says.

"I know."

Emily has compassion in her eyes even though she's frowning. "Sweetie, you can't live like this."

Normally someone saying that, it would make Chloe feel like she was in trouble, like there was something wrong with her. It would make

Chloe mad. But Emily doesn't give her the chance to react. "Let's fix it," she says. She reaches under the cabinet and pulls the dishes out, pile by pile. She doesn't seem to mind when she touches a blotch of semidried ketchup. She stacks everything in the sink.

"I ran out of detergent," says Chloe.

"Right." Emily opens the refrigerator. It's empty except for a bottle of mustard. Emily closes the fridge. Chloe is on the edge of embarrassment, of defensiveness. But Emily is acting all detached and matter of fact, like she's a doctor or a jail guard. Professional. "Stay here," Emily says. "I'll be back in an hour." She pulls her purse over her shoulder and heads outside.

Emily buzzes the intercom again an hour later. She asks Chloe to come down and help her. She's standing at the front gate with eight grocery bags gathered at her feet. She hands Chloe two of them. Chloe looks past her, to the street.

"Where did you park?" she asks.

Emily turns. She waves to the stretch of empty space next to the sidewalk. "A truck was here a second ago," says Emily. "I'm on the next block."

They bring the groceries up in two trips.

"You want to unpack?" asks Emily. "I'll do the dishes."

Chloe lifts the brown paper bags onto the counter. The groceries smell cold. They smell like promise. She runs her fingers over each avocado, each orange, the cardboard on her brand-new carton of eggs.

"Thank you," she says.

Emily pulls a dishrag from one of the bags and moves closer to Chloe. "It's nothing," she says. She puts a hand on Chloe's shoulder and leans in. Her breath is seductive. Her voice vibrates close to Chloe's ear. "Doug and I are through," she says. "You can count on me, okay? Can we count on each other?"

CHAPTER FORTY-FOUR

EMILY

Gaining Chloe's trust was ultimately depressing. I was used to elite circles. I'd never sought out a relationship with a vulnerable, possibly ill person before. It required zero effort. She was a sign of what Doug had done to me, of how far I'd fallen. She didn't even own a dishwasher.

I was in the kitchen with her, drying the last of her bowls with the dish towel. I covered my fingers with the terry cloth as I touched it all so I wouldn't leave fingerprints. I asked if she liked chicken soup.

"I love it," she said. Of course she did. I set aside carrots, celery, and an onion from the groceries.

"Where are your knives?"

She opened a drawer to reveal a few pieces of mismatched silverware and a long serrated bread knife. It would have to do. I sawed at the onion, my eyes stinging from the fumes, as she sat on a stool.

"That smells so good," she said. She reminded me of Bella, the way she tracked me as I moved from cutting board to stove top and back, sighing occasionally in contentment. I missed my dog.

"How do you do it?" she asked.

"Do what?"

"Make friends so easily?"

I stirred the sizzling onion in the pot and thought of my sorority sisters, my old posse. The video had come out the day before, and not one of them had checked to see how I was doing.

"Seriously," Chloe said. "We were, like, enemies yesterday, and now you're making me soup."

"I guess it helps to have something in common," I said and winked at her. She gave me a shy, flirty smile. I wiped my fingerprints off the knife with a wet paper towel. I did it right in front of her. She reached for one of my peeled carrots and snapped off a bite.

"You know what I mean," she said as she crunched. An edge crept into her voice. "You're, like, a popular-girl type."

I nodded. I didn't like where the conversation was headed. "I forgot to get bay leaves," I said. I opened the refrigerator and pulled out a new carrot to replace the one she was eating. "LA is tough," I said. "It's not like I'm comfortable all the time." I peeled the carrot with long strokes. "You know, when I first started out, I was backstage at a concert with these rock stars. I mean, the guys were legends. It was one of the first signs that I'd made it, you know? Then at one point, they started telling stories about being in marching band in high school. I couldn't believe it. I even said to them, 'You were in *band*?' and they were like, 'Of course. We're musicians.'"

Chloe stared at me. Her mouth was open.

"The point is, Chloe, I'm surrounded by nerds here in LA. I'm out of my element. But I make it work."

"I'm a nerd," she said.

I pointed at her. "I suspected as much."

"Not a band nerd. I was a dancer. It kind of saved me, having somewhere to go every day. My grandparents didn't have a lot of money."

She quieted down and focused on the counter. She was about to tell me something. I could feel it. I could smell the loneliness coming off her.

"I was bullied pretty bad," she said, her tone a mix of confession and confrontation. I narrowed my eyes at her, waiting for her to continue, but she didn't. She looked straight at me. I wasn't sure what she wanted. An apology? Was I now the spokesperson for the former cool kids?

"Was it an ugly duckling–type thing?"

"No," she said. "My mom tried to kill me."

I dropped the carrot peeler, like she'd yanked me, pulled on my arm. The kitchen turned vivid. I blinked, aware of her skin, of her youth and lack of wrinkles. How old was she? She'd told me once, but I couldn't remember.

"I think the other kids just didn't know how to be around me," she said.

Chloe looked down. I stopped blinking. "Are you fucking with me?" I asked. I was having crazy thoughts, wondering if Destiny Stimpson had something to do with this, with Chloe being in my life.

"What?" she asked, all clueless sounding.

She wasn't a helpless person, not at all. I backed up to the middle of the kitchen as I ran through the major events in my head. She'd come to *my* office. She'd pursued *my* husband. The emails. The ease with which she'd let me enter her life. Chloe was a stalker. Or something. The fear was just a sliver, an irrational one, but it was sharp, that Chloe was somehow Destiny's baby come back to life, come to seek revenge.

My voice came at her hard. "What did your mother do to you?"

She shrank in her seat. "Are you mad at me?"

I hammered her. "How old are you?"

"Twenty-four." She was just about the right age.

"Where are you from?"

"Phoenix!"

"Phoenix?" I said. "Have you ever been to Figblossom Valley?"

"I don't even know what that is."

"What did your family do?"

Her eyes widened. "Why are you asking me this?"

"You lived with your grandparents? What did they do?"

"My grandpa was a golf pro."

"Where?"

"Oh my God, Emily."

I didn't let up. "Where did your grandfather work?"

"He was at the Phoenician."

I smiled. I had her. The Phoenician was an ultralux resort at the base of Camelback Mountain. I knew it well. "One of the pools there is lined in something unusual. What is it?"

Chloe brought her hand to her face. She looked like she was about to cry. "Are you talking about the mother-of-pearl thing? Why are you being so mean?"

No, Emily. I shook my head, like I was shaking something off. Destiny's baby died. I crossed my arms over my chest. *The baby died.* I repeated the fact to myself, standing in Chloe's kitchen. I didn't believe in ghosts.

Chloe wiped the counter in front of her with frantic movements, sweeping bits of crumb and paper onto the floor. "I can never tell anyone about my mom. They always freak out."

"I'm not freaking out," I said. I was spooked. My actions, my plans—this whole situation was terrifying.

"You are," she said. Her chin was jutting forward, like a toddler holding back tears.

I was losing her, ruining my plans with a reckless detour into paranoia. "Okay," I said. "You're right. I am freaking out."

Chloe looked at me, not satisfied but willing to listen. I had to explain myself. I closed my eyes and wished I were a more nimble liar, that I were more like Doug. But it was a long story, and it was easiest just to play it straight.

"Something happened when I was a kid," I said. "It's stayed with me."

I told her about Destiny Stimpson, about getting her in trouble for shoplifting, ghosting her in middle school. I told her about the pregnancy, about the fact that my friends and I hadn't known for sure she was pregnant, but we'd spread the rumors anyway.

"There were a lot of news stories that year with teen parents literally throwing babies away. One girl gave birth at her prom, in the bathroom. She went back to the party and danced afterward, like nothing happened."

Chloe's face grew injured looking, as if I were relaying facts that had to do with her. I clenched my jaw, furious at her self-absorption. "I made a crack in the cafeteria. I said that Destiny's baby would end up in a dumpster. I didn't realize, until one of my friends shushed me, she was sitting right behind me." Chloe looked away, to the window. I wanted her to turn back, to see me. I was about to tell her something I'd never shared with anyone. "At least that's one way I remember it," I said. "That's the version I told the principal. But I also remember saying it deliberately, knowing Destiny would hear. I honestly can't tell you which version is true."

Chloe nodded. She kept her face turned. "My mom left me," she said in a monotone. "She left me alone in an empty apartment to be with her boyfriend."

I raised a hand to my mouth. I'd just told her exactly who I was. It was a warning. She didn't get it. She started picking at a scab on her thumb.

"I was seven," she said. "All I had to eat was a loaf of Wonder Bread and a jar of peanut butter. After a few days, I started knocking on the neighbor lady's door. She fed me. She gave me a bar of soap and told me to take a shower."

Chloe winced and took a shaky, brutal inhale. Her eyes took on a narrow, wounded look.

"The thing that gets me was this woman," she said. "She'd open the door just a crack and slip me cookies or chips. But she never invited me in. She never called anyone."

I grimaced. I didn't understand. "Is that how your mom tried to kill you?"

Chloe laughed. Her face relaxed into a cheerful expression. "Of course not! Gosh, that would have taken forever." She came around the counter and lifted one leg of her yoga pants, almost to the crotch. There was a long scar on her thigh, raised and red against her pale skin. It looked like a gummy worm. "She stabbed me."

I took a step back. Chloe's smile was bright. Her eyes were twinkly.

"To be fair," she said. "She only meant to *threaten* me with the knife. And she took me to the emergency room and didn't even try pretending that she hadn't done it. That's when I went to live with my grandparents."

I straightened, waiting for a cue that she needed comfort. She went to the stove and lifted the lid to the soup pot. She smelled it.

"Why are people so awful to children?" she asked.

I slid my hands into the back pockets of my jeans and shrugged. "Kids are weak."

CHAPTER
FORTY-FIVE

CHLOE

Emily comes every day that week. And then every day the next. Sometimes she texts first. Sometimes she just shows up with breakfast. She brings egg sandwiches and cereal, and then she starts bringing clothes. Long-sleeved shirts for the coming winter weather and a black, puffy down jacket. She brings orange juice, too, and even though Chloe's never been a juice person, she drinks it because it's so thoughtful, Emily helping her out like this.

They do a lot of talking, and they never leave Chloe's apartment. It's nice at first. Chloe starts to hate the outside. She stops going out, even on her own. She doesn't have to, not with Emily coming over and bringing her food and coffee.

But after two weeks of this, Chloe feels jumbly, like she's filling up with white noise, and she gets the idea that maybe fresh air will help her. She doesn't open a window on her own, no. She doesn't know why, but the idea of that makes her nervous. The next time Emily comes over, though, Chloe makes a suggestion. She asks if maybe they can go someplace together. Like instead of watching Netflix on her computer, maybe they can go out to a movie. But Emily stands up, all worried and shaking, and says she can't risk it. She walks to the window and looks through two slats of Chloe's blinds.

"I have to tell you the truth," Emily says. "I'm scared of Doug. He's a coke addict. He's out of control and he rages, especially now that everyone knows he's a criminal." She thinks Doug has a private investigator on her. She tells Chloe she's scared to leave him. "He told the dog breeder I was dead," Emily says. "Sometimes I think he wants to kill me."

As Emily tells her these things, Chloe looks to the dead bolt to make sure it's locked. She tries to remember her time with Doug. She doesn't recall him doing drugs or having a bad temper, so this is surprising.

"He gets death threats too," Emily says. "It's a nightmare. They even threaten me and the baby." Emily comes back and sits next to Chloe on the carpet. "Honestly, I think it would be best if someone actually did just come along and kill him." Emily pauses for just a moment before going off again. She's on a tear. "Do you know I actually found his drugs? He's hiding them in the cabinet. In this dummy can of baking powder."

Emily sidles up closer to Chloe. She points at the laptop on the floor, just out of Chloe's reach. "Can you google that? Google *hiding place baking powder false bottom*." Chloe opens her laptop and searches. "That's it!" says Emily when the image results load. The picture is from a spy shop. "Can you follow the link?" she asks.

There's other stuff they sell in the spy shop, like hidden cameras and keystroke loggers. "Let me see what the GPS trackers look like," Emily says. "I know he's tracking me. I keep my phone at the house, so I think he put something on my car."

"You think?" Chloe asks. It's the first thing she's said in the last half hour.

That night, after Emily leaves, Chloe has dreams about GPS trackers, about a malevolent force following, controlling, her every move. She texts Emily as soon as she wakes the next morning:

Did you find tracker?

Yes.

Chloe backs up to the head of her bed, panicked. If Doug put one on Emily's car, he must know where she goes every day.

"What is happening?" she whispers. This isn't the same Doug Chloe remembers. He's a shadow Doug. Menacing. Violent. Chloe knows she should check her car too. She looks up the spy shop again. She studies the picture of the GPS tracker.

She doesn't think it will be hard, going down to her parking lot, not until she tries it. As soon as she steps out her door, as the breeze hits her skin, it feels like she's being splashed with scalding water. She looks past the gate to her parking lot and almost loses her balance. A man is standing near her car. He's in his thirties and has wavy brown hair, and she doesn't recognize him from her building. He stares at her. He raises a vape pen to his mouth. A cloud of steam escapes from his face.

Chloe backs up inside. She slams the door and locks it. She looks out the peephole. The outside walkway is empty. She stays there for a few minutes, checking to make sure the guy isn't coming for her. She texts Emily:

Will I see you today?

Emily doesn't text back for a whole hour.

Yes. Later. Visiting Bella.

Everything okay?

Chloe thinks. The guy in the parking lot, should she tell Emily about him? She crawls to the living room window and peeks out the bottom blind. She can see the street from here. A neighbor she knows is walking her dog. A car with a loud radio whizzes by. Chloe reaches for a slim ray of sunlight. No, she won't say anything to Emily about the guy. It will make her sound crazy.

The guy in the parking lot worried her; that's all. Chloe needs to leave her apartment; she knows this. She needs to get used to seeing random people she doesn't know again. She opens her blinds. She opens her windows. The air smells like spring.

CHAPTER FORTY-SIX

EMILY

I shouldn't have left Chloe alone for a full day. But circumstances forced me to stay away. First, I had to see Bella. She'd attacked another dog at the ranch, and the breeder's daughter, who'd been fostering Bella, wanted money. It was an opportunity to introduce my dog to Grace, to see how she reacted. I had to make sure she was okay around the baby before I brought her home.

The place was an hour away. I brought my regular cell phone and my burner phone and parked at the edge of the driveway. I could hear Bella as soon as I started down the patchwork of uneven pavement leading toward the breeder's daughter's ranch house. Bella must have seen me through the slats of the side yard fence, or maybe she caught my scent. I recognized her bark. I started running toward the gate. Grace's stroller wheel caught in a mini pothole, almost toppling her.

"Shit," I said. Grace started to wake. Bella's barks grew more urgent, hoarse even. I could hear her desperation as I unbuckled Grace from her stroller. "Come on, Grace," I said. Bella jumped up and pawed at the wood.

"Hi, Bella!" I called from the driveway. "Hi, baby!" She gave a happy series of barks. Grace began to cry. "No, Grace," I said. "This is a good sound. Good girl, Bella!" I wanted to run to Bella, but I had to give Grace a gentle introduction.

The breeder's daughter joined me. She had a nose ring and wore flowy purple pants. "Pup remembers you," she said.

"Of course she does," I said.

The breeder's daughter considered me. "You want me to hold the baby?"

I looked at Bella. She was jumping, happy, not at all threatening. "No, it's better if I have the baby with me when I approach."

I shifted Grace to one arm and leaned my opposite side toward Bella. I let my dog lick my cheeks. I scratched her ears and welled up and started laughing, remembering a dream I had a month after my mother died. I dreamed she came back to visit. I held her hands in the dream and said over and over, "I'm so happy to see you."

"Do you want to meet Grace?" I took a step back. "Sitz!" I said and showed her the baby. Bella stayed seated and gave a high-pitched moan, no growling, no showing her teeth. This was a good sign. I spent an hour with Bella, playing fetch, lying together on the grass, giving her a minute here and there to investigate the baby. I took a picture while Bella nuzzled Grace's belly. "We're going to be a family," I said. "Just the three of us."

Before I left, I gave the breeder's daughter $1,200 cash for the other dog's medical bills and asked if I could see the receipt from the animal hospital.

"Sure," said the breeder's daughter. She started into the house. Then she stopped. She turned to me. "My mom told you what your husband said?"

I raised my eyebrows. "About me being dead?"

She put a hand on her hip. "He's that guy that ripped off Dr. Maryn?"

"That's him."

"He's going to jail, right? Is that why you're keeping Bella here? You're waiting?"

I shook my head slowly, giving nothing away. "I have no idea what's going to happen."

She stepped closer, assuming a more intimate tone. "You know, there are places you can go."

I tilted my head. "What places?"

"You know . . . shelters." She gestured to Grace. "They'll take both of you."

I smirked. All I knew about this woman was that she was bilking me. In a month she'd make up some other phony reason for me to fork over $1,000. And yet she thought it appropriate to give me advice. "Don't you worry," I said. "I have it under control."

I left. I was going to visit Chloe later that morning. The plan was for me to meet the nanny at my house, drop off Grace, and hide my iPhone back under the mattress.

I was almost home when I saw the news vans. There were three of them, parked across PCH from our house. Five police cars were in front, blocking my neighbor's driveway and flanking a navy-blue armored truck with the gold lettering of *FBI*.

I kept driving.

I drove for ten minutes, thinking of Doug's computer, the one he'd used to transfer money into my Nauru account. We'd destroyed it only a few days before, along with my laptop, smashing them to bits with hammers and dropping the pieces into the ocean from our kayaks. Even if some of it washed ashore, the data was unrecoverable.

And I'd already moved the money to a Swiss bank. I'd memorized the account numbers, the complicated password. They were in only one place: my head.

Grace started crying. I was still on PCH. "Not now, Gracie," I said. She kept crying. "Not now!" She wailed even harder.

I pulled over and fixed a bottle for her in the back seat. I called Doug's cell. It rang once before a heavy male voice answered, "Agent Schroeder."

"Hello?" I said. "Can I speak to Doug?"

"Not on this phone."

I heard Doug's voice in the background. "Is that Emily?"

"That your wife?" asked the agent.

"Tell her to call the office line," said Doug.

Grace spit up. I unbuckled her from the car seat and wiped her neck, some of the sour liquid seeping into her shirt, onto my jeans. I called Doug's office number. "Oh, good, you have your cell phone on you," he said.

I blinked. I didn't have time to process what he was saying. "Are you getting arrested?" I asked.

"No," said Doug. His voice was matter of fact, accepting. He'd already lost about 70 percent of his clients. His employees were quitting en masse. "My lawyer says it might take them months to build a case."

"The FBI is at the house," I said.

Doug lowered his voice. "I can't really talk right now."

He hung up. My rage spiked. I dug through the diaper bag for a clean shirt for Grace. The nanny hadn't packed one. I looked back, in the direction of my home. I couldn't even get a change of clothes. I cursed Doug and blotted Grace's spit-up off her shirt. I buckled her back into her car seat and spoke to her in singsong. "We're going to a park now. You like that? There'll be grass there and other babies."

I got back in the driver's seat. I couldn't see Chloe now, not while I had Grace with me. And my regular cell phone would ping at her place.

But there was still work to be done. I reached into the glove compartment for the burner phone and texted her.

Something's come up. Can come tomorrow.

She didn't write back.

I drove south, to a park in Santa Monica next to the municipal airport where Doug kept his Cessna. I took Grace out of her car seat and carried her to the playground, blending in with the other moms and kids. I carried her through the playground, past the tennis courts and baseball diamonds, to the barbed wire–topped fence separating the park from the airport tarmac.

"Look!" I bent and pointed to the dozen small jets and prop planes parked just a few feet away. "That one in the middle, that's Daddy's!" Grace reached forward. "You want to touch the fence?" I squatted with her next to the weigela bushes lining the fence. I pulled my sleeve over my fingers and felt the slim steel weaving into chain link. I looked for wires or an alarm-company insignia. There was only a battered and bent **NO TRESPASSING** sign.

"Do you see the trees?" I asked Grace. I pointed up to the nearby treetops and scanned for surveillance cameras.

I stayed at the park for an hour afterward, making myself appear as normal as possible. I even spread out a baby blanket on the grass. I put Grace on her back and kissed her. I rolled her over onto her tummy. "This is how you roll over," I said. The most advanced babies were able to roll from back to front by three months old.

"See? You roooollll over." I rolled her over again in slow motion and laid her on her back. "Now you do it," I said. "Roll over, Grace."

"Awooo!" she said and pumped her fists in the air.

I opened my flip phone. Chloe still hadn't texted back. All I needed was a Google search, inspiration for how to sabotage a plane. I couldn't do it myself. I texted Chloe:

I'm scared.

What's wrong?

Search warrant on my house.

Oh no.

FBI was there.

Geez.

I'll see you tomorrow?

She didn't write back right away. She hadn't responded earlier. Something was going on.

How are you btw?

I had a good day.

Went for a walk.

I think I'm ready to find a job.

"Fuck," I said. A nearby mom of a toddler flashed me a look. One day. I spent one day away from Chloe, and suddenly she was feeling empowered. That wasn't going to work for me. For now, though, I had to play along. I picked up my phone and texted:

Go Chloe! Amazing!!!!

CHAPTER FORTY-SEVEN

CHLOE

Emily texts at 8:00 a.m. She's on her way over. Chloe ventures out to wait for her. It doesn't frighten her as much anymore, the idea of being outside. She sits on the front steps of her building and slips her hands in her sweatshirt pockets. Chloe has been thinking. She's been up most of the night, going over everything. She has a plan now, for her life. Or the beginnings of one, at least.

The fact is, she's been drifting, relying on Emily, and Emily has been so helpful. Chloe will tell her that. Chloe rehearses what she's going to say. She'll tell Emily how grateful she is. But it's time for Chloe to stop hiding. She's going to look for a job. A waitressing job so she can be on her feet and talking to a million different people, and she'll be rushing around, not giving anyone time to settle into hating her. Then, once she starts making money, once she gets a little stability, she can start thinking about what she wants her life to look like.

But the most important part is that Chloe has to get back to work. She needs to stop counting on others. They swoop in, these people, and they're full of promises, but it never pans out.

Chloe shivers. She doesn't know why, but she has this feeling that Emily won't like it, that she'll get mad or be jealous. Chloe will have to speak gently, then. She'll involve Emily in the idea. She'll ask her for help. "Do you know any restaurants you think I should apply to?" she can say. She'll ask Emily if she thinks she's too old to be a model. Or maybe Emily can help her with commercials like they talked about.

Chloe sees Emily's car slow as it approaches the building. Chloe waves. Emily drives past her. Chloe watches her park up the block. Her flip phone vibrates. Emily is texting her.

Go inside.

Chloe gets a jolt; it's fluttery and jittery, and it makes her look up and down the wide boulevard, makes her look into the passing cars. She texts back.

Why?

I think I'm being followed.

She heads back upstairs and wonders, briefly, who would be following Emily. The police? Doug? She moves into her apartment. The lack of furniture is heavy all of a sudden, like it's going to crush her. She doesn't want to be here. And she's starting to wonder why, if Emily has a bad marriage, if Doug might be going to jail, why that means that Chloe can't be out in the fresh air.

Emily locks Chloe's dead bolt as soon as she enters. She's breathing heavily. "Here," she says. She has a plastic grocery bag in one hand and a debit card in the other. She slides the card into Chloe's fingers. "It's prepaid. I put fifteen hundred dollars on it. You can go to IKEA, get a futon, maybe even a couch. Let me know if things are more expensive."

Chloe brings the card to her chest. She'd given up on ever having a place to sit. "This is too much," she says.

"Chloe, you need help."

"I know, but I—"

"Save your money. You're going to need it." Emily walks into the kitchen. She plops the bag on the counter. "Do you like couscous?"

Again with the food. Chloe wishes she hadn't told Emily about her mother abandoning her. "Emily," she says. She clears her throat. "I was thinking of looking for a waitressing job."

Emily turns. Her gaze is like a tractor beam. "At a restaurant?" she asks. She sounds enthusiastic, with high, breathy words, like she's happy for Chloe. But Chloe feels trapped. Emily's personality is too strong. Chloe will never be able to escape it. She brings the side of her thumb to her teeth.

"Stop that," says Emily. "Your cuticles are ragged."

Chloe pulls her thumb away. Emily considers the grocery bag on the counter before clapping her hands together. "Let's get mani-pedis." She raises her eyebrows at Chloe. "Would you like that?"

An exuberant "Yeah!" bubbles up out of Chloe. She can't believe Emily is actually suggesting they go out. "You're not worried about Doug?"

"I—" Emily cuts herself off and crosses her arms in a jerky motion. She tightens her lips and says nothing else.

Emily is keeping something from her. Chloe moves to the kitchen. She puts her hands on the counter. "Emily? Is everything okay? Who do you think was following you?"

Emily rubs her forehead with her fingers. "I can't believe I'm about to say this." She brings her hands to the other side of the counter, mirroring Chloe. "The FBI wants me to talk."

Chloe shakes her head. "About what?"

Emily looks behind her, like she's making sure there are no eavesdroppers in the vacant room. "Chloe, they want to put me in witness protection."

Chloe inhales, sharp and anxious. "Why? Why would they do that?"

"Doug is a really bad guy." Emily whispers this. It's like she's afraid to even say it. "He's dangerous."

"How?"

"I'm sorry. I can't talk about it. But the people he's involved with . . ."

Chloe looks to her door. She looks to her window. The blinds are open.

"Are you okay?" asks Emily.

Chloe touches her palm to her own cheek. "I think so."

"I'm worried about you." Emily comes around the counter and reaches for Chloe's arm, steadying her with the lightest touch. "Are you crying?"

"No," says Chloe. She's not. She's not even tearing up.

"You look like you're crying," Emily says. "Your eyes are all red."

Chloe's not crying. She knows this. But she swipes her fingers under her eyelids anyway. She sniffles.

"Sit," says Emily.

"There was a guy in my parking lot yesterday," Chloe says. "He was acting like he just went out for a vape, but something about him was weird."

"What did he look like?"

"He was white, light-brown hair. Maybe six feet."

Emily rushes to the window and spins the blinds closed. Chloe puts her hands out in front of her, panicked, like she's about to be hit by a car. "Why are you doing that?"

"Just in case," Emily says.

"Just in case what?"

Emily puts her hands on Chloe's shoulders and talks square in her face. "Chloe, listen to me. I'm not going to let anything happen to you. We're gonna fight this. We can beat Doug."

Chloe leans forward. It's almost as if she can't stand up under her own weight anymore. She's in Emily's arms now. And she doesn't know what's happening.

"I didn't get any sleep last night," she says.

"Take a nap then."

Emily leads Chloe to the bedroom. She lays her down and shakes out the comforter. The top sheet falls over Chloe, reminding her of a safe sensation, except it's not really a memory of something that happened to her. It's more like a thing she saw in a movie once. Emily smooths the covers snug across her shoulders and whispers, "Do you want me to stay until you fall asleep?"

It's dark when Chloe wakes. Her flip phone is on her nightstand. Chloe didn't put it there. Emily must have moved it for her. Chloe opens the phone. There is a text from a number Chloe doesn't know. She doesn't even recognize the area code.

What do u think u r doing?

Who is this?

Don't you dare talk to police.

Chloe sits up. Doug must have found Emily's phone. She hears glass shattering a second later, in the front of the apartment. She doesn't scream. She bolts. She runs. She's running into danger, she knows this, but she's not thinking, she's just running, and there's nowhere to run to but the front of the apartment. Her kitchen window, the one facing the alley, has a hole in it. There is a rock in her sink the size of a fist.

CHAPTER FORTY-EIGHT

EMILY

I heard somewhere that the difference between the successful and the unsuccessful is a willingness to have difficult conversations: breakthrough, next-level conversations. Successful people are okay with discomfort.

Of course, I didn't start my relationship with Chloe by asking her to kill Doug. I worked up to it. I laid the foundation. I scared her. I improvised. That story about the witness protection program and Doug being gangster-level dangerous: I made it up on the spot. It was exhilarating, delving into a lie, realizing I was better at it than I thought. Doug must have felt that way all the time.

I broke Chloe's window. And I helped her clean it up the next morning.

"He knows about us," I said. We were both kneeling on her linoleum floor, wearing dish gloves and wiping up the last of the glass shards with wet paper towels.

"We should call someone," she said.

"No," I said. "We have to think through our options."

She stood and threw her paper towel away. "I want to call the police," she said. She was shaking.

"And say what, Chloe? You got a prank call on your burner phone?" She opened her mouth, shocked. I pushed harder. "You know, they always go after the mistresses."

"Who does?"

I reached into my purse for the masking tape I'd bought and unfurled a large piece. I climbed on the counter and placed it diagonally over the hole, creating the silhouette of a no-smoking sign.

"We have to deal with Doug," I said.

I stopped what I was doing then and stared at her hard, thinking my intentions, transmitting without words. I waited for her eyes to clear, to show some understanding.

She wrapped her arms around her torso. "Oh," she said.

"You understand?" I asked. She nodded, staring off to the side. "We can sabotage his plane."

Her body gave a tiny jerk. She smiled, and her voice came out distracted and dreamy. "I always thought I'd use poison."

"Can you help me look it up?" I took off my gloves and pointed to her computer in the living room. She turned to it like a robot, like a dog I'd just commanded. I followed and sat next to her on the carpet.

"Try *sabotage Cessna 172*," I said.

She typed. She tried to hand me the computer so I could read the results. I wasn't touching it. I'd been so careful. I wiped down everything. I wore a baseball cap whenever I entered her apartment, parking out of view of any cameras.

"Cut the fuel line?" she said.

I read over her shoulder. The fuel line wasn't easily accessible. We couldn't cut it without drawing attention to ourselves. And it might not cause a crash. It would most likely just prevent his plane from starting.

"Loosen the wings?" she asked.

"Maybe. I feel like that's one of the things he consistently checks."

"Sugar in the gas tank?" She clicked on the link. This was a good one. It would let the plane take off, but eventually, the sugar would dissolve and turn to sludge, gunking up the engine in midflight.

Chloe slid her computer off her lap. We both sat, not speaking. I put my arm around her and dug in my pocket for cash.

"We can do it tonight," I said. "We'll need sugar. One-pound bags should do it."

She pulled away and faced me. "Wait," she said. "Are you serious?"

"Of course," I said.

She rose to her feet. "I thought we were fantasizing."

I stood to meet her. I had to keep talking, make it sound inevitable. "We'll go in from Clover Park. Doug's plane is parked along the fence next to the baseball diamonds. You know the area?"

"No," she said.

"It's off Ocean Park Boulevard. You can park in the lot near the playground. There's only one camera there, in the southeast corner. Get some electrical tape. You can tape the letters on your license plate to obscure them. If you have a *J*, you can turn it into an *O*, got it?"

Chloe nodded.

"You have the puffy coat I got you?"

She nodded again.

"Wear it. It'll obscure your figure. And tuck your hair into the hat I bought you. They'll think we're men."

She backed against her window, into her blinds, and picked at her thumb. "You've thought this through," she said.

"There's a small wooded area where Twenty-Fifth and Hill Street intersect. Meet me there at two a.m. I'll be lying against a tree, pretending to be a homeless person."

She pushed off from the windowsill and moved into her empty dining room. "I need to think about this," she said.

"No. You need to decide."

She started pacing, in quick pivots. She shook out her hands. "This is really heavy."

"I can't do it alone."

She hid her face in her hands.

"Chloe, you have to help me!"

"I don't know," she said. "I don't know what I'm supposed to do."

I grabbed her arms. I pulled her hands away from her face. "People push you around, Chloe! People take advantage of you! Aren't you sick of it?" All my life I'd been able to get people to do what I wanted, through charm or the threat of social isolation. "Are you my friend?" I asked.

She stepped back. "Of course I'm your friend."

This wasn't working. I realized it would take months. I'd have to induce some kind of psychological breakdown to compel someone to help me kill.

But it didn't matter. I could steal the box of sugar from her cabinet, the one labeled *S!!!!* Her fingerprints were all over it. And she'd just done the internet search I needed. Even if she erased her browser history, her internet service provider would have a record of it.

Still, it would be helpful to have her there, to direct her in front of the cameras. I pointed at her. "You emailed *me*," I said. "You started this."

She stared at me, wide eyed and panicked.

"He's evil," I said.

"I know," she said.

"You'll come?"

She nodded swiftly, tensely. I wondered if she even knew she was lying.

"Good," I said. "Now give me your burner phone back."

———

319

At nine p.m., I called my father. It wasn't that I thought I would be arrested or hurt that night. But I was uneasy, being the sole possessor of account information for millions of dollars.

"I'm sending you a letter," I said.

"I love letters."

"Dad, you have to promise me you won't open it. I just need you to keep it safe, okay?"

My dad was the only person I could think of to trust, the only person aside from my mom who truly loved me. He exhaled a phlegmy rattle. "Everything okay, Em?"

"I'm fine."

"You can come stay here, you know. You and the baby."

"Dad, I've got it under control."

I wrote out instructions on how to access the money in case anything happened to me. I wrote that I loved him and asked him to make sure Grace was taken care of. There was a mailbox just up the road. There were no houses, no cameras, near it. I held my breath as I dropped the letter inside.

———

I drove to the airport at midnight. I parked a mile away and jogged on quiet residential sidewalks lined with jacaranda trees and middle-class-looking homes priced in the millions. I wore all black, with the same kind of black down jacket I'd bought Chloe. I hid my hair in a hat. I had gloves on and a backpack with two pounds of sugar in it.

Running made me feel like I belonged in the area, like I was participating in some boot-campy trend, even at this odd hour. The two people I passed on the street didn't even look up. But the sugar in my bag grew heavier, slipping to lopsided and smacking the right side of my back. My C-section scar, which was supposed to be completely healed, began aching.

I slowed to a brisk walk. I was only a few blocks from the park, but slowing down made me feel like a target, a suspicious person. I approached a car parked at the curb. A man was inside, looking at his phone. He glanced up, and we made eye contact.

What if he called 911? I was dressed like a cat burglar. What if the cops asked to see inside my bag? It would get messy. The sugar, I could explain. I could say I'd just gone to the store. The funnel, maybe. It was the wire cutters and the duct tape. There would be questions about that.

Fucking Doug. Making me do this. Fuck him.

The park was empty. I decided not to wait for Chloe. I went to the fence and hid, crouching between two weigela shrubs. I waited a half hour for a Santa Monica Police SUV to make its slow patrol down the tarmac. My heart dipped and hollowed out my chest as it passed. I didn't dare turn my head to check the SUV's progress. I waited until twenty minutes after the air had gone still and quiet. Only then did it feel safe to breathe, to move my head and fingers.

I unzipped my backpack. The sound of it seemed to echo across the park. I pulled out Chloe's crumpled sugar carton with the *S!!!!* on it. I had to hide it somewhere, out of plain sight. I didn't know when Doug would be flying next, and I didn't want it to be picked up by a litter collector. I shoved it deep in the bushes and looked up. I was still alone.

I repositioned myself in one swift move so my back was against the fence post and went still again. Anyone nearby, who might have noticed movement in their periphery would now see only shadow. I sat in the dirt, acclimating myself to my new surroundings. My bag was in my lap, unzipped.

I took out the fence cutters. I only needed to clip a few of the wires near the ground, just enough to peel it back and crawl through. I slid the blades into position and paused. I hadn't committed a crime yet. I could still go back.

Fucking Doug.

I clenched my jaw and grabbed the handles in each hand. I felt the blades sink into the metal. They didn't go all the way through. I bit my lip and tried harder. Snip. I worked my way up, cutting about two feet of chain link. I tried to peel it back. It wouldn't move.

Fucking Doug.

Never had I had so much riding on an act of physical fucking labor. I pried. I peeled. I stood up, committing a felony, a possible act of terrorism, out in the open. I didn't belong here.

Fucking Doug.

I braced my foot against the fence pole and yanked the hole wide enough to shove my backpack in, to shimmy through. As I did, the ragged edge of one of the wires snagged my jacket pocket, but I wasn't letting that stop me. I clawed at the dirt and kicked and shoved myself through. The wire ripped my jacket and my black yoga pants. It scraped my leg, drawing blood.

Fucking Doug.

I could explain my DNA being all over his plane. I couldn't explain it on the fence. I looked back, to see which wire had done it. I retraced my moves and decided on a culprit. I clipped it shorter and put the metal shaving in my pocket.

The rest was simple. I'd hoisted myself onto Doug's wings before. Once on top, I lay on my stomach and arched my upper back to reach the fuel tank. I uncapped it, inserted the funnel, and tore open one corner of the sugar bag I'd bought. The sweet crystals dissipated into the air like talc. I blinked them off my eyelashes and licked my lips.

Before I screwed the cap back on, I took out a Ziploc bag. It had Chloe's leg hair in it, the stuff I'd scraped from my razor. I tucked it in the threads of the screw cap.

I was almost back through the fence when I heard her voice: a stage whisper, crawling up the hill to me. "Emily!"

I checked my watch. It was 2:00 a.m.

"Shhh!" I said.

CHAPTER
FORTY-NINE

CHLOE

Emily's smile is animated. Her teeth are white and perfect and the first thing Chloe sees as she approaches through the dark. "I'm so happy to see you!" Emily says in a high whisper. She hugs her tight.

Chloe hugs Emily back. It feels right, being here. She can trust this exuberance. She can trust Emily's embrace. Chloe means something to Emily. She hadn't been sure until just now.

Earlier, at her apartment, when she was going over the plan, it was like Emily *needed* Chloe too badly. It was the first time she'd ever seen Emily want anything, and it was savage and desperate and suddenly unveiled, like she'd been keeping it from Chloe the whole time. Like she'd been hiding the fact that she needed Chloe's help to murder—not just talk about it but *actually* kill—Doug.

It was enough to make her want to skip tonight. She almost did. She was listening to this part of herself that kept saying, *Get out of this situation. Just get out.* She called two restaurants that had posted want ads. She lined up waitressing interviews.

But then later, when she went to bed, she couldn't sleep. She couldn't stop thinking about Emily waiting all alone in the middle of a park, in the dark. How long before she realized Chloe wasn't coming? Chloe wanted to text her, to apologize, to ask if Emily had really just been using her this whole time, but Emily had taken her flip phone.

And Doug. Chloe can't stop picturing him. He's awful, yes. He's a terrible person who's done terrible things to Chloe and Emily and all of Dr. Maryn's customers and who knows how many other people. But death, making him dead, when she can't stop visualizing him as this person just like her who thinks and squirms and doesn't want to die any more than she does. The image in her head of him realizing that his plane is crashing, that he's about to die, it makes her feel like she's suffocating.

She's had that terror before, and it's not a feeling or anything human. It's monster claws. It's running through glass. She can't bring that horror into the world on purpose.

No one wants to be a murderer. It's one of the basics. You're not supposed to kill other people. And the solution is simple. *If you don't want to be a murderer, all you have to do is not murder.* She's been repeating the phrase in her head all night.

Chloe grabs both of Emily's hands. "I need to talk to you," she whispers. "I don't think you should do this."

Emily waves her off with a satisfied grin. "It's done."

"What?"

Emily holds up her arm. "It's all over my jacket." Chloe swipes her index finger over Emily's sleeve and rubs it against her thumb. The powder is stiff and grainy. She puts her thumb in her mouth.

"Holy crap." Chloe glances in the direction of her car. She has an idea that maybe she can walk back to it, rewind, erase herself from the moment, but Emily grabs her arm.

"Stay with me."

"I wasn't going to come," says Chloe.

"I know."

Chloe doesn't know if it's worth saying now. She doesn't know what to do. The sugar is in the gas tank. There's no way to take it out without getting in trouble. Emily reaches into her backpack, around the sharp point of a cutting tool. She pulls out a spool of silver duct tape. "You can help," she says. "See where I cut the fence? We need to tape it together so there's no obvious tear. It'll take them longer to notice the break-in."

She hands her the roll of tape. Chloe rubs the outside with her thumb. The tape is so smooth it feels wet. She puts it down on the ground between them.

"Emily," she whispers. It's not too late. "I've been thinking about this."

"Nope. No thinking now."

Chloe shakes her head. She has to say it. "When my mom stabbed me, when I thought I was going to die, I knew—I mean, my soul knew. It was terrifying. I kicked and bucked and fought because my soul knew it was headed toward nothing."

Emily grabs Chloe's wrist, tight. Chloe tries to pull back, but Emily doesn't let go. "There is nothing," Emily says. "There's just us. Now, whose side are you on?"

"Emily, please," Chloe says. "That baby, from the dumpster. You felt guilty your whole life."

Emily digs her nails into Chloe's skin. "If you're not on my side," Emily says, "I can't be on yours."

Finally. There's the threat. It's been lurking in Emily the whole time. There's a small piece of Chloe that feels gratified. It's like a gift Chloe has, the way she makes people reveal the worst of themselves.

Chloe lowers her head. She picks up the duct tape and slivers her fingernail under the edge. She rips off a ribbon.

"Shhh!"

"Sorry."

Chloe peels more slowly. She cuts the tape with her teeth and hands Emily the pieces.

CHAPTER FIFTY

DOUG

Doug sits up in bed and wonders where his wife is. It's 3:00 a.m. She's been out all night. He walks across the hall to Grace's room. The baby is sleeping soundly at least. He stands there a moment, listening to her breathe.

Emily is gone all the time now. In the mornings, at night. She doesn't even have a job. Well, not one she can go back to. The nanny is raising their daughter. Doug's been arguing that they should let the nanny go, that they have to save money. But Emily says they may as well spend while they have it, before they're sued for everything. She's right. Plus, there's all that offshore money. They'll be okay once things die down and they can safely access the funds.

He's been on a buying spree himself, flying to shops in Nevada and Arizona, paying cash for watches—Rolex, Patek Phillipe—portable and with high resale values. At first he would fly them down to his parents' house. But his dad said it made him uncomfortable, being a storehouse for his son's loot.

His dad. His wife. He can't trust anyone anymore. His last client left him today.

Doug walks down to the living room. He sits on a stool at the breakfast bar and holds his cell phone in front of his face. He takes a picture. He doesn't look right in the photo. It's not a question of aging, really. Something seedy has crept into his expression. Into his eyes. He first noticed it on a watch-shopping trip to Scottsdale, when he took a selfie for a local hookup app. Doug scrolls through his recent images. He's shifty, a guilty man in all of them.

He opens his texts. He wants to message Emily. Ask where the hell she is. But her phone is tucked under the mattress upstairs. And he needs her. He needs the money she transferred to her Nauru account.

Doug hangs his head and covers the back of his neck with his hand. Why did he let Emily take his money? She exploited him. She caught him at a vulnerable moment. All this time, he assumed she had some humanity in her. That was where they met, he thought, at the intersection of their desires to be good people.

He turns and gazes out the sliding glass door. It's windy. Before, whenever he imagined getting caught, he pictured terrible scenes. Every moment filled with drama. He didn't realize how tedious the whole thing would be. Waiting to hear his fate. He can't sit still. He can't move on. Maybe that's what jail is like.

Doug lifts his phone once more to eye level and turns the camera on. He relaxes his face into an unassuming smile and tries to clear his mind of everything but sweetness. He thinks of puppies. Innocence. He takes a picture. He looks deranged in this one.

He shouldn't be on a hookup app anyway. All it would take would be one screenshot. He's had enough bad press. And Emily. She's such an operator. She'd find a way to use it against him. He doesn't trust her anymore. She's planning something. The way she's been looking at him lately. Like he's a specimen.

It's not that he's in denial. He knows what he did. He stole Dr. Maryn's data. He sold it. Emily didn't do that part. But she set it up for him. She tempted him, no matter how much she pretends she didn't.

He hears her car pull in and runs up to the bedroom. He pulls the covers to his chest.

"You're up," she says when she comes in. Her face is calm. Her breath is unhurried. She takes off her puffy winter jacket and starts to hang it in the closet. But then she stops. She brings it to the laundry room. Doug hears her start the washer.

They've stopped asking about each other's whereabouts. *Where were you? Why are you dressed like a Mossad agent?* They don't ask these sorts of questions anymore.

She pauses in the bedroom door and watches him with a spark in her eyes, a burst of animosity, before her expression goes back to opaque.

"I was just with Chloe," she says.

He studies her. Her skin. Her eyes. It's clear now. He's never known her. She's only given him access to a set of honed behaviors. Maybe that's all she is.

CHAPTER
FIFTY-ONE

EMILY

If Doug hadn't been awake at that moment, I'd have let it go, let him die in his plane thinking his death was random, an accident. But I wanted him to know, when it happened, that it was me.

I moved to the foot of the bed and crossed my arms. "What did you do to my dog?"

I saw fear on his face. It was all I wanted at this point, to be the cause of one small piece of his downfall, take some credit from Dr. Maryn.

"Nothing," he said.

"Liar."

"I had nothing to do with it."

"You told the breeder I was dead."

He looked away.

"You staged the scene." He covered his face with his hands. "You left the gate open." I kept on. I started pointing, accusing, screaming. "You made me think it was my fault! I thought I killed her!"

He said nothing.

"You're a fucking monster."

"Jesus Christ!" He punched the comforter and swung his feet to the floor. "I'm a human being!" The tendons of his neck were bulging. He slapped the backs of his fingers against his palm. "Do you have any idea what it's like? I had a business! I had hundreds of people depending on me. You, Grace, my employees. And their families and their fucking holidays, and all it took was five minutes. That bitch, your doctor, took five minutes to ruin everything! It's like they couldn't take that I wasn't perfect. And they left. Do you know how much work that was? Being that guy that everyone wants to be, and I had to be that guy all the time. Convince everyone over and over again that I'm special because that's all that's allowed at the top. And I didn't even want it! I didn't!"

He chopped the air with his hands like a conductor ending a symphony, the last of his cry reverberating into silence. I couldn't help it. I smirked.

"At least you don't have to worry about being on top anymore," I said.

He whimpered and stretched his torso away from me, straining, uncomfortable. "What are we going to do about Grace?"

I shrugged. Grace was better off, losing him before she formed any real memories. "So we're breaking up?" I asked.

"We hate each other," he said.

I nodded, conceding his point. He pulled a suitcase from the top shelf of the closet. I moved to the bed and watched him pack. He counted out seven T-shirts and seven pairs of underwear. Before he left, he sat next to me on the bed. He took my hand. I jerked it back, refusing him a parting ceremony.

"Do you want to know where I'm going?"

"Not really."

He reached for my hair then. I tried to move away, but he gripped a handful of it, immobilizing me. He pulled my head down and brought his face close. "If you steal my money, I'll kill you."

I smiled at him.

And then he was gone. I lay back on the bed fully clothed. I didn't sleep. Grace woke at six thirty. The nanny arrived at eight.

I pulled my phone out from under the corner of the mattress. There was a notification on the home screen, from my work calendar. In two hours, I was supposed to be on a conference call. It was Monday. My maternity leave was officially over.

I texted Ron Faulman, the managing partner.

Should I come in?

You work here, don't you?

They were going to inflict as much pain as possible, move me out of my office, to a cubicle probably, maybe a desk in the hallway. I'd have nothing to do: no clients, no assistant, no one speaking to me for as long as I could take it. I'd orchestrated one of these demotions years ago. I'd instructed the staff not to give the guy so much as a pen. I texted back:

You win.

I win?

I give up.

Give up what?

I won't make trouble.

Call me.

They put me right through. Ron was conciliatory. He didn't want to be "punitive," but they'd divvied up my clients. Dr. Maryn was staying

331

with him. He offered a settlement, a lump sum for my current and future commissions, on the condition I never defend Doug in public, never write a book, never discuss Dr. Maryn with anyone. He offered less than I was worth, but it was still a ton of money. We made arrangements for our lawyers to start talking.

After I hung up the phone, I lay back, stared out at the ocean, and laughed. So that was what I'd worked so hard for. A buyout. I'd spent my career aiming in one direction, and my reward landed like a canon shot from a completely different angle.

CHAPTER FIFTY-TWO

CHLOE

Chloe drives through Hollywood to Larchmont Village. There's a restaurant hiring waitresses. They said to come at 4:00 p.m. She called them last night, before she became an accessory to murder. "Are you still hiring?" she asked.

She turns onto Larchmont Boulevard and squints even though she's wearing sunglasses. The harsh sun, the pavement: these things make her think of bubble gum melting onto her tires and sticking to her shoes. It makes her queasy, the daylight, like she no longer belongs here. But she wants to be a regular, daytime kind of a person. She wants to be normal. That's the whole point of today.

All she has to do is follow through, go to the interview, stick to the mundane, the handshakes and the *nice to meet you*s. Boring. If she can keep it boring, she has a chance.

It's 3:45. She scans the angled parking spots on Larchmont for an empty space. There is nothing. Chloe turns onto First Street. She turns onto Gower.

"It's only street parking." That's what the restaurant manager said when she talked to him. It's 3:48. There's plenty of time. And there are people everywhere. Sunny people. Sunny storefronts. Sunny sidewalks. Walking and talking. Chloe can be one of these folks again.

She hears a rip. The sound of duct tape unspooling. The ripping is so loud. It's as if she's hearing it live, like it's happening not in her mind but in the passenger seat of her car. "Shhh," she says.

The clock on her dash turns to 3:51. She turns again onto First Street. She turns onto Gower. There's a car in every space. She taps the steering wheel with her palm. "Please," she whispers. "Please."

She turns onto Larchmont, and then Emily flickers through her thoughts, uninvited. She smiles at Chloe. She says, *It's done.*

No. Chloe focuses on the cars to her right. There are four of them, parallel parked. The second car's rear lights come on. Chloe brakes. It's 3:56. Chloe can do this. She can wait for the spot. She can run the two blocks to the restaurant. She pulls ahead. The car edges out and does a U-turn. Chloe puts her car in reverse, to back into the space, and looks over her shoulder. A red BMW noses into the spot. The driver is blonde and doesn't make eye contact. Chloe gets out of her car.

"Excuse me," Chloe says.

The woman raises her face to Chloe with a sulky look. She doesn't roll down her window.

"That's my spot."

The woman offers a wan shake of her head. Chloe knocks on the window.

"That's my spot!"

The woman motions for Chloe to move back and gets out of her car. She's just a few feet away. Her expression is impassive. A scream rises inside Chloe, and she's about to let it out. She's about to kick the woman, about to slam her into the window, but she stops herself.

Emily, Chloe thinks. *Emily would wait.*

Chloe counts. By the time she gets to four, she's calm. "Did you see my car?"

"I'm parked here now," says the woman.

"I was backing up."

"I don't care."

Chloe can feel people across the street, watching them. She can shame this woman. That's something. She looks to the opposite sidewalk. There's a bemused-looking tech type at a café table and an older couple who've paused their stroll. The couple jerk their heads forward and continue walking. The bemused guy keeps watching. Chloe points her finger an inch from the blonde driver's face.

"You don't care?" she yells.

The woman ducks away from Chloe's hand and runs across the street. A car honks as it passes. Chloe's driver's side door is wide open, swinging into the road. She can still chase after the woman, knock her down, kick her in the face.

But Emily wouldn't do that.

And it's not like Chloe's going to start acting like Emily now and meticulously planning murder in the first degree, but Emily has shown her something. Another way to be.

Chloe composes herself and gets back into her car. It's 4:04. She's late. But she stays calm. She makes another loop. There's an open spot as she turns back onto Larchmont, just a few feet away from the red BMW. It's like that book, *The Secret*. The world is opening to her now that she does things like wait when she's mad. She pays the meter with a dime and three nickels and walks toward the BMW. The café tables across the street are now empty.

She fingers her keys. The ignition one is longer, but her apartment key is sharper. She grips it between her thumb and forefinger, and it's amazing how she doesn't feel angry at all right now. She's composed, relaxed.

She strides toward the BMW and scrapes her key along the length of it. She keeps an even pace and continues. She rounds the corner and waits. She counts to thirty. Then she saunters back. The scratch comes into view. It's straight, a mix of pale yellow and pink.

She checks her watch. It's 4:15. It's too late to become a waitress.

Chloe is back in her car now. She has to think, to figure out what she's going to do with the rest of her life now that she's not going to be a waitress. She needs a friend. *Who is a friend?* Emily is a friend. But Emily is trying to kill someone. Emily is death. She'll die if she sees Emily again.

Dylan. Dylan has a crush on her. He lives in Echo Park in a house with uneven floors. Chloe drives there. She stands on the sidewalk outside Dylan's front fence. She listens to his roommates on the other side. They sound happy. They're playing music. She pulls the bungee on the wooden gate and opens it. The roommates are drinking beer in the patchy front yard, volleying a badminton birdie over a Ping-Pong table. They stop their game when they see her. They group together like they want to block her. Dylan's not there, they tell her. They don't elaborate.

Chloe backs up. She says, "Okay, thanks," and gives them a thumbs-up. Even though Dylan's roommates are being rude and weird, Chloe is being calm. She is doing everything right.

She leaves and sees a tree with roots breaking up the sidewalk. There is a chunk of cement, broken off, about the size of a shoe. Chloe picks it up. She walks back to Dylan's gate. She throws it over the edge and hears it hit the Ping-Pong table. The guys in the yard go quiet.

"Psycho," Chloe hears one of them say before she runs away.

Chloe is back in her car. Sheralyn. Chloe knows her forwarding address. She drives there, propelled by a desire for nothing more than to reach out, to get in touch with the people she knows. It's a rational thing to want: connection.

She takes Sunset. Santa Monica. Highland. Fountain. Sweetzer. A parking space is open right in front of Sheralyn's new high-rise. See?

There it is again. The world is already working in her favor. Chloe stands outside the apartment building's front door and runs her finger down the silver-plated directory. She sees Sheralyn's last name and dials her code on the intercom.

"Hello?" comes Sheralyn's voice.

"It's Chloe."

Sheralyn pauses before saying, "No."

Chloe presses the talk button. She can't think of anything to say. She releases it.

"—you hear me?" says Sheralyn. She's yelling. "Just go."

Chloe peers through the glass door of Sheralyn's building. There's a carpeted hallway and an elevator off to the side. A professional-looking couple comes out of it. Chloe starts to scoot in as they open the door. The woman glances at Chloe a moment before she passes her, then stops. She spends a little more time looking at her.

"Can I help you?" she asks.

"Can I help you?" Chloe mimics.

The man is behind Chloe, outside. The woman is in front of her. He says, "Do you live here?" Chloe turns back. He's tall and muscular. All he'll have to do is grab her shoulder to stop her. She leaves. She gets in her car.

There's another place she can try. She doesn't want to do this. She hates to, actually. She never thought it would come to this.

She dials her grandpa. She listens to his phone ringing and imagines him making his way to his wall-mounted slimline, the violet one with the curlicue cord. She knows her grandpa only uses a cell phone now, but that old phone, she picked the color herself.

He answers with a pause and a suspicious, "Chloe?"

"Simon?"

"Yeah?"

"I'm in trouble."

"What happened?"

"I don't know where to go."

"Chloe, slow down."

"I was with this guy. He was my boss, actually, and when he was done with me, he, like, drove me away. He got everyone in the company to rise up against me. But then the guy's wife, and this is the really weird part, his wife and I started hanging out."

"Hold on," says her grandpa.

"But she's trying to kill her husband." Chloe's throat catches. "But I'm good, Grandpa. I'm a good person."

There is silence on the line. Her grandpa blows air into the receiver.

"I know you are, Chloe," he finally says.

"Grandpa?" She's never asked what she's about to ask. She's been too scared of the answer. "Can I come home?"

Her grandpa doesn't speak.

"Simon?"

"Chloe . . ."

"Please."

"Chloe, honey, your grandma still can't talk right. She can't even feed herself."

That was so long ago! Chloe is a different person now. It's not fair. And the last thing she needs now is these images in her mind, not when she's trying to get it together, get on with her life. She covers her ears and closes her eyes, trying to shut out the replay of the old lady howling on a dirty carpet, shielding her head from Chloe's kicks and punches.

A police car slows as it passes. Chloe starts her engine. She gets on the road. The late-afternoon shadows talk to her—they say, *Come closer. Come west.* It's not clear to her where she's headed until she finds herself there, at the edge of a playground, a few spots away from where she parked last night. She watches the families through the windshield. The parents stick close to the littlest, the babies. Big kids run in a pack and pretend their fingers are guns. A mom walks over to them and shakes her head no.

The light turns golden and brilliant until it fades to blue and shadowless. The sun sets. The air cools. The last of the families pack up and leave.

Chloe waits until it's completely dark. Then she gets out of her car. She crosses to the swing set and sits. She kicks off, pumping her legs and soaring as high as she can, back and forth, and for a second she feels it, the abandon, the sense of pure being, the feeling she's had from dancing, from sex, from being the center of attention.

She looks past the soccer fields and baseball diamonds to the fence separating the park from the airport. She walks toward it. She doesn't see any damage as she approaches. Maybe last night was a dream. She gets close to where they mended the wire with duct tape. You wouldn't know the chain link was cut unless you were looking for it.

She lifts her eyes in the direction of Doug's plane. Someone's out there. She doesn't recognize him at first. He's just a figure, a man like any other, emerging from behind the hangar. He stops under a lamp and checks his phone. He's more disheveled than usual, like the mess of his hair and bloat to his face aren't on purpose anymore. He looks at the sky.

Chloe stands. He doesn't notice her. It's like she's invisible, like she has superpowers. The low branches of the bush poke Chloe's sandaled feet, but she remains still as she watches him walk toward his Cessna with a slouch, with the cautious steps of an old man. Chloe tries to remember what it was like having sex with him. But it's like trying to recall what the flu feels like when you're not sick.

He circles his aircraft, feeling the joints, shaking the wings. A corporate jet taxies to the end of the runway, flooding the air with the stink of fuel. Doug disappears in front of the prop, moving it from side to side.

Check the gas tank! Chloe wants to shout, but she can't. It's a nightmare how she can't say anything, like she's running down a hallway, and a trick of perspective is making it longer and longer, and she'll never reach the end of it.

She'll go to jail if she says something. But he'll die if she doesn't. She'll be a killer.

She doesn't feel invincible anymore. She steps farther into the bushes, to a palm tree that can shield her. She presses her hands into its trunk. It's not a rational decision, the one she's about to make. It's not weighing pros and cons. She has no idea what's going to happen, whether she's about to save his life or not.

The corporate jet takes off. Chloe moves from her hiding place. Doug opens his pilot door. He takes a step up. Chloe starts toward the fence with her mouth open, her voice ready, but she hits something with her big toe. It feels like a corner, like cardboard. She glances down, not really thinking. At first it looks like a random piece of litter. But something about it is familiar.

It's a sugar carton, scrunched up and beaten. Chloe reaches for it. She sees it, before she even uncrumples the box. A giant markered *S!!!!* for *Sheralyn* scrawled across the logo.

Chloe can hear a plane starting up, a propeller with a deep motor, sputtering, catching before rising to a higher and higher pitch. It sounds like insects, like a horde of angry wasps. It's all she can hear as she falls to her knees and tears the bush with her fingers. What else? What else has Emily hidden there?

CHAPTER
FIFTY-THREE

DOUG

Doug doesn't like flying at night. But the traffic is bad. It would take him four hours at least to get to his parents' house. He does one last check, mapping his flight plan against his pilot weather app. Partly cloudy skies all the way to San Diego. He switches on the radio.

"On the ground Foxtrot seven nine Delta Quebec ready to taxi VFR to the south."

He steers his plane down the tarmac. He barely notices the din of his propellers, he's so familiar with this machinery. He's comfortable here. And he doesn't know where else to go.

He checked into a hotel earlier. He had lunch at the bar and tried to make eye contact with a woman, a business traveler, sitting by herself. The look on her face. Doug can only describe it as revulsion.

He reaches the edge of the runway and turns around. "Foxtrot seven nine Delta Quebec ready for takeoff." He gets the all clear and accelerates, relaxing into his seat as the plane bumps and dips, and then it's as if God has scooped him up. The city shrinks below him. He needs this, to be in the air.

His parents. They'll give him a place to hide. To plot his next journey. It will be a humbling one. He already knows that. There are moments, actually, when he thinks about it, where he's almost giddy. Humility. It will be a new experience.

Doug maneuvers his plane over the Orange County shoreline, with the ocean to his right. He sniffs. He smells smoke. He looks from side to side, to both of his engines. It's not coming from his plane. He glances out toward the ocean and sees a thin trail of darkness floating along a moonlit cloud. The smoke from a forest fire has blown out to sea. He doesn't bother scanning the horizon for an orange glow. There's always a fire somewhere.

Doug clenches his jaw, wondering what Emily is doing at that exact moment. Curling up on his couch, probably. Puttering around his kitchen. That's his house. He should have made *her* leave.

He should do it. Kick her out. Apply for sole custody of Grace.

Little Grace. That little angel. She fussed when he picked her up from her baby swing yesterday. He cupped his hand around her fuzzy scalp and kissed her forehead. "Amazing Grace," he called her, mainly because he knows Emily hates it. She wants them to agree on nicknames.

"What about Gracie?" she asked. "Grace-aroonie?"

He should have taken her with him this morning. It would have been easy. He could have just picked her up and run. Where does it say she's supposed to live with Emily? She's not even a good mom. She's turning crazy, forcing Grace to exercise with that ridiculous tummy time. And today. When he called Emily. All he did was suggest, just floated the idea, that Grace fly with him sometime, that she could visit her grandparents. Emily had to start in with the histrionics, screaming, "Grace will never get on that plane!"

The divorce will be messy. He can already tell.

Doug is hit with nausea. Dizziness. It's not just Emily. Something is wrong. He's distracted. It was the smoke. His eyes were on the clouds over the ocean. He turns his head to the left, to where the lights of Orange County should be, but there's only dark sky out his window.

"Jesus," he says. He's been banking to the right, not even realizing.

He concentrates on his instrument panel. His altitude indicator says he's in a twenty-degree turn. He rolls his shoulders back and ignores the urgency inside him, the desperation to lift his eyes, restore his sense of balance by looking out the window. That will kill him. It's a trick, his eyes and body telling him one thing, his instruments saying another. He keeps his head down as he guides the yoke gently to the left, until the lines of his indicator match the fixed horizontal horizon. He looks up. He's now pointed due west, out to sea. Patience. He turns south, to get back over land. Only five degrees this time, making a wide circle.

He rejoins the coastline at Camp Pendleton. A high-pitched ambience signals the takeoff of a stealth helicopter below him. The black chopper glides away and hovers over the sea, invisible except for a single blue light.

He's afraid. Of what, he doesn't know. It's almost like he's just realized, after all these years of flying, that he's up in the goddamned *air*. None of his knowledge or experience, the principles of flight or his accumulated hours, can help the fact that as a human, he's not really supposed to be here.

The lights of Montgomery-Gibbs Airport appear ahead of him. He calls to the radio, requesting permission to land, half hoping they'll say, *No, stay there. We'll come and get you.* He circles the airport and has to remind himself that he knows what he's doing. He knows how to land a plane. He approaches the runway from the south. He tracks his descent on his altimeter. He doesn't trust his vision anymore.

Emily flashes in his mind. He has an urge to abort the landing, race back to Malibu, protect his daughter. From Emily? He's not sure. But something isn't right. He feels it in his torso, in the set of his jaw.

He lands, hitting the ground harder than he wanted. He's unnerved. That's all it is. He's going through a lot. Air traffic control directs him to park outside a hangar. He calls Emily's cell. It goes to voice mail. He tries the landline. She doesn't answer. She's letting it ring out of spite.

He orders an Uber. His parents are expecting him. But he directs the driver to the beach instead. He wants to be alone.

Emily is on his mind. So is Grace. And Chloe. And Harper. Everyone he's ever hurt. The dog, Bella. Dr. Maryn's customers. The driver stops at the entrance to the pier. Doug gets out. He can see the ocean from here, but he can't hear the waves, not with the noisy restaurants on the strand. He takes off his shoes and socks and walks down the beach, past the hotels, to a dark stretch of sand.

He walks to the shoreline. He lets the tide run over his feet. Random people push into his thoughts, people he's never seen before, people he doesn't know. But he can picture them. He sees them when they realize their mental health data is no longer private.

He scratches his arms, suddenly overwhelmed. A question dances, hovers over him. What did it feel like? That moment when Dr. Maryn's customers realized that data brokers knew everything, that their most vulnerable selves had been sold. Was it panic? Shame? He wades deeper into the surf, not caring that he's soaking his pant legs.

No. He can't start worrying about how other people feel.

Because it's not enough. Because seeing things through someone else's eyes has never been the point. Because the truth is he's a smart guy, and even though he pretends differently, he's always known what other people go through.

The horror is that he doesn't care.

No one knows me, he thinks. There isn't a single person on this earth who does. He lies. He steals. He steps farther into the ocean. The water is above his knees now. He has a brief urge to continue fully clothed. He can float or even sink. The thing is to let the cool drench his skin.

"I'm an asshole," he says. A large wave breaks across his thighs.

He backs up onto the sand and sits.

A pigeon flutters down, landing a few feet away. It folds its wings against its sides. "What are you doing up?" Doug asks. The pigeon steps toward him. Doug gives a little laugh. He throws a handful of sand at it. But the bird stands its ground, cocks its head to the side, and eyes him before flying away.

"Come back," Doug whispers.

Shush, go the waves, and in the lull between breaks, he swears he can hear a new sound. Footsteps. He turns. The sound stops. No one is there. He looks back at the water. It starts up again. It's unmistakable, the soft crunch of feet. He looks back. The beach is empty, but he can hear it still. It's getting louder. A single pair of footsteps in the sand. It comes closer and stops next to Doug. An awesome, hovering presence.

Of course, Doug thinks. He's having an epiphany. Just like the one he had decades ago, on this very same beach. Only this time he has the words. He knows how to move forward.

Organized religion.

He won't even have to do much work. Just some research. He's a good speaker. All he'll have to do is start talking. He's spent so much energy, goodwill, his whole goddamned life, building his business, his worldview, all of it from scratch. But religion. It's set up already.

Doug gasps and buries his face in his arms. "Oh Jesus," he says. And a warm creep of forgiveness trickles in, oozing and soothing, a balm inside his body. "No," he cries, resisting. He doesn't want this. He wants things to be like they were before.

But that's impossible. There is only this. He has to do it. He has to make it real. And then he'll tell the story of this moment for the rest of his life.

He drops his arms in surrender. "I've done some terrible things."

CHAPTER FIFTY-FOUR

EMILY

Chloe rang my doorbell. "What are you doing?" I called through the door. She wasn't supposed to show up like that.

"I was at the airport," she said.

Shit. I opened the door and pulled her inside. She shrank into the wall, all narrow and shivering, clutching her hands to her chest like a frightened rodent. I stepped out to the driveway, looking for potential witnesses, neighbors or stray paparazzi still trying to get a shot of Doug. I didn't see anyone.

"Chloe, we can't see each other. I told you this."

"Doug took his plane," she said. She was shaking.

I took a sharp inhale. So this was it. At every instant in this process, I kept thinking, *There's no turning back.* But now there truly wasn't.

"What do we do?" she asked. She looked terrified. Her eyes stood out, round and pitiful, like the waif from the *Les Misérables* poster.

"Come with me," I said.

She followed me down the hall and slowed as we neared the open door to the nursery. The nanny was in the rocker with Grace, the tinkling notes of "Brahms' Lullaby" sounding from the mobile above her crib. Chloe stopped. She pointed to the mobile.

"Is that a real Calder?" she asked. She sounded caustic. I'd never heard that tone from her before.

"What?"

"At your office," she said. "I asked you about the Calder."

"I don't remember that," I said. I closed the door to Grace's room. "Come downstairs."

I went to the couch. Chloe stood behind me as I opened my new laptop. I pulled up the KTLA and Fox 11 pages. There was no news of a plane crash. "Shit," I said. "I wish I could google this."

Chloe cocked her head. "Why can't you?"

"They can get a warrant for your searches," I said and shut my lips tight.

I realized what I'd just done. I'd had Chloe google everything for me. I kept my eyes on my computer a few moments, hoping she wouldn't put it together.

"Have a seat," I said. I offered her space on the couch. She considered it a few moments before strolling to the breakfast bar and perching on a stool.

Fuck.

"Do you want something to drink?" I asked. "Water? Tea?"

She said nothing but looked at me so strangely. Her eyes were glassy. She seemed like she was suppressing a smile.

"Chloe?"

"I'll have wine."

"There's no wine," I said.

"That's not true," she said in a low, bursting register. She pointed to the pantry behind the refrigerator, where Doug had installed a wine locker. "You have a whole room of it back there."

I stood, suddenly aware that she was different, confident. She seemed to have gathered strength on the walk from my front door. She slapped a hand on the counter and kept it there. "I get it, what Doug saw in you," she said. "You're both hard people."

"Ms. Markham?" The nanny was coming down the stairs. She stopped a few steps from the bottom. She frowned in Chloe's direction before raising her eyebrows at me. "It's okay?"

"Yes, Gloria, it's fine, thank you. Is Grace asleep?"

"She's asleep."

"I'll see you tomorrow, then."

Gloria glanced at Chloe, took one step up, and hovered. I wanted her out of there. I had no idea what Chloe might say, how she might incriminate me.

"You need, I can stay," she said.

"No need. You have a good night. Thank you."

I waited until I heard the front door open and shut. I turned back to Chloe. She'd moved farther into my kitchen, walking the perimeter and touching everything: my toaster, my spatula carousel, my knife block, my faucet.

I pushed my hair away from my face and cleared my throat. "I didn't think about the internet searches until tonight," I said.

She ran her fingers along the vertical dowels of our cold drip coffee maker.

"How much did this cost?" she asked.

"I have no idea."

"It's funny," she said. "In the back of my mind, I've always hoped for some huge disaster. Something that would plunge the world into chaos. You know, level the playing field? Like, if we could all start from scratch, then maybe I'd have a chance. But people like you, people like Doug, you'll always be the first ones out of the muck."

Something dark and heavy dropped in my chest. All this time, I'd assumed Chloe wanted me on her side, wanted me to like her. She opened my refrigerator. She opened my freezer, peering in with one hand on the door. My kitchen had somehow turned into a seat of power.

"There was this lady today," she said. "I was backing up to parallel park, and she scooted in behind me. I told her. I got out of my car and told her that was my spot. And you know what she said? She said, 'I don't care.'"

I needed to get her out of there. I needed my phone. It was in my purse. Somewhere. Upstairs or on the floor in the living room. My landline was in the office.

"She had a red BMW, just like you."

"I drive a Mercedes," I said. "And I think you should leave."

I took a step back, opening a path to the stairs. She slid forward from the fridge and gripped the rim of the countertop. The freezer was still open, hurtling me toward a world where melted ice cubes and thawed gyoza no longer mattered.

"I stabbed her," she said.

"Get out."

"That doesn't scare you?"

"Are you trying to scare me?"

"I found the sugar box," she said.

"Okay," I said.

"Okay?" She raised her voice. "That's all you can say?"

I had no fear at that moment. I had only grim calculation. My daughter was upstairs. It was too dangerous now to let Chloe pass the nursery. She'd have to take the sliding glass door. It was high tide. She'd be stuck on the balcony.

"What do you want?" I asked.

She scoffed and hung her mouth open in outrage. "You used me!"

I took a breath. I had to keep cool.

"Don't take it personally," I said. "I've used lots of people."

My cell phone rang. The sound was muffled through my purse, but at least I knew the phone was downstairs, near the couch. If only it could have been in my hand like it usually was. I was incredulous that I couldn't simply make it materialize there.

"Do you want to get that?" She was smirking, challenging me.

To not answer it was to admit I was aware of looming violence, to make it real. But I didn't dare turn my back on her. The ringing stopped. Chloe lifted her chin in triumph.

I needed an advantage, a deterrent. I strode past her with a burst of bravado. I went deep into the kitchen, straight for my knife block. I pulled out my chef's knife and turned.

All I could see was her eyes. They were so pointed, so sharp. The rest of her blurred in contrast, into a silhouette haloed with undulating shades of a rage I could never hope to match.

The landline started ringing in the office. Doug was the only one besides me who knew the number. He was alive. He was throwing me a lifeline. Chloe glanced toward the sound. I sprinted past her, bumping my ribs on the counter. The phone was in the corner of the office, on the other side of the bulky swivel chair. I swept it aside with my arm, but it caught on the rolling mat. I stumbled over it. The knife was in my right hand. I grabbed the cordless receiver with my left. My fingers were stiff, like I'd been out in the freezing cold. I couldn't make them move. I stared at the buttons. In that moment, I couldn't remember which one would let me answer.

Chloe slammed into me with her whole body and slapped the phone out of my hand. It bounced to the ground, still ringing. I dived for it. I dropped the knife. Then she was on top of me, yanking my hair. I elbowed her. I punched her thigh. I reached for the arm of the chair and pulled it over us.

"Let go!" I screamed. And she did. I pushed her off me and rose to a crouch. She stood. Her eyes were wide and frozen. She looked even more freaked out than I was.

The knife was under the chair, behind her. My instinct was to lead her away from it. I backed out of the office into the living room, feeling for obstacles with my hands. She moved forward at an even distance. There was no menace to her just then. She looked like a kid sister, tagging along.

"Doug's alive," I said.

"How do you know that?"

"No one else calls that number," I said. "You want to go back? Pretend like none of this happened?"

"What do we do?" she asked.

I reached the sliding glass door. "We have to keep everyone safe, okay?" I touched the door handle.

Some understanding rushed to her face like a blush. She crossed her arms. "You mean keep you safe."

"Chloe," I said. "I have a child upstairs. I have to protect my child."

Her expression didn't change.

"I'm going to open this door, okay? I have to unlock it first."

"Okay."

I kept my eyes on her as I bent to unlatch the floor lock. I slid the door open.

"Come outside with me," I said. "We can call Doug."

"I thought we were going to kill him."

I tilted my head toward her and summoned something soft and sweet inside me. "No, no," I said. "That was a mistake. And I'm so relieved he's alive."

Chloe pursed her lips and swished them to the side like a kindergartener.

"It's a mess," I said. "But Doug's alive. He doesn't know anything. It's like it never happened." I moved out, keeping my hand on the door. "Come on out. We'll call him. We'll tell him we're friends. He'll think it's funny." She joined me outside. I stepped back in, straddling the screen track. "I just have to get my phone." I moved both feet inside. "I'm going to close this and come back with my phone, okay?"

She started back to me. I put my hand up. "It's okay." I slid the door closed as inoffensively as I could. "I'll be right back," I said and locked the plastic handle. She was six inches away. But she was out of my house.

I moved to the other side of the living room. She tracked me, pacing the glass like a caged tiger. My purse was under the couch. I took my phone out and dialed 911.

Chloe knocked on the window and yelled, "Are you calling Doug?"

"Of course!" The emergency line rang. They picked up. I heard voices in the background. I was safe.

Chloe shook the door handle. I went up to the glass and slid the bottom lock into place.

"Nine one one emergency, what is the address you are calling from?" The dispatcher was female.

Chloe's face scrunched. I turned my back to her. "Hello," I said. "I have a disturbed person in my house. She won't leave."

"What is the address you are calling from?"

I heard a loud bang. I turned. Chloe had the garden table in her hands.

"She's banging on the window," I yelled into the phone. "She's on the balcony."

"Ma'am."

Chloe hit the glass again.

"Holy shit!"

"Ma'am, I need you to calm down and tell me your address."

Bam!

"19472 Pacific Coast Highway."

"Repeat that?"

Bam!

I screamed into the phone. "I'm in Malibu!"

Bam!

"Slow down." The dispatcher was firm and deliberate.

Bam!

"Chloe, stop!"

I was calling the police. That was what I was supposed to do. That was supposed to be the end of it.

Bam!

"I have Pacific Coast Highway," said the dispatcher. "I need the house number."

Chloe cracked the glass, making a bullet-size hole in the center of a shattering circle.

"Oh my God!"

She kept hitting, hard and fast. The hole was now the size of a fist.

"Your address!" The operator was screaming now too. "Your address!"

"One nine four seven two!"

Chloe pawed at the crumbling glass. I dropped the phone. I ran. I used my hands and feet to climb the stairs as she reentered the house. I rounded the top railing and ran across the hall into Grace's room and grabbed her from her crib. We got as far as her bedroom door.

Chloe was at the top of the stairs, blocking my exit. She had blood on her face and hands. Grace wriggled in my arms.

"The police are coming," I said. I saw a glint of something at her side. It was my chef's knife. She flexed her fingers and closed her fist around the handle.

"Emily, all I want is an apology."

The front door was behind her, just down the hallway. But I couldn't make a run for it, not with Grace in my arms.

I pointed to the knife. "You want to kill us?"

She refastened her grip and focused her eyes on Grace.

"What's the plan, Chloe?"

The police were coming. I needed to keep Chloe calm until they got there. I needed to remove Grace from her line of vision. I laid Grace on the floor, just inside the doorway. Chloe was still staring at her. I stepped past her and pulled the bedroom door closed behind me.

"I wasn't setting you up," I said.

"Bullshit!" She waved the blade at me. I backed up. She lunged. She swiped my forearm and backed up. We looked at each other in shock. I held up my arm. There was no blood at first. I thought for a moment maybe nothing had happened. But then a clean, burning line of red appeared. Chloe watched, fascinated.

"Time-out," I said and made a T with my hands. I had a sense we should break before we did this. She should give me a chance to turn on the light or use the bathroom.

She sliced my other arm and retreated, quick on her feet like a prizefighter. I pushed her in the chest. She stumbled and recovered quickly. She jabbed again and again. I circled my hands in wax-on-wax-off defense moves.

My arms were dripping. They were on fire. I reached for the knife. I grabbed the blade. She pulled back, cutting through the bridge of skin between my thumb and finger.

"Say you're sorry," she said.

I cupped my hand. Blood was pooling into my other palm.

"Emily, I just want you to say sorry."

"I'm sorry," I said.

"What are you sorry for?"

"For everything."

"I don't believe you."

And I never knew what *sorry* meant. Did I wish I'd never met Chloe? Did I regret the fact that she was stabbing me?

"I'm so sorry," I said. I started crying. "I'm so, so, so sorry. I'm sorry."

I kept crying. I kept apologizing as her face twisted in gruesome satisfaction. She was going to kill me. I knew this. She was going to kill Grace.

I could hear the traffic on the other side of my front door. The rest of the world, rescue, was close, just a few feet away. I conjured an image of a football tackle and led with my shoulder, aiming for her middle. She flew back and held on to the railing.

I slipped on my blood. I landed at her calves. I grabbed at her feet and pulled them toward me. She fell. I climbed up her body and grabbed a handful of her face. She beat the top of my head with the knife handle. I kept climbing up her body until my knees were at her shoulders. I pinned her arms down with my shins. She chomped the air like a zombie, trying to catch a piece of my flesh in her jaws.

But she couldn't. I had her.

I had her until her arm started sliding out from underneath my leg. I pressed harder, but everything was slippery. I couldn't keep her there. I scrambled forward. I kept going. I crawled up the front door and reached for the dead bolt.

It was unnatural, the force of what came next. The blows were steel, but they felt like water, waves of rage breaking over me and folding back in on themselves before crashing forward again, each surge stronger than the last. It started with my shoulders and sank into my neck, my ribs, my back.

I hadn't known what pain was until then, not until pain was the only thing that was. It was a lake, and I was drowning. It was an ocean of pain. It was a universe, paper thin and shimmering out to eternity, and I was a flattened speck inside.

I didn't start panicking until I heard myself screaming. I gurgled and trilled, and I covered my head with my hands. I'd never heard such screams before. "Please don't let me die!" I could hear myself screaming. "I don't want to die!" I'd be stuck there if I died, trapped in the beginning and end of my death, my terror wide open and echoing into the dark forever.

I heard a baby cry. I tried to say hush, to say it would be all right, but I couldn't stop screaming.

Something pushed against me then. It was coming from the opposite direction. My front door. It was shoving me toward Chloe.

"Please," I whispered.

Glass broke. It shattered all over. I barely felt it. There were people in the house now. They were yelling, and their voices were commanding. Chloe was yelling too.

I could hear my name. I could hear them telling me to stay with them.

"I don't want to die," I responded, but no sound came out. I don't know if my lips moved. "I don't want to die."

But I did. I died in the ambulance. The EMTs kept calling my name, but the pain was ebbing, and it felt so nice.

And I wish I could say what happened next, where I went, what I'm doing now. But I'm afraid we've reached the limit of our understanding. I have no idea what happens after we die. I'm a ghost, you see. I'm a fiction. I am words on a page.

EPILOGUE
GRACE

GRACE

Hi Diary!

It's nice to meet you. I got you for my birthday. I'm 12 years old (happy birthday to me!), and I'm in the 6th grade and I can't wait for summer. That's a lot of ANDs. Anyhow, next year I go to middle school which is gonna be weird because I only went to one school in my whole entire life. We're gonna join up with kids from the other elementary school across the freeway which is also weird because that's where all the poor kids go.

I mean, there are poor kids who go to school with me now but there's also regular kids to balance it out. Not that I have anything against poor kids either. My mom tells me that those kids just aren't as lucky as me but seriously, I'm soooo not lucky. Sometimes I think I'm like the unluckiest person in the whole world.

What else? Oh my gosh I forgot to tell you my name. I'm Grace. I live at 8 Glenside Trail, Figblossom Valley, California, United States of America, North America, Planet Earth, The Solar System, The Milky Way, The Universe, Whatever Is Past The Universe, 90511.

Oh, and my last name is Markham. That's the funny thing. I literally don't have the same last name as my mom and dad. And here, Dear Diary, is where I cannot tell a lie. The truth is, my mom and dad aren't really my mom and dad. They're my Aunt Jessica and Uncle Wally. I don't even call them mom and dad except if I'm talking to someone I don't know, like if I meet some kids on a beach, and I'm never going to see them again, I'll be like, "Yeah, my mom and dad, whatever." That way I don't have to deal with them asking where my real parents are. It's so embarrassing. I mean, everyone in my school knows the story, but they've all known me my whole life basically, and reporters don't come to town anymore. I mean, sometimes they do, but Aunt Jessica is really good at telling them to fuck off. (Her words not mine!!!! I don't have to put money in the swear jar because I'm just saying what she says!) That's funny. I'm imagining somebody is gonna read this diary and be like, you shouldn't say fuck. Fuck Fuck Fuck Fuck Fuck. And BY THE WAY if someone is reading this diary MIND YOUR OWN BUSINESS!

I don't remember what I was talking about now. Oh yeah, my real mom. She was murdered when I was a baby. I don't remember her at all.

Now I'm sure you're wondering why my mom got murdered. That's what everybody wants to know. Uncle Wally says that my mom was a good person who made bad choices. And that makes me so mad because even now, I'm 12 years old. I've been double digits for OVER TWO YEARS and they STILL won't tell me what he means by bad choices. Aunt Jessica just says that's why we go to church and why I can't get a phone yet and have to eat hamburger casserole which I HATE. I hate tomatoes and she puts them in EVERY TIME.

Chopped tomatoes are NOT the same thing as tomato sauce. Do you:

AGREE or DISAGREE
(circle one).

Besides, I already know everything about my mom. Hello? I have the internet! She got killed by this lady who had an affair with my dad. I even saw a picture from where she stabbed my mom to death. My mom wasn't in the picture but her blood was. It was all over the floor and smeared up the door of the house I lived in when I was a baby.

Okay. I have to be honest now. I didn't just see the picture once. I saw it a lot. And I wanted to stop looking at it, I swear. Every day I would wake up and say, "I'm not looking at that picture today." But I kept going back to the website. Aunt Jessica and Uncle Wally finally went through my history and said I wasn't allowed to have my laptop in my room anymore. I got really mad at them. I mean, I was there when my mom got killed. I found out from the website. I yelled at Aunt Jessica and Uncle Wally and called them liars for not telling me the truth. And that's how we all ended up in therapy together. Even Jayden and Asher come to sessions when they visit. They're my cousins, but they call me their little sister.

So I guess I should tell you about my real dad. First off, he's really famous, but not the good kind of famous where you get to be a movie star. Second, the reason it's not the good kind of famous is because he's in jail. And here's where it gets really complicated . . . (drum roll) . . . The murderer lady who killed my mom tried to kill him too.

She put sugar in his plane's gas tank. But duh, sugar doesn't dissolve in gasoline, so nothing happened. I learned about it in science class. If you want to dissolve sugar, you have to do it in water. It's like this:

Sugar (solute) + Water (solvent) = Sugar Water (solution)

I raised my hand in class and asked my teacher, Mr. Travers, if gasoline could ever be solvent for sugar. That's when it got weird. Mr. Travers got a funny look on his face, and the other kids started making shocked eyes at each other like they couldn't believe what I was asking. Like I said, the whole town knows everything about me.

Mr. Travers coughed and said that gasoline was a solvent for things like oil and wax. So then it would be:

Oil (solute) + Gasoline (solvent) = Oil and Gas Solution

Anyhow, the murderer lady has a lot of nerve. I mean, I guess if you're a murderer you're probably not the most polite person, but she keeps saying it was my *mom's* idea to kill my dad. She's a total liar.

Because there is NO WAY that's true. My mom would NEVER do something like that.

Anyway, the murderer lady didn't go to jail. She pleaded temporary insanity and self defense, so she ended up in a hospital instead. And me and Aunt Jessica and Uncle Wally are really mad about that. Every time they think about letting her out, we all go and tell the judge and doctors she should stay locked up. Like, every year, I have to talk about how sad it is that I don't have a mom. We even went on *The Dr. Maryn Show* to complain about it once. But we hate Dr. Maryn now. She lied to us. She said we'd be on the show by ourselves, but she interviewed the murderer lady on the same episode.

The problem is, the murderer lady is all of a sudden like, the good kind of famous. And it's because of Dr. Maryn. She interviews the lady on her show like all the time to defend herself and now the murderer lady has her own podcast. She's allowed to record it in the hospital. It's called *Cracked!* and she interviews all these other murderer ladies. They all talk about how they were really good people before they met so and so, or did such and such, and the real problem was that they didn't take care of themselves to begin with. Like, supposedly nobody would have killed anyone if they'd taken bubble baths every night or something.

What bugs me the most, though, is that part of the reason my dad is in jail is because his and the lady's cell phones both pinged at his airport right before my mom got murdered. (Seriously can you believe my dad used to have his own plane???) Anyway because they had proof my dad and the lady were together right before she went to my mom's, that means that the lady only got charged with temporary insanity manslaughter instead of first degree murder like she should have been. Her lawyer did this whole song and dance about how she was under my dad's influence or something stupid like that. But my dad swears he didn't talk to her. He didn't even know she was there.

I totally believe him by the way because he never got charged with murder. He always says that. "I never got charged with murder." He sounds really proud when he says it too which grosses me out a little because you're supposed to be proud of cool things, like getting an A on a test or winning a race. But anyway, he's in jail because they kept telling him they would charge him with murder if he didn't agree to a super long sentence for stuff like fraud and stealing data. Like I said, it's complicated.

I'm glad my dad copped a plea though because I get to sit at a picnic table when I visit him. The only other kids with parents in jail are the poor kids at my school and they have to deal with handcuffs and partitions and all sorts of craziness. When I tell them I get to hug my dad, they're all like, "No fair!" The poor kids make me sad sometimes.

Anyway, my dad's kind of weird. He looks like he wears a wig, but Aunt Jessica called it a combover. I mean, what's he trying to do? Look good for his cellmate? Some other lady married him, so I guess I have a stepmom now. Her name is Anna. She keeps trying to meet me but Uncle Wally and Aunt Jessica keep going to court about it. Oh, and they revoke my dad's privileges with me all the time so sometimes I go months without visiting or talking to him on the phone.

The first time was when I was like 6. He told me that Jesus was the one that sent him to jail because he could only help people if he'd actually been through some shit. (His words! No swear jar!) He showed me his arm and how he couldn't straighten it anymore. He told me what the other prisoners did to him.

"It was the missing piece," he said. "Now I know what it means to suffer."

We took a break from my dad for a while after that and then I had to have my social worker sitting with us and listening in on our phone calls. Seriously there is so much drama. She interrupted him once when he started talking about Jesus, and then he got a court order saying he had a right to tell me about Jesus.

Everybody calls my dad a phony but he swears he met Jesus on the beach before he even knew my mom was dead. When he gets out he's going to start his own church. And it won't be boring like the church I go to with Sister Destiny making us sing songs about redemption and lost coins and sheep and all that. I ask Sister Destiny about my mom sometimes because Uncle Wally told me they were friends when they were little. All she'll say is that God loved my mom because God loves everybody which makes me think that she didn't like my mom and that Uncle Wally doesn't know what he's talking about.

Anyway, my dad's church isn't going to be small and uncomfortable with everybody sitting on wooden benches. It's gonna be huge like a stadium with big screens and there's gonna be guys in suits with walkie talkies escorting him to the podium and then back to his Escalade when he's done with his sermons.

And that's pretty much all he would say for years. But when the social worker finally stopped coming on our visits he started telling me he's gonna need my help to start the church. Because it turns out there's money. Secret money. And it's on an island way, way out in the Pacific Ocean. My dad won't tell me which one, but he promises he'll take me there when he gets out, and it'll be like we're pirates hunting buried treasure. Before we do any of that, though, my dad told me I had to find my mom's death certificate.

Well. I don't have to tell you that Aunt Jessica and Uncle Wally got soooo pissed when they caught me going through the filing cabinet. The next time my dad called collect, Uncle Wally screamed at him, "YOU SONOFABITCH! YOU LEAVE THAT LITTLE GIRL OUT OF YOUR SCAMS!"

We were about to take another long break from seeing him after that but my dad started crying and begging Uncle Wally to let me keep visiting. I could hear him through the phone on the other side of the room. "She's all I have, Wally. She's all I have."

Anyway, I don't know if my dad is telling the truth about that Pacific island money or living in a fantasy world or what, but if there's one thing I know, it's that you have to be rich. Especially with the economy and everything. I mean, all the grownups talk about is how hard things have gotten. A bunch of my friends had to leave their houses. That's super bizarre, when they just stop showing up for school. Everyone's like, "Where's so and so?" and it's like, "They had to move." And we're all like, "Wow. Did they turn into poor kids all of a sudden?"

Anyway, we're super lucky because we moved into my grandpa's house after he died last year. It's all paid off, so we don't have to pay anything except the taxes. And seriously, that was totally enough for us. Uncle Wally was going to take the carpet up because there were hardwood floors underneath and we were pretty excited about it.

But then—and I swear this is where the story gets totally bonkers—it turned out my grandpa was RICH. We didn't even know! He had MILLIONS of dollars that he didn't tell anybody about. When I first found out, I was like, let's get a mansion! Let's get a limousine! But Aunt Jessica and Uncle Wally said we can't start acting like showoffs and they told me I especially can't talk to my dad about it which is kind of lame, but then they got me a horse. Her name is Bessie Junior, and she's a pinto with the best personality. I'm learning how to ride both English and Western styles.

Anyway, we put a new roof on Grandpa's house and bought one of those stair lift elevator things so that our dog, Bella, can go up to my room at night. She was my mom's dog and she's super old and can't climb the stairs anymore. I sleep in my mom's old room, by the way. The one she grew up in. I asked Uncle Wally where her bed was, and I put mine in the same place. Uncle Wally said she was a neat freak too, so I keep my room really clean, and even though he doesn't remember how the walls were painted when she was a kid, I'm pretty sure she would have liked mauve because that's my favorite color.

Okay. I have to admit something now. Even though my aunt and uncle show me pictures of her and stuff, I didn't really think of my mom as a real person before I moved into her room. Like, I knew she used to exist, but I never pictured her breathing and thinking and feeling. But now, it's almost like we're sharing a room. Is that a weird thing to say? Some nights I stay up and stare ahead at my closet and think about the fact that she had the same exact view at my age. It makes me feel like I know her. Like she's a friend. My favorite thing, though, is to open the window and climb out and sit on the roof. I bet my mom did this too. Who wouldn't? I'm out here right now actually. It's the only place I feel calm.

I can see the whole town by the way. It's midnight here in Figblossom Valley and everything is dark except for the gas stations lit up near the freeway, and I don't know why everybody is asleep right now. How can anyone be in bed with all these stars out? It's like billions of them.

Sometimes I wonder what's out there. Like, is it just fire and rocks or whatever? I hope so. I really hope there's nothing. I hate to think I'm looking up at planets full of people just like us with everybody straining away all the time to do stuff and causing each other problems. I mean, what if there are murderer ladies up there? And economies and court orders and weirdo dads who pretend to be nice but you never really know what they're planning?

I know it's crazy, but I'd rather look at outer space and think that the universe only cares about infinity or whatever. That it doesn't care about me at all. And sure that thought is scary. Sometimes if I think about it too long, it feels like all that nothingness is going to swallow me up. But sometimes (and this is going to make me sound like a maniac) but sometimes it feels like I have a tiny piece of outer space inside me. Is that weird? Like a tiny piece of sky is inside me, and if I'm really still, that part of me will talk to the rest of it and tell me what the night sky says. That none of it matters. Nothing matters.

I don't know about you, but I find that really peaceful.

ACKNOWLEDGMENTS

This book would not have been possible without the support, generosity, and wisdom of the following:

My husband, Peter, the best reader in the world, and Neil, the best kid in the world.

My sisters and cheerleaders, Molly Fagan and Jane Ward.

Laurie Horowitz, who taught me how to write.

Great people and institutions, including Stephen Cooper and UCLA Extension, Jim Krusoe and Santa Monica College, and Beyond Baroque.

Friends, critiquers, and experts: Lene Amalfi, Julia Lee Barclay-Morton, Ilona Brown, Jill Caryl Weiner, Jennifer Clay, Ryan Hilary, Tamara Holub, Chris Lawson, Shelli Margolin-Mayer, Frank Matcha, JoBeth McDaniel, Greg Moore, Jason Peugh, Frank Possemato, Victor Rauch, Chris Richardson, Katie Saunders, Jan Shure-Hurwitz, Signe Sorstein, Anna Stigen, Matt Sullivan, and A. K. Whitney.

My agent, Noah Ballard, and his unceasing support.

And my wonderful editor, Liz Pearsons, and everyone at Thomas & Mercer. Thank you for believing in this book!

ABOUT THE AUTHOR

Kate Myles is a television producer for networks such as the Food Network and OWN. Before producing, she worked as an actor and comedian, enjoying a two-year stint as a host and video journalist for the Travel Channel series *Not Your Average Travel Guide*, among other adventures. Her fiction has appeared in *Necessary Fiction, Quarterly West,* and *Storm Cellar Quarterly. The Receptionist* is her first novel.